THE CASE OF THE FLYING TRAPEZE

DOUBLE DETECTIVES BOOK ONE

LARKYN SIMONY

SimonySays

PUBLISHING & MEDIA

First paperback edition August 2020

Cover design by Liam Relph

ISBN 978-0-578-69446-7 (paperback)
ISBN 978-0-578-69447-4 (ebook)

www.simonysays.com

PART I

SATURDAY, TWO DAYS BEFORE MEMORIAL DAY

I f it hadn't been for Joey Taylor's bar mitzvah afterparty, none of it would have happened. The party was one of those huge to-dos, more appropriate for a college graduation than for the celebration of a boy turning thirteen. There was a cover band, catering with attending waiters, and multiple tents covered in fairy lights erected all over the backyard. Joey Taylor's bar mitzvah afterparty was, in fact, the reason Maureen McNair could not find a place to park at her parents' house when she stopped by to drop off the decorations for her sister's upcoming baby shower. And, because of this lack of suitable parking, all hell would soon break loose.

As Maureen drove down Gardenia Lane, she noticed her parents' driveway had been rendered unusable by a hideous maroon Range Rover parked right in front of it. Maureen tried to park next door in her Aunt Oleen and Uncle Gary's driveway, but their driveway, too, was blocked, only by an ostentatious yellow Hummer rather than by a maroon monstrosity of a Range Rover. So, it was with incredulity and some irritation that Maureen parked around the corner on O'Connell Street, and not on Gardenia Lane, the street on which her parents still lived in the house in which she had grown up.

Maureen got out of her eight-year-old silver Honda Accord, and huffed around the corner toward her parents' house carrying two Trader Joe's bags full of decorations she had bought at Party City not even three hours ago. After she had dropped each bag twice, she found herself standing next to the maroon Range Rover in front of 32 Gardenia Lane. Maureen wondered why she hadn't thought to leave the bags at the house before she'd found a place to park her car, but then she remembered there wouldn't have been any place to park the car while she dropped off the bags anyway. To drop the bags off, she would've needed to have stopped in the middle of the street and blocked the entire road, and blocking the entire road seemed to be the exclusive domain of the guests of Joey Taylor's bar mitzvah afterparty.

Maureen's mother's car, a dark-blue Ford Expedition the size of a small tank, was not in her parents' driveway. Since it was Saturday afternoon, Maureen assumed her mom and her Aunt Oleen, her mom's identical twin sister, were having what her mom, Ida, called "tea" with Agnes, her Uncle Gary's mother. Having "tea" amounted to the three women drinking margaritas at the Silver Kettle for four hours, two of which were spent sobering up enough to be able to drive home. Some family members thought the three women had drinking problems, but Ida, Oleen, and Agnes usually confined their drinking to these Saturday afternoon jaunts, which was okay with Maureen. It amused her to consider them getting plastered on a weekly basis like nineteen year olds at a frat party. Maureen was glad they still went out and had fun and hoped when she was their age, she wouldn't be some shriveled-up old fig who only left her sofa to change the remote control batteries.

As she trudged up the driveway, Maureen noticed her

parents' garage door was open, which wasn't unusual because both her dad and her Uncle Gary loved to work on cars and restored old cars together all the time. They always worked in her parents' garage, since lord only knew what crap Oleen had shoved into her and Gary's garage. Oleen called their garage a storage unit, which, to anyone familiar with her aunt's general lack of organization, meant "repository of crap."

Maureen stood near the driveway and looked at her parents' house. She was ready to unload the two bags in their living room, since with every passing moment they seemed to get heavier. She walked into the yard and stood in the shade of the blooming magnolia, which grew near the curb, and set the Trader Joe's bags down. Maureen decided she better start exercising again, because not being able to carry two bags of baby shower decorations a short distance without getting winded was really kind of sad. Maureen wiped sweat from her forehead with her left hand and, as she did so, movement caught her eye. Maureen stared at the peculiar scene unfolding in front of her. What she thought she saw was, in fact, so odd that she rubbed her eyes twice to be sure she wasn't imagining things.

Maureen walked out from under the tree toward the house and saw her father in the garage, leaning face-first up against his everyday car, a Ford F-150, and there appeared to be a woman pushed up against the car underneath him. And they were kissing! It wasn't the usual, discreet kissing most people would do in public, say when pushed up against a truck in an open garage in plain view of the street. It was teenagers-in-the-back-of-a-station-wagon kissing!

Oh. My. God. Surely Delbert McNair wouldn't decide to cheat on her mother at the age of sixty-five! He was way past the age of a midlife crisis, wasn't he? Maureen crept toward the garage. She watched the ground to avoid stepping on anything or making any noise because she didn't want the woman underneath Delbert to hear her approach and have time to run away. But Maureen was not blessed with the gifts of stealth or coordination, and when she got about ten feet from the open garage door and leaned forward to get a better look at her dad and that hussy, she tripped over a tree root and fell flat on her face on the driveway. Her elbows scraped across the cement and left a trail of blood. She must have made a lot of noise when she fell because she heard movement from the direction of the garage.

"Oh my god!" her dad yelled. "Are you okay?"

And when Maureen looked up, her whole world tipped ass over teakettle as she saw that the "woman" leaning with her back against the truck, breathing as though having run a race, was her Uncle Gary. Maureen screamed and screamed and screamed until her vocal cords almost gave out. Then she lay her forehead down on the driveway, facing away from the horrible scene before her, and wondered what the hell to do.

2

SATURDAY

Wisps of Maureen's shoulder-length brown hair stuck to her face. She was aware that her knees ached and her elbows were sore. She could hear the cover band across the street at Joey Taylor's bar mitzvah afterparty playing a terrible version of N'Sync's hit song "Bye Bye Bye", which was much better than the song the band had been playing a second ago when she'd spotted her dad and Gary making out; a song which she'd never be able to enjoy again. As Maureen listened to the dulcet tones of a boy band which was now as defunct as her former version of reality, she hoped Joey Taylor, the cover band, and Justin Timberlake himself would all perish in a fiery tent collapse as soon as possible. Maureen turned her head toward the garage, and was startled to see two giant eyes mere inches from her face. Maureen screamed again for good measure. She raised herself up on her elbows, and felt two stabs of pain. She dropped back down and rested her head on her arms. Her dad's face loomed over her, and she put her right hand out in the universal "stop" gesture.

"Ow! You get back!" Maureen said with a blankness of intonation that frightened her.

In the distance, she saw Gary propped face-first against the inside wall of the garage. He appeared to be weeping, which wasn't a surprise, as Gary cried more each week than Maureen had during all three of her pregnancies combined.

"Reenie," said her dad's soft voice; the voice that had comforted her when Jeremy Philpot had stood her up at the junior prom; the voice that had explained to her why she couldn't have a giraffe as a pet when they had gone to the zoo when Maureen was three.

"Dad!" Maureen said. "I really don't want to talk to you right now. Just get back. Go back to the garage or something."

Delbert retreated to the garage. Gary had stopped leaning against the wall and was now sitting on one side of an old wooden bench. He stroked his enormous bushy brown mustache as though doing so might cause him to teleport to another location. Maureen was pretty sure Gary used Just for Men on both his hair and his mustache, though she had always been too tactful to mention this hunch to anyone else. At that moment, though, she had the urge to create fliers advertising the idea and to place them under the windshield wipers of each of the illegally parked cars littering both sides of Gardenia Lane.

Gary cut a dashing figure on that bench in his Hawaiian shirt, grease-streaked khaki shorts, knee-high black socks, and brown sandals. Maureen had never understood people who wore Hawaiian shirts when they were not in Hawaii.

Delbert sat down on the opposite side of the bench and turned his back on Gary to face the same wall Gary had just been leaned up against. Delbert, like Gary, was quite the fashion plate. His clothes were also stained with grease. He had on blue denim overalls and his ugly black Reebok sneakers poked out of the bottom of his overall pant legs. His light-blue button-down mechanic's shirt, with his name emblazoned in red across a patch on the right breast pocket, stuck out of the top of the overalls. This uniform was also what Delbert wore at the body shop he had bought fifteen years ago, and which he still ran himself. To Maureen's dismay, Delbert did not confine this ensemble to the times he spent working in the garage at home and working at the body shop. He wore it to run errands, and sometimes even out to dinner! Maureen shook her head, as she understood people who wore their work uniforms outside of work even less than she understood people who wore Hawaiian shirts outside of Hawaii.

Maureen laughed like a maniac as she mentally compared her dad and her uncle to the stereotype of the well-dressed, immaculately groomed gay man because apparently her dad and her uncle were gay now. Maureen's brother, Scott, fit this stereotype, except when he found it necessary to wear tank tops outside his house, which no man, regardless of age, race, or sexual preference should ever do.

Maureen observed how both her dad's and her Uncle Gary's general appearances made them look like they had been in a horrible accident at Big Lots. It was like they were hanging out there with the worst hairstylist from Great Clips when an unexpected tornado had lifted them all up, spun them around, and dropped Delbert and Gary out looking the way they did now, with their horrible clothes and haircuts, hopefully throwing the hairstylist and his scissors all the way across the store into the housewares section.

At least Gary looked like he had attempted to make himself presentable when he had exited the tornado. Even in ugly clothes and with unsightly hair, Gary always appeared neat and clean, even when he had grease on his shorts like he did now. Her father looked like he had just been the victim of a vicious attacking cloud of grime and dust that had flown off the top of a grand piano which hadn't been cleaned in sixteen years.

With his enormous brown mustache, close-cropped brown hair, and small build, Gary resembled Ned Flanders from the *Simpsons*, particularly in the winter when he wore many sweaters, although Maureen wasn't sure if Ned Flanders had a large bald spot on top of his head. She was pretty sure, though, that Ned Flanders had never sported a combover, as Gary had when he had begun to lose his hair in the late 1980s. At least Oleen had convinced him to give that up.

Maureen's own father had a full head of graying hair, which looked like he styled it with an egg beater. Delbert was tall and beefy and beginning to sport a belly that protruded from beneath his overalls, stretching the hard, crunchy denim as far as it could go. Maureen knew those overalls had been around way before stretch denim had been invented, which made the belly protrusion even more prominent. Hell, those overalls were so old they were actually frosted. Maureen had always thought her dad bore a slight resemblance to Archie Bunker from *All in the Family*, only much taller. At six foot three, Delbert towered over Gary, who was only five foot eight.

"Maureen," Gary said, tears running down his face. Maureen couldn't make out what he was saying from her spot on the driveway, but, whatever it was, she felt a rude response was in order.

"Shut up, Gary. Let me think. You both just stay there and don't move."

As she told Gary to shut up, Maureen realized that lying halfway on and halfway off her parents' driveway with blood dripping down her elbows and her face resting on the cement wasn't an inconspicuous look. Someone might stop to help, believing her to be injured or dead, though as there would be no place for said person to park, maybe it wasn't a problem after all.

She sat up and wiped her bloody elbows with the hem of her purple t-shirt. She'd have to remember to ask her mom the best way to get blood stains out of clothing. Her mom always seemed to know how to do that kind of stuff. Maureen looked around the yard and noticed it was alight with pink streamers emblazoned with the words, "It's a Girl." The streamers had blown out of the Trader Joe's bags, buffeted by an unexpected gust of wind. They covered the ground under the magnolia and inched toward the bushes at the front of the house like snakes on their way home to their burrow.

She decided she must first remove the lurid pink streamers from the yard. Then she could deal with her dad and Gary. At the speed of a blind man disarming a bomb, she limped across the yard and picked up the Trader Joe's bags from underneath the magnolia. She located all the party streamers, none of which were damaged, picked them up and stuffed them back into the bags. While performing this task, Maureen noticed that both her elbows and her knees were cut up and streaked with blood. Great. Hopefully she wouldn't be dealing with flesh-eating bacteria while trying to figure out how her dad and her uncle could be gay, while also trying to decorate her parents' living room for a baby shower. When she had finished collecting the streamers, she put the bags on the ground under the magnolia and sat next to them with her back to the tree. She stared at her dad and Gary.

Inside Maureen an uncomfortable feeling simmered. It was a combination of how she had felt when she was eleven and her dad, who was notoriously bad about not knocking before entering a room, had walked in on her changing into her swim-suit, and of how she had felt a few years ago when someone had broken into her car and stolen her laptop. It was shame and anger, and wondering how she could be so stupid as to not notice she'd left her computer in plain view on the backseat of her car.

Ida and Delbert had been married for forty-five years, and Gary and Oleen had also been married for forty-five years. How long had this affair been going on? Oh my god! Maureen couldn't think about it without her head breaking in half, and her brain congealing into a gelatinous liquid and running out of her ears and down the arms of her shirt. That was all she needed on top of the bloody elbows and knees. She'd have to figure out not only how to get bloodstains out of clothing, but brain stains as well.

So, Maureen did all she could think to do. First, she called her younger sister, Janie. Janie was seven months' pregnant, but could surely drive herself over for such a perilous situation. Janie's phone rang six times and went to voicemail. Maureen needed some damn help, like five minutes ago, so she texted her sister:

"Call immediately. Need help. It's Dad."

Maureen knew it wasn't fair to write words that might make her sister think her dad was on the way to the hospital, but she also knew these words would generate a fast response from Janie.

Within fifteen seconds the theme song from *The Jeffersons* exploded from Maureen's phone. Without saying hello, Maureen said,

"Come over. Mom and Dad's house. Right now!"

"Oh my god! Is Dad okay? Is he dead?" said Janie.

"No, he's not dead, moron. I wouldn't have started to tell you that Dad's dead through a text. Don't you think I'd at least call you if Dad were dead? In fact, he's perfectly healthy. But you're gonna want to hear this in person."

"Okay. Should I bring Jason?"

"No. Just us three. And what time is it? How much longer do you think Mom has at the Silver Kettle?"

"Well, it's about two, so maybe two more hours? Three if it's Bottomless Pitcher Day."

"Okay, well, on your way over, think of ways we can keep her there longer if we need to."

"Um, okay. Are you alright, Reenie?"

"Yeah, I'm fine. Just do it. Come now. I'll explain when you get here."

Maureen hung up.

Next, Maureen contacted her brother, Scott. Who the hell knew what Scott was up to right now. Scott was ten years younger than Maureen and not known to be the most reliable person on the planet, but he had mellowed and straightened his life out since he'd met Steve six years ago, so she was now optimistic about his ability to come through for her in a crisis.

Scott liked to communicate only by text or Snapchat, a program she couldn't begin to understand, so she texted him, "Mom and Dad's. Come immediately. Emergency. It's Dad."

Since Scott watched his phone like her old college math professor had watched the co-eds' cleavage, she received an immediate response.

"What's up? Is Dad dead?"

What the hell was wrong with her siblings?

"No, idiot, Dad's not dead. Do you really think I'd tell you Dad was dead in a text?"

"Maybe?"

"What moron would break that news over a text? I'd call you if Dad were dead. Possibly I'd even Facetime you."

"Jeez. Sorry. What's going on?"

"Just get here as quick as you can."

"Steve and I are at brunch, so let us pay, and we'll be right there. Twenty minutes tops."

Maureen sent a thumbs-up. Scott was always at brunch. She didn't bother telling Scott not to bring Steve. Steve might be helpful in this situation, unlike Jason who would be more interested in if there was a cooler of beer in the garage than in the problem at hand.

Maureen stared at her dad and Gary from her spot beneath the magnolia. Both were weeping on separate ends of the bench, but her dad was trying to hide his tears, and Gary was not. At one point her dad yelled that he had to go to the bathroom to which Maureen yelled back across the yard,

"Sit down and shut the fuck up, Dad."

Delbert McNair's eyes popped out of his head since the worst word he had ever heard Maureen say was "dammit" that time when she was in tenth grade and had dropped a can of beans on her toe in her one-and-only attempt to cook chili.

Maureen clutched the handles of the Trader Joe's bags like they were all that was keeping her from being sucked out of a plane in which the door had been blown off at twenty-five thousand feet. And she waited.

3

SATURDAY

Maureen eyed Delbert and Gary as though they were two highly questionable terror suspects rather than two closeted gay men with wives, families, and likely many hours of lurid behavior in a garage. She heard someone call her name. The word "Reenie," said in her sister's voice, startled her. Maureen looked toward the street and saw Janie, sitting in her green Jeep Grand Cherokee, idling in front of the house. Janie sported a sleek, layered, blonde bob with not a hair out of place, and her blue eyes were made up as though she'd spent hours preparing for this trip to learn about the detonation of her family. Maureen knew Janie loved makeup to the point of insanity, and it had probably taken her all of ten minutes to achieve her current look, which was both natural, and showed off her eyes to their best advantage. Everyone knew a natural makeup look took way longer to achieve than something dramatic, but not for Janie. Janie was good at anything she tried. Janie was the only person Maureen knew who would don bright-red lipstick to drive to her sister's aid in a situation she knew was not going to be pleasant.

Since cars lined both sides of the street, and there was no

access to either Maureen's parents' driveway or to Oleen and
Gary's driveway, Maureen told Janie to drive her car up into
their parents' yard and to park in the shade of the magnolia.
Janie was in no condition to traipse to the house from two
blocks away just because some guests of Joey Taylor's bar
mitzvah afterparty couldn't park like normal people.

Janie, who found the idea of illegal parking scandalous, as
she was someone who followed every rule she encountered,
down to not removing the tags from pillows, said,

"But won't that mess up the yard?"

"If it does, we can hire a yard boy to come and fix it, and
then maybe Dad and Gary and the yard boy can have a
threesome."

"Maureen!" Janie called from her car window, both shocked
by her sister's brazenness, and clueless as to what Maureen
meant.

"Why would Dad and Gary, you know, want to go be with a
'yard boy,' as you call it? Why would they do that when they
have wives and kids and fix a lot of cars and watch an awful lot
of football?" asked Janie.

As Janie exited her Jeep, stomach protruding ahead of the
rest of her, Maureen noticed how Janie's slender, athletic form
remained, despite the large belly. Janie was tall, about five foot
nine, whereas Maureen was just a shade over five foot three.
Every time Maureen had been pregnant, she had just looked
fat. But Janie looked as beautiful as always. Janie didn't even
look pregnant from the back.

Maureen was beginning to sport a muffin top over the
waistband of her jeans, and she didn't have being pregnant to
use as an excuse for this horror. Developing a muffin top was a
sin of which she doubted her sister would ever be guilty. You
couldn't help but love Janie, even if her beauty sometimes
made you want to stab her in the eye. She was one of the nicest
people in the world.

Maureen pointed with disdain toward the garage. Gary was still crying on the bench, while Delbert was turned away from Gary and staring at the garage wall as though the door to Narnia was just moments from appearing there.

"Huh?" Janie asked, following Maureen's finger with her eyes and not understanding at all what the gesture meant.

"Maureen, are you okay? Are you sick? And why are you sitting under that tree? And what are all these cars from? I mean, I know the McGruders have their annual barbecue on Memorial Day weekend, but this seems a little excessive. There are never so many people at that barbecue that the guests would need to park several blocks away from their house."

The McGruder's Memorial Day barbecue was something all three McNair children had started to avoid many years ago. There were dishes like Jell-O filled with fruit, which Mrs. McGruder called congealed salad, a name that made Maureen throw up in her mouth a little. There was also pimiento cheese with a ratio of three-quarters pimientos to one-quarter cheese, and then there was the notorious seven-layer salad, a monstrosity Maureen couldn't even contemplate without needing nausea medication.

And then there was creepy Mr. McGruder, who always seemed to "accidentally" brush up against all the women's butts. It was an event which held little appeal for the three McNair offspring, or for any sane person, really. Even Scott, who shouldn't have needed to worry about having his backside felt up since Mr. McGruder liked the ladies, didn't want to go.

Scott had always claimed that when he was fifteen, Mr. McGruder had cornered him in the walk-in kitchen pantry and complimented him on his "shapely buttocks," but no one had ever believed Scott, because sometimes he made up things like that.

Maureen tried to envision all the times she had seen Mr. McGruder over the years. Hadn't there been a year at the barbecue when Mr. McGruder had asked her dad to help him carry a large keg of Heineken into the house from the garage? Oh my god. Was "carrying a keg of Heineken" just some code for "Meet me in the garage so I can compliment your shapely buttocks?" Granted, Delbert McNair did not have shapely buttocks, while his son, Scott, did since Scott seemed to spend more time at the gym than he did at work. Eww. Why was she thinking about her dad's and brother's butts anyway, Maureen wondered.

Maureen's heart pounded as she stood up and abandoned her Trader Joe's bags. She hugged her sister tightly at the same moment Janie tried to close the car door. This ill-timed gesture nearly knocked Janie to the ground.

"Careful, you don't want to send me into early labor underneath this tree, right now, do you?"

"Well, if I did it would be the most normal thing to happen today."

"Maureen," Janie said, grabbing her sister by the shoulders and taking a step back to get a better look at her. "What's wrong? You don't look right. I mean, at all. You look like you just ate some of Mrs. McGruder's seven-layer salad the year she somehow added guacamole under that disgusting marshmallow topping."

Janie's stomach turned thinking about how awful it had been. Being pregnant, smells and tastes, and even the thought of smells and tastes affected Janie viscerally. She reached her hand out and placed it against the magnolia's sizable trunk to steady herself.

Sensing Janie's disgust, and possible vomiting spell, Maureen limped to the front of the house and grabbed two lawn chairs from next to the front porch. She dragged them back toward Janie and unfolded them side-by-side under the magnolia. Maureen helped Janie lower herself into one. Then she sat down next to her sister.

"Reenie, why are we sitting under this tree, and why are Dad and Gary sitting in the garage on that bench acting weird? Did the classic Mustang die again or something? And have you just been sitting on the ground under the tree watching them? What's wrong? Oh my god! Are you pregnant again?"

"No, Janie! I'm not pregnant! Three boys are quite enough children for me. And what would sitting under a tree have to do with my being pregnant? Wouldn't I be less likely to be sitting on the ground under a tree if I were pregnant? Wouldn't I be more likely to want to sit in a chair or something?"

"Maybe you aren't very far along?"

Maureen took Janie's left hand in her right hand in a sympathetic, motherly way.

"Janie, pregnancy, and sitting on the ground have nothing to do with each other. But, if you want to know what's going on, I'll tell you. I caught Dad and Gary making out in the garage."

"Wait, what? You caught them making what in the garage? Were they building some kit car again like they tried with that Fiero in 1987? I remember that went very badly."

Maureen watched a film of denial slide over her sister's eyes.

"No, Janie," Maureen said more slowly. "I caught them making out up against Dad's truck with the garage door open, while Joey Taylor's bar mitzvah afterparty cover band played a terrible version of that old song, "I'll Make Love to You." That one by Boyz II Men, you know? In fact, I think that song made it ten times worse. And also, how is that song in any way appropriate for a bar mitzvah afterparty?"

Tears flowed from Maureen's eyes.

"Wait, what?" Janie asked, thinking she must have misheard her sister. "What do you mean they were making out against a truck? Like, fixing it, somehow?"

"Oh my god, Janie! Is being pregnant really making you this stupid? Making out! Like, pushed up against Dad's truck going at it like they were starring in that old movie *Body Heat*. Like Dad was Patrick Swayze helping Gary make a pot on a pottery wheel. Making out in a way that leads to, well, this," Maureen said, gesturing to Janie's stomach.

Janie's eyes went wide and her mouth gaped, but she still didn't seem to get it.

"Janie, Dad, and Gary are having a gay love affair."

And Janie, who had never said any word worse than bitch, which she had directed at Maureen that time Maureen had spilled ketchup all over Janie's brand-new pink Hypercolor t-shirt, which Maureen had borrowed without asking, said, "Well fuck me." Janie squeezed her sister's hand as, across the yard, Gary's moist and frightened eyes raised up to meet hers.

4

SATURDAY

From behind them, in the shade of the magnolia, Maureen and Janie heard guffawing, knee-slapping laughter.

"A gay love affair?" a loud, slightly effeminate and very flamboyant voice cackled. "Who's having a gay love affair? Is it Mr. McGruder? We all know how much he loves a pair of shapely buttocks on a man."

Maureen and Janie's flashy younger brother, Scott, laughed so hard he shook. Scott, unlike Maureen, had inherited Delbert's height genes. Scott was almost six feet tall, with an athletically toned form like Janie's, though his came from the hours he spent at the gym, while Janie kept in shape by running two miles a day, well, walking now that she was pregnant. Janie had been on the track team in high school, while Maureen had been in the marching band. Maureen sighed. Maureen could run two miles a day and eat only lettuce, and she still wouldn't be able to get below a size 14. But to adequately run two miles a day, she'd need an ice cream truck driving ahead of her and a bloodthirsty lion on her tail.

Maureen had lately taken to wearing high-waisted "mom

jeans," the kind her own mother had worn in the 1980s and 90s, to hide her expanding belly. At least mom jeans had been in fashion when her own mom had worn them. Now they were hideous, and only used for hiding muffin tops. But the tag on Maureen's jeans read "high-waisted," which was of some comfort to her, and, of course, she covered the high-waist with long shirts to avoid mortification. Only Janie knew her secret, a secret that Janie knew revealing would result in Janie's drawn-out and painful death. Seriously, though, what non-delusional woman in her early forties would either want to or find it appropriate to wear jeans that barely covered her hip bones? If Maureen had the body to pull off those kinds of jeans, she wouldn't even bother with jeans at all. She'd just wear a string bikini everywhere she went. Maureen laughed as she pictured herself accompanying her mother to book club in a shocking-pink string bikini and pink spangled high heels for good measure. Maureen sighed. Life just wasn't fair sometimes.

Scott and Steve walked around the tree until they stood in front of Maureen and Janie's chairs, and looked down at the two women, seeming not to have noticed Delbert and Gary who were still sitting in distress on the bench in the garage.

Next to Scott, who was clothed in a white tank top and long khaki shorts that showed off his gym-toned form, Scott's husband of two years, Steve, was a study in contrast. Steve, who at six foot four, was about five inches taller than Scott, wore old-looking jeans that were really old, not made to look old by the manufacturer. With his jeans, Steve wore an old *Jurassic Park* t-shirt, Converse sneakers, and two days of beard stubble. His dark-brown hair was a bit too long and messy. His nose, which was slightly too big for his face, worked for him in the way unusual facial features sometimes do to make people more attractive.

Scott, who would have been horrified if his own light-brown hair was even slightly off-kilter, had his hair cut at an expensive salon every four weeks. Maureen remembered the time she had caught Scott applying her pink Dep hair gel to his hair with her favorite comb, the one she'd used to tease her bangs when she was in her early teens. When she had caught Scott doing this, she no longer teased her bangs or used Dep hair gel. Scott had not realized that the gel was very old and therefore smelled very gross and was very oily, and he had used so much of it that his hair looked like he'd taken a ride on the back of the Exxon Valdez. Maureen's comb required three hours of soaking in dish soap to get the greasy, oily smell off, and it was never the same again. Lucky for Scott, he was back to normal after two rounds of Pert Plus though, even as a child, he had maintained that shampoo and conditioner should never be combined into one step.

It was likely no one would guess Steve even had a husband were they to run into him at the grocery store. They would assume he was out doing the weekly shopping for his wife and child. With his hipster sense of fashion and "dad bod," Janie, who had been the first one in the family to meet Steve, had a crush on him for several weeks before realizing he preferred men.

Scott continued laughing until tears ran down his cheeks and said, "But who doesn't love a pair of shapely buttocks?"

"Come on, Scott," Steve answered in a voice so deep it conjured visions of Barry White, "Everyone knows you made that story up."

Maureen, Janie, and Scott all stared at Steve as though he had jumped off the pages of *Teen Beat* magazine. Steve's was a voice with an appeal that transcended all genders and sexual orientations.

"Steve, I know Jenny and I have both told you this before, but right now you look so much like Thomas Arroyo. Even more than you usually do. Maybe it's the light, or being in the shade or something since his skin color is a little darker than yours is," said Janie. "You're lucky you do. After all, he's the Spanish Sean Connery, you know. Well, according to the media he is. You know who I mean, Scott?" she asked. "He and Steve have, like, identical noses and they both have blue eyes. Jenny thinks Steve looks like him too. And you know, Thomas Arroyo is Jenny's age-inappropriate celebrity crush, so she's studied his looks pretty carefully. Scott, you're married to Thomas Arroyo and Jenny is in love with him, so your cousin is in love with your husband by default."

"Oh my god, Janie, of course I know who Thomas Arroyo is!" Scott said. "Even mom knows who he is, but she calls him 'Thomas Arroz.' And, yes, Steve gets that a lot, and you've only mentioned it about five hundred times. But, Jenny is not in love with Steve, and Steve is not from Spain, and Steve is clearly too young to be Thomas Arroyo. I've suggested to Steve he work for one of those celebrity lookalike businesses. They could use makeup and age him, but he won't do it."

"That would be so boring," said Steve. "I don't even like his movies that much. He's not that young and he always ends up with women half his age. And, Scott, whether or not I look like Thomas Arroyo, you still made that 'shapely buttocks' story up."

"I did not!" And you gotta admit, I do have a nice pair of shapely buttocks."

Scott laughed, turned around, and stuck his butt out toward his sisters. He put his arms around Steve's neck. Steve tried not to smile as he said to Scott, "Get back. How can anyone be expected to control themselves around a pair of shapely buttocks such as yours?"

Scott jumped back, leading with his butt, knocking it into Maureen's stomach, nearly upending her chair and tipping it backward in the process. The front legs landed back on the ground. The high waist of Maureen's jeans would have protected her from a lower back injury, had it come to that.

Scott turned around to face Maureen and Janie, looked down at them, and said, "Okay, my sisters, just who is having this 'gay love affair,' as you call it?"

Maureen and Janie pointed toward the garage, where Delbert and Gary were trying not to look out into the yard. Both men were still sitting on the old wooden bench, staring at the garage floor. Scott and Steve turned around and eyed them, though each appeared to be more curious than distressed.

"Oh my god. It's Dad and Uncle Gary? I knew it! Didn't I tell you that, Steve?" Scott said, and slapped his husband on the arm.

"He did tell me that," said Steve.

"Something squirrely is going on between those two. I've been telling Steve that since right after we met. I mean, nobody fixes cars THAT much. Plus, have you ever noticed how feminine Uncle Gary is? And Gary has that big pornstache. You know, that bushy mustache with no beard? Only police officers, gross, dirty people in 1970s movies, and incredibly tacky gay men have a pornstache. And his name is Gary. What person named Gary ISN'T gay? It's like nurses in the maternity ward somehow know which babies are gonna be gay and they attach name tags to their cribs that say 'Gary.' And Dad and Uncle Gary touch each other a lot. Steve pointed that out."

Maureen and Janie stared at Steve.

"I did point that out once," Steve said. "Not about the name Gary being gay or about Gary having a pornstache. But I always have kind of wondered about your dad and your uncle. I mean, they just seem to exchange so many intimate looks and unnecessary touches. It made me think of John, in high school. It was before I told my parents I was gay, but I really liked John, and we were definitely more than friends, but we had to hide it, or at least we felt like we did.

"Of course, after college, once I told my parents I was gay, they told me they'd wondered if I was since I was little, and they always knew John and I weren't just friends, ever since the first time he came over. They never cared, but they knew I cared, so my parents were always extra careful never to interrupt us when we had a door closed, unless they knocked. They didn't want to embarrass me. So, yeah, it kind of always seemed like that with Delbert and Gary too, you know, like something has always been going on between them, and they've been trying to hide it. But I would never have said anything if Scott hadn't asked me."

Maureen and Janie looked at Steve. "And this doesn't upset you?" Maureen turned toward Scott and stared at him like a suspicious detective on an episode of *Law and Order*.

"Well, not really. Steve and I have known for years. I mean, it's kind of weird, and I feel bad about how Mom and Aunt Oleen are gonna feel when they find out, but what were Dad and Gary gonna do? I mean, it's not like they could implode two families, and pretending you're someone you're not gets old after a while."

"Scott, you have never pretended you are someone you're not," Maureen pointed out. "Our whole family knew you were gay even when Janie and I didn't understand what gay was."

"True, but I'm unusual, and I have a very kind and understanding family, some members notwithstanding." Scott stared at Delbert from across the yard. "Not everyone is so lucky. Steve's parents have always been amazing, though."

Scott looked to Steve for affirmation.

"Yeah, he's right, my parents have always been sensitive and wonderful, and I have no idea how I got so lucky. I don't know how I got so lucky to find Scott, either," Steve said, looking at Scott. "It's hard not to love someone who's so, well, himself. And it is true many, many gay people pretend in the presence of their families and friends that they aren't gay because they're afraid of being rejected, even though a fair amount of people I know later found out that everyone else already knew or suspected they were gay and just didn't mention it. I guess they didn't know what to say. Pretending to be someone you're not is exhausting, and it kind of destroys your soul. It would be like if Scott tried to pretend he didn't like coleslaw when anyone who's ever been out to eat barbecue with him has noticed this is false."

"My soul would be destroyed if I could never eat coleslaw again," Scott said, nodding.

"I'm just so angry!" Maureen raised her voice, clenched her fists and cried openly. "How could they do this to us, and to our family?"

"Babe," said Scott, putting his arm around her. "First, they did not do this to our family or to us. I'm sure they weren't trying to make this happen, it just happened. And second, aside from Uncle Gary being the most effeminate "straight" man you or anyone else has ever met, how did you find this out?"

Maureen repeated the story of seeing Delbert and Gary making out against the truck, of the terrible Boyz II Men soundtrack that had accompanied the scene, and of falling down while trying to sneak around the tree.

"The least surprising part of this story, Reenie, is that you fell down trying to sneak around a tree."

Janie smiled for the first time in an hour.

"Why did they do this to us?" Maureen repeated.

"It sounds more like they did it to the truck," Steve said.

"Well, if you want to know why, let's just ask them," Scott said.

And so, Steve helped Janie up out of her chair, Maureen stood up, adjusting the waistband of her jeans, and the whole contingent approached the garage, where Delbert and Gary still sat on the bench like two men floating across an endless ocean in a lifeboat with a hole in the bottom.

5

SATURDAY

Maureen, Janie, Scott, and Steve stood just outside the open garage door and stared in at Delbert and Gary. No one seemed to know quite what to say, and in situations in which no one knew what to say, Scott started talking, whether he had any idea what to say or not.

"So, Dad, Uncle Gary, how's this gay thing working out for you? Listened to any Gloria Gaynor songs lately?"

Gary began weeping again, and Delbert stared at Scott like he wanted to murder him. Janie smacked Scott on the arm.

"First, Son," Delbert said, with a disdainful emphasis on the word son, "Isn't it Barbara Streisand gay people like? And, second, Gary and I are not gay."

"Dad, I guess some like Barbara Streisand, but I prefer Gloria Gaynor. Anyway, how are you not gay? Maureen saw you and Uncle Gary making out against your truck."

"We're not. That was a mistake."

"You fell on him trying to pick up a wrench? I'm sure it was a tool of some kind." Scott cackled.

"Delbert, just stop! Stop pretending!" Gary said in a whisper. "When you're a man and you do things with another man, you're gay. This isn't *Brokeback Mountain*. You and I have known how we felt since we met. So don't pretend you don't know that! It hurts my feelings!"

After this brief, lucid speech, Gary returned to weeping, only now he wept into an old shop towel rather than into his hands. Black grease marks streaked Gary's face, reminding Maureen of the time when Janie was four and had used her mother's eyeliner to make herself into a tiger.

"Wait! What?" Janie said. "What do you mean you've known how you felt since you met? Didn't you two meet, like, two hundred years ago?"

Maureen's look of chagrin returned as she sat down on the bench between the two men, shoved Gary over, and wept right along with him. Her display of emotion calmed Gary, who grabbed another shop towel from the box next to the bench and handed it to Maureen. She wiped her nose with the towel, smearing black grease across her forehead, and tried to calm herself down by breathing deeply.

"Are you..." Maureen gulped and sputtered. "Are you saying you never loved Mom and Oleen?"

And then Maureen put her face back into the shop towel and cried like she hadn't cried since she was twelve years old and Janie, who had been nine at the time, had finally told her Santa Claus wasn't real.

"Of course we love your mother and Oleen," Gary said, with a tinge of anger in his voice. "Don't you ever question that. We always have and always will love them."

"Well, Uncle Gary," Scott said, "If you and Dad love them so much, then why were you making out against a truck to a song that, having to watch your tonsil hockey while listening to it, almost made Maureen here throw up?"

"It's complicated," said Delbert, clenching his fists to keep his hands from reaching up on their own and throttling Scott.

"Of course it is," Maureen sobbed, "Everything's

complicated."

"Dad," Janie interrupted, "I don't think you get to say 'it's complicated' in real life. That's just some online relationship status thing. I'm pretty sure in real life you have to, like, explain and everything."

"Wait!" Maureen sat up from her slouch, and looked at her watch. "It's 3:45! Mom, Oleen, and Agnes will be home soon. What are we gonna do? They could be home any minute."

"Well, by the time they're able to park, it will be Halloween," said Scott, "So that should help."

At the sound of Ida and Oleen's names, both Gary and Delbert sat up, looks of horror appearing in their eyes.

"Oh my god!" said Janie, "You're right! They'll be home soon. Thank god you remembered. We don't want them coming home to this. We need a plan!"

"Well, what do you suggest, Daphne?" Scott said. "Should I dress up like a sea monster and scare them away with my chains and net of seaweed?"

"Shut up, Scott!" Maureen, Janie, Delbert, and Gary all said at once.

"We should tell Jenny and Mike before we tell Mom and Oleen. This affects them too," said Janie.

At the mention of his children, Gary pressed his face further into the shop towel, hoping it would suffocate him if he tried hard enough.

"Then we can all agree on what to do next," Janie said.

"Just let Gary and me tell your mom and your aunt," Delbert said. "There's no need for any of you to be involved."

"No," said Maureen, regaining her composure. "This is a problem for all of us. And you don't even think you're gay, but Gary says this, well, this whatever it is, has been going on for, like, seven hundred years. No way do I trust you to tell anyone!"

Gary nodded and whispered, "It has. It really has."

"Scott, are Jenny and Mike in town this weekend? Do you

know?" Maureen asked.

"Why would I know that?"

"Fine, let me rephrase. Steve, do you know if Jenny and Mike are in town this weekend?"

Steve, Jenny, and Janie had all worked together at a Starbucks years before, and Steve and Jenny had become good friends, which is how Steve and Scott had met. According to Janie, Janie had wanted to introduce them for a while, but Jenny had been skeptical that anyone would want to date her obnoxious, flamboyant cousin. She had wondered though, if Steve, who was so calm and even, might mellow Scott a bit, so she decided to introduce them. There was always a disagreement between Janie and Jenny about whose idea it had been to introduce the pair, though Scott believed it to have been Janie's idea, and Steve thought it to have been Jenny's idea.

"Jenny is in town, I know," Steve said. "She had to go to a couples' wedding shower, and she wasn't too excited about it. I don't even think Jenny knows the girl who's getting married that well, and she mentioned to me she thought the girl only invited her to get an extra present. Also, she didn't want to go without a date because she was the only one going who isn't already married. I think that the shower is going on right now, and I'm sure Jenny would be delighted to leave. Let me call her, and I'll ask her where Mike is too."

"When did people start needing a date to go to a bridal shower?" Delbert asked. "That's stupid."

"Well, Dad," Scott said, "When you and Uncle Gary get married, you don't have to have a couples' shower. It can just be the two of you and a bunch of women."

Scott laughed until his eyes filled with tears.

Delbert stood up, but Maureen, who was still sitting on the bench between her dad and her uncle, grabbed Delbert's wrist and pulled him back down.

"Gary and I are not gay," Delbert said, and Gary began to

cry again.

Steve nudged Scott and turned away from the dispute. He put his cell phone to his ear and pointed toward Oleen and Gary's house. He walked away almost into the middle of their front yard to drown out the sound of Gary's crying. Steve spoke into his phone, and when he turned back a couple of minutes later, he said,

"Jenny's on her way. She was so happy I called, even though I told her she may not be pleased with the reason. But she said Mike is out of town with Lauren. They're at the beach, and he may be asking her to marry him this weekend! Jenny isn't supposed to tell anyone that, so pretend you don't know. You know how Jenny is about that stuff, though."

Everyone nodded in agreement.

"We're gonna have to go someplace else to talk about this, aren't we?" asked Steve. "I mean, Ida, Oleen, and Agnes will be home soon. And Gary is still gonna be crying, and Delbert is still gonna be angrily staring at the wall. The rest of us could try, but I don't think they can pretend they're okay."

"That's true," Scott said, "Why have we just been standing around? We're all dumb. And we better move everyone's cars. How are we gonna explain why Maureen, Janie, you, and I, plus Jenny all have our cars in the neighborhood? I mean, no way are Mom, Oleen and Agnes gonna believe we all went to the bar mitzvah afterparty to hear 'I'll Make Love to You' played by the cover band, and they certainly won't believe we all went to the McGruders' barbecue."

At the mention of the song, Maureen looked like she was going to throw up, and she knew the image of her dad and Gary making out would be inextricably linked to that song and burned into her memory for the remainder of her life.

"I'll call Jenny and see if we can meet at her house," Steve said. "It's just a small apartment but, under the circumstances, who cares?"

"Does Jenny even have a car anymore?" asked Janie. "I thought she told me she sold it because she needed the money. It was an expensive car, but I thought maybe she would have bought a cheaper car. I'm not sure if she did, though."

"Yeah, it was an obscenely expensive BMW," Steve said. "I will never understand spending the equivalent of more than a down payment on a house on a car."

"Oh, you just don't understand the value of anything nice," Scott said, bumping Steve with his hip.

"Hmm," said Steve, "That might explain how I ended up married to you, Scott." Steve widened his eyes at Scott, and they both laughed.

"Jenny, I think," said Steve, "may have some debt. I'm not going to get into it; it's not my business. She mostly takes Uber and Lyft everywhere, or she walks. I think that could be why she lives in the middle of Midtown. Lots of places to walk to. We better go now, though." Steve looked at his watch. "We don't want Ida and Oleen drunk AND angry."

"You can't get drunk on tea,'" Scott said, making air quotes with his fingers when he said the word tea. "I wonder if Mom will ever give that up. The Silver Kettle only stopped serving tea, when? During the Triassic Period?"

"I doubt she ever will," said Maureen.

"I'll call Jenny on our way to her apartment and tell her to meet us there," said Steve. "And I'll text the address, the gate code, and the apartment number to you two, Maureen and Janie."

While everyone else returned to their cars, Maureen deposited the Trader Joe's bags in her parents' garage, as far away from her dad's truck as she could. Then she marched Delbert and Gary over to O'Connell street, where this whole mess of an afternoon had started. Delbert and Gary climbed into the backseat of her Silver Honda Accord, each shoving himself as firmly into different doors as was physically possible.

Maureen didn't trust either of them, especially not her dad. She wouldn't let either one leave her sight, as she was afraid one of them might make a run for it. Well, Gary would just cry, but her dad might try to escape. During the drive to Jenny's apartment, Maureen received a call from Ida. The first part of the call consisted of Ida ranting and raving about the parking situation on Gardenia Lane, and then came the question of where everyone had gone.

Before she knew what she was saying, Maureen had announced, "We're all going to the outlet mall. You know how Scott loves to shop, and Janie needs some new maternity clothes, and Jenny's even coming because she loves the shoe store up there."

"And Gary and Delbert are with you?" Her mom asked suspiciously. "Why?"

Delbert motioned for Maureen to hand him the phone.

"Hey, hon," he said. "Yes, I know it seems strange, but there's a little car show up that way today, and also a huge Bass Pro Shop. Maureen has been telling us about the Bass Pro Shop forever, and I want to look at the fishing gear, so we all thought it might be fun to go and have dinner, and also that gives us a good excuse for missing the McGruders' barbecue. I know how you don't like having your butt touched without your permission, either, so you can pretend you came with us. Yeah, I know you think it's weird Gary and I want to go to the outlet mall. But we didn't think you'd want to go, Ida. You've been drinking for four hours. Go put your feet up and drink a lot of water. Sit on the porch or something. We won't be too long."

"It was tea," Ida insisted. "We were having tea. And it was three hours, not four. But putting my feet up on the porch with a good book and some lemonade doesn't sound like a bad idea."

And so, satisfied with this answer, Ida hung up, just as the convoy approached Jenny's apartment.

6

SATURDAY

There were only six parking spaces in the garage under Jenny's apartment building, and Maureen's, Janie's, and Scott's cars took up half of them. Above the visitor parking area were several more levels of parking, which Maureen assumed were for residents.

The building itself was pretty extensive. It was about five stories tall and looked like it housed at least thirty to forty apartments per floor. Assuming the first floor held things like the leasing office, common areas, and a fitness center, that still left four stories with at least thirty apartments per floor on the low end. *Six visitor spaces?* Maureen thought. *For a minimum of one hundred and twenty people?* And that was assuming all the apartments were studios or one bedrooms, which they couldn't be. Who designed these things? Only two people lived in her parents' house, and they alone could easily have six or seven visitors at a time parked in their driveway and in front of their house. Maureen wondered where the rest of the visitors to the apartment building would park this afternoon, and then decided she didn't care.

Maureen snapped out of her pointless analysis of Jenny's

apartment building parking garage and realized no one was moving to exit her car. She turned around to find Gary and Delbert, each with his arms crossed and each looking out different car windows, sitting so far apart it reminded her of those old TV shows where teachers at high school dances would stick a balloon in between couples to make sure they weren't dancing too closely together. Gary and Delbert had gone from close lovers to two people who appeared to hate each other in a span of fewer than two hours.

"Come on," Maureen said to them. "Get out of the car."

Gary unbuckled his seatbelt and exited the vehicle.

"Dad?"

"I'm not going in there, Reenie."

Maureen sighed. Delbert had always been as stubborn as a mule on steroids.

"You have to, Dad. We have to talk about this. You don't really have a choice."

"Actually, I do have a choice," Delbert said. "We all always have a choice. The only things in life that aren't optional are eating, sleeping, and going to the bathroom. Everything else is a choice, and I choose to stay in this car."

"Fine," Maureen said, getting out of her car and slamming the door.

She knew there was no way Delbert could escape because they had used a code to get into the visitors' area of the parking garage, and he didn't know what it was. While Gary might know the code to get into his daughter's apartment building, Maureen knew there was no way he'd tell Delbert anything under the current circumstances. There was also a keypad next to the door that led from the parking area into the apartments, which used the same code. Maureen double-clicked the alarm button on her key fob, causing her car horn to honk twice, and leaving her dad inside to bake in the heat.

There. Now, if Delbert tried to exit the car, her car alarm

would go off, and if he wanted to come inside, he would have to call someone to let him in, and he couldn't leave the parking garage because he didn't have the car keys. Maureen knew her dad had his cell phone, which would eventually die since you couldn't charge things in Maureen's car with the car turned off. All the windows were automatic, and were rolled up, and it was pushing eighty-five degrees outside. Maureen gave him five minutes before he gave up and called someone to come get him.

Scott and Steve were waiting with Janie at the door to the apartment building when Maureen approached. Gary stood off to the side, trying to disappear behind a post.

"I called Jason," Janie said. "He's on his way over."

"Janie!" Maureen said, "Why'd you do that?"

"Jason's a part of this family too, Maureen. Even if he isn't your favorite person in the world. And he's about to be the father of, so far, the only female grandchild in this family," Janie said, looking from Scott to Steve as though each had just told her she had a face for radio.

Scott held up his hands.

"We've only been married two years, Jane. Give us some time to decide if we want kids. If we have them anytime soon, you're gonna be the surrogate."

Janie, who had terrible morning sickness throughout her entire pregnancy, looked at Scott with hatred, and then turned back to Maureen.

"Maureen, I think you should call Alex too since he's the smartest, most wonderful person in the world. Perhaps he'll have some good ideas about what to do next."

Janie glared at Maureen and Maureen glared right back.

"Fine," said Maureen.

"Awesome," said Janie.

Jenny appeared at the door leading from the parking garage to the apartment building. She opened the door, and a welcome gust of cold air swept outside. Jenny seemed to be doing a mental count of her guests.

"Where are Dad and Uncle Delbert?" she asked.

"Well," said Scott, pointing just to the left of the door, "Uncle Gary's just over there hiding behind a post, and Dad is refusing to exit the car. He's locked in with the security alarm on and is gonna end up like one of those toddlers people forget in their cars in the summer when they go to work and is probably gonna die of heatstroke."

"Scott!" both Maureen and Janie said.

"You shouldn't joke about that!" Janie said.

Jenny stifled a laugh by turning it into a cough.

"See," said Scott, squeezing Steve's hand. "Reason one Steve and I shouldn't have kids."

Steve smiled tightly, so a laugh wouldn't escape.

"Well, let me get Dad," Jenny said. "You guys can go up to the apartment if you want. It's on the fifth floor, unit 5612. The door's unlocked."

Janie, Scott, and Steve filed into the building, but Maureen stayed behind in the lobby to call Alex.

He picked up on the first ring.

"Hi, Reenie, how's the decorating going?"

"I never got around to decorating," Maureen said. "There was a problem. With Dad."

"Oh my god!" Alex said, sounding worried. "What's wrong with your dad? He didn't have another heart attack, did he? Wait, he didn't die, did he? Oh my god! Oh my god!"

Good god, Maureen thought, *were people really this stupid?*

"Alex," she said. "Dad's fine. And if he were dead, don't you think I'd warn you first that I had bad news, so you wouldn't freak out on the phone with the boys around and terrify them?"

"Oh, good point," Alex said.

"What's wrong with your dad, then? I guess he's not sick or anything?"

"No, but it's not good. It's way too hard to explain on the phone. Can you come over to Jenny's apartment? We're all having a meeting to talk about it."

"A meeting? Like an intervention? Maureen, is your dad on drugs? I would never have expected your dad to have an addiction problem. Possibly your mom, yes, but never your dad."

"What do you mean you wouldn't be surprised if my mom had an addiction problem?" Maureen asked, feeling her face grow hot.

"Well, you know, sometimes she, Oleen, and Agnes do drink a lot."

"That's just on Saturday afternoons. Can you come over or not?" Maureen said in a clipped tone.

"Okay, okay. I'm sorry!" Alex said. "Yeah, my mom can watch the boys. Let me call her, and then you text me the address."

Maureen explained to Alex about the parking garage gate code and the apartment door code, promising to text it, along with the address and apartment number.

Before she hung up, Maureen said, "And Alex?"

"Yes?"

"Stop at the liquor store, will you?"

"The liquor store? What do you need from the liquor store?"

"Everything," Maureen said. "I don't care what you get. Just get a lot."

7

SATURDAY

Maureen entered the apartment building and stood in front of the bank of elevators. She looked back through the glass doors that led to the parking deck. Maureen could see Delbert sitting in the car. She hoped it was hot as hell in that car and that there wasn't enough reception on his phone for him to play Farmville. In fact, she hoped it was so hot that his phone exploded, and she'd never receive another damn Facebook Farmville notification from him for the rest of her life. Her dad was the only person in the world who still played that damn game, having hopped on the Farm-Ville train about ten years after everyone else had disembarked.

Maureen didn't see Jenny or Gary outside the doors, so she assumed they had gone up to the apartment while she'd been talking to Alex and she just hadn't noticed. She rode the elevator up to the fifth floor and located Jenny's apartment. Inside, she found Janie, Scott, and Steve all crammed, cross-legged, onto a futon just inside the entrance. In front of them sat a huge wooden Chinese horse. It was made of weathered brown wood with many red and green accents painted all over it. It resembled a gargantuan rocking horse, but with no rockers on the bottom. Janie, Scott, and Steve each leaned hard into the back of the futon to avoid moving forward, as moving even as little as a half-inch would cause them to smack their knees on it, a fact confirmed by the bruise appearing on Janie's left knee. They also had to sit cross-legged because there was no space between the giant thing and the futon, preventing them from putting their feet on the floor.

"What the hell is that?" Maureen asked, pointing at the horse.

"I think Satan might be in the apartment and he rode that here," Scott said.

"I'm not sure," said Steve, ruffling Scott's hair, "But I know Jenny has been selling things on eBay, so my guess is it must have something to do with that. Still, this seems overboard, even for Jenny. I think it would cost a few hundred dollars just to ship that thing."

"Not the hair, Steve!" Scott said, "Or I'm gonna stick you on Satan's horse and send you and it straight back to Hell."

Jenny's studio apartment was about five hundred square feet, and the futon, which sat in the small alcove just off the main entrance, combined with the big-ass damn horse, made it nearly impossible for anyone to stand inside the door, much less to enter the apartment.

"Why didn't you guys go in?" Maureen asked. "Why are you just sitting there next to this fucking horse?"

"Maureen!" Scott said, "I've never heard you talk like this before. It's so beautiful it brings tears to my eyes. And, let's see, we didn't go in because we'd need incredible mountaineering skills to climb over this damn horse."

"Oh my god! Just go in!" said Maureen. "Move it or something."

"We tried," Janie said. "We can't. It must be filled with

cement or made of lead that's painted to look like wood. I bet that's why Jenny never got it any further inside than right here."

"Satan's a big dude," said Scott. "He needs a sturdy horse."

Maureen glared first at Janie, then at Scott and Steve, and then at the horse. Scott and Steve, in reaction to the thunderous look on Maureen's face, got up off the futon and tilted the horse enough for Janie to walk around it on the side opposite the futon and to fit her now-sizable belly through the opening and into the apartment. Maureen followed Janie.

"I can't hold it anymore!" Steve yelled.

With a thud, the horse hit the floor. Steve lifted up the bottom of his t-shirt and wiped sweat from his face.

"It's a good thing that sucker is concrete," Scott said, pointing to the floor. "Otherwise some poor dude on the fourth floor would be dead from that hideous thing falling on top of him."

"I think we can squeeze through, Scott," Steve said, moving around to the side of the horse that was close to the wall opposite the futon. He smooshed himself against the wall, lifted a leg over the horse's back, caught his foot on the horse's head, and fell onto Jenny's living-room rug.

Scott glided past the horse with the grace of an Olympic ice skater.

"How do you do that?" Steve asked

"It's a trade secret," said Scott.

Scott, Maureen, and Janie stood looking into Jenny's apartment as Steve lay on his back on the living room rug. Gazing into the apartment was similar to looking at pictures of apartments online, and then, upon viewing them in real life, realizing that whoever took the photos clearly used a wide-angle lens to make the places appear habitable.

"Wow, this place is tiny," said Maureen.

"It's like a house where all those Precious Moments figurines you used to collect could live," Janie said.

"Don't talk about that!" 'Maureen said. "It was just a phase. I was only thirteen."

"Precious Moments figurines and Satan's horse all living together in harmony in a confined space," said Scott. "Gives me real hope for world peace."

The apartment was so tiny that there weren't any actual rooms. Jenny's bed, which was pushed against the back wall of the apartment and was only a twin, was up in a loft with a desk underneath it, and was separated from the rest of the apartment by a curtain, which was now open. To the right of the bedroom area was some wall space with attached clothing racks that appeared to function as Jenny's closet. The kitchen, which was the size of Maureen's guest bathroom, sat off to the right just in front of where they stood, while on the left was a small living area with enough seating for five people.

Somewhere there had to be a bathroom, but Maureen hadn't yet figured out where.

"Why would anyone live here?" Janie asked. "And I bet the rent on this place is still higher than my entire monthly mortgage payment. And how can there only be six visitor parking spaces?"

"You're probably right about the rent," said Scott. "But this is trendy central. Midtown. Look out the window. She even lives right next to one of those rainbow crosswalks."

"There are actually way more than six visitor spaces," said Steve. "Each resident is issued one visitor pass, which allows them to have a visitor park up in resident parking. I think Agnes usually uses Jenny's visitor pass. She's been coming over a lot to hang out with Jenny since everything happened."

"Hey! Dad and Uncle Gary should feel right at home here! You know, rainbow crosswalks and everything." Scott cackled with delighted laughter.

"Scott," said Steve, "You sure are heavy on the stereotypes

today. I don't care if you use them, but sometimes gay stereotypes make you mad."

Scott shrugged.

"This has to be hard for Jenny to get used to," said Maureen. "No car, and she used to live in a huge condo in a high-rise, right? I never went there or saw how big it was, but it had to be better than this. That's gotta hurt."

"Yeah, she did," Steve said, sitting up to look at Maureen. "And it was huge and had a great view of Downtown. Things haven't been easy for her."

"I feel like I barely know her anymore," said Janie. "She's hardly talked to us for the past couple of years and at family gatherings she just sits in the corner on her phone. But Maureen and I figured it was the drinking and we wondered if she and Brandon were having issues, so we've never mentioned it."

Janie looked at her sister, who nodded in agreement.

"Where are Jenny and Gary?" Maureen asked. "I thought they came up right after you two did."

"We haven't seen them," said Steve. "Last I knew, Jenny was downstairs trying to coax Gary out from behind that post."

"Does Jenny have any libations?" Scott asked, opening all of Jenny's cabinets and even her refrigerator and freezer, all of which were empty. "Wow! Jenny doesn't have anything! Maybe that horse is like a piñata or something, with food and drinks inside. But we'll never get them out. Wait, does anyone have a jackhammer?"

"Steve, what exactly does Jenny do for a living now?" asked Maureen.

"Jenny is...finding herself," Steve said. "You know, she lived with Brandon for three years. And after she figured out her mental health issues, and he realized what it meant, he kind of left her. She's been having a tough time since then. That was about six months ago and, for a long time, she wasn't able to work a lot. Coming off those wrong medications took nearly this whole six months, and the side effects were terrible. When she's been able, I'd say she's sort of worked 'odd jobs.'"

"Definitely odd," Scott said, turning around to look at the horse.

"But Jenny has an MBA!" Maureen said, shaking her head. "And she was some big deal at Home Depot headquarters."

"She was," said Steve, "But everything sort of fell apart for her when she got her diagnosis and Brandon left. Since he owned the condo, she had to find a new place to live and ended up here. She quit her job because she couldn't take the pressure and because coming off those medications was making her so sick, and she's been trying to figure things out since then."

"But who pays for this apartment?" asked Janie. "It seems like a lot of money for someone selling strange Chinese horses on eBay to come up with each month."

Steve shrugged. "Somehow she's doing it, I guess. Maybe she has a lot of savings. She used to make a lot of money."

"But then why would she sell her car if she had enough money?" Maureen asked.

"Can we lay Brandon down on the floor in front of that horse and topple it over on him?" Janie asked.

"I wasn't around him much," said Maureen, "But he always seemed solid. Not like someone who would leave if things got hard. I wondered if Jenny's drinking was an issue between them, but I've never really known how much Jenny drinks."

"Yeah, I thought he was solid too," Janie said. "So did Jenny, I think. But, apparently, he's a dick who deserves to have a large wooden horse knocked onto his head. But, now that I think about it, it's kind of weird that he barely ever came to any family events with her and he didn't come to dinner with us when we used to go all the time. Back before Maureen had Jack."

"Brandon had some issues too," Steve said, "but that's not my business to talk about."

"I'm starting to wonder if Brandon's main issue was that he was a giant dick," Maureen said.

Scott pretended to wipe a tear from his eye.

"I don't think I've ever heard this much cursing from my sisters in my life. It's so touching."

Steve stood up off the floor. Scott, Steve, Maureen, and Janie sat down on the living room couches to wait for everyone else to arrive. Maureen tapped her foot on the rug and looked at her watch.

"How is Dad still sitting in the car?" she asked.

The apartment door opened and Alex's voice said, "What the hell is this thing, Jenny?"

"It's an authentic wooden horse from the Ming dynasty," Jenny's muffled voice called from somewhere behind him in the hallway.

"Okay, under the circumstances I'm not even going to ask how you know this or why you don't move it someplace else so people can get in the door," Alex said.

"Dammit!" he yelled, accompanied by a thud and the sound of bottles knocking together. "I almost dropped the box."

Then Alex appeared in the living area, having shoved himself past the horse while carrying a large box full of what could only be alcohol. Alex was only about five foot nine, but because Maureen was short, she made him look like a giant. He was stocky, though not fat, a fact which Maureen appreciated because it made her feel thinner. Alex's wavy black hair was tucked behind his ears, and stylish, rimless eyeglasses adorned his face. His gray t-shirt and basketball shorts indicated that he'd either been exercising or playing outside with the kids.

"Sorry I'm sweaty," Alex said. "I was playing Horse with Tyler and Devin on the driveway when you called, Maureen. Jack was sitting in the yard in the baby pool and playing with a bucket not three feet from us and, somehow, he still managed to fill the pool up with dirt without any of us noticing. The other two thought it was hilarious, of course. That'll be fun to clean up later."

"I'm glad you made it safely past the guardian of the Gates of Hell," said Scott. "Mainly, because you brought liquor."

Jenny and Gary entered the apartment behind Alex, with a minimum of banging and no cursing. Jenny closed the apartment door, and she and Gary scooted past the horse.

Alex, Jenny, and Gary walked to the kitchen counter, where Alex set the box from the liquor store. Scott followed them, craning his neck to look into the box and bouncing on his feet as though he were five and it was Christmas morning.

The apartment door opened again, and there was a loud bang.

"Oh shit! Shit, that hurt!"

More banging followed, and then a loud slamming noise, which Maureen hoped was not the horse making a hole in Jenny's wall.

Delbert appeared in the apartment, standing on his left foot and shaking his right foot, gritting his teeth in obvious pain.

"I think I broke my toe," he said. "Jenny, what in the name of god is that thing and why is it blocking the way into your apartment?"

"Are you okay?" Gary asked, rushing toward Delbert.

"Oh my god!" said Scott, approaching Delbert with open arms. "The prodigal Delbert returns!"

Throwing a murderous look at his son, and rubbing his right foot, Delbert jumped, one-footed, traversing a wide path around Gary as though Gary were a canister of plutonium. Then Delbert sat down, hard, on the edge of Jenny's living room rug and turned his back to the rest of them, muttering to himself, and continuing to rub his right foot.

8

SATURDAY

J enny's living room consisted of two couches set up in an L-shape, one of which could hold three people, and one of which could hold two. Steve and Janie occupied the three-person couch with Janie on the end furthest from the other sofa, and Steve in the middle. Maureen sat alone on the two-person couch. A low square coffee table squatted in the corner between the two couches, but the table was unusable as it was covered with small beaded bracelets woven together with pieces of leather.

"What do you want, Steve?" Scott asked, tearing his eyes away from the box of liquor and noticing the table of bracelets. He looked at them as though he smelled something foul, but didn't say anything, and turned back to the box.

"Never mind," Scott said before Steve had a chance to answer, "I'll just bring you something."

"Uh, okay," said Steve.

"Dammit, we need cups," said Scott.

Scott stopped his pillaging of the box of liquor and rummaged through Jenny's cabinets for the second time.

"Maybe since now I'm looking for cups and not refreshments, I'll find some food," he said.

Jenny had returned to the entrance hall, and grunting noises indicated she was trying to move the horse, so she didn't hear Scott as he discussed her apartment's lack of suitable drinkware. The rest of the group sat quietly, waiting for Scott to locate something that would hold liquid, seeming to understand that copious amounts of alcohol would be needed to have this discussion.

Gary leaned against the kitchen counter, stealing frequent looks at Delbert, while Delbert sat on the carpet looking down at his now-bare foot and rubbing his toes. His black Reebok sneaker lay discarded to his left. Alex, who had been standing by the box of liquor, moved to the small sofa and sat down next to Maureen.

Everyone watched Scott as he plundered the kitchen for cups. After several tense moments during which the terror of an unlubricated conversation about his dad's and uncle's sexual orientations and apparent affair overtook the group, Scott found an enormous bag of large pink plastic cups sitting, inexplicably, inside Jenny's refrigerator crisper drawer. Maureen began to cry into Alex's shoulder, and Alex put his arm around her and stroked her hair.

"I should have checked down there earlier," Scott said. "Don't cry, Reenie. Now you can be drunk when we discuss the unambiguously gay duo here."

Delbert looked up from his foot and gave Scott a death stare.

"Dad," Maureen asked, "Why didn't I hear my car alarm go off? How did you get up here without setting it off?"

"Oh, that," said Delbert. "I went up under the dashboard and disabled it, as well as the automatic door locks. Don't worry, I can fix it."

Maureen glared at him.

No one asked what the hell cups were doing in the refrigerator. Scott opened the bag of cups and set a stack on the counter. He removed the bottles from the box. He opened a massive bottle of clear liquid, lifted the cups, one by one from the stack, and filled each cup from the bottle without mixing anything else into them. Them he handed out the cups like pieces of cake at a child's birthday party.

"Sorry," Scott said. "There was no ice. I checked. I even checked for ice in the cabinets."

"I need more than this," said Maureen, taking a cup from Scott's hand.

"You get what you get, Reenie," he said. "You can go back for more later."

"I can't even drink anything," said Janie, staring at the bottles of alcohol on the counter as though they were piles of the expensive makeup she so loved.

"Yes you can!" Alex said. "Scott, there's a bottle of sparkling grape juice in there somewhere. Pour some for Janie, will you?"

Janie looked at Alex thinking, against her will, that he was pretty perfect and wonderful despite the snide comments she had made about him earlier to Maureen. Jason would never have thought to bring her grape juice.

When Scott handed a cup to Delbert, Delbert pushed the cup away.

"You know I don't drink that shit, Son," he spat. "Gary and I only like beer. Heineken."

Then Delbert looked down at the floor, having realized he had mentioned his and Gary's names in the same sentence. Gary, hearing Delbert say his name and mention their shared love of Heineken, moved from his place leaning against the kitchen counter and walked to the living room rug. Gary sat down next to Delbert, eyes brimming with tears, and tried to squeeze Delbert's hand. Delbert yanked his hand away and glared at Gary as though Gary were a grizzly bear that was likely to bite off several of his fingers if given the opportunity. Delbert scooted away from Gary on the rug. He slowly inched his rear end toward the windows, and Gary crossed his arms and turned his back to Delbert.

"Two six-packs of Heineken are in there, Scott. I think they might even be cold." Alex called from the couch.

Thinking that a search for a bottle opener in this atrocity of an apartment would be a fruitless endeavor, Scott pulled a small multi-tool from the pocket of his shorts and unfolded the bottle opener. He cracked open bottles of beer for Delbert and Gary, and walked over to hand one to each of them.

Jenny reappeared in the living room, sweat streaming down her face, and dust covering her shirt. Jenny was about five foot eleven, and her height must have been passed down to her from her grandfather, because neither her mother nor her father was tall, and Jenny's brother, Mike, also happened to be tall. It was hard to understand. Jenny was glad she was tall because the fifty pounds she had gained from being on incorrect medication for the past five years didn't show quite as much as it might have otherwise.

Jenny had never been what she'd call thin, but she had been average and then, a month after starting a new medication which her old psychiatrist swore was helping her, she began to eat like she'd never see food again. She binged on all kinds of foods to the point that she gained fifty pounds and considered seeking treatment for an eating disorder. But then her new doctor took her off that medication and, like David Copperfield making the Statue of Liberty disappear, her desire to shove everything edible into her mouth went away too.

With her long, wavy, dark-brown hair, wide brown eyes, and full lips, Jenny was quite pretty. She knew she didn't look fat, exactly, thanks to her height, but she didn't look thin, or even average either, which bothered her very much and also caused her to try not to stand next to Janie unless she absolutely had to. Jenny might soon have to resort to wearing mom jeans like Maureen did. Janie had told Jenny about Maureen's mom jeans, but told Jenny she'd kill her if Jenny told anyone else. Jenny didn't fault Maureen for wearing mom jeans. She doubted her own mom jeans days were very far away, as, even though she was exercising and eating healthy foods, she couldn't seem to lose any weight. Jenny sighed at the cruelty of life.

"I was trying to move that horse," Jenny said. "Delbert's right. It's really in the way. I left it there because I want to get it appraised and that way it's closer to the door."

"You left it there," said Scott, "Because it's so big and heavy it could have easily defeated André the Giant at the height of his wrasslin' days, though I doubt that horse could have pulled itself up onto the ropes to do a dive attack, so André would have had an advantage there."

"Shut up, Scott. It's valuable," Jenny said. "And do you still watch wrestling? I thought that was something you quit doing when you were a kid."

"No," said Scott at the same time Steve said, "Yes."

"Maybe occasionally," Scott said.

"Sometimes he makes us get Pay-Per-View," said Steve.

"Thanks, Steve," Scott said. "At least I don't watch terrible movies on Lifetime and the Hallmark Channel."

Having handed everyone a cup of liquor or grape juice, Scott took a seat on one of the two uncomfortable bar chairs behind Jenny's kitchen counter. Jenny sat down next to him, brushing the dust off her shirt and onto the floor. Scott offered her a pink cup of liquor.

"I'm good," said Jenny, "I'll just pour myself some grape juice."

Jenny poured grape juice into a pink cup, and Scott grabbed a pink cup of clear liquid that was made up of way more alcohol than cup. Eager to get off the bar chair, Scott made his way to the couch and sat down next to Steve. The smell from

Scott's cup combined with the smell from Steve's cup made Janie wave her hand in front of her nose.

"What the hell is that, Scott? Moonshine?" Janie asked.

"It's Everclear," Alex said. "I figured that right now getting the job done was more important than flavor."

Maureen looked at her husband in surprise and smiled. Alex had never been a big drinker, but even he held a large cup of Everclear in his hand.

"Gee," said Janie, with a snort, "Now you're gonna be like Mom, Oleen, and Agnes at the Silver Kettle."

"Janie, I have a feeling Mom, Oleen, and Agnes are going to be spending a lot more time drinking at the Silver Kettle from now on," said Scott with obvious glee on his face. "And they may need to start requesting a splash of Everclear be added to each of their margaritas."

"Son," said Delbert from his seat on the carpet, "shut the fuck up."

"I'm so proud of all this cursing," Scott said, attempting to clap his hands before realizing he held a large cup of flammable liquid in one, and so he slapped his other hand on his knee instead.

Everyone was either sipping grape juice or on their way to drunk. Scott noticed that everyone was looking his way, so, with a considerable swallow of Everclear that made him wince as though he'd just ingested pure ethanol, Scott nudged some of the bracelets across Jenny's side table, put his cup down, and began.

9

SATURDAY

Scott looked down into his lap.

"Dearly beloved," he said, lifting his head toward the rest of the room in triple slow-motion.

"Don't even start with your Prince thing, Scott. You start every dramatic story that way!" said Janie

Scott looked around at the irritated faces staring at him.

"Okay, okay," he said, "We are gathered here today because Dad and Uncle Gary are gay lovers and Maureen caught them making out against a truck to Boyz II Men's classic hit, 'I'll Make Love to You.'"

"Scott!" Janie and Maureen shouted at the same time, while Steve tried not to snort Everclear out of his nose. Alex stopped drinking, mid-sip, mouth agape, and Jenny choked and spit grape juice into her cup.

Delbert scooted nearer to the window and stared out as though all the mysteries of life were contained just outside the dusty window pane of a five hundred-square-foot studio apartment that lacked a proper bedroom. Gary began weeping into a bright-red throw pillow he had taken off Jenny's kitchen counter. When he had moved to the carpet from the kitchen, he had taken the pillow, thinking there would likely be some crying. He hadn't stopped to wonder what a throw pillow was doing on the kitchen counter in the first place. Now he was grateful he had thought to grab something to cry into.

"Well, at least that was succinct," Scott," Alex said. "Wait, are you serious? Delbert and Gary? Gay? How can Delbert and Gary be gay? They're married, Scott. To your mom and your aunt. And making out against a truck? What?"

"As I've said before," Scott said, "Being married doesn't mean anything, though I'd argue that making out against a truck does."

"We are here, you know," Delbert said, gripping the fringe at the edge of the throw rug and twisting it as though it had done him a great personal wrong. "You don't have to talk about us like we're little kids. Next, are you going to start spelling out words, so we don't know what you're saying?"

"Yes," said Scott, "G-A-Y. Oh wait, that's an easy one, they might know how to spell it."

Delbert stared at Scott with a depth of hatred in his eyes Scott had rarely witnessed, and Scott was a lawyer.

"Gee, Dad, that's a good look for you."

Then Scott began to sing the words "Spiteful Delbert Eyes," to the tune of the old Kim Carnes hit, "Bette Davis Eyes," complete with accompanying jazz hands.

"Wow, Scott, that's a throwback, and it's helping so much," Janie said, as she observed her father glaring out the window again.

Scott stopped singing and put his hands in his lap, then grabbed his pink cup and took a large gulp. He tried not to smile.

Ignoring Scott, Maureen said, "Dad and Gary have been secret lovers for years. I just happened to catch them at their shenanigans this afternoon."

Jenny spit more grape juice into her cup and said, "Lovers? Shenanigans? Maureen, you're too much!"

"Why don't you seem more surprised, Jenny?" asked Maureen. "You should be angry. Did you already know or something? I don't see how you could have."

Jenny waved her hand.

"Remember five years ago when I drank so much at the McGruder's Memorial Day barbecue that I got alcohol poisoning and had to go to the hospital? It's because I spotted Dad and Delbert caressing each other's faces and kissing in the back of the McGruders' walk-in pantry. I never told anyone because I didn't even know how to bring it up. 'Hey, everyone, our dads are gay!' That just didn't seem like a good conversation starter."

"That pantry has been the site of so much debauchery," Scott said, attempting to lift his butt up off the couch and rub it on Steve's lap.

"Get off, Scott!" said Steve. "We all know you have shapely buttocks."

"Ohh," said Janie, "That's the year Dad and Gary went to the barbecue because Mr. McGruder ordered two times the amount of Heineken he meant to. I remember that. Wait, Jenny, why did you go? None of us had gone in years. Had it been a while and you needed your butt touched?"

Jenny laughed.

"No, I just went to take a picture of a piece of Mrs. McGruder's seven-layer salad because my friend, Leah, didn't believe anything so disgusting could even exist and I wanted to take a picture of it to prove it to her. I'd been telling her about it every year, and she never believed me, and I wanted to settle it once and for all. She was smart and never went to one of those barbecues, even though I used to invite her every year starting when we were eighteen. She'd heard enough about Mr. McGruder rubbing up against women's butts to have the sense to stay away, so she'd never glimpsed the seven-layer salad in person, lucky for her.

"I cut a piece, put it on a plate, took a picture of it and texted it to her. I might add that her response was a vomiting emoji, which was also, oddly, an accurate foreshadowing of the remainder of my day. The trash can was by the pantry, and when I went to dump the piece I'd cut into the trash, I caught a glimpse of Dad and Delbert in there pressed up against the rolling ladder in front of a shelf of soup cans. You know how that pantry has a big window in the door. They were kissing. It was shocking, to say the least. Then I went to the garage and sat with the extra kegs of Heineken and just started drinking until I woke up in the ER."

"Well," said Alex, "I have to say, this is a huge shock. I'm sorry, guys," he said, looking at Delbert and Gary. "I'm sorry to be talking about you like you're little kids or something, but I guess the best place to start is for you to tell us how this happened, and I guess when."

Gary, who had managed to stop crying into the throw pillow and calm himself enough to speak, looked up and said,

"You saw that, Jenny?"

"Unfortunately," Jenny said.

"I'm so sorry."

Jenny shrugged.

"I don't suppose drinking myself into the ER was a good choice, either."

Gary sniffed into his pillow, his nose streaming. He wiped his nose on the pillow, and Scott made a mental note never to touch it. In fact, he would steal it and stick its unsanitary ass in the trash can as soon as he got the chance.

"Well, as you all know," said Gary, in a whisper, "I met Oleen, and Delbert met Ida when we were in college. Delbert and I were roommates, and Ida and Oleen were roommates, and we were in the same year. We met Ida and Oleen at a fraternity party during our sophomore year. Only Delbert was in the fraternity. I just went to the parties, and the girls always came, too. That's just what you did for fun back then. Well, within two weeks of meeting her, Delbert had given Ida his lavalier to wear.

"I was kind of jealous because I'd had a crush on Delbert since I first laid eyes on him." Gary gazed at Delbert in admiration. "I still have a crush on Delbert."

Scott, Janie, Jenny, and Maureen all looked like they'd just eaten some of Mrs. McGruder's seven-layer salad upon hearing this admission. Steve, who was quite drunk at this point, giggled, and Alex looked perplexed. Delbert moved so near to the window that he almost had his nose pressed up against it.

"So," Gary said with a sigh, his voice gaining strength, "I accepted that Delbert liked women, and then I realized that Oleen seemed to like me, and I really did like her because she's a great girl, Oleen is. And she liked my mustache and always made me laugh. I liked spending time with her and being with her meant we could double date with Delbert and Ida, so I just went with it. Since they were twins, I figured if Delbert was with Ida, and I was with Oleen, then Delbert would always be in my life."

Jenny stared at her dad, climbed off her tall bar chair, walked to the carpet, and grabbed the red throw pillow off Gary's lap. Then she returned to her spot at the counter and sobbed into the pillow.

"So," she snorted, through tears, "You never loved Mom!"

Shaking, nose running into the pillow, Jenny retreated to her bedroom area, shutting the curtain behind her. Steve stood up from the sofa and followed her, walking with a slight wobble.

Scott, who had started drinking much faster after watching all the bodily fluids that were being forced into that throw pillow, stood up and shouted in a slurred voice, "Steve, be careful!"

"Why do I need to be careful?" Steve asked, still wobbling, but not yet slurring his words.

Scott jumped up off the couch, pulled a small bottle of hand sanitizer from his pocket, and handed it to Steve.

"Don't touch the pillow!" Scott whispered at the volume of a football coach psyching his team up for a game.

"Oh my god, Scott, learn to whisper," Steve said, taking the hand sanitizer and disappearing behind the curtain.

10

SATURDAY

Muffled noises escaped from behind Jenny's curtained "bedroom." The noises sounded like uncontrollable sobbing and occasional comforting murmurs. None of the noises sounded like someone opening a bottle of hand sanitizer.

"Steve must be really drunk," said Janie. "Steve is only not polite when he's drunk."

"He wasn't that impolite," said Alex.

"That's true," said Maureen. "Since he always has to endure Scott 'whispering' and also being a germaphobe, I'd call his response downright saintly."

"Oh shut up, Maureen," Scott slurred. "I wasn't that loud."

"Ha!" said Maureen. "Your whispering is about as successful as my efforts at stealth."

"Maureen!" Scott said, as though congratulating a small child who had just hit a home run in a little league game. "Way to go! Your face is pink. Are you drunk?"

"I don't think I am yet," she said. "But I'm working on it. I'm gonna make you proud, Scott."

"The meanest thing Steve ever said to me he said when he

was drunk," Janie said. "And, looking back, it wasn't that mean. In fact, it was kind of true."

"What was it?" Scott asked, delight in his eyes.

"Well, he said my shoes were ugly. And they were. You know how with fashion it seems okay at the time, and then a few years later you see a picture of yourself, and you're like, 'Oh my god, what was I thinking?' It was like that."

"What kind of shoes were you wearing?" Maureen asked.

"Remember those foam platform flip-flops from the early 2000s? They were, like, three inches tall, but the whole way down the shoe, not like a wedge heel. And they had rhinestones on the straps. They were black, and the rhinestones were silver."

"I thought those were cute back then!" Maureen said.

"Well, I was a little late to the party. It was 2009," said Janie.

"Honey, the party was over by then." Scott cackled. "Steve was right. In 2009 those were hideous."

"Oh shut up," said Janie. "You wear tank tops when you go out in public."

"I wear them to work out."

"You wear them to brunch! I've seen you do it loads of times. You're wearing one now. I bet if I ask Steve he'll tell me you didn't work out this morning and then go straight to brunch. You'd never go anywhere after working out without taking a shower."

"Yeah, Jane, I'll give you that. The hair wouldn't be right. I'm guilty of wearing a tank top in public. But not," Scott said, pointing first to Delbert and then to Gary, "Of having a secret gay love affair for forty years. My gay love affairs aren't secret. And none has lasted forty years just yet."

"I'm sure Steve will be pleased to know that none of the many gay love affairs you're having has lasted forty years yet," Janie said.

"You know how I love my Stevie," Scott slurred, pink in the face. "I'd never do that to him."

"Your Stevie!" Janie snorted. "I wish I were recording this."

Having been pointed at by Scott in a thoroughly drunken, yet still accusatory, manner Gary began crying again. Lacking a throw pillow or any other suitable item to cry into, Gary stood and walked through Jenny's tiny kitchen to her even more minuscule bathroom. He didn't understand how having your bathroom directly attached to your kitchen could be remotely sanitary.

Gary dug through the small linen closet inside the bathroom until he located a hand towel. It was old, and it smelled funny, but in this situation it would have to do. Unable to bear hearing his daughter's cries of anguish from behind the curtain, Gary moved from the living room into the alcove near the front door of the apartment, and sat down on the futon.

He rested his arms over the massive wooden Chinese horse's back and wept quietly into the hand towel. Though he made no noise, his shoulders shook, and his position over the horse made him look like he was in one of those antiquated contraptions used long ago for public punishment, in which a person's head and hands were stuck through holes while he knelt on a wooden bench.

Any kind of punishment would have been okay with Gary at that moment. His daughter hated him and soon his wife and son would too. Oh, and also his mother. Boy, was it a good thing his dad had died two years ago, or Gary would have had to flee the country for his own safety. And Delbert, Delbert, who had been so loving and kind to him earlier in the day, and who now wanted nothing to do with him. Delbert hated him too.

As Jenny's crying subsided, Gary dared to lift his head. He extricated himself from behind the horse. As he stood, he banged his foot into one of the horse's legs.

"Dammit!" he shouted. Now he understood why Delbert

had been hopping around and rubbing his foot earlier. Gary had wondered at the time if Delbert's supposed pain and the related drama of his saying he had possibly broken his toe had been a diversionary tactic, but now Gary knew better. Banging his own foot against that goddamn horse had hurt like a son of a bitch.

Gary limped back into the living room to see his daughter sitting on the couch next to Maureen. Maureen had her arm around Jenny's shoulder and was stroking her hair and speaking quietly into her ear. Alex had moved to the kitchen counter and was sitting on one of those horrible bar chairs. He was also refilling his sizable pink cup with more Everclear.

Oh my god! Even Alex couldn't take the stress any longer, Gary thought. This was very, very bad. Gary knew what he had to do. With quivering legs, he walked toward Jenny, dropping the odd-smelling, now soaking-wet towel onto the floor without even noticing. He crossed the tiny space to the couch to stand in front of his daughter.

"Jenny," Gary said, "I'm so sorry I've put you through this. I always have loved your mother. I promise to explain it to you and answer any questions you have. You said you saw us in the pantry five years ago."

Gary could not contain his tears.

"Jenny, sweetheart, is that what caused, you know, your problems? If it is, I'll never forgive myself."

Gary bent down to hug Jenny, who pushed him away in a huff.

"Dad, don't call them 'my problems.' There's too much secrecy in this family already."

Jenny stood up and faced as much of the crowd as possible.

"Since we're all learning things about each other today I'll just say it. I have bipolar disorder. That's why I'm not drinking. You all know that, ordinarily, in a situation like this, I'd be drinking *a lot*."

Everyone in the group looked around, nodding at one another in agreement. Jenny was definitely the biggest lush of all of them, with Ida, Oleen, and Agnes in second place, and Scott running a close third.

"I don't drink now because it's not good with my meds and I'm trying to get stable. And while we're confessing, as you may have suspected, that's why Brandon left me. In a way, I don't blame him. I put him through a lot. But in another way, I think he is a giant asshole."

Maureen and Janie both nodded.

"He's a giant asshole," said Maureen.

"Jenny," Gary said in a shaky voice. "Did seeing Delbert and me cause it?"

"No, you idiot! Bipolar disorder is highly genetic! Didn't you ever notice how batshit crazy your dad was? I'm nearly certain he had it, and Grandma agrees, but it was untreated which is like triple-time batshit crazy. Only back then they wouldn't have called it bipolar disorder, they would've just called it batshit crazy. But I guess you never noticed because you were too busy living a lie!"

Jenny sat down on the couch with such force that Maureen bounced upwards.

Gary bent down to comfort Jenny, who still had the throw pillow in her lap. Jenny began hitting Gary with the throw pillow, hard, fast, and many, many times, until Gary threw his arms up to protect his face.

"Whoa, whoa, whoa, Jenny! Stop beating your dad with the crying pillow!" Scott said, jumping up to intervene. He fell back down onto the couch, then stood up and walked toward Jenny with great concentration.

Scott grabbed the pillow from Jenny's hands, and Gary retreated to the kitchen counter, climbing onto one of the tall bar chairs and banging his foot into the chair leg. It was the same foot he had just banged on that stupid horse.

"Goddammit!" Gary shouted.

"First, Jenny," said Scott, "You just shouldn't hit your dad, not even with a pillow. Second, do you have any idea how many germs you're spreading hitting Gary with the pillow both of you snotted all over? Eww!"

Scott picked the pillow up with two fingers and held it out in front of him like it was a dead rat. Then he hurried to the bathroom and threw it into the bathtub.

"Fuck you, Scott!" Jenny called from the other room. "That's my best pillow!"

"If that's your best pillow then that giant fucking horse isn't your biggest problem, Jenny, so that's a good thing!" Scott yelled back.

Scott smiled as he noticed the odd collection of hotel toiletries lined up along Jenny's bathroom sink. While he knew Jenny had thought he was obnoxious for most of their lives, they *had* always been able to bond over their love of cursing. With a chuckle, Scott left the bathroom and reappeared in the living room. He noticed he was very, very drunk, and that Steve's head was resting against the back of the sofa and his eyes were closed.

Scott sat down next to him.

"Drunk as a skunk," Scott said, nudging Steve with his elbow.

"Go away," said Steve, not bothering to open his eyes. "You're way drunker than I am. In fact, I'd call your baseline level of existence drunk."

"You're right, Janie," Scott said. "He's a saucy drunk."

"Hey, Delbert!" Scott called to his dad, who sat so still and quietly by the window, and who had so much sweat soaking through the back of his shirt that he could be mistaken for an old-time radiator. "We haven't heard from you in a while. What say you?"

Scott's slurring problem was getting worse, though he was still remarkably lucid.

Delbert raised his middle finger into the air without even turning around.

"Seems like a good analysis," said Scott.

11

SATURDAY

Alex watched Scott as he flitted from person to person, heckling each and causing mayhem like a toddler running amok in a restaurant. Alex watched Delbert staring out the window, and then looked at Gary, who sat next to him on one of the horrible bar chairs. Gary had his head down on the counter and was resting it on his arms. He was crying into the sleeve of his shirt now. Though Gary was crying over the situation at hand, he could also have been crying about how much these damn bar chairs hurt his butt, Alex thought. Alex stood up. It was time someone did something, or they would be here until Christmas, when Delbert and Gary could make out against a truck with a wreath on the front, or, if they celebrated the holiday at Scott and Steve's beach house, perhaps against a festively decorated boat.

"Look, we've wasted a lot of time here and haven't made any real progress," Alex said. It's been an hour since we got here and the most helpful thing that's happened is Scott throwing that disgusting red throw pillow into the bathtub. I don't know how long this story of a trip to the outlet mall is going to hold, either, but I'd say we have an hour at most to figure out what to do.

"Scott, Steve, get up and sit on the floor. Janie, you stay there and Delbert and Gary, you sit on the couch with Janie."

Everyone followed Alex's instructions. As Janie scooted to the edge of the couch nearest Maureen, Delbert appeared from nowhere like a leopard launching itself out of a tree. He rocketed onto the sofa next to Janie, into the spot nearest Maureen, shoving Janie back into the middle, and forcing Gary to take the spot on Janie's other side. Janie looked with disgust from one man to the other. Her large belly made it virtually impossible for them to even see each other, which Janie supposed was the point.

Janie marveled at how quickly her father had moved when he had dived onto the sofa. Delbert sometimes walked with a slight limp, but his launch onto the couch had been nothing short of impressive. Janie would have to keep in mind that Delbert could haul ass when needed, say, for after she'd had the baby and wanted him to take the stroller down the street with her. He'd try to get out of it so he could sit on his butt watching sports in that fancy lounge chair he kept in the garage, but if he tried to beg off, she'd remind him of this moment.

Maureen continued to calm Jenny as Steve and Scott sat down on the floor where Delbert had been, against the wall near the window, so they could see Alex as he spoke.

"Guys," Alex said, looking at Gary and Delbert and, by default, Janie, "I'm sorry to be less than gentle about such a difficult topic, but we need to get home by seven at the latest to avoid raising suspicion with Ida and Oleen. So, I'm going to ask you some questions, and I'd appreciate honest answers."

Both men nodded and frowned.

"Gary, you said that in college Delbert seemed taken with Ida, and so you started dating Oleen, right?"

"Yes," Gary said, head hung low.

"So, then, when did this, 'love affair,' or whatever you want to call it, start? I mean, if Delbert was into girls how did this even happen?"

"Well," Gary began, "All during our freshman year I got the sense that Delbert might feel something for me. Of course, I would never, ever have said anything, Delbert being so manly and all. How would I be lucky enough that he'd be interested in me? But, one night, I think it was Halloween—"

"It was Halloween," Delbert interrupted.

Maureen gagged at hearing her uncle refer to her dad as "manly."

"Well, on Halloween, the two girls, Delbert and I went to a party. I don't think I wore a costume, I can't remember."

"You were dressed as the Green Hornet," said Delbert. "You wore a leotard."

"Okay, well that's not important. We got back to our dorm room after the party, and we were both highly inebriated. I remember getting into my bed, and a few minutes later I heard Delbert retching, only he wasn't in the bathroom, he was in his bed! His bed was so disgusting, and we were both so impaired that there was no way we could have cleaned it up right then. Delbert began walking to the little couch next to the mini fridge, but I asked if he'd like to sleep with me, and, somehow, he came and got in my bed. He lay behind me with his arm over me, and then, after a few minutes he reached down and started to touch my—"

"We get it, we get it!" Alex said, holding up his hands and hoping Gary would stop.

"So, did this happen all through college?" Alex asked.

"Yes," Delbert sighed, shocking everyone by speaking. "We shared a bed almost every night."

Scott laughed like a hyena.

"Nice one, Dad. I can really see how you're not gay."

Alex gave Scott a stern look and continued talking.

"And so, the whole time you were 'sharing a bed' you dated Ida and Oleen too?"

"Yes," Gary and Delbert said in unison, not daring to raise their eyes to meet the crowd.

"Mom and Aunt Oleen aren't dumb," Maureen said. "I mean, Mom is, but only about the names of TV shows and movies. Not about anything else. So, how did they not figure this out during three years of dating you two?"

"Well," said Delbert, "Your mom and your aunt were not 'loose women' as some people might say."

"They're called floozies, Dad!" Scott called merrily from the window. "And why the sudden honesty? Are you gonna have to go to the bathroom soon? The bathroom for avoidant people?"

Delbert ignored him.

"They were the 'wait until marriage' type. While I much preferred kissing Gary, kissing your mother was not unpleasant. And, while you may not know this, neither Ida nor Oleen likes to spend too much time in the bedroom, if you get my drift."

Maureen, Janie, Scott, Jenny, and even Steve and Alex cringed at this thought.

"Well," said Alex, feeling shocked that Delbert was speaking at all, much less sharing information about his mother-in-law's bedroom behaviors and his own feelings about kissing Gary.

"Delbert, you married Ida, and Gary married Oleen, and you even live next door to each other. So how have you put the brakes on this affair while living in such close proximity? And why did you marry Ida and Oleen? If you wanted to be with each other, I mean?"

"It was 1975," said Gary, "And it was much easier to be a married man with a family than it was to be a gay man living out in a hostile world. Delbert and I both wanted kids and, as I said, we both thought Ida and Oleen were great girls, so getting married to them, having kids, and being in a situation where we could still see each other seemed like the best choice at the time."

"Can anyone spell used?" Scott asked. "Because that's how Mom and Aunt Oleen are going to feel when they find this out. You might want to, you know, find a better way to relay that story, Gary."

Delbert slouched and looked at the floor, his face turning maroon, while Gary sat up a little straighter.

"But," Alex continued, "How did you manage to stay away from each other for all these years? I mean, I don't think I could live so close to Maureen and not want to be with her, so how did you two do it?"

"Well," Delbert began, looking like he was going to throw up on the beaded leather bracelets that covered Jenny's side table, "There were only four times during our marriages when anything happened between Gary and me, and those were all isolated incidents. That's why we're not gay."

Scott guffawed until Steve elbowed him in the ribs and he became silent.

"One was, as you know, when Jenny saw us in the McGruder's pantry. There were also three other times. But things started up what I would call, 'full time' again about two years ago when Ida, Oleen, and Agnes took a spring break trip to the beach."

Maureen and Janie each put their heads in their hands. Alex and Steve stared at Delbert and Gary, and Jenny began crying into Maureen's shoulder again.

"You've been having a full-time affair for the past TWO YEARS?" Maureen asked, and then began to cry into Jenny's right shoulder, as Jenny continued to cry into Maureen's left.

A look of amusement crossed Scott's face. "Oh my god! This has been going on now for TWO YEARS? For two freaking years right under our noses and none of us realized it? I mean, I didn't know it was ongoing. I just thought it was something that happened from time to time and the rest of the time you just pined for each other. It's amazing you don't possess the gift of stealth, Maureen, since Dad obviously does."

"Wait, Scott. Did you, I mean, did you know about this too? I mean, not just speculating with Steve, but did you *know*?" Maureen asked, between sobs.

Before Scott could answer, the front door opened and a female voice called, "Yoo-hoo! Jenny! I've got those plates you've been asking about. I hope it's okay I just came in. The door was open a crack. I didn't think anything was wrong like you'd been robbed or something. I thought you were just letting in some air."

The door shut, and noises from the entryway indicated someone moving around the horse, without cursing or injuring herself.

Then Agnes stepped into the living room, and looked from face to face, her eyes finally landing on the large bottle of Everclear on the counter.

Agnes, like Scott, liked to look good. At eighty-two, she took care of herself, exercising regularly and having her hair colored regularly at a salon, platinum gray with tasteful lowlights and highlights. Her hair was straight and hung past her shoulders, and today the highlights had an almost imperceptible tinge of lavender to them. Janie was pretty sure Agnes spent nearly as much time on her hair as Scott did, as such a sleek, straight look was not possible without freshly washing and drying your hair and using a high-quality flat iron. Agnes wore a pair of yellow Capri pants with a black boatneck t-shirt and a pair of black sandals. She carried a black tote bag on her left arm and held the plates with both her hands. Her fingernails and toenails were painted in matching light gray. Agnes frequently mentioned that old ladies with brightly-colored fingernails looked tacky, and if there was one thing Agnes hated, it was tacky.

Agnes walked across the living room to the kitchen and set the plates in the sink, picked up a pink plastic cup, and poured herself enough Everclear to keep an army in the desert hydrated, yet impaired, for three weeks. Agnes sat in one of the high-backed chairs, the one Alex had recently vacated and slowly brought the pink cup to her lips.

"Uh-oh," she said. "I think I know what's happened here, and this isn't good."

12

SATURDAY

"Well, I understand now why we're all drinking in Jenny's tiny apartment that everyone clearly doesn't fit into," said Agnes, taking another sip from her pink cup.

She looked at the couch, where Gary sat with tears welling in his eyes at the sight of his mother, and at Delbert, who was staring down at his feet.

"Yes," said Agnes, her eyes sweeping the room, "There's only one thing this could be. I've always wondered if this would happen. I would have asked where Ida and Oleen are. You know how they love drinking. Oh, sorry," Agnes said, "They love having 'tea.' Agnes made air quotes with her fingers as she said the word tea. "But I'm assuming they're not here because the jig is up."

Everyone stared at Agnes, with facial expressions ranging from Janie's puzzlement to Scott's obvious delight, to Gary's countenance of abject terror.

Gary looked at his mother, his face a mask of fright typically found on the faces of recently-slaughtered victims in horror movies.

"Uh, uh, uh..." said Gary.

"It's okay, honey, I know. I've always known."

"Oh my god," Gary said, sliding down on the couch until his knees almost touched the floor.

"You've always known what?" Maureen asked.

"Grandma's always known that Gary is gay, and she's also known for a long time that Delbert and Gary have been secret lovers for, like, two hundred years," said Jenny.

Agnes studied each face in the room, and with a dismissive wave of her hand said, "You all are just now figuring this out? I thought it was pretty obvious."

Maureen, Janie, Scott, Steve, Alex, Delbert, and Gary looked as though they'd just had their heads smashed, in turn, into the side of Jenny's wooden Chinese horse.

"Since when do you call your dad Gary?" Scott asked Jenny.

"Since I found out my life is a lie and I don't know my own dad," said Jenny.

"Wait, wait, wait, wait!" said Maureen, "You knew this, and you didn't tell anyone, Agnes? And Jenny knew too? That Gary has always been gay, I mean."

"I didn't know THAT," Jenny said. "Until Grandma told me, but it does make sense."

Gary slid further down on the sofa until he was sitting on the floor. He covered his face with his hands. Delbert slumped, refusing to look up.

"Well, I didn't KNOW, not exactly," said Agnes. "Not at first. It's just, well, ever since Gary was five his father and I figured he might be. I mean, it wasn't as easy to tell as it was with Scott. I'm pretty sure Scott exited the womb waving a rainbow flag and liking brunch. But it became evident to us pretty quickly."

Scott waved at Agnes. "You are one perceptive lady." He laughed.

"But how did you know?" Janie asked. "And you and Jenny have talked about this?"

"Mostly it was that Gary is pretty effeminate. Surely you've noticed that." Agnes said.

Everyone in the room, including Gary, nodded their heads.

"And Jenny came to me after she saw Gary and Delbert together in the McGruders' pantry several years ago. Bad juju in that pantry. Once, long ago, Mr. McGruder found me in there getting some more paper towels and 'accidentally' grabbed my butt while claiming to be reaching for more paper plates. When Jenny came to talk to me and mentioned the McGruders' pantry, at first, I thought Bill McGruder had grabbed her butt, too. But then she told me the story. She said she needed to tell someone who knew Gary and Delbert very well. And I told her I already knew."

"That was a big relief," Jenny said, "To know that I wasn't crazy, and Grandma knew it too, even though maybe sometimes I am a little crazy."

"Now, Gary was never into sports or anything either," Agnes said, "As a kid, I mean, but that wouldn't by itself mean he was gay. It was lots of little things. Herman was always trying to get him interested in sports, but it never took. Herman was pretty disappointed to have a gay son. I wouldn't say that in front of Gary, but I do because Gary already knows. Unfortunately, Herman made that fact pretty clear."

Gary's shoulders drooped and he pulled himself back up onto the couch. He faced the room. "He really did," said Gary.

"He made Gary feel like something was wrong with him without ever accusing Gary of being gay, and without ever saying why he thought there was something wrong with Gary. I didn't realize until later how hard Herman had been on Gary. Gary never understood why his dad seemed to dislike him so much, not that he ever told me. I wish I'd done more to put a stop to that, Gary," Agnes said, looking across the room. Her voice quavered, but she controlled it. "Your father could be difficult, though, when he had one of his 'spells.'"

"Jenny's right," Gary said. "Dad was batshit crazy. And I did know why he didn't like me, but not until I was about fourteen. Before that I suspected, but I just thought he hated me all around."

"I agree he acted crazy sometimes, Gary," Agnes said. "Still, I loved your father. When he wasn't going through one of his 'spells,' he could be pretty great."

"I remember that," said Gary. "It's too bad that in between them he was insane. And mean."

"Sound familiar, Dad?" Scott called from his seat up against the wall.

"Shut the hell up, Son," Delbert called back.

Agnes continued.

"Things got better when Gary was about eight or nine and developed an interest in cars. Herman loved cars too, only he loved them for their speed and the statement they made. Gary loved them for their aesthetic qualities and because he was interested in how the appearance of a car related to how it worked. So they had something to bond over. I was quite shocked when Gary was in college and announced he had a girlfriend, and even more shocked when he told me he was getting married. Herman was shocked too, and that was the first time we openly discussed the fact that we both thought Gary was gay. But because Gary never dated in high school and we'd never discussed it previously, we had always just let it go and decided that maybe there was a small possibility we were wrong and Gary wasn't gay. When Gary decided to marry Oleen, though, we were worried. We loved Oleen, of course, but we wondered, even Herman wondered, if Gary would truly be happy. But we decided it wasn't our place to butt in and say anything."

"*Dad* was worried about me being happy?" Gary asked, tears running down his cheeks again.

"Yes, honey, he was," Agnes said, her voice catching in her throat.

Gary looked around for a pillow or dish towel, and Agnes pulled a package of tissues from her tote bag and tossed it to Gary. Gary hated tissues, but he supposed he didn't have much choice.

"But how could you not be surprised about Dad?" Janie asked. "Never in a million years would I think my dad was gay. I mean, he's such a, a man! He's dirty and messy and wears overalls to restaurants."

Delbert scowled at Janie.

"Now that did surprise me when I found out, Janie. I was shocked when I discovered that not only was Gary gay, but that it was Delbert he was interested in. I don't seem shocked now, but, believe me, when I found out I was downright flabbergasted. I thought Ida and Delbert were a real couple, and that Gary and Oleen had somehow ended up together just because they were so close to Ida and Delbert. I know I don't seem bothered now, but that's because I found out so long ago—right after Gary and Oleen got married."

13

SATURDAY

Everyone stared at Agnes in silence.

"Oh my god, Mom! I'm so embarrassed!" Gary said. "You *knew* way back then?"

Gary held his head in his hands, resuming his most recent crying jag, two tissues having disintegrated onto the floor. Delbert continued staring at his feet.

"How did you find out?" Gary asked in a whisper.

"It was 1975," Agnes said. "That was back when Caroline, Ida and Oleen's mom, was still with us. It was about a year before she got sick with cancer. It was the second year the McGruders had their annual Memorial Day barbecue. The McGruders had moved to Magnolia Manor the year before, and, since Caroline, Ida, and Oleen had always lived just around the corner from where the McGruders lived, and Caroline still lived there, everyone in the family always ended up being invited to the barbecue. The McGruders were always good about inviting whoever wanted to come, but the crowd dwindled as more and more women realized how handsy Bill McGruder was. But still, many women continued going just to be polite, and because their husbands were thrilled with the amount of beer Mr. McGruder always bought for the occasion, so I guess the women felt like they had no choice. I'm getting off topic."

"Wow!" said Scott. "Mr. McGruder should have a slogan, you know, like products in stores do. Like, 'Bounty, the Quicker Picker Upper.' I can see it now on a billboard, or at least on a yard sign on Magnolia Manor. I know! A yard sign in the McGruder's front yard: 'Mr. McGruder: Grabbing women's asses since 1975.'"

Agnes chuckled.

"Well, Bill McGruder certainly has been doing that since well before any of you were alive. Okay, back to the story now. So, I was in the house with Caroline, and she was making some kind of taco casserole. All the women brought food to the barbecue. This was partly because it's polite, and partly because, aside from the hamburgers Bill cooked on the grill, the rest of the food was pretty bad. Grace McGruder's cooking was atrocious. If no one had brought other food, there wouldn't have been anything, well, anything *edible* to eat. I haven't been in years, because Bill McGruder has no age preference when it comes to butts, but I seem to remember some disgusting salad with marshmallows on top. That was the worst."

Everyone nodded. Janie, who began to picture the salad, including the only time she had sampled it, remembered its taste and looked like she was going to throw up.

"So, Caroline and I were cooking—well, she was cooking and I was sitting in a chair talking to her—you know how she loved cooking. I love cooking too, but she never seemed to want any help, so I would just watch her cook and chat with her. I think Herman was over at the McGruders', he said he was going to help Bill make the hamburgers, but really it was so he could get a head start on the beer. Ida and Oleen left Caroline's house through the side door in the kitchen. They wanted to go play with the McGruders' dog before the party got too crowded.

They loved the McGruders' dog. He could do interesting tricks, like jumping through a hula hoop, and he loved to fetch. He was a border collie, and those are very smart dogs, but he had quite an unusual name for a dog: Michael. I always chuckled about it because giving your dog a very common human name strikes me as funny. Like Jessica, or David. Okay, back to the story.

"Caroline got a phone call, and she answered it, and it appeared it might be a long conversation, so I took the opportunity to use the powder room off the kitchen. Just as I was about to go into the bathroom, I saw that the bathroom door was open a crack. I could see that there was someone in there. I thought, 'Why is this door open at all if someone's in there? I don't want to see anyone going to the bathroom.'

"As I stood thinking that thought, I looked through the crack where the door was open, and I was able to make out Delbert, sitting on the lid of the commode, turned to the side toward the tub, and Gary, standing behind him giving him a shoulder massage. It's good they were turned away from the door, and also that no one was using the bathroom. I thought, 'Boy is that weird! Who gives someone a shoulder massage while they sit on the commode?' And then it struck me that most men don't give each other massages, on the commode or anywhere else. I stood very still because I didn't want them to see or hear me, but I saw Delbert lean his head back and kiss Gary on the lips. And not a quick kiss you could attribute to some cultural thing, but I mean a kiss like in that movie where that man and that woman are making out on the beach. What *is* the name of that movie? This is gonna drive me crazy all day."

"From *Here to Eternity*," Scott called.

"That's it!" said Agnes, snapping her fingers. "Thank you, Scott."

"You're welcome, Agnes," Scott said with a smile. "But why

the thing about the kiss being cultural? I mean, that's not exactly an American custom."

"I was trying to make the story less embarrassing for your dad and your uncle," Agnes said in a loud whisper.

"Oh, Jesus Christ!" Delbert yelled, throwing one of Jenny's beaded leather bracelets against the wall. "We can hear you! Why are you whispering? And what the hell are these?" Delbert asked, holding a second bracelet and looking at Jenny.

"They're bracelets I made to sell on Etsy," said Jenny.

"Well they," Delbert said, narrowing his eyes at Jenny, "are ugly."

Gary jumped up in shock.

"Delbert!" he said, moving to stand in front of the man he had just hours earlier been kissing up against the door of a Ford F-150, "Don't you dare speak that way about Jenny's bracelets. Jenny is trying very hard to get back on her feet."

Jenny began crying into Maureen's shoulder again, and Maureen stroked Jenny's hair and glared at Delbert.

"I know you're angry, and evidently hate me now, Delbert, and you want to deny our love," Gary said, "And you go ahead and you do that, but don't you dare speak that way to my daughter."

Gary walked over to Jenny, who stood up and hugged him.

"I love you, Dad," she sniffled, "and I'm sorry for hitting you with a pillow."

"It's okay, honey. I love you, too."

Staring at the floor again, Delbert ground his shoe into the carpet like a bull pawing the dirt before attacking a matador.

14

SATURDAY

"Okay," said Alex, standing up from his chair at the kitchen counter. "So we've established that this affair has been going on for a long, long time, and Agnes, Jenny, and Maureen have all caught Delbert and Gary together. Guys," Alex said, looking from Delbert to Gary and back, "Believe me. I know this is embarrassing, and I'm trying my best to be gentle here, but you said there were only four times you were together between when you got married and two years ago, right?"

Gary and Delbert both nodded.

"Did anyone else ever catch you all together? I mean, if both Agnes and Jenny did, then isn't it possible Ida and Oleen know? Did anyone else in here ever see them together?" Alex asked, looking around at the crowd.

Both Scott and Steve raised their hands, then stared at each other like each was watching the other turn into a unicorn.

"No!" said Scott, with an excitement reserved for seven-year-old girls receiving ponies for their birthdays. "You saw them, too? I can't believe you didn't tell me!"

"Well, you didn't tell me, either," said Steve.

"Oh. My. God. Where did you catch them, Steve? This is gonna be good, because Steve is so discreet it could be baaaaaaaaaaad, and Steve would never tell anyone."

"He told me," Jenny said. "When he came to the hospital the night I had alcohol poisoning. I think he told me to make me feel better after I told him I caught them in the pantry, but he did tell me. And he didn't tell you, Scott."

Jenny laughed and Scott rolled his eyes at her.

"What happened, Steve?" Alex asked.

Both Delbert and Gary looked as though they wanted to crawl under the couch, obviously remembering the incident in question.

Delbert got up and raced out of the room.

"Gotta go to the bathroom!" Delbert yelled. Gary slid back down on the couch again.

Maureen wondered how, with two incidents left to choose from, both men seemed to know what was coming. They hadn't realized anyone else had seen them together, after all. She wasn't sure she wanted to find out about this incident.

"Okay," Steve said. "Well, I'm just going to make this as quick and as painless as possible. Sometimes I go to the gym. Scott tries to get me to go to that awful Gray's Gym that's about a mile from here. I call it Gays' Gym because it's just a lot of gay guys strutting around trying to impress each other, and they all have Lycra on, and I just want to wear my ratty shorts and t-shirt, so I go to the YMCA near the townhouse. I'm not in shape like those guys. They make me want to hide."

"Scott always has liked to strut," Janie said, and she, Maureen, and Jenny cackled.

"Well, when I finish my workout, I go into the steam room. It's relaxing, you know? It's in the locker room, and I take my shirt off when I go in because I always wear these moisture-wicking shorts that dry fast, but I wear regular t-shirts so they just get gross and wet in the steam room. Still, I don't take my shirt off until I'm right outside the steam room and then I just hang it on a hook, and nobody bothers it, probably because it smells. So, the year before Jenny got alcohol poisoning, not long after Scott and I met, I was at the Y, and I was headed to the steam room when I thought I saw Gary walk around the corner ahead of me. I wasn't sure it was him, because I'd only met him one time at that point, and when I saw him at the Y it was from the back. Then he bent down to drink from the water fountain, and I saw his mustache, and then I was sure it was him.

"I was wondering why he was at a YMCA so far away from where he lived. Then some guy walked by and knocked into me by accident, and I ended up behind a potted tree. I'm glad I did because when I looked back out, I saw Delbert walk up behind Gary and hit him on the butt with his hand. I thought that was weird because most people don't do that. I'd never even do that to Scott, especially not in public. And if a guy did that to a girl in public or vice versa, that would be really weird, too. Then Delbert kind of glanced toward the tree and examined it like he saw me or something, but eventually he turned away. They both hurried into the steam room in their workout clothes. And Gary had on long pants, like wind pants. It's bizarre to go into the steam room fully clothed, and in wind pants I think you might die. I stood behind the tree a minute longer, and I saw Gary stick his head out of the steam room door and look around like he was relieved, so I guess maybe Delbert did think he saw me and Gary was double-checking."

"Oh my god," Gary moaned, head in his hands. "Don't go on, Steve. Please!"

"It's okay, Gary, I won't say much more. I decided to go sit in the lobby for a few minutes and cool down. I know I could have just gone home, but steam rooms are relaxing, if you've never tried one, and it's part of my routine, so I like to stick to it. I waited about twenty minutes thinking Delbert and Gary would have left by that time. Let's just say when I peeked into the steam room twenty minutes later and found that they hadn't left, I knew what was going on between them, but neither of them, uh, saw me. I closed the door quickly and quietly, and I skipped the steam room that day."

"Oh my god! Steve! I can't believe you didn't tell me! Right after that was when you started asking me if I noticed how much my dad and Gary touched each other unnecessarily. Oh my god, I am so dumb!"

"So, it *was* you. Oh my god," Gary said. "I told Delbert if he thought he saw you we shouldn't chance it, but he said you went to the gym with Scott so it couldn't be you, and I looked out and didn't see you."

"Dad!" Scott called, "You can come out now. Release the Kraken! Return, Delbert! Oh, I guess you and Gary already released the Kraken in the YMCA steam room!" Scott giggled.

Delbert walked out of the bathroom, but stood next to the kitchen counter, either not having heard what Scott said, or ignoring him. Scott leaned toward the rest of the group like it was story-time at the library.

"Uncle Scotty has quite the tale for you," he said.

15

SATURDAY

"Uncle Scotty?" Janie asked. "Eww! That sounds like you're going to lure small kids into your windowless white van with balloons and candy."

"Oh, shut it, Janie," said Scott. "Even if that were the case I would never, ever drive a windowless white van. That's so tacky."

"That would be tacky," Agnes agreed.

"The year was 1998," Scott said, "And there was a very gay little boy named Scott. No one had ever questioned whether little Scott was gay from the time he was five and tried to kiss Barry Jensen underneath the termite tower in kindergarten."

"What's a termite tower?" asked Steve.

"It's code for a playground play structure, but it's made totally out of wood," Scott said, "So I guess termites could eat the whole thing. This boy, Scott, his dad didn't like him being gay and made him feel like he was no good for a long time, until Scott was eleven. Because the year Scott was eleven was a very important year. It was the year of an event young Scott would from then on refer to as 'The Reckoning.'"

"Oh my god, Scott, get to the point, and stop talking about

yourself in the third person. That's so annoying!" said Janie. "I'll have this baby before you finish your story."

"If you do, will you name the baby after me?"

"It's a girl, Scott! What do you want me to call her? Oh, I know! How about Scotty Beth?"

"Okay, okay," Scott said, talking faster and dropping the story-time voice. "Basically, when I was eleven, Mom asked me to go out back and cut the grass. She paid me like $5 to do it, which I thought was a fortune at the time. If I had $5, I could get some decent hair gel at the drugstore. So, I went to the shed to get the lawn mower, and I thought I heard something. It sounded like giggling. I crept quietly around the shed because, unlike Maureen, I possess the gift of stealth."

Maureen rolled her eyes at Scott.

"I saw Dad and Uncle Gary sitting in the grass up against the shed. They were both wearing Zubaz pants. It was the late 90s, and well past the heyday of Zubaz pants, but you know how fashionable Dad and Uncle Gary are. Hell, I think even I was wearing Zubaz pants. In my defense, I was a kid and Uncle Gary gave me those pants for my birthday, and, even though I knew they weren't in style, the fact that they weren't made me seem more mysterious at school. The pants make sense, because Mom always made me wear long pants and tennis shoes when I cut the grass. The tennis shoes I understand, but how would long pants have protected me from a flying rock? It would still have hurt, even through the pants. Zubaz pants were ugly as sin, but I'm pretty sure I had some on, and I found my brown zebra-striped pair to be quite fetching. My sisters know I went through a phase where I would only wear neutral colors."

Janie and Maureen nodded.

"It was so weird," said Maureen.

"So, I saw Dad and Uncle Gary giggling behind the shed. Dad was stroking Uncle Gary's thigh through Gary's pink leopard-print Zubaz pants, and I remember thinking, 'How tacky!

Those pants are hideous!' And then Gary lovingly pushed the hair off Delbert's forehead, and—"

"Oh, enough!" Delbert said. "Everyone gets the picture, Scott. I had no idea you saw that. But now it makes a lot of sense. After that, you ignored anything negative I said to you. Your mom was always on me about the things I said, and around the time I think this happened she pointed out how much happier you seemed, and so I just tried my best to stop saying negative things altogether. Once I did that you would talk to me sometimes, and so I was glad I did. But I know I made your first eleven years hard."

"I believe the word is hell, Dad," Scott said with less enthusiasm than usual, looking down at his lap.

Alex stood back up.

"Okay. Wow, man. I can't believe so many of you knew about this and didn't say anything to the rest of us. I mean, I get it. What would you even say? But I'd be willing to bet Ida and Oleen don't know if those of us who didn't catch Delbert and Gary firsthand didn't know."

"For all we know, they found out some other way, and they do know. I mean, maybe they noticed the excessive touching or something," said Jenny. "But I never noticed it until the alcohol poisoning incident, so who knows?"

"I'm wondering how we didn't see this," Janie said. "It seems so obvious now."

"When you get used to someone you tend to stop noticing things about them, so it makes sense," said Maureen. "Like, before I met Alex, I dated this guy who used to snort whenever he laughed. I liked him, so I overlooked it. We dated for about six months and, then, one day I introduced him to one of my friends he'd never met before, and someone told a joke, and he laughed really hard and snorted a lot, and my friend said, 'Oh my god, how do you stand that snorting?' After that, it was the only thing I noticed about him, and it made him less and less attractive to me until I had to break up with him. But for six months, I just stopped noticing that he snorted like a farm animal anytime he laughed. I don't know how I quit noticing! It's okay, though, because I met Alex a week later."

"Well, I think maybe we should talk to Ida and Oleen tomorrow, after Janie's baby shower," said Agnes.

Janie smiled and clapped her hands.

"I had a hunch it was a baby shower tomorrow and not just lunch," she said, smiling. "Thanks, Reenie!"

"I'm sorry to tell you in advance, Janie," Maureen said, but I think we've all had enough surprises."

"That sounds like the best plan," said Agnes. "At least let them enjoy the baby shower before we obliterate their lives."

Everyone, even Delbert, agreed to this plan. Delbert looked defeated. As they were about to head home, the outlet mall story losing credibility by the minute, Jenny's door opened, and there was a noise that sounded like someone tripping over the giant wooden horse.

"Goddammit!" they heard a man's voice yell.

Scott unsuccessfully tried to stifle a giggle. Jason appeared next to the couch.

"I'm not even gonna ask," he said to Jenny. Jason was about six feet tall, with curly blonde hair, mischievous blue eyes, and a perpetual grin on his face. He wore a green polo shirt tucked into khaki pants. Jason came off as very charming at first, until he opened his mouth.

"Hey, babe," he said, kissing Janie on top of her head. "Sorry I'm late."

"You're not late," Janie said. "You missed everything."

Tears brimmed in her eyes, but she held them back.

"You know how it is when you manage a restaurant, Janie. Stuff happens, I couldn't get away. Let's just argue about this later, okay?"

Janie stood up and stomped toward the door, holding her

belly as she went. They heard her huff past the horse without running into it at all. As Jason raided the liquor box for all the leftover Heineken, Scott stood up, no longer wobbling, and walked over to the counter, positioning himself right in front of Jason.

"You, my friend," Scott said, poking Jason in the chest, "Are a motherfucker."

Then Scott turned and strode toward the door of the apartment, grabbing Steve's hand and pulling him up as he walked past the couch. He and Steve left, making no noise at all as they passed the wooden horse.

PART II

16

SUNDAY, THE DAY BEFORE MEMORIAL DAY

I da McNair woke up and looked at the clock on her iPhone. 7:30. In the morning. Why couldn't she ever sleep past eight? She had just the tiniest headache from yesterday's tea. Delbert hadn't gotten home until 9 p.m., which Ida had thought was strange because she'd asked him loads of times to go to the outlet mall with her, and he had always refused. Then, when he finally did go, most of her family had gone too, without her, and had stayed almost until the place closed! Ida was a little miffed, if she was honest with herself.

She rolled over, expecting to see Delbert, but instead she saw a Delbert-shaped indentation in the bed. The baby shower decorations hadn't been put up yesterday for some reason she didn't yet know. Ida had lain on a lounge chair on the porch all afternoon and had taken a long nap in the heat, from which she woke herself several times with her own snoring. Too much tea did that to her. It had started to get dark and, with a momentous effort, she had moved inside and lain down on the living room sofa.

By the time she woke up and shook off the grogginess of the drinking, the nap, and an afternoon in the sunlight, Delbert had appeared in the living room with some Taco Bell for her. She had eaten it and gone right back to sleep, the food making her even more exhausted. She had been too tired at that point to care if she even went to the bathroom before getting into bed so as not to pee in her sheets, much less to care about if baby shower decorations had been put up. Somewhere in the dim recesses of her brain, though, she had noticed there weren't any decorations in the living room. At that point, she was happy she had even made an effort to climb the stairs up to her bedroom rather than lying down on the living room rug and falling into a deep slumber.

She was going to have to cut down on the drinking. She simply couldn't recover from knocking them back the way she used to be able to. Somehow, though, the alcohol never seemed to affect Agnes, and she was eighty-two and drank more than anyone else! Ida bet that even after six margaritas, Agnes could still install a baby car seat, erect a large tent, and put together a piece of IKEA furniture more competently than almost any sober person on earth. And those margaritas at The Silver Kettle were *strong*. It was astounding.

Ida's hair hung in her eyes, and she tried to arrange her frosted-blonde, shoulder-length hair back into something presentable, which wasn't possible as she was ninety-nine percent sure the last time she had taken a shower was Friday night. Ida showered at night because she couldn't stand the idea of getting into bed dirty, and it seemed silly to take a shower in the morning when she had taken one the night before. She would have to take one before the baby shower, though, unless she wanted all the guests to think she'd spent the weekend lying drunk in a gutter somewhere.

Ida wondered where Delbert was. She climbed out of bed, her head throbbing as though someone had placed a large metal trash can over it and then hit the trash can with a rubber mallet. She put a bathrobe on over her knee-length "Knightshirt." Yes, it was called a Knightshirt because it had a picture of a knight on the front and letters that spelled out "Knightshirt" underneath the image of the knight. Delbert had gotten it for her last year when they had visited Scotland with Oleen and Gary. Delbert and Gary were both fascinated by the idea of visiting a castle, and even though neither of them cared much about castles, Ida and Oleen had accompanied Delbert and Gary on a tour of one, just to be polite. Ida and Oleen hadn't had any interest in looking at more castles after that, and had sat in a pub for two hours while their husbands visited two more castles. One was quite enough for Ida and Oleen. There were lots of women sitting in that pub, so maybe Scottish castles played some siren song only men could hear. When Delbert and Gary returned, Delbert had presented Ida with her Knightshirt, which he had bought in a gift shop in one of the castles, and which he had thought was hilarious. Ida had always thought the shirt was kind of stupid, but she wore it because it was long and comfortable, and because Delbert had bought it for her.

Ida padded down the stairs in bare feet and found Delbert in the kitchen. To her astonishment, all the baby shower decorations were hanging in the living room. The entire bottom floor of the house had also been tidied up, with only the vacuuming left to do. Did they possess a live-in maid Ida had never before been aware of? Ida supposed it could be a man, but then would he be called a butler if he were a man? Ida wondered if this mysterious, and possibly mythical cleaning professional might live in what Ida and Delbert referred to as "the crap room;" a small room downstairs that was meant to serve as an office, but which instead served as a repository for random junk Ida and Delbert didn't know quite what to do with, but weren't yet prepared to throw away.

Ida tried never to go into the crap room. She also never allowed her eyes to stray inside the room when she opened the door to throw junk in and, at this point, she and Delbert had both taken to opening the door and tossing whatever junk it was into the room, sometimes with too much force. There was no gently setting anything on the floor anymore, nor was there any looking as they threw items inside.

Most of the time, out of sheer terror of seeing the horror that was the crap room, both of them looked in the opposite direction when tossing objects inside. Even hearing the thuds and clunks that almost certainly indicated some object's obliteration didn't deter them. They just couldn't face it. If a cleaning professional now lived in there, then it probably wasn't so crappy anymore. Ida would have to look inside later, if she could stomach it.

"What did you do, Delbert?" Ida asked. "Are you having an affair or something? You never clean."

Ida poked Delbert in the side and then hugged him as he tried very hard not to vomit on top of her head.

"I just wanted to help out, sweetheart. I was gone a long time yesterday, and I felt bad about not being here to cut the grass. So, I thought I'd get up early and do some setting up, and then cut the grass after you got up. I can even vacuum if you like. I know you have cooking to do."

Ida stared at Delbert as though his head had just popped off and rolled across the kitchen floor.

"Are you okay, Delbert?" she asked.

"Can't a man just want to be helpful to his wife?"

"Yes, a man can, but this man," she said, gesturing in Delbert's direction, "this man, well, this man usually wouldn't be. The last time you cleaned the house without me nagging you about it was when you ran over my bed of petunias with the lawnmower, and you wanted to soften the blow before I noticed."

"Well, maybe I want to be different now," Delbert said, his face feeling hotter and hotter with every moment he spent in that kitchen. "I'm going to go cut the grass now and *not* run over any of your flowers. When I'm done, I can vacuum if you like."

Well, thank you, dear," Ida said, kissing him on the cheek.

Delbert was so tall, and Ida so short, that Ida had to stand on tiptoe and Delbert had to bend down for her to reach his cheek. Sometimes, when they went out together, Ida wondered if people might think she was a midget. With no person of average height in the vicinity for comparison, she was pretty sure she looked like the long-lost eighth dwarf, the only female dwarf: Frumpy.

"Whatever the reason, I appreciate it, and I think I will let you vacuum. I have some baking to do for this afternoon. Janie will be so surprised!"

Delbert doubted anything would surprise Janie today, but he wasn't dumb enough to say so. He walked outside and went to the shed to get the lawnmower. *The* shed. The one beside which his son had seen him in the 1990s, wearing Zubaz pants and stroking Gary's thigh. Delbert cut the grass, stopping only twice to throw up in the bushes.

Next door, Oleen Johnson had baked a cake and made two casseroles. Oleen was both a night owl and an early bird, and neither bird ever seemed to win out over the other. Oleen was tired. She was always tired. She was so tired she could remember each individual night during the past ten years during which she had slept all the way through without waking up. That was sad. The only night she had slept well recently was when Agnes had given her an Ambien to try.

Oleen had slept like a baby when she had taken the Ambien, but had woken in the morning on the living room couch with a box of Ho Hos on her chest, surrounded by cellophane wrappers, and with no memory of how she had gotten there. Gary also had no idea why she was on the couch covered in Ho Ho wrappers, but they both decided she shouldn't take Ambien again. Gary had been suggesting for a while that Oleen see a sleep specialist, and she was starting to consider it.

Gary showed up in the kitchen around 8:55, toasted his usual English muffin and then proceeded to the living room to sit on the couch, eat his breakfast, and drink his coffee while watching *Sunday Morning* with the volume set to sonic boom. She swore that man was losing his hearing. She knew he would get crumbs all over the couch too, but at least he would clean them up. He had bought a hand vac specifically for this purpose. He was so obsessed with that hand vac Oleen was surprised he hadn't given it a name.

Oleen wished Gary would put on some pants before he came downstairs in the mornings. Gary had slept in a long nightshirt every night since they were first married, like he was Wee Willie Winkie, or something, and Oleen had always found this habit odd. She had always wondered why he didn't sleep in pajama pants and a t-shirt, like a normal man. Gary had his favorite nightshirt on today, his "Knightshirt." He'd gotten it at some dumb castle in Scotland while she and Ida had sat in a pub. Delbert had bought an identical one for Ida, and both she and Ida had thought it was stupid, but Ida wore hers anyway. Delbert and Gary had returned from the last castle they'd visited, and walked into the pub. Delbert had held the gift-shop bag out to Ida and grinned as though the bag contained $50,000, and not some ugly nightshirt. Oleen thought she had seen Gary stick a similar bag into the back waistband of his pants. That night, in their hotel room as they got ready for bed, she learned this assumption had been correct.

Gary had come strutting out of the bathroom in his Knight-shirt as though he were John Travolta in *Saturday Night Fever*. Oleen had no idea why such a stupid shirt would inspire such confidence in her husband, nor why any man would feel such confidence while wearing a nightshirt of any sort, but just thinking of it now made her giggle, while simultaneously annoying her.

Oleen continued working in the kitchen as *Sunday Morning* blared fifteen feet away from her. She hoped she wouldn't develop a need for hearing aids in the next hour. When she was done with the last casserole, she walked out onto the front porch to get away from the heat of her kitchen and the noise of the television. She saw that next door, Delbert had just finished cutting the front yard, and he looked overheated.

"Delbert! Are you okay?" Oleen called across the yard to him.

"I'm fine!" he yelled back. "Just a little hot. Don't worry, I've got water!" he said, holding up a plastic water bottle.

Oleen went back inside, forgetting why she had gone out onto the porch in the first place, and not noticing Delbert throwing up for the second time into the rose bush beside her sister's house.

17

SUNDAY

The baby shower was scheduled to start at 2 p.m., but, by one, Ida's entire family had arrived and was standing in her living room. The men had decided to go off together and do something which she supposed was much manlier than attending a baby shower. Maybe they were going off to fix things with duct tape or to visit castles in Scotland. Whatever they were doing, Ida knew it was a celebration for Jason. Ida had never thought of Jason as something to celebrate.

"But why, Steve?" Scott asked. "Why the hell do you want to go to a baby shower? There aren't even going to be any other men there. You'll be the only one. Baby showers are so lame."

"I think all those little baby clothes are so cute," Steve said, with a sigh. "And the little stuffed animals and toys are so sweet."

All the men, his husband included, stared at Steve as though he had just announced his undying love for Richard Simmons videos.

"And, you know," Steve said, cottoning on to the looks the men were giving him.

"I want to be there for Jenny. She asked me to come. For moral support."

"Who needs moral support to go to a baby shower?" Jason asked.

"Well Jenny, apparently," said Scott. "You, Jason, just need moron support."

Jason mouthed "fuck you" at Scott in a way he must have thought was surreptitious, but which he executed poorly enough that Ida noticed.

"Jason! We don't say those kinds of words in this house!" Ida called to him from the kitchen.

"I didn't say it, I mouthed it. At Scott. He started it."

"I don't care who started it. Just stop it. And, Scott, don't antagonize people. We all know you like to do that."

"Way to go, moron," said Scott, clapping Jason on the back. "Piss off your wife's mom. Good job!"

Scott stood up very straight and applauded like Jason had just won an award. Scott pretended to wipe a tear from his eye, and Jason made a rude gesture at Scott, which Ida squelched from the kitchen with one direct glare at Jason.

"Jenny was with Brandon for three years," Steve said, interrupting the hi-jinks and touching Jenny's arm. "She thought they were gonna get married and have kids, and now, six months ago, that ended, and she's afraid she'll never get to have kids now. She's afraid she'll feel bad at the baby shower, so I'll be there, you know, just in case."

"Oh my god, Steve! Why did you tell everyone that?" said Jenny. "It's so embarrassing."

She looked at her feet.

"Why are you afraid you'll never have kids?" asked Maureen, a puzzled look on her face.

"I'm thirty-seven now, and I'm getting up there when it comes to having a baby," said Jenny. "I may be too old by the time I find anyone, since right now I feel like a lunatic half the time."

"All women are lunatics half the time," said Jason.

"That's so rude, Jason," Janie said.

"I think you have lots of options," said Maureen, ignoring Jason. "Even if you don't meet someone you like anytime soon you can still have a baby on your own, or adopt a baby and then when the right man does come along the baby won't be brand new anymore. It will be 'gently used,' like a pair of nice shoes at Goodwill, and then your new husband will have gotten by without changing any diapers, which is likely to make him happy. Nobody in the world likes changing diapers, moms or dads. If they say they do, they're lying. Even though Alex has always been super sweet about it and said he sees it as 'bonding time,' everyone knows a diaper blowout is disgusting."

Alex shrugged, then nodded his assent. "Yeah, they are pretty gross. I'm not gonna lie."

Alex walked into the kitchen to offer Ida some help as Jason shrugged and located the punch bowl on the kitchen island. Ida had spiked the punch with champagne, and Jason poured a generous amount of punch into a plastic wine glass. Ida, who had overheard Jason's comment about all women being lunatics sometimes, and who also didn't like people digging into the refreshments before a party started, looked like she wanted to dump the punch bowl over Jason's head, but instead walked into the living room and began straightening pillows. When Ida was irritated or angry and trying not to show it, she straightened things up, particularly things that were already in perfect order. Jason sat down in the living room on a chair Ida had just tidied and began drinking his punch. Alex sat down on a bar chair behind Ida's kitchen island.

"God, Jenny, Maureen didn't have Jack till she was forty," said Scott. "You're not old. Geena Davis has twins, and she's like five hundred years old now, and her kids are like toddlers or something. Come on, Steve," Scott said. "Seriously?"

"Seriously," said Steve.

"I hope you have to guess what kind of chocolate is in a diaper," Scott said.

"I hope so too," said Steve, rubbing his hands together in mock anticipation.

Alex, who was enjoying sitting on the comfy stool behind the kitchen island, and who was thinking about how much nicer this stool was than those horrible high-backed chairs in Jenny's kitchen, looked at his watch and realized it was time to get the men moving. Alex clapped his hands with way more force than was necessary, and everyone looked in his direction.

Alex stood up.

"Okay, guys," he said. "Where is it we're going?"

"Anywhere where there's not a steam room!" whispered Scott.

For the first time in his life, though, Scott had managed to whisper correctly in front of his family, so no one heard him.

"Johnny's Real Pit Barbecue," said Delbert. "There's a new one on Cheshire Bridge Road. That's not too far from here."

Scott laughed out loud.

"What?" asked Gary.

"Oh, nothing," said Scott, giggling.

After all the men except Steve had filed out the front door, Jason abandoning his half-empty wine glass on Ida's oak side table without a coaster underneath it, Oleen and Agnes moved the gifts that were from themselves, Ida, Jenny, Maureen, and Steve next to the chair in the living room where Janie now sat. Ida grabbed Jason's plastic wine glass from the side table, dumped the remaining contents into the sink, and put the glass in the kitchen trash can.

"I'm gonna get up," said Janie.

"Don't bother. I'm not," said Maureen flopping onto the sofa.

"Well, we have about twenty minutes before anyone gets here," said Oleen.

"You know how Grace McGruder is always early to *every-thing*," said Ida. "You'd think at her age she'd understand no one wants you to be early to a party. In fact, come late. That's better. But she never does."

"I think it's too late for her," Oleen said with a sigh.

"Haha, too late!" said Maureen. "Grace isn't capable of being late."

"Reenie, dear, have you already had some champagne punch?" asked Agnes.

"No, I'm just tired, so that seemed way funnier than it should have," said Maureen. "Jack thought it would be fun to play in the cat box last night. At 10 p.m. He wouldn't go to sleep last night. He got in there right after Gordon finished pooping, and he got it all over himself when it was fresh, and then he even managed to get it in his hair!"

"Eww!" said Janie. "That stinks. Ha-ha, stinks. Too bad it wasn't just two minutes later. Cat poop becomes fossilized in, like, five seconds."

"I wish two year olds knew that," said Maureen.

"That's gross," said Janie.

"Janie, when you were two, we caught you eating out of the dog-food bowl, twice," said Ida. "And I believe Jenny used to eat dirt."

"She did," said Oleen, nodding her head.

"Well, that explains a lot," said Jenny, looking down into her lap.

Janie looked like she was about to throw up. She rested her head back and inhaled deeply.

"This is all very unappetizing," said Agnes. "Could we please talk about something else? We don't want Janie to have afternoon sickness when she's made it through the morning okay."

"Don't feel bad, guys," said Steve, "My mom says when they were potty training me, I would run outside all the time and pee on a tree. Right in the front yard."

Everyone laughed.

"That sounds more like something Scott would do! Maybe even now!" Jenny said, shaking with laughter.

The doorbell interrupted the group giggling fit Jenny's comment had provoked.

"I'll bet you twenty million dollars that's Grace," Ida said.

"I don't have twenty million dollars," said Oleen.

Ida hoisted herself off the sofa, walked to the door, and opened it. On the other side was Grace McGruder.

"Hi, Grace!" said Ida, plastering a smile on her face and speaking mechanically, "How are you?"

"I'm great!" said Grace, walking past Ida into the living room and placing an oddly shaped gift onto the gift pile.

Grace sat down on the end of the sofa next to Steve's chair.

"I think I know everyone here except you," she said, holding out her hand to Steve. "Grace. Grace McGruder. Maybe I have met you before, but I'm not sure. I'm a bit tired, and I had some wine last night."

"I'm Steve," Steve said, shaking her hand.

Steve recoiled, no doubt catching a whiff of Grace's sickly sweet floral perfume, which she seemed to have applied with a crop duster.

"It's so nice of you to come and be supportive," she said. "Most men wouldn't do that. Are you a friend of Janie's?"

"I'm—"

Ida interrupted Steve.

"He's more a friend of Scott's," said Ida. But he's always been very supportive of the girls too."

Steve looked at Ida, confused, as there had never been a

time when she hadn't introduced him as Scott's boyfriend or husband.

Ida looked back at Steve. "I'm going to get some appetizers and the punch. Steve, would you mind helping me?"

Once they were behind the kitchen island, not truly far enough away from the living room to have a hushed conversation, but with Grace's sweet-tea accent booming like a train derailing, Ida figured it was okay. Plus, Grace was oblivious to almost everything.

"I'm so sorry, dear," she said, touching Steve's arm. "I hope I didn't hurt your feelings. It's just that Grace is very homophobic, and I didn't want to get her started because I don't want you to have to listen to that. The woman hasn't ever believed Scott was gay. Scott! And Scott is clearly the gayest human being on the planet."

Steve laughed.

"Wow," he said, "That is some denial. I am excited to meet the other half of the famous Bill McGruder, though. I've met him enough, but only heard about her."

"She'd never think you were gay, so I figured it would be less hassle not to mention it. Bill has always told her Scott is gay and she won't listen to him. And Scott would tell you that Bill is an authority on Scott's sexual preference, I'm sure, as the famous 'shapely buttocks' story suggests."

"It's okay, Ida, I understand. That's probably the best idea in this situation," Steve said with a laugh.

Ida gave Steve a quick kiss on the cheek.

"You're such a dear," she said.

They gathered trays and the punch bowl and returned to the living room.

"Thanks for making us this special punch, Ida," Jenny said, holding up her plastic wine glass.

"Yeah, thanks, Mom," Janie said.

"Oh, I was happy to," Ida said. "I just put sparkling grape

juice in it instead of champagne. There's more in the refrigerator, if you like."

"It will be funny if people think you're drinking," Jenny said to Janie.

"It will be funny if people think you're not," Janie said.

Jenny was glad to know Janie had made that comment, not with malice but with love. The two women had talked at length about Jenny deciding to give up drinking, and about how great it was, so Jenny didn't have to wonder about Janie's intent as she might have had to if someone else had said the same thing. The two continued to sip their modified punch, looking at the clock over the fireplace and wondering when the rest of the guests would arrive.

18

SUNDAY

"Look at her ass," said Jason, as the only female waitress at Johnny's Real Pit Barbecue walked by.

No one looked at her ass.

"Jason," said Delbert, from across the booth, "Don't you think it would be good not to point out other women's butts to your wife's entire family? Maybe keep that with your friends?"

"Yeah. Sorry," said Jason, as he continued to stare at the waitress, who was now taking orders at a table across the room.

"Why are all the waiters here men?" asked Gary. "Except her, I mean," he said, gesturing to the female waitress. "That's strange."

"Yeah, I noticed that too," said Delbert.

"Well, she's not a man," Jason said, gesturing toward the waitress.

Scott shook his head and hit his palm against his forehead.

"You're brilliant!" he said, nearly yelling to be heard over the crowd.

Jason held his middle finger out toward Scott, accompanying the gesture with a thrust of his hand.

"Come on, guys, can't you cut it out for just a couple of hours?" asked Alex.

"Nope," said Jason.

"Not a chance," said Scott.

Alex took a breath and went on.

"I get that you guys don't like each other and, Jason, that comment was uncalled for, not to mention disrespectful of your wife and her family. I'm not even blood-related to Janie, and it makes me mad. She's pregnant, for god's sake. And you're out staring at other women. That sucks. Even so, we're here to celebrate Jason and Janie's baby, and it's a lot easier to do that without you two being rude to each other. Just stop while we're in this restaurant, and you can start again out in the parking lot if you want."

Both Jason and Scott had the decency to look apologetic.

"Okay," said Scott.

"Alright," said Jason.

Scott bit his lip and gripped the edge of the table, his knuckles turning white. He opened his mouth to speak, then closed it again. Alex looked at him and nodded his head. Jason glared at Scott, but neither of them said anything.

A waiter approached the booth, and said, in a voice that was strikingly similar to Scott's, "Hello, my name is Jerry, and I'll be taking care of you today. How are we all doing this afternoon?"

Gary and Delbert stared at each other across the table, and Scott stifled a giggle.

"We're doing great," said Alex. "How are you?"

"I'm just dandy this afternoon," said Jerry. "Would you like to hear our specials or are we ready to order?"

"We can order," said Scott. "I'm starving. Who eats lunch at 2 p.m.?"

"Uh, plenty of people," said Jason, looking around at the crowd.

"I'll give you that," said Scott.

Each man ordered the all-you-can-eat ribs, and non-alcoholic drinks, because the restaurant lacked a liquor license.

"Please make extra sure my tea is unsweet and not sweet," said Gary. "Doctor says I gotta watch my sugar level."

"Okay, dear," said Jerry, collecting the menus and walking away.

"There sure are a lot of male waiters here," Delbert said.

"Jason doesn't see that, because he won't stop staring at that poor woman's butt," Scott said, gesturing toward the lone female waitress, at whom Jason was still sneaking glances. "Come on Jason, pay attention to the conversation."

Alex made a slashing motion across his throat as he looked at Scott.

"I can't help it," said Jason. "I'm ADHD. I have trouble paying attention."

"You shouldn't say you're ADHD," Scott said. "You are a person who has ADHD. Don't sell yourself short. You've gotta use person-centered language."

"What's person-centered language?" asked Jason.

"It's used in schools," said Scott, "Mostly in special education. When kids have a disability, you're not supposed to say, like, 'autistic child.' You're supposed to say, 'child with autism.' The idea is it recognizes that the person isn't just a disorder, but a whole person."

"How the hell do you know that?" Jason asked.

"A couple of my cases a few years ago involved discrimination in schools, and a principal explained it to me."

"I get that," said Jason. "I had ADHD growing up, and lots of people just thought I was bad or annoying or something. It would have helped a lot if someone had explained that to me the way you just did."

"Where's all this sudden insight coming from, Jason?" Scott asked, without even a hint of sarcasm for what might have been the first time in the annals of his and Jason's conversational history. Jason shrugged and became interested in his silverware. Alex mouthed "Thank you," at Scott, who just shrugged and said, "Where the hell are our beverages?"

"I see our waiter. Looks like he's bringing them," said Delbert.

As Jerry set the drinks down on the table, Scott said, gesturing to his own waist, "You know, Dad, you should watch your sugar level too. You're, um, putting some on around the middle."

"Son, don't say that to me when you're about to eat a pile of ribs. I've seen how you can pack it in, and it's not a small amount," said Delbert.

"This is the *only* time I don't eat well," said Scott. "I have a weakness for barbecue places. I'm always telling Steve he has to help me go only once a month. But you know Steve. He's too polite to do that. But I also work out a lot. So, it's okay if I do this sometimes. Besides, I like the coleslaw way more than I like the ribs."

Jerry returned with the food, and everyone started to eat.

"You may want to set aside a lot of coleslaw," Jason said to Jerry as Jerry walked away.

19

SUNDAY

Ida and Steve set the food on the large oak coffee table, and Ida made sure there was a sizable stack of coasters next to the plastic wine glasses. Then she sat down next to Oleen on the sofa across the coffee table from where Grace sat.

A few seats away, Agnes examined Grace. Grace always dressed as though she were attending a particularly cheery funeral. She was fond of sheath dresses with matching jackets and sweaters, and low-heeled sandals and pumps. If her outfits had been entirely black, Agnes thought, she could be ready at a moment's notice if anyone she knew happened to die suddenly. Agnes remembered an article she had read somewhere about the royal family in England that told about how members of the royal family had to keep a "mourning outfit" with them at all times when they traveled, in case another royal died during their trip. It was because once, when they were young, Queen Elizabeth and Prince Phillip had been traveling when some or other crucial royal person had died, and the queen was horrified not to have had a mourning outfit on hand, so she made this decree. Agnes sure was glad she wasn't a member of the royal family.

Grace would have made a good royal, though, if only there were some special spray paint one could use to change the color of one's outfit to black on a whim. Today Grace's outfit was a cherry-red sheath dress with a lightweight, short-sleeved red cardigan and low-heeled red sandals. Agnes pictured Grace with a black veil over her head and nearly laughed. Agnes did have to give it to the woman for taking good care of herself, though. Grace, like Agnes, liked to look good. Agnes knew that, under that cardigan, Grace's arms did not look like the arms of a woman who had recently turned sixty, but were well-defined and muscular, and looked like the arms of someone at least twenty years younger than Grace was. Agnes also doubted that Grace would ever have to resort to wearing mom jeans the way Maureen had. Agnes had to remember never to mention this fact to anyone as Jenny had told her about the mom jeans under penalty of a slow and painful death if she ever revealed the information to anyone. Grace's layered, chin-length haircut had a slight red tint, but not enough to look tacky on a woman her age, and Agnes was pleased to see that Grace's nail polish did not match her outfit and was, instead, a tasteful light blue.

Grace leaned back on the couch to examine Ida and Oleen.

"I know it's been a couple of years since we've seen each other, which is crazy since we live so close to each other," Grace said. "We'll have to get together more often from now on. You two still look exactly alike. I mean, exactly." Surveying the room, she asked, "How do you all tell them apart?"

Steve winced as Grace's loud Southern voice almost burst his eardrums.

"They don't look alike," said Janie.

"My mom has different-shaped eyes," said Jenny.

"And their smiles are different," added Janie.

"Even though they're pretty much the same size, I never confuse them, even from the back," said Maureen.

"I've known them both a long time, and I never have a problem. One time they even tried to trick me by pretending to be each other, but I had their number," said Agnes.

"Really? How funny," Grace said.

"What about you?" she asked Steve. "Can you tell them apart?"

"At first I couldn't. But now I have, I'd say, about an eighty-five percent success rate, if no context tells me who it is."

"Sometimes we wear similar outfits without even talking about it. Like today." Oleen gestured down at her own clothes. She and Ida both wore cropped jeans in dark denim. Ida had on an oversized pink tunic shirt, while Oleen wore an identical oversized blue one. The two women had bought the shirts together during a shopping trip to Chico's, and had been careful not to buy the same color. Each also wore similar, though not identical, light-blue flat sandals with ankle straps.

"It's terrible sometimes when we show up in almost the same clothes," Oleen said, wrinkling her nose.

"It's not that terrible," said Ida. "Though since you decided to copy my hairstyle, Oleen, it is hard for us not to look exactly the same."

"I did not copy your hairstyle, Ida," said Oleen. "It just happens to be a flattering style and color for both of us. At least that's what Patrick says every time we go in for a cut and color which, I might add, you always insist we do together."

"Well, it's Patrick's fault, then," Ida said.

"You all look great, so this Patrick must have some wisdom," Grace said, lifting her plastic wine glass to her lips and taking a swig of punch, then setting the glass down on the coffee table. Ida quickly picked it up and placed a coaster underneath it.

"Rings," she said, "are for trees. Not for coffee tables. And thank you, Grace."

"Yes, thanks for the compliment," Oleen said.

The doorbell rang.

"I'll get it," said Oleen.

"That's probably Piper," said Grace. "I tried to get her to come here with me, but she wouldn't because she said we'd be way too early. I'm glad she made it on time."

Ida glanced at the clock over the fireplace. It showed 1:55 p.m.

Oleen opened the door, and Piper entered the room. Oleen took her gift from her and handed it to Ida to place atop the gift pile. As Oleen started to close the door behind her, Piper reached her hand out to stop it. In the doorway stood Matilda, Piper's twelve-year-old daughter.

"Andy had a work thing. He had to do emergency surgery, and since Mom is here and I couldn't find anyone else, I had to bring her. I'm sorry," said Piper, herding Matilda into the living room and onto the sofa next to Grace, who was Piper's mother and Matilda's grandmother. Piper sat on Matilda's other side.

"None of your brothers babysits?" asked Agnes.

"They would, but every single one of them, all four, and my dad, are on a fishing trip, though they might be home by now. And their wives decided to go together for margaritas at some Mexican place. That's not my thing. I don't drink much," Piper said, rubbing her hands together absently.

"You know, I have no idea what they did with my nieces and nephews, surely they didn't take them out for an adult activity like drinking. I guess I should have tried to find out who's looking after the kids, but I didn't think of it."

"It's okay!" Ida said with a game show host smile and voice. "We're glad to have her, aren't we?" she asked, looking around at her family with wide eyes and a huge smile that, together, made her look demented.

After a brief pause Maureen nodded, and, noticing this gesture, Agnes, Janie, Jenny, and Steve nodded too.

Piper, like her mother, also favored sheath dresses, but without sweaters and jackets. Piper tended to accompany her dresses with pearls and wedge-heeled sandals. Agnes bet Piper wore such outfits when she vacuumed too. No, wait, Piper almost certainly had a maid.

Piper was between the ages of Janie and Maureen, though Agnes couldn't remember how old Piper was. Janie was thirty-seven and Maureen was forty-two. Agnes supposed Piper wasn't yet worried about how her arms looked the way women tended to worry as they got older. Piper was in even better physical shape than Grace was, but only because of their age difference. Piper's sheath dress was a pale shade of lilac.

Matilda looked bored sitting between her mother and grandmother at a baby shower for a woman she barely knew. She looked much older than twelve. Her long, straight blond hair, full, pouty lips and—was that makeup? Well, Matilda looked about sixteen, and she most certainly did not need to be wearing makeup at her age! Agnes had noticed when Piper and Matilda came in that Matilda was only about three or four inches shorter than her mother, who was already tall; about Janie's height. Agnes also noticed Matilda's denim shorts were too short, her pink t-shirt was too tight, and her pink sandals sported a heel that was too high.

"Hi, Matilda!" said Oleen, like Bob Barker heading into the *Showcase Showdown*. "Let me find you something to drink from the kitchen. How about some lemonade? Or tea? There's tea, too."

"I'll have some of this," Matilda said, reaching across the coffee table for a plastic wine glass and grabbing the ladle from the punch bowl.

"Uh no, honey," Grace said, as Piper stopped Matilda from taking the wine glass and removed her hand from the ladle.

"That punch is for grown-ups only," Piper said. Janie, Jenny, and Maureen exchanged looks.

"Matilda, I'll put your drink in one of those glasses. How about that?" Oleen said.

"Then you can have the same glass as everyone else."

"They're cups," Matilda said.

"What, dear?" asked Grace.

"These," Matilda said, gesturing to the plastic wine glasses, "Are cups. They're plastic, so that makes them cups. Glasses are made of glass."

"Okay, I'll put your drink in a cup. Lemonade or tea?" said Oleen with a wide, creepy smile, like the Joker.

"Punch," said Matilda.

"An Arnold Palmer it is!" said Oleen, grabbing a plastic wine glass and speeding into the kitchen.

Oleen returned with Matilda's "cup" full of a mixture of half lemonade and half tea, which Matilda took and set on the coffee table. Ida picked it up and placed a coaster underneath it. Matilda sat back against the couch and started typing on her iPhone.

Watching the scene unfold from her chair, Janie began making a mental list of ways to make her daughter turn out well.

"Where's the bathroom?" asked Matilda.

Maureen pointed Matilda to the bathroom off the kitchen, and Matilda got up, taking her phone with her. Maureen watched Matilda enter the bathroom and close the door.

As the guests slowly trickled in and the gift pile grew, Ida circled the room ensuring everyone had a coaster. Once all fifteen guests had arrived and assembled in the living room with glasses of punch and plates of casseroles, appetizers, and cakes, Ida stood up and clapped her hands together.

"Thanks for coming, everyone," she said. "I'm sorry we're a bit cramped with these extra chairs, but I suppose we'll make do. We'll go ahead and let Janie open the gifts now."

Ida didn't like long, drawn-out social occasions.

"What, Ida? We aren't going to guess what melted chocolate is inside a diaper?" Grace asked with wide eyes and an innocent smile.

"No, we're saving that activity just for you, Grace," Ida said. "You can stay late for it. I've heard Steve enjoys doing that too."

Grace roared with laughter and slapped her knee, sloshing some of her punch onto the carpet. Ida was glad the punch was light pink, and not red.

Maureen grabbed a notepad and a pen from the side table and Steve, who was seated in the chair next to Janie, handed Janie the first gift from the gift pile which sat between their chairs.

Janie tore the paper off to reveal a set of baby monitors.

"Ooh, these are great! They're just the ones I wanted. Thank you, Piper!"

Maureen wrote: "Piper—baby monitors" on the notepad.

Steve slid the next gift, which was huge, across the floor to Janie. Janie opened it to reveal a deluxe-model luxury stroller with the price tag of a small yacht from Agnes, Ida, Oleen, Delbert, and Gary

"Oh my god! Mom! Oleen! Agnes! This is too much! This is way nicer than the one I put on the registry! It's the WiFi and Bluetooth-enabled one. Wow! Thank you so much! If I wouldn't roll around on the floor like a Weeble, I'd get up and hug all three of you."

"You're welcome, dear," said Ida. "It's from your dad and Gary too."

Oleen reached over from the adjacent sofa and squeezed Janie's hand.

Agnes said, "We hope you enjoy it. I don't understand all that blue WiFi stuff, though."

Janie laughed.

"Has Matilda not come back from the bathroom yet?" Piper said. "I guess she hasn't. I swear, that girl..."

Piper got up and walked toward the bathroom. A couple of minutes later she returned with Matilda.

"She was in there watching videos on YouTube," said Piper, shaking her head. "I'm not sure she even used the bathroom."

Piper sat Matilda back down on the couch.

"Don't get up again. Your rear end stays parked here until we leave. Got it?"

Matilda rolled her eyes and returned to typing on her phone.

Steve continued to hand Janie gifts, and Maureen continued to make note of who each gift was from so Janie could write thank-you cards later. Janie opened a huge gift which clearly contained a basket of some sort. The basket was full of diapers, bath toys, teething toys, and stuffed animals.

"Thanks, Steve! Thanks, Maureen!" Janie said. "This stuff is adorable!"

"That's from Alex and Scott too," said Maureen. "Scott and Alex went with us to pick everything out. Would you believe Scott insisted we add stuffed animals?"

"It was weird," said Steve. "He was just fixated on that zebra."

Janie opened Jenny's gift to reveal a set of three beautiful knitted baby hats that looked like animals.

"Wow!" said Janie, "Where did you get these? I've never seen anything like them before. They're so cool!"

"I made them," said Jenny.

"You MADE them?" asked Piper.

Jenny nodded.

"You should seriously think about selling these, Jenny. I know Etsy is full of baby hats, but I've never seen any animal hats with such unusual animals. An ostrich? You'd think it wouldn't work, but it does. And you can even tell it's an ostrich!"

"Those are so nice, Jenny!" said Agnes. "You're so good at

knitting. I never knew you still did it. I thought you stopped in college."

"Lately it's been helping me feel better," said Jenny, looking down into her lap.

"Too bad you didn't make a zebra," said Steve. "I'd ask you to make an adult-sized one for Scott."

"I might do that anyway!" said Jenny with a diabolical laugh.

"Why would you ask her to do th—?" Grace began to ask Steve.

"There's still a gift left, Steve, would you hand it to Janie?" Ida cut in.

Steve, who had been avoiding the final, oddly-shaped package because he had a bad feeling about it, handed Janie the gift he had slowly inched to the bottom of the pile earlier.

"This is from Mrs. McGruder," said Steve.

"Please, Steve, call me Grace. It's also from Bill," Grace said.

"I bet it's one of those long-reaching grabber tools, but it folds up to make it portable," Oleen whispered to Ida. "You know, for grabbing butts."

Ida gasped and choked on her punch. Oleen patted her on the back until she stopped coughing.

"Are you okay?" asked Grace.

"I'm fine," Ida spluttered. "It just went down the wrong pipe."

Ida glared at Oleen out of the side of her eyes.

Janie opened Grace's gift, turning it around and around in her hands, trying to decide what to say.

"Thank you so much, Grace," said Janie, sounding perplexed.

The gift was a standard-sized bed pillow with two rubbery hands attached to one of the flat sides. Each hand was slightly open, as though it were petting a dog.

"Uh, what's the best way to use that?" asked Maureen. "Is it good for toddlers? I was thinking about Jack."

"It's a pillow that helps your baby feel safe when she's sleeping, and you're not right there with her. You position the pillow behind her or underneath her in the crib, and you put the hands around her like they're your hands holding her. It helps with bonding and attachment."

"It's so unique!" said Ida, struggling to hold up the corners of her mouth.

"I thought so," said Grace.

"See, they modeled those hands after her husband's, since his hands are usually in that cupped position," Oleen said into Ida's ear. Ida reached over and squeezed her sister's hand until Oleen's eyes watered and she tapped Ida on the back to get her to stop.

On the notepad, Maureen wrote: "Grace—effing insane."

20

SUNDAY

"Oh my god," said Oleen, after all the food was put away and the dishes were in the dishwasher. She flopped onto a chair. "Kill me."

"I don't think it was THAT bad, honey," said Agnes. "Although that pillow with the hands does look quite frightening. It's like those hands are coming to get you. I'm afraid it will scare the baby, not soothe her!"

Janie burst out laughing.

"No way am I gonna use that thing!" she said. "Why would anyone think that would make a good gift? But the upside is we can find a way to scare Scott with it. You know how easily he gets creeped out by random stuff. Like clowns. Maybe we can draw a clown face on that pillow and he can run away from the scary clown hands. Someone can hide in the sewer and hold it up as he walks by. It'll be like in *It*."

"That'll be hilarious," said Jenny. "I think Steve should do it because Scott would never suspect him. Steve's always so nice about Scott's weird phobias."

"Yeah, it will be a lot funnier if you do it than if one of us does it, Steve," said Maureen.

"Okay," said Steve. "Somebody needs to distract him. Get him talking. You know how he doesn't notice anything around him when he starts talking. Get him with his back to the kitchen, and I'll hide behind the kitchen island with the pillow. Just tell him I'm in the bathroom or something. Then I'll sneak up behind him from the kitchen and do something with the pillow."

"Everybody else just act natural. Wait—you guys can act natural, right?" Jenny laughed, and looked at Ida and Oleen.

"You know, don't do those weird smiles, Mom and Aunt Ida. They make you look like you escaped from the lunatic asylum."

"That is true," said Agnes. "A long time ago, when she was still with us and healthy, Caroline even told me that's the way both of them used to smile in photos when they were little. She tried to get them to do it differently, but that didn't seem to take until high school. She even showed me several photos. The only pictures where they didn't have those smiles on their faces were their yearbook photos from their junior year of high school. Caroline had no idea why, but they smiled normally in those photos, so she got those pictures printed as 8 x 10s, framed them and hung them on the wall. Caroline was their mom, and even she said their senior pictures are the worst."

"Hello!" Oleen called from the sofa. "Over here! It's Ida and Oleen. We ARE in the room."

"But we do love when people talk about us like we're not here, so thank you," Ida said.

"You must be irritable after that shower," Oleen said to Ida. "You're never this sarcastic."

Ida leaned her head back onto the couch and closed her eyes.

"I think I need Vicodin," she said.

"Why have we never seen these photos?" Janie asked.

"Don't you two have all of your mom's photo albums?"

Agnes said to Ida and Oleen. "We should get them out one day. I'm sure there will be quite a few of those pictures in there."

Oleen rolled her eyes.

"Yeah, that'll be great," she said.

"Wasn't that Matilda something?" Ida asked. "Between Matilda and Grace's booming voice, I wished I were deaf, blind, and on hard drugs."

"Matilda was something alright. Something awful!" said Oleen. "But the McGruders, every single one of them, even all the boys, have always been odd, and when they were kids, none of them behaved. I guess that's why Matilda not being that well-behaved and polite didn't surprise me very much. Do you remember when Piper was little?" she asked, turning toward Ida and Agnes.

"One time, when she came over to Mom's house, she sprayed whipped cream on the toilet seat!" said Oleen. "It was on Labor Day, and we were having a cookout. Well, I guess Mom was having one, but it always felt like our house, even when we moved out. Gary and I were living in an apartment back then. It was before our houses here were even built, and all this land just had our old house on it. This neighborhood seems to still be plagued by cookouts, though that's an aside."

"I seem to remember that," said Agnes. "Didn't Gary sit in it?"

"That's right!" said Oleen. "He did."

"I don't remember that!" Maureen said. "Gary sat on the toilet seat with the whipped cream? With a bare butt?"

"Yes, with a bare butt," said Oleen with a giggle. "We didn't ever mention it to anyone, because we couldn't prove it was Piper," Oleen said. "And, Maureen, you were pretty young. How old is Piper now?"

"I think forty-two, same as me," said Maureen.

"Well, Piper was about four, so you were about the same age, Maureen," said Agnes, "and then that means Jenny, Janie,

Mike, and Scott weren't even born yet. And Grace was so young! She was only twenty-two, and she hadn't had any of the boys yet either. And the girls and Delbert and Gary were, let's see, about twenty-seven, and Bill was thirty. He liked them young. And, gee, I, I was only forty-four. Those were the days! That's when Ida and Delbert lived in that weird duplex."

"Yeah, I remember that duplex a little," said Maureen. "It smelled funny, and it was right next to the railroad tracks."

"Okay, we're getting off topic," said Agnes. "Right after Gary sat in it, I caught Piper in the kitchen spraying whipped cream in her mouth."

"I know it was her," said Oleen, "So I guess it's genetic."

Jenny cackled like a hyena and gasped, "Dad sat in it?" She laughed until she shook. "Let's hope Piper didn't touch the canister to the toilet seat before she sprayed it in her mouth. Eww!" Jenny threw her head back and laughed some more.

"Come on, Jenny," said Maureen. "It's funny, but it's not THAT funny."

"Yes it is!" Jenny said, continuing to giggle. "It's funny because of how much my dad hates messy stuff. I can only imagine him with whipped cream on his butt."

"I'm glad to see you laughing again, Jenny," said Agnes, "Even if it is over your dad having whipped cream on his butt."

"Yeah," Jenny said, looking thoughtful. "I guess I'm glad I'm laughing too. It just feels weird is all. I didn't even notice I was doing it. I suppose that's good, though."

"Hey, Janie," said Jenny, "Do you know what you're going to name the baby? Because I think you should call her Jenny."

She laughed.

"See, Grandma, now I'm smiling even more because Janie's baby and I can have exactly the same name and then we can get the baby little outfits that exactly match mine, kind of how you can with those American Girl Dolls."

"Uh, Jenny, yeah, just no," said Janie. "I think you're kidding.

I mean, I hope you're kidding. But we've been over this so many times, Jenny! Jason may have many flaws, and I mean *many* flaws, but having the same last name as you do is one of the smaller ones."

"Why'd you have to change your last name when you got married, Janie?" Jenny drew the phrase out so she sounded like a whiny toddler. "You know I never wanted us to be Jenny Johnson and Janie Johnson. We sound like some weird circus act."

"I've told you, Jenny, like eight hundred times, I've always thought, since I was a kid, that when I got married I'd take my husband's last name. How did I know I'd end up with a husband that has the same last name as you? I mean, I know it sounds dumb, and we do sound kind of like the same person. It's almost like being identical twins like our moms are. Maybe one day it will come in handy like it did for them and we can benefit, or at least laugh at people, by making them think each of us is the other. But, some days, if I had to return either the name or the husband, I'm not sure which I'd choose."

Janie sighed.

"I've always wanted to take my husband's last name if I get married, Janie. And now I may not be able to. I mean, what if I marry someone with a horrible last name like Alex used to have? No way would I want that as my last name. Then I'd have to keep the name Johnson, but my future husband or whatever you call someone who currently doesn't exist, won't be as cool as Alex is and then no one will know we're married, and all our kids' teachers will be confused."

"Yeah," Maureen added. "Alex's last name was horrible. Atrocious. I really don't understand why his parents didn't change it when he was a kid, at least unofficially. When we started dating, that was my only concern. What if I had to take that horrible name? Alex told me pretty early on that he knew his last name was horrible, and when he got married he didn't care what his wife's last name was, he was going to take it. But I was still surprised, years later, when Alex proposed and said he wanted to take my last name. He said that when we were in college, so I hadn't thought about it in a long time. At first I thought he was really progressive, but after his dad told me that both he and Alex's mom also wished they could change their last names to McNair, I decided it really was because of how horrible a last name he had. I mean, come on, who'd want that? And who'd want their kids to have to go through life with a last name of—"

The front door burst open, interrupting Maureen's explanation and Jenny's ensuing giggling fit. Delbert, Gary, Scott, Alex, and Jason stepped into the house. They were talking and not looking into the room. Janie handed Steve the pillow with the creepy, rubbery hands.

"Hide, quick!" she said.

Steve grabbed the pillow, hurried behind the kitchen island, and crouched down.

"See, Son?" said Delbert, "I knew you would pack it in, and I was right."

Scott sat down on the sofa next to Maureen.

"Move over," he said, pushing her toward the other end of the couch with his shoulder. "I think I might die."

He lay down facing the fireplace, and put his feet in Maureen's lap.

"You really did eat a lot," said Gary. "I've never been with you anywhere where you ate that much."

"It was kind of astounding," said Alex. "I didn't have any idea one person could eat that much coleslaw."

"I can't move," said Scott, "If I do, I'll throw up."

He put his right arm up over his eyes and lay very still.

Steve peeked over the top of the kitchen island and saw Scott lying with his arm over his eyes. Then Steve tiptoed toward the sofa, holding the pillow and arranging the rubber hands in his own hands as he walked. The rest of the men stared at Steve like he had just taken all his clothes off in the middle of the living room. Jason opened his mouth to speak, but Janie motioned for him to be quiet. Jason smiled and covered his mouth with his hand to keep his laugh from escaping.

Delbert, Gary, and Alex also tried not to laugh, Delbert had to put both his hands over his mouth to stay quiet. Janie held a finger up to her mouth and glared at them.

Steve approached the couch where Scott lay and stood over Scott. He ran the fingers of the rubbery left hand through Scott's hair.

"Stop it, whoever's doing that. Or I'll throw up all over Reenie. That's how awful the throwing up is gonna be."

Steve stroked Scott's face with the rubbery right hand.

"Steve, is that you?" Scott asked, opening his eyes as Steve wiggled the rubber fingers right in front of Scott's face.

"Aah! Aah!" Scott screamed, jumping up and running away from the hands.

He knocked into Alex, who laughed as he helped Scott steady himself.

"Oh my god, Steve! What the hell is that thing? Oh my god!" Scott held his hand over his heart.

Every single person in the room roared with laughter. Delbert doubled over so far, he fell on the floor and, on his hands and knees, slapped the carpet, unable to control himself.

"That," said Jason, "is the most magnificent thing I've ever seen in my life."

"It sure is!" called Jenny.

"Where did you get that thing?" asked Scott. "Is that from the Halloween store they open every October? I can't even figure out how that would be useful for a costume. But it is terrifying."

"It was a baby shower gift," said Maureen.

"A baby shower gift?" Scott said with a look of shocked surprise on his face. "Well, whoever gave that gift should be drawn and quartered. Not to mention whatever person thought it would be a good idea to manufacture that abomination. They can be punished together. Who the hell thought that was a good gift? And what the hell is it even supposed to do?"

"Do you remember who was invited to the baby shower?" Maureen asked.

"No," said Scott.

"Think about barbecues. And pantries."

Scott's eyes lit up, and he shook with laughter.

"That monstrosity," he said, pointing at the pillow in Steve's hands, "Is from the McGruders?"

All the women nodded.

"I had no idea what to do when I opened it," said Janie. "I had no idea what it even was! Thankfully, Maureen asked Grace McGruder how you use it."

"How the hell do you use it other than to make sure everyone who sees it never sleeps again?" Scott asked

"It's supposed to help your baby sleep!" Jenny said.

"And have awful nightmares?" asked Scott. "Those hands literally look the way I used to imagine the hands of some crazy thing hiding in my closet that was coming to kill me would look. Back when I was, like, seven or eight."

"That's about the size of it," said Agnes.

As Janie explained the pillow's intended use to the men, Scott stared at her as though he smelled something putrid.

"Good god," he said.

"It does seem to have cured you of your vomiting spell, dear," said Ida.

"Yeah, maybe that's the only thing it's useful for," Scott said. "I'm feeling pretty good now," he said, patting his stomach. "The old tum's feeling much better."

"The old tum?" asked Jason.

"Yep," said Scott, patting his stomach twice more. "The old tum."

Scott went back to the couch and sat in the middle, shoving himself up against Maureen, who tried to push him over.

"I've been thrown up on enough in my life by kids, Scott," she said. "Go away."

Steve put the pillow with the attached hands on the coffee table, sat next to Scott on his other side. and pulled Scott toward him and away from Maureen.

"Be civil, Scott. Just because you're terrified of that pillow doesn't mean you need to be rude," Steve said.

"I'm not terrified. It's simply not to my liking," said Scott.

Alex sat down on the couch between Maureen and Scott.

"Go sit somewhere else, Maureen, or Alex," Scott said. "This couch isn't meant for four."

Steve shook his head as Alex stood up and moved to a spot on the floor near Maureen's end of the couch.

"I'm sorry my brother has the sensitivity of one of Mom and Dad's steak knives," Maureen said to Alex.

"There's nothing wrong with our steak knives," said Delbert.

"You never sharpen them!" said Maureen. "You've had them forever and the last time you sharpened them was during Operation Desert Storm when the first George Bush was president."

"I'm sorry to say, they are pretty blunt," Agnes said.

"Like Scott!" shouted Janie.

"Duh, that's the point," said Maureen.

Janie, who had never gotten up from her chair after the baby shower, patted the empty chair next to her and motioned for Jason to sit down. Ida, Agnes, Oleen, and Jenny occupied the couch opposite Scott, Steve, and Maureen. Delbert and Gary still stood, eyeing the remaining sofa that faced both the fireplace and Janie's and Jason's chairs.

"Aren't you guys gonna sit?" asked Scott. "*Plenty* of room on that couch."

Gary and Delbert sat down, each scooting as far as possible toward opposite ends of the sofa. Gary held a throw pillow in his lap. Delbert glanced toward the bathroom.

"Why are we all sitting in here like this?" asked Oleen, "I want to go lie down. It looks like we're having a meeting in here. Should I go fetch *Robert's Rules of Order*?"

"Ida. Oleen, honey. We need to talk to you," said Agnes, patting each woman on the hand.

"All of you?" Ida said. "All of you need to talk to us?"

"Yes, all of us," said Agnes. "There's something we need to tell you."

21

SUNDAY

"**O**kay. Well, yesterday I came over here to put up the baby shower decorations," Maureen began, inhaling deeply.

"*You* came over to put them up?" said Ida. "But Delbert put them up this morning. It was odd, but I was grateful. I'm confused."

"I never did end up putting them up, so I guess Dad did. That *is* out of character for Dad; to be so helpful, I mean. I came to put them up yesterday and Joey Taylor's bar mitzvah afterparty was going on, and the guests took up all the parking, so I had to park somewhere else and walk here."

"Those people had no couth," said Ida. "What were they, born in a barn?"

"My guess is no, said Scott. "Probably in hospitals."

"When I got here, I noticed Dad doing something weird," said Maureen.

"Your father does a lot of weird things," Ida said. "What weird thing was he doing yesterday? Was he standing out in the front yard scratching his behind again? I always tell him no one wants to see that."

"No," said Maureen. "He was in the garage. And he was leaned up against his truck, and he was, uh, kissing someone."

"Your father does love that truck," Ida said, her brain trailing behind her mouth. "But kissing the truck is weird, even for him."

"He was KISSING someone?" Oleen boomed. "Oh my god, Delbert! Are you having an affair? You're too old to be doing that. I can't believe you'd do that to Ida! And in the garage. Was the door open, Maureen?"

"Uh, yeah, the door was open. They were pretty, uh, visible. And it wasn't the truck Dad was kissing,"

"Was it that hussy Julie Wellington?" asked Oleen. "Grace McGruder told me she thought Julie and Thomas got divorced because Julie was having an affair. Maybe with Bill, because Julie enjoys having her butt grabbed. Ida, why was she invited to the baby shower?"

Ida shrugged and stared at Delbert.

"That's not confirmed, honey," said Agnes. "I wouldn't go spreading that around. We don't know why they got divorced, though the few times I met him I did think Thomas seemed a bit dodgy, so Julie cheating on him wouldn't be a surprise. Maybe she caught some of it by osmosis."

"Dodgy?" Jenny laughed, "You've been watching BBC America again, haven't you, Grandma?"

"A bit," said Agnes.

"Shut up, everyone, and let Maureen get on with it," Scott said.

Maureen breathed in deeply and swallowed.

"Dad was not kissing Julie Wellington." Maureen looked down at the floor, trying not to hyperventilate. "Dad was, uh, he was kissing Gary."

Ida and Oleen stared at Maureen.

"What?" they said at the same time, exchanging looks of profound confusion.

"Kissing Gary? Delbert?" Ida said. "I don't understand."

"Um, um, well, I think that, I mean, they were kissing, and—"

"Gary and Delbert are lovers and have been getting it on, so to speak, since they were in college," said Scott. "There, now it's said."

"Scott!" Maureen said, "I was going to say that gently."

"Gotta rip off the Band-Aid, Reenie," Scott said.

Ida and Oleen stared at Scott, and then at Delbert and Gary. "Huh?" said Oleen.

"What do you mean, Gary and Delbert are lovers?" asked Ida. "Lovers like *lovers*, lovers? Like in a soap opera where they meet in secret in some seedy hotel room?"

Delbert started to stand.

"You don't need to go to the bathroom, Dad," Scott said. "You went right before we left the restaurant. Sit down. Think of this as your coming-out party. We are in the South, after all."

"I do," said Delbert, standing up to his full height.

"Well, hold it, then," Scott said.

Delbert sat back down on the sofa and crossed his arms like a toddler who had just been denied candy at the grocery store. Then he turned his whole body toward the kitchen and stared at the refrigerator. Gary curled into the other side of the sofa and began sobbing into the throw pillow he had been holding in his lap.

"Mom, if it's seedy it's a motel, not a hotel. And, yes, like that," Scott said. "Likely it was the No-Tell Motel, also known as the garage."

"Good god, Scott," Alex said. "I don't mean to be rude, but don't you think you should tone it down a bit?"

"Let me think about that," Scott said, putting his left hand under his chin and touching the index finger of his right hand to his temple. He held the pose for a moment and then removed both his hand and his finger. "Uh, no," he said, looking at Alex.

"But why would they do that?" Ida asked.

"Ida, honey," said Agnes, touching Ida's arm, "Gary and Delbert are gay."

"Gary and Delbert can't be gay. We've been married to them for a long time," Oleen said.

"I'm not gay!" called Delbert, whose words were slightly hard to make out on account of his back being to the group as he stared at the refrigerator.

"They can't be gay because they're married to us," Ida said.

"Uh, yeah," said Scott "They can be. Happens all the time when people don't want to admit it."

"Admit what?" asked Ida.

"Admit that they're gay, Ida," said Agnes. "Gary and Delbert are gay. They prefer men."

"Specifically, each other," Scott said.

"No, I don't believe that," said Ida. "I'm not sure why all of you think they are, but we know they're not."

Oleen nodded her head. She reached behind Agnes and took her sister's hand in what she seemed to think was a gesture of solidarity but, due to their distance from one another and the odd positions of their arms, looked more like a contortionist's trick.

"That's just crazy talk," said Oleen. "I'm not sure why all of you would get together and say this. Are you still mad we lost those football tickets? I know it was a big game, but..."

Scott stood up and moved to the adjacent sofa, sitting down in between Gary and Delbert.

"This man," he said, gesturing toward Gary, "and this man," he said, nodding toward Delbert, "are together, like a couple. They are secret lovers. I swear to god I'm not making this up. Maureen caught them together, Agnes caught them together, I caught them together, and Jenny and Steve have each caught them together, too."

"No," said Oleen. "That just can't be true."

"It's true," said Agnes.

"Ida, Oleen, I hope I'm not out of bounds here," said Alex, "But Scott's telling you the truth. Both Gary and Delbert even said it was true when we all talked yesterday."

"You all talked yesterday?" asked Oleen. "How did you all talk about this? You were all at the outlet mall. I hope you weren't talking about this in the middle of the outlet mall."

"We weren't at the outlet mall," Alex said. "We were all talking at Jenny's apartment. And then Agnes came over to bring Jenny some plates. She didn't know we were there, but she stayed and told us she knew about Gary and Delbert. And we had a long talk, and we decided to tell you after the baby shower. You have to know. It's only fair. We thought maybe you knew but, obviously, you don't."

Oleen stared straight ahead with blank eyes. Ida stood up and grabbed the first pillow she saw, which was sitting on the coffee table. Tears exploded from her eyes, and she wept into the pillow. On the opposite side of the pillow, two rubbery hands waved at everyone in the room.

Ida cried harder, and the hands waved faster and faster.

"I thought you went to the outlet mall without me!" she sobbed, pointing at Delbert. "You knew how much I wanted you to go with me! Why would you say you went when you didn't? That's so awful, Delbert!"

Ida continued crying, and sat back down on the sofa. She turned to face the couch where Gary, Delbert, and Scott sat. Scott recoiled from the waving hands.

"Mom," he said, "I know you're upset, but can we please get you another pillow to cry into? Those hands are creeping me out."

Maureen got up and reached across the coffee table,

handing Ida a throw pillow with tassels at the corners. Ida gave Maureen the creepy hand pillow, which Maureen put behind the couch.

"You sure do have a lot of pillows," said Jason.

Ida cried into the tasseled pillow.

"Ida," Delbert said, "I didn't go to the outlet mall without you. We really were at Jenny's house talking. Not like I wanted to be there or anything, but that's where we were."

Gary looked up from his pillow, tears running down his face.

"I didn't want to be there either," he said.

Oleen said, "So you're telling us that Gary and Delbert are gay, and they've been having an affair for the past forty-five years? And that you all knew, and nobody said anything? Gary, is this true? Are you gay? Have you been having an affair with Delbert?"

"Yes," Gary said, at the same time Delbert said, "No."

"It's actually been more like forty-eight years," Gary whispered. ""It started in college."

Ida stood up.

"It's either true or it isn't, and Gary says it's true. Delbert McNair, this is hard for me to believe, but I know how you avoid conflict. So I'm not listening to you, and even though I can't wrap my head around this right now, I just know I need to be alone."

Ida turned away from Delbert and walked around the sofa to the stairs. Then Ida stomped up the stairs as though each step had deeply offended her, turned the corner at the top, and vanished out of sight.

22

SUNDAY

I n the living room Oleen sat without speaking or moving. Jenny turned toward her.

"Mom?" she said, putting her arm around Oleen, "Are you okay?"

Oleen opened her mouth but didn't say anything. She stared at Gary with wide eyes, mouth agape.

"You're gay?"

Gary nodded.

"I've always thought you did some weird things, and I've always thought you were a little bit less masculine than, say, Delbert, but I figured that some men can be that way. I've always loved you so much I overlooked it. I mean, you're not like Scott or anything."

"Thanks, Oleen!" called Scott, standing up and walking past Delbert to sit down between Steve and Maureen.

"I'm sorry, Oleen," said Gary. "You have no idea how sorry I am."

"I have no idea what to say. The only thing you do that would ever have made me think you were gay is that you sleep in a nightshirt. I've always thought that was, uh, pretty unusual for a man not living in the 1850s."

"Trust me, Oleen," said Scott, "that has nothing to do with being gay. That's just weird. No man I've ever met, gay or straight, sleeps in a nightshirt. I think that's just some odd, eccentric, and highly unfashionable behavior right there."

Scott turned to his left.

"You sleep in a nightshirt?" Scott said. No wonder no one's ever known that. I see why you'd both keep that a secret. Wait, I hope you have one of those Knightshirts that Mom wears. The one with the little knight on the front where it says Knightshirt underneath. That thing is so tacky it's hysterical and awesome."

Gary turned a very dark shade of red.

"Oh my god!" Scott said, leaning back into the couch and pointing at Gary, "You do!"

Seeing an opportunity to deflect some of the negativity, Delbert said, "He found it first. He said it was, and I quote, 'amazing,' and he sighed when he said it. Then he said he had to have it and I should get one for Ida."

"You didn't seem to mind my nightshirts when we were in college!" Gary said, turning toward Delbert.

"That's because I bet you rarely wore one," Scott said.

"Eww, Scott!" Maureen said.

"Yeah, I even grossed myself out there, Reenie. Sorry about that. That's just a little bit less weird than that atrocious pillow."

"I'm going to have to agree with Scott," said Steve. "I had a lot of relationships before I met Scott, all with gay men, and not a single one even owned a nightshirt. I don't think the nightshirt thing has anything to do with the gay thing."

"I always thought the nightshirt thing was weird!" Jenny said. "I never met a straight guy who sleeps in a nightshirt either."

"You sleep in a nightshirt?" Jason said, withholding a laugh as he looked at Gary.

"Yes I do," Gary said, sitting up straight and putting the pillow down in his lap. "There is nothing wrong with a man sleeping in a nightshirt. My father did it his whole life."

"Your father was crazy," said Jenny. "Believe me, I deal with what I think he did, and I've made lots of decisions that have later seemed weird to me. He wore a nightshirt because he was crazy, not because he was gay, because he wasn't gay."

"My dad wasn't crazy, Jenny!" said Gary. "He was eccentric."

"Okay, Dad, I guess I'm just eccentric too," said Jenny.

"You're not eccentric, Jenny," said Scott. "Or crazy."

Jenny stared at him.

"Scott, did you just say something nice to Jenny?" Janie asked.

"Yeah, I did," said Scott. "Don't know where that came from."

Tears escaped Jenny's eyes, though she tried to hide them. "Let's get back to the discussion," she said.

"Oleen, Gary and my dad are gay. Do you think we made that up? We don't have a reason to," said Maureen.

"I just can't believe it," said Oleen. "We've been together forty-five years. I don't understand how this could have happened, and how I wouldn't know. That's just not possible. I'm going home," she said, gathering her bag and hurrying out the front door. With Ida and Oleen gone, no one said anything. Everyone just looked around at everyone else. Delbert got up, went into the bathroom and closed the door.

"I don't think I'll try to talk to her right now," said Gary. "It might take her a while to forgive me."

Jenny looked at her father. "Dad, you know she might not forgive you, right? I'm not trying to be mean, but I think you need to be prepared for that."

Jenny rested her face in her hands and looked down at the arm of the sofa as she began softly crying.

"Oleen always forgives me," Gary said. "And I've done a lot of stupid things. She's a very forgiving person."

"Gary," said Janie, "People don't always forgive people when they have affairs. I don't think I'd be able to forgive Jason if he did. Would you forgive me?" she asked, turning toward Jason. He shrugged. "I don't know, but you'd never do that."

"No," Janie said. "I wouldn't."

"I don't think it's just the affair, Gary," said Scott. "Don't you think she might be a teensy bit upset that, I don't know, you pretended to be straight for forty-five years? If Steve were only pretending to be gay and wasn't, and we'd been married forty-five years or even just the two we have now, I think I'd be just a little miffed. It's a trust thing, and I think I'd feel stupid for not noticing, too."

Gary started crying again.

Delbert returned from the bathroom and said, "I'm going to the garage." He walked through the kitchen and out the door that led to the garage.

"Maybe we should bet on how long old Delbert is gonna deny this. I'm going with six months at least," Scott said.

"I think Delbert is always going to deny our love," said Gary with a sniffle. "After the conversation yesterday, I thought things were getting better, but now I doubt he'll ever want to talk to me again. I'll have to move." Gary tried to hide his crying by grabbing the blue throw blanket off the back of the sofa and crying into it instead of into the pillow. The blanket hid his entire face and most of his head.

"I think maybe we should go," said Steve. "Let's go, Scott." Steve took Scott's hand and led him out the front door.

A moment later Janie stood, with some effort, and said, "We should go too. We can get all these gifts tomorrow. Come on, Jason." Janie and Jason left, followed by Alex and Maureen. Only Agnes, Jenny, and Gary remained in the living room.

Agnes put her arm around Jenny and pulled Jenny against

her. "I'm so sorry, Jenny," she said. Jenny allowed the tears that had been lined up for hours, ready to pour out of her eyes like lemmings jumping off a cliff, to fall against her grandma's shoulder.

"I'm sorry too," she whispered.

23

SUNDAY

After Agnes and Jenny left, Gary spent a long time
sitting on the left side of the fireplace-facing couch.
Once everyone else had gone, Gary had remained on
the sofa, crying on and off for two hours. He then fell asleep,
and when he woke up and looked up at the clock over the fireplace, it read 8:15 p.m. Gary examined the pillow and the throw
blanket he had used as makeshift tissues. He had always found
it easier to cry into something other than tissues. You just used
way too many of them. Since he was a child he had mostly
cried into towels, and when there weren't any towels around,
into whatever was handy. And Gary cried a lot.

Gary sat with his legs curled underneath him, his left arm
on the armrest of the sofa. He hadn't seen Delbert or Ida since
they had left the room earlier. About an hour before, just
before he fell asleep, Gary had peeked through the window in
the door to the garage and seen Delbert lying in the lounge
chair he kept there. It was a very comfortable and sturdy
lounge chair, very high quality. He guessed it was unusual to
keep a chair that nice in a garage that served as a shop, but he
thought it was the place in the house in which Delbert felt

most comfortable, so he guessed it wasn't that surprising. Delbert had his eyes closed and appeared to be sleeping.

Gary went to the refrigerator, opened the door, and looked inside. There was a lot of leftover food from the baby shower in there, and he was getting hungry. He hadn't eaten much at the barbecue place earlier because he had been thinking about what was going to happen after the baby shower. He still felt bad, but now that the "intervention" was over, at least he could eat again. Gary got a plate from one of the cabinets and selected two dishes of casserole, several plates of appetizers, and a lemon pound cake from the refrigerator. Ida always kept cakes and desserts in the refrigerator, even when they had no business being there. As he set the dishes on the counter, he heard a noise on the stairs and looked up to see Ida coming down.

Ida saw Gary and jumped.

"Gary, you surprised me," she said. "I wasn't expecting to see you here."

"Sorry, I've been sitting on your sofa for the past few hours, and I got hungry. I didn't eat that much earlier. Not nearly as much as Scott did."

Ida reached the kitchen and pulled a stool around the island to face the spot where Gary stood on the other side.

"Scott really can eat a ton at all-you-can-eat barbecue places. Always could, even as a kid. Other than that, he never had a big appetite, which is why he never seemed to put on weight, even after eating what seemed like fifty pounds of coleslaw," said Ida. "Delbert could eat like that when he was younger, but in the past few years he's started getting a little thicker around the middle."

Gary nodded and sat down on the stool facing Ida, with only the kitchen island between them. Gary was glad for the kitchen island. While Ida seemed okay now, who knew if she might snap and try to strangle him with a dish towel? Ida was usually calm, but he could see how the current situation could make even the most peaceful person go off his or her rocker.

"I didn't think you'd ever want to talk to me again," he said.

Ida shrugged.

"I don't see the point in being mad. This is terrible, but you can't change the facts. While I was upstairs, I was thinking back to the past, and I started to understand how this could be true. I can even see specific incidents differently. But, truth be told, it will be much harder to be calm with Delbert."

"Do you want some food?" Gary asked.

"I don't know why, but I'm starving," said Ida. "I'm usually not hungry at all when something difficult is happening. When Maureen had that high blood pressure while she was pregnant with Jack—I can't remember the name, but it has a special name—that was so scary I barely ate anything for four days."

"Yeah, that was scary," Gary said.

Gary handed Ida a plate, and they each chose some casseroles and appetizers.

"I'm glad no one made anything we had to heat for the baby shower," she said. "That's always a pain. Well, I say no one, but it was just Oleen and me. You know, I felt like something was off this morning when Delbert put the baby shower decorations up and cut the grass without being asked. Maybe I always felt something was off, you know, subconsciously."

Gary thought for a moment and, to his own surprise, he didn't feel like crying.

"I'm so sorry, Ida. So sorry. I didn't mean for this to happen. I just didn't think and didn't know what to do."

"Thank you," Ida said. "I think I'm still in shock. Maybe after everything sinks in, I'll be furious at both of you. But, at least right now, I feel strangely calm."

"Oleen is in denial, I guess," Gary said. "I can see why. This is a pretty hard thing to believe. In a couple of days, I bet she'll be really mad. After she gets mad, she always forgives me. But maybe not this time."

Ida shrugged again. "I don't know. Too soon to tell. I don't even know how I feel."

"I'm not sure what I feel either, Ida," Gary said. "I'm mad at myself, sad and scared. But I'm also relieved. I had no idea how much stress keeping this secret was causing me. I'm just sorry that to make me feel better it's making you and Oleen feel terrible."

"I'm actually a lot more worried about all the kids," she said. "And also, about Tyler. He's about to be ten now, and I'm sure he knows about being gay and stuff. Alex and Maureen have taught him to be accepting of people who aren't the same as he is, but I'm still worried about how it will affect him. The other two are young enough they won't understand."

"They probably won't," Gary agreed.

"And even though our own kids are adults, I don't think we should assume they'll handle it well either. When Julie and Thomas Wellington got divorced a couple of years ago... remember that?"

"I do," said Gary.

"Julie told me Ed and Joseph kept it together, but it sent Sarah into a terrible depression. And Sarah is the same age as Janie. In fact, she was even at the baby shower yesterday, she and Julie. Sarah got put on some medication and went to therapy, and she's doing much better now."

"Well, we *know* Scott will be fine. And Mike will deal okay, and so will Maureen," Gary said. "I'm not saying they won't be upset, but they'll manage to get past it without any major damage. I think Scott is enjoying this."

"After how his dad treated him when he was younger that wouldn't surprise me," said Ida. "I think that's how he perfected his sarcasm. It became his defense mechanism."

"I'm mostly worried about Jenny," Gary said. "She's going

through so much. If this makes her worse, I don't know what I'll do. I'll never forgive myself."

"She seems to be handling it okay, Gary. Much better than I would expect. And way better than she would have before," said Ida. "I'm glad she's doing better. I know how hard life has always been for her. It's such a relief to finally know why, and that her medication and therapy seem to be helping."

"Yeah," said Gary, "She's doing a lot better. I just hope she keeps doing better. I know handling all this is hard on her, even when she doesn't say so."

"Jenny's a really strong person, Gary," Ida said.

Tears began to run down Gary's cheeks, and Ida handed him a dish towel. Gary wiped his eyes.

"I think Janie will handle things okay," Ida said. "But I'm just worried about it putting stress on her and on the baby. And you know Jason isn't all that helpful. I hope it will be okay."

Gary cut both himself and Ida a piece of lemon pound cake.

"I never thought I'd be in this position," said Ida. "Seeing my marriage fall apart at my age."

"You think you and Delbert won't stay together?" asked Gary.

Ida stared at him.

"Well, how could we, Gary? How could you and Oleen, either?"

As Ida took small bites of her pound cake, Gary abandoned his dessert, returned to his seat on the couch, and sobbed into the dish towel.

24

MONDAY, MEMORIAL DAY

The next morning, Oleen awoke to a very loud bird chirping just outside her window. She looked at the clock on her phone. It read 10 a.m., and Oleen never slept until 10 a.m., or really at all. She had fallen asleep at 1 a.m. and had thought she heard Gary come in around midnight, but she didn't feel like going downstairs to check. She wondered why he never came to bed. Then she remembered what had happened the afternoon before and her stomach felt like she had swallowed a boulder. After a few minutes, Oleen ran across the bedroom to the bathroom. Anything that worried her always gave her stomach problems. When Maureen had that blood pressure issue when she had Jack a couple of years ago, Oleen, Gary, Mike, and Jenny had attended the wedding of one of Mike's childhood friends, and Oleen had run back and forth from her seat to the bathroom about fifteen times. She was terrified and would much rather have been at the hospital than at some wedding. It was a good thing she had been seated at the end of the aisle.

Once Oleen had returned from the bathroom and gotten dressed, fixed her hair, and put on her makeup, she sat down on the bed and took a deep breath, still trying to figure out how Gary and Delbert could be gay. She went downstairs to find Gary sitting on the living room sofa, still wearing his pajamas but, today, he had on a pair of sweatpants under his nightshirt. She guessed that was a step toward regular pajamas. That conversation yesterday about nightshirts must have gotten to him. Even though Oleen didn't believe Gary was gay, or that he had been kissing Delbert against a truck yesterday, she still felt mad at him.

"Hi, honey," Gary said as Oleen entered the living room.

"Hello," Oleen said.

Oleen never said hello, except when she was mad. She was never that formal.

"How are you?" asked Gary.

"Okay, I guess," she said.

Oleen never responded in such short sentences when people asked how she was, either.

"Got any plans for the day?"

"I think I'll see if Ida and Agnes want to go to lunch," said Oleen. "I better call them now, or Agnes will have eaten."

Oleen took her phone and walked outside to the front porch, taking a seat in a red rocking chair. She called Ida and Agnes, who both sounded tired but agreed to lunch at the Silver Kettle in an hour. They would take Ida's car and pick up Agnes on the way. It was always best to take only one car when they went to the Silver Kettle. You never knew which of them would be able to drive home, but certainly not more than one of them.

Oleen saw Delbert trimming the bushes next door. Whenever Delbert did something wrong, he always became very helpful around the house and the yard. Since it was a beautiful day today, she guessed the yard made more sense.

"Hello, Delbert!" she called.

Delbert turned around.

"Hi, Oleen," he said, waving.

He turned back to the bush he had been working on. Oleen usually tried to say more than this to people when things were strained. She guessed she thought she could fix everything that way. But today she didn't know what to say, so she didn't say anything.

At 10:45, Oleen went inside and got her purse.

"I'm going to lunch now," she said to Gary. "I don't know when I'll be back."

Gary was still wearing the nightshirt and sweatpants which, for some reason, made Oleen feel murderous. It had always aggravated her that he didn't get dressed until 11 a.m. on weekends and holidays, but his wearing those sweatpants was really irritating her. Oleen walked down the steps and noticed that Delbert was nowhere to be found, though his hedge clippers and gloves, and the pieces of bushes he had trimmed off lay on the ground where she had seen him a few minutes ago. Like Ida had said yesterday, Delbert avoided conflict. He hadn't always been that way, but Oleen thought he'd started getting that way around the time Scott was eleven. That was when he had seemed to stop hassling Scott too, and Scott seemed to feel a lot better than he ever had after that. If it was becoming conflict-avoidant that had made Delbert stop being how he'd been to Scott, she guessed she was glad for it.

The hostess at the Silver Kettle greeted Agnes, Oleen, and Ida by name, and led them to their favorite booth. They had been going there for years, so they knew everyone in the place. The Silver Kettle would be crowded today, as it usually was on minor holidays like Memorial Day and Labor Day, but every time the women went there, they arrived right when the place opened, so they always got their favorite booth. Agnes was glad the Silver Kettle only served brunch on weekends, Thanksgiving, and Christmas. She didn't feel like being in a noisy crowd today.

Their waitress arrived. Agnes was glad to see it was their favorite waitress, Megan. Megan was about thirty and had worked at the Silver Kettle for ten years. She was always extra-attentive to the women and sometimes snuck them a free pitcher of margaritas, when she could do it without getting caught. The Silver Kettle was, Agnes supposed, a little bit odd as far as restaurants went, almost like it was having an identity crisis. Its name made it sound like it would serve Southern food, but it actually served Mexican food. The restaurant used to serve a lot of different types of cuisines and used to have a large selection of teas, but about fifteen years ago the place had changed ownership and the new owner, who was from Mexico, had changed the food to Mexican food and gotten rid of all the teas. Because the Silver Kettle was well known, though, he had kept the name, even though it didn't fit. Agnes liked it much better here now. It was bright and airy, and the food was much better. She also liked the staff better, and the owner took more of an interest in the restaurant because he worked as the restaurant manager, too.

"Hi, ladies!" said Megan, "Glad to see you today. We usually only see you on Saturdays."

"We needed a drink today, dear," Ida said, surprising herself.

She always told the waitresses they had come for "tea," which she had started saying when the Silver Kettle quit serving tea. But just then Ida didn't see the point in pretending she had come to do anything but drink herself into a coma.

Megan looked surprised.

"Well, after Allison seated you, she told Lina to start making your pitcher, so I'll have it out in a second."

Ida thanked Megan, and the women ordered their food.

Once Megan was gone, Agnes looked at Ida and Oleen, who were sitting across from her in the booth.

"How are you two doing today?" she asked.

Oleen shrugged.

"I don't think we should talk about this until we've had a couple of margaritas," said Ida.

Agnes made small talk about the weather and the upcoming week until the pitcher arrived. Megan set the large glass pitcher of frozen strawberry margaritas on the table, along with three margarita glasses, some chips and salsa, and a bowl of cheese dip. They didn't usually order cheese dip since the margaritas they drank had enough calories on their own, but today no one seemed to care.

Agnes poured each of them a margarita, and both Ida and Oleen began guzzling them as though they were in a race. Agnes took a sip of her margarita and contemplated what might be the best thing to say to two half-drunk women who had just discovered their husbands were having a love affair with one another.

25

MONDAY

Today was the only day in the history of their trips to the Silver Kettle when Agnes drank less than either Ida or Oleen did. In fact, Agnes didn't even finish one margarita. Today she figured someone needed to stay sane, and she doubted either Ida or Oleen were good candidates. Getting drunk was the best thing for them today, Agnes thought. Even Maureen, who she'd never seen drink much at all until yesterday, would have to get drunk daily to handle this kind of news.

Ida and Oleen each finished a second margarita and ate half the chips and cheese dip while Agnes barely ate at all and drank even less, though neither Ida nor Oleen seemed to notice. It was funny how no one ate the salsa when there was cheese dip. Not even Agnes ate the salsa when there was cheese dip.

Ida and Oleen were laughing and talking about some funny commercial they had seen.

During a pause in the conversation, Agnes said, "How are you two doing?"

Oleen burst out laughing.

"My husband wears a nightshirt!" she said.

"Are you feeling angry? Sad? I think it would be good to talk about this."

Oleen, who was usually more talkative than Ida was, and who, when she was drunk, could even get going like Scott did, said, "The thing that made me really mad this morning was how Gary was wearing sweatpants under his nightshirt. Sweatpants! As though a plain nightshirt wasn't bad enough. Get some damn pajamas, Gary!"

Ida laughed loud and long.

"Sweatpants?" she said. "Now that right there is really hilarious."

Seeing that neither Oleen nor Ida was going to talk about anything serious, Agnes took a breath and moved on to another topic.

"So, I guess Scott and Steve's anniversary is coming up in June, right? Won't it be three years? Do you know if they're doing anything special?"

Megan put the plates on the table in front of each woman. She looked at Agnes.

"We're having some family issues," Agnes said. "I know we aren't usually so loud. I'm sorry."

"It's okay, Agnes," said Megan, "We have lots of loud, drunk people here, especially in the spring and summer. You can't serve margaritas and not have loud, drunk people."

Ida giggled.

"Megan, did you know our husbands are having an affair? We had no idea, but Delbert and Gary have been having a secret love affair the whole time we've been married!"

"You know," Megan said, tapping her fingers on the table without seeming shocked at all, "they come here together a lot, and one time I did think I saw them holding hands across the table, so I'm not too surprised. I've kind of wondered for a long time if they were."

"Really?" asked Ida. "I never even suspected."

"I hope I'm not talking out of turn," said Megan, "But most of the waiters and waitresses here think Gary and Delbert behave strangely. They touch each other a lot, more than you'd think two men who are married to women would touch each other. Delbert tries to hide it, and Gary is more obvious about it. But don't feel bad, I could see how if you're that close to them you wouldn't realize it. So many people don't realize their husband or wife is having an affair. I've heard lots of stories like that from loud, drunk people."

Agnes thought for a moment.

"I think that's a pretty good point, Megan. I don't think they're going to remember this conversation tomorrow, or maybe even later today," she said, gesturing toward Oleen and Ida. "So please do me a favor and don't mention it to them the next time we come in."

"Sure thing, Agnes," said Megan. "Can I get you all anything else?"

"Just, well, I didn't know that a lot of people knew Gary and Delbert were having an affair," said Agnes. "This is a big city we live in."

"Well," Megan said, "I only know about what goes on here but people, not just the staff, but people who eat here, mostly the regulars, have gossiped about it for a while. I thought maybe Ida and Oleen had some kind of arrangement with Delbert and Gary, but stayed married out of convenience or something."

"No, the girls really didn't know," said Agnes, putting her head in her hands.

"I thought they did," said Megan. "It seems kind of apparent to me about Delbert and Gary."

Agnes thanked Megan and tried to eat her bean burrito, which didn't taste quite as good as it usually did.

26

MONDAY

Agnes, Ida, and Oleen left the Silver Kettle and, as neither Ida nor Oleen could drive, Agnes drove Ida's car. Once they were done eating, rather than staying at the restaurant and waiting to sober up as they usually did, Agnes had decided it was time to go. There was no reason to sit there while people in the restaurant might be looking at Ida and Oleen and talking about them. She decided to take them back to her house.

Agnes didn't think it was a good idea to take either woman back to their own homes. Who knew what they might say to Delbert and Gary right now? Whatever it was, she was sure It wouldn't help matters. She couldn't imagine any conversation between the women and their husbands would be very productive, considering both Ida and Oleen were very drunk. Gary would cry, and Delbert would develop a sudden need to go to the bathroom.

After arriving home and making sure both Ida and Oleen got into her house without falling, Agnes put on a pot of tea. Her house was smaller than either Ida's or Oleen's. Their houses were large and two stories with open floor plans and beautiful kitchens, which looked onto spacious living rooms. Sometimes Agnes wished she had a house like theirs, but other times she thought about how she and Herman had raised Gary and his brother, Marcus, in her one-story brick ranch house, and both Gary and his brother had turned out okay. Well, sort of okay.

Agnes supposed it was a generational thing, thinking you needed a massive house for only two or three kids. Still, as Agnes stood in her galley kitchen and poured three cups of tea, she thought about how she did envy Ida's and Oleen's kitchens. If Agnes were honest with herself, her kitchen had always been somewhat of a pain in the ass to maneuver in. As Scott would say, whoever came up with the galley kitchen should be drawn and quartered.

Agnes took the cups of tea, along with sugar packets, packets of artificial sweetener, and three spoons, into the living room. Agnes used to try to be fancy with a special sugar bowl with a tiny silver spoon and artificial sweetener packets arranged in a decorative container, and sometimes she even had honey, but now she just bought packets of everything and they all sat jumbled together in a freezer bag in the cabinet. When she had used a sugar bowl the sugar would always clump up and stick to the side of the container, and someone always managed to stir their tea or coffee with the sugar spoon, and it just wasn't worth it anymore. Agnes had grown tired of trying to be so damn decorative. She handed mugs of tea to Ida and Oleen, and let each of them select their preferred sweeteners. Once everyone was done stirring, and the spoons were set on paper towel, Agnes again attempted to bring up the issue. Oleen sipped her tea and said,

"I love how hot drinks make my head not hurt. Why don't we have tea every time we drink?"

"Because by the time we leave we're usually not this drunk

anymore," said Ida. "In fact, by this point, at least one of us is sober. But, Oleen, I think we're still drunk now."

Ida giggled. "Agnes, are we still drunk?"

"We're sloshed!" Oleen sang like she was performing in the *Music Man*.

"I think you're still drunk," said Agnes.

Agnes's cat, Louie, entered the living room, jumped onto Oleen's lap, and tried to stick his paw into her mug.

"No, Louie!" said Oleen.

Ida set her mug down on the coffee table, stood up from her chair, and started singing "Louie Louie" by the Kingsmen. When she got past the first two words to the part where the lyrics are indiscernible, Oleen jumped up from the chair next to her to accompany her. Louie fell onto the floor and jumped up onto Oleen's chair.

"Louie, Louie, oh we gotta go."

Agnes shook her head and rubbed her temples with her fingertips.

Oleen sang, grabbing Louie's tail to use as a microphone, "A fine little girl, na, na, na, na, Gary and Delbert are liars!" Oleen put Louie's tail above her lip like it was a mustache. Louie jerked away from Oleen and ran out of the room.

Ida put her arm around her sister and sang, "Gary and Delbert are liars!"

"Honey," Agnes said to Ida, "Let's both of you sit down on the sofa. I think what you need is water."

Ida and Oleen collapsed onto the sofa in giggles. Agnes went to the kitchen and returned with two large bottles of water.

"They're not cold, but you won't notice," Agnes said.

Ida and Oleen took the bottles and began drinking. After they had finished their water, Ida said, "I'm tired, and my head hurts. Agnes, would you hand me my tea?"

Agnes put Ida's and Oleen's mugs in front of them, and each woman began sipping her tea again.

"I think I'm not drunk anymore," said Oleen. "Well, a little maybe. But not like I was."

"Oleen, honey," said Agnes, "I'm worried about you."

"Don't worry about me," said Oleen, "I'm not *that* drunk. I'm not gonna throw up or anything."

"I'm not worried about you throwing up, honey," said Agnes, "I'm worried about how you're dealing with learning about Gary and Delbert being together and keeping it from you."

"Oh," said Oleen. "Oh, that."

"Yes," said Agnes. "That."

"I believe it!" said Ida. "Delbert has been acting way weirder than usual. And Maureen never lies. None of my children are good liars. Maureen and Janie stopped trying after the time when Maureen was twelve and Janie was seven, and I caught them watching *Nightmare on Elm Street* on the VCR the day after Christmas. That was sometime in the late 80s."

"Really?" asked Oleen.

"Yes!" Ida said. "And when I asked them where the movie came from, would you believe Janie said Santa left it in her stocking? Maureen even agreed with her and insisted that Santa brought it. Maureen believed in Santa Claus for a long, long time."

"Where did they get it?" asked Agnes.

"Some school friend of Maureen's gave her the VHS," said Ida. "It turns out the girl who gave it to her had been passing it around the class and charging a rental fee for it, but Maureen was able to get it for free because she gave the girl two rolls of Bubble Tape or something. Both Maureen and Janie had nightmares for a week after seeing that movie, and I don't recall them lying much again after that. I could always tell if they did, though."

"And when Scott lies it's always something ridiculous that no one believes anyway," said Oleen. "Like saying Mr. McGruder cornered him in the pantry to compliment him on his 'shapely buttocks,' or whatever it is Scott said."

"It *was* shapely buttocks," said Ida. "Believe me, when he was fifteen, he told that story so many times the phrase is seared into my memory."

"Getting back to my question," Agnes said, "Oleen, how are you doing? And, Ida, are you saying you believe it now?"

"I don't know why I'm so calm right now," said Ida. "Maybe I'm in shock, or it's the alcohol, but I do believe it. I have no idea how I'll feel in a few days, and I can't quite get my head around it yet."

"I still can't believe it," said Oleen. "I know everyone else seems to believe it, but I don't see how we could live with them and not know for the two hundred years we've been married. If that's true then we're just stupid, and I know we're not stupid, so I don't believe it. I know I was just singing about them being liars, but that was the margaritas talking."

Agnes and Ida looked at each other. Louie returned to the living room, jumping up on the sofa and curling up in Ida's lap.

27

MONDAY

G ary was sitting on a wicker bench on the front porch of his house when Mike's car pulled into the driveway. Mike and his girlfriend, Lauren, got out of the car and walked up the steps onto the porch. Lauren had her long dirty-blonde hair pulled back into a braid. Her red, flowered strapless sundress cascaded over her thin frame, stopping just above the tops of her red wedge-heeled platform sandals. Her blue eyes sparkled as she looked at Gary, and her small upturned nose, wide smile, perfectly straight teeth, and lack of makeup made her look like she had stepped out of a Noxzema commercial.

"How was the beach trip?" Gary asked. "You two sure are tan."

"Hi, Dad! It was great!" Mike said. "Where's Mom? We've got something to tell you."

Lauren took Mike's arm and kissed him on the cheek. She had to tiptoe, even on three-inch platform sandals, to reach Mike's cheek. Lauren was five foot six and Mike towered over her at six foot five. Oleen and Gary were both pretty short, so everyone assumed Mike and Jenny got their height from Gary's side of the family because Agnes was tall and her husband, Herman, had been even taller. Mike was also large, and broad-shouldered, and almost everyone he met assumed he had played football at some time in his life, though he had played soccer and didn't even like to watch football. Mike had wavy brown hair, brown eyes, and he wore a blue polo shirt, khaki shorts, and brown loafers.

Gary looked both Mike and Lauren over and thought about how the two of them would one day join a country club.

"Your mother went to lunch with Ida and Agnes," said Gary. "You know how it is when they go to the Silver Kettle. They might not get back for three or four hours."

"Oh, yeah," said Mike, "I guess you're right. Well, Dad, Lauren has something to show you."

Lauren held her left hand out to Gary to show off the large, shiny, diamond ring adorning her ring finger.

Gary jumped up from the wicker bench to examine it.

"Oh my god!" said Gary, his voice cracking. "You guys are engaged?"

Mike and Lauren both nodded and smiled.

Gary jumped up and down, clapping.

"I'm so happy for you!" he said, wiping a tear from his eye. "This is so great."

"Welcome to the family, Lauren," Gary said, pulling Lauren into a tight hug. "I'm so happy for you," he said, putting his arm around Mike.

Mike looked next door toward Ida and Delbert's house.

"We should go tell Uncle Delbert, too," he said to Lauren. "I'm sure he'll want to know."

Mike turned toward Gary.

"Dad, why don't you come with us?"

"Oh, I wouldn't want to intrude," said Gary.

"You're not intruding, Dad," Mike said. "We're excited, and we want to share it with you guys."

Lauren touched Gary's shoulder.

"Please come, Gary. It would mean a lot to us."

"Okay," Gary said, crossing his arms.

"Are you okay, Dad?" Mike asked.

"I'm fine," said Gary, "Just a little tired. We had a busy weekend with going out to lunch with Jason to celebrate the baby, and I had some work I had to bring home."

Gary continued and, having no idea why, said, "And the trip to the outlet mall took a long time too."

"Wait," said Mike. "*You* went to the outlet mall? Since when do you like shopping? Every time I see you, you have on, like, the same five things all the time."

"Well," Gary said, "it was a bunch of us. Maureen came by to decorate for the baby shower, and she and Janie were going, and then she told Delbert and me about a car show, and Scott and Steve showed up, and even Jenny and Agnes came."

Gary shifted from one foot to the other and clasped his hands together behind his back.

"That's, uh, weird," said Mike. "But, whatever. Let's go tell Uncle Delbert. Come on, Dad."

Mike took Lauren's hand and led her down the steps and across the front yard. Gary trailed behind, wishing he'd fall into a sinkhole or that the dead tree in Ida and Delbert's backyard would fall right on his head.

Mike, Lauren, and Gary stood on Ida and Delbert's front porch. Mike rang the doorbell and heard loud footsteps approaching the front door from inside. Gary stood behind Mike, whom he hoped would block Delbert from seeing him. Gary saw Delbert looking out the window next to the front door. Delbert opened the door to greet them.

"Hey, guys, what's going on?" Delbert asked, wiping his hands on his overalls. "Sorry I'm dirty, I was working on that Mustang your dad and I have been restoring, Mike."

"Don't you all do that together?" Mike asked.

"Yeah, but your dad didn't feel like it today. I guess he was tired or something."

Gary stepped out from behind Mike and poked his head between Mike and Lauren.

"I was not tired, Delbert," said Gary, poking his finger into Delbert's face, or as close as he could get to Delbert's face from his spot behind Mike and Lauren. "You just didn't tell me you were working on it today. And I bet you were reupholstering the seats, weren't you? You know that's my favorite part, and I bet you did it anyway!"

"I was not reupholstering the seats, Gary. Calm down."

Mike looked from Delbert to Gary, then back to Delbert.

"You know he gets emotional sometimes," Delbert said to Mike.

"I am not emotional, Delbert!" said Gary. "I just don't like it when you leave me out of something we were supposed to do together."

"Dad," Mike said. "Calm down. It's not that big a deal."

"Oh, it's a big deal, Mike. It's a very, very big deal."

Delbert ignored Gary. "Why don't you guys come in," he said.

"We can't right now, Uncle Delbert," said Mike. "We just wanted to show you something, but then we're going to run by the Silver Kettle and show Mom, Agnes, and Ida. We need to hurry so we get there before they're totally plastered."

Lauren held out her left hand to show Delbert her ring.

"We're engaged!" she said.

Delbert looked at the large diamond, then at Mike.

"You must be doing pretty well for yourself, there, Son," said Delbert.

Mike laughed. "I do okay."

"Well, I'm very happy for both of you," Delbert said.

Delbert grabbed Mike's hand and shook it, then hugged

Lauren, patting her on the back. Mike had always thought Delbert hugged like a robot.

"Well, we'd better get going," Mike said to Lauren. "I want to tell Mom while she'll still be able to remember we told her."

Mike and Lauren walked down the steps and across the yard to Mike's Prius. They pulled out of the driveway and turned the corner at the end of Gardenia Lane.

Delbert stood just inside the open door and stared at Gary, who was standing a couple of feet away on the porch.

"I can't believe you have the gall to deny our love, Delbert!" Gary said. "Just this time yesterday you were so kind and sensitive."

"I'm not gay, Gary!" Delbert said, slamming the door in his face.

28

MONDAY

Ida and Oleen seemed to be getting back to normal when Agnes's doorbell rang. She opened the door to find Jenny, Scott, and Steve standing on her front steps.

"Well, this is a nice surprise," she said, hugging Jenny and motioning all three inside.

"Hi, Scott," she said, giving him a quick kiss on the cheek. "Hi, Steve," she said, enveloping Steve in a hug.

"Hi, Agnes," Scott and Steve said at the same time.

"Come on in and sit down," said Agnes. "Your mothers and I were just having some tea."

"Real tea or Ida tea?" Scott asked.

"Real tea," said Agnes. "Believe me, no one needs anymore Ida tea today, but it seems like they're doing better now."

Scott and Steve sat down in adjacent chairs, and Jenny joined her mom and aunt on the sofa.

"Would anyone like anything to eat or drink?" asked Agnes.

"No thanks," said Scott. "We just had brunch."

"And it was delicious," Jenny said.

Ida burst out laughing.

"Jenny, did you know your mom sings very well but only when she uses a cat's tail for a microphone?"

Ida and Oleen laughed and fell further into the couch.

"Wow," said Scott, looking at Agnes. "They are so trashed. What did you give them, Sterno?"

"They each had several margaritas," said Agnes, sitting down in the chair by the front window. "I guess they're still drunk," she said, running her hand through her hair.

"How many did they have, Grandma?" asked Jenny.

"I think they each had about four, maybe four and a half."

"Jeez," said Steve, "And the Silver Kettle makes theirs extra-strong. I think four of their margaritas would even flatten Scott."

Scott held his hand over his mouth, trying not to laugh as Oleen put her arm around her sister and loudly sang, "We're sloshed!" into Ida's ear.

"You two are hammered, and Gary and Delbert are enamored," Scott said.

Scott smiled and ran his hand through his hair.

"He's so proud of himself for that rhyme," Jenny said to Steve, who smiled and nodded. "He runs his hand through his hair when he's proud of himself," Steve said.

Scott looked at Jenny and dropped his hand to his lap. Ida and Oleen both giggled.

"I've never seen them this way," said Jenny. "It's kind of funny, and it makes me glad I don't drink anymore, because at least now I know I'll never start talking about what kind of underwear I wear in public again."

"When did you talk about your underwear in public?" asked Steve.

"Oh, it was back when we worked at Starbucks," Jenny said. "I told several customers that I had tried to wear a thong and that it was very uncomfortable. I kind of went to work drunk that day. Don't worry, I didn't drive there. That was the day the manager sent me home and told everyone I had stomach flu."

"I remember that!" said Steve. "That was right after I started there and I barely knew you. When you left you looked at me and said, 'Did you ever dance with the Devil in the pale moonlight?' I thought you were weird for a while."

"That's when I was obsessed with that Michael Keaton Batman movie," Jenny said. "You know, the one with Jack Nicholson? I used to say that a lot when I was drunk."

"Why are you three here?" asked Oleen, gesturing toward Scott, Steve, and Jenny.

Jenny laughed.

"You're so polite, Mom. You sound like Leah's four-year-old daughter, Rachel. One time I went over to take Rachel this hat I made for her, this was when she was three, and after I'd been there a few minutes, Rachel turned to me and said, 'Can you go home now, Jenny?' It was hilarious."

Oleen stuck her tongue out at Jenny, who giggled.

"How are you all doing?" asked Steve. "Agnes, what about you?"

Agnes gestured toward the sofa, where Louie was still curled up in Ida's lap. Oleen was holding his tail under her nose again like a mustache.

"This is how I'm doing," she said, rubbing her head and looking at Oleen.

Scott laughed. "Oh my god, you should sell them off as a circus sideshow, Agnes."

"Oleen's been bothering the cat the whole time she's been here. She won't stop doing things to his tail. I don't know what's gotten into her."

"I'd say four margaritas have gotten into her," said Jenny. "This is fun. It's making me feel so much better about myself. It's like therapy, except there's a cat. And Scott. I'd love to have a cat at therapy, but probably not Scott."

"Thanks there, Jen," said Scott.

"Well," said Agnes, "I think we're having some denial issues."

Agnes motioned toward Oleen, who was now using the cat's tail to tickle her sister under the chin. Ida pushed Oleen away and Louie, who had managed to sleep through Oleen's harassment of his tail, rolled over in Ida's lap so his tail curled underneath him.

"That is the most tolerant cat I've ever seen," said Scott, fascinated.

"I love cats," said Jenny.

"So, she doesn't believe it?" said Steve, nodding in Oleen's direction.

"No," said Agnes. "Her reason is that if she and Ida have lived with Gary and Delbert that long and never noticed they were gay or that they were having an affair, then that would make them stupid, and since they're not stupid, it isn't true."

"Seems legit," said Scott, laughing as Oleen lifted Louie's back leg up to pull his tail out.

"But Ida believes it?" Steve asked Agnes.

"I think so," Agnes said. "She's in shock and has a lot to think about, but I'm pretty sure she does."

"I wonder how Gary and Delbert are dealing with things," said Steve.

"I would venture a guess that Gary is crying," said Scott.

"You're probably right," Jenny said. "And I bet your dad is hiding in the bathroom to avoid people, Scott!"

"Delbert sure does like spending time in the bathroom," agreed Scott. "That's his favorite place to go to keep from having to talk about things. When I was little, I thought that if you went to the bathroom and had to do anything but pee, it took twenty minutes or more. When my dad would be in there for so long, I just figured it took a long time for Delbert to do the old number two."

"The old number two?" Steve laughed, reaching for Scott's hand. "I hope you're not going to start taking twenty minutes to do the old number two. You hog the big bathroom as it is."

"It's because I use product in my hair and you have to use just the right amount or it doesn't look right," said Scott. "Sometimes it takes a while."

"Product?" Steve laughed. "It doesn't even get a 'the' or an 'a' before it. Just product? Like Cher or Beyoncé?"

"Just product," agreed Scott. "You wouldn't know, Steve, because don't you get your hair cut at Fantastic Sam's?"

"Supercuts," Steve corrected him. "And no one at Supercuts has ever advised me to use 'product.'"

"That's because haircuts cost, like, $1.99 at Supercuts. It's like buying your wedding dress at Kmart," said Scott.

"Your father used to buy nightshirts at Kmart," Oleen said to Jenny. "That was the first time I realized you could only buy nightshirts in the women's section, but your father never seemed to care. I thought it was weird, though."

Oleen held Louie's tail up to her mouth like a microphone and sang the old Jefferson Starship classic, "We Built this City." Then the doorbell rang.

"I'll get it, Agnes," said Steve, standing up. "You stay there."

"That might be the worst song ever written," Scott said in Oleen's general direction.

Steve opened the front door, and Mike and Lauren walked through. Scott saw Mike and stood up.

"Mikey!" he called, pointing at Mike.

"Scotty!" Mike replied, pointing back at Scott.

"Scotty?" Steve asked.

Mike put his arm around Lauren. "We've got something to tell you," he said.

29

MONDAY

Jenny jumped up from the couch and ran to her brother.

"Oh my god, oh my god, oh my god! Did you do it?" she asked in a semi-whisper, trying not to move her mouth as she said the words.

"You tell them, Lauren," Mike said.

Lauren held her left hand up to show off her ring.

"We're engaged!" she said.

Jenny grabbed Lauren's hand to examine the ring.

"That is so beautiful!" she said. "I'm so excited!"

Scott, Steve, and Agnes all walked over to look at the ring. Scott whistled.

"That is a *nice* ring, Mike. Are you selling drugs?"

"You mean, like painkillers?" asked Mike, "To the people who have to be around you so they can stand it?"

"No, I was thinking more like hallucinogens," Scott said. "So when people look at your face it won't seem quite so ugly."

Both Mike and Scott burst out laughing.

"Congratulations, man," said Scott, giving Mike a hug. "I'm so happy for you."

Scott turned to Lauren. "I don't know how he managed to get you, but you're a brave woman," Scott laughed.

"In all seriousness, Mike and Lauren, I'm so glad you're getting married," said Scott. "You know, before I met Steve, I wasn't a happy person. I was sarcastic and I didn't listen to people because I just talked all the time, and—"

"And now you're a happy person who's sarcastic and talks all the time?" asked Mike.

"Well, yeah." Scott laughed. "The thing is," he said, putting his arm around Steve and pulling him close, "before I met Steve I just wasn't...right, you know? And I'm just grateful I did."

Scott's eyes glistened.

"Scott!" said Jenny "Are you *crying*?"

"No, no," Scott said, wiping his eyes with the back of the hand that wasn't resting on Steve's shoulder. I just wish Lauren and Mike all the happiness I feel."

Steve kissed Scott on the cheek.

"And I introduced them," said Jenny, gesturing towards Scott and Steve.

"Congratulations, honey," Agnes said to Mike, stepping past Scott to give Mike a hug. She turned to Lauren and said, "You'll be a beautiful bride."

A crash from the other side of the room caused Agnes to turn away from Lauren mid-hug. Agnes felt something whoosh by her feet and caught sight of Louie as he skittered out of the room.

From the sofa Oleen said, "Scott thinks it's the worst song ever written, Louie thinks it's the worst song ever written, nobody knows good music these days."

One of the mugs of tea lay overturned on the coffee table, though it appeared to be empty.

"It *is* a terrible song, dear," said Ida, patting Oleen's arm, "But that's not your fault. It wasn't your singing. I remember Delbert used to make me listen to that song in the car. It was our old tan station wagon with the wood paneling on the side. Okay, the paneling was fake, but it looked like wood. I think you and Gary had a purple one."

"We did!" said Oleen. "Gary insisted it had to be purple. I had no idea why."

"Well," said Ida, "Whenever that song came on the radio it just made me feel depressed. Because it's not good, but it's also not so terrible you can laugh at it. Not like that awful movie, that one where that girl from *Saved by the Bell* is swinging on a pole. What was that called?"

"*Showgirls!*" called Scott.

"Yes, dear, that's it," Ida said. "Now that movie was really terrible, but it was so terrible that all I could do was laugh. But that song—that Build the City song you were just singing, Oleen—every time it came on the radio Delbert turned it way up, and when we were in the station wagon it felt like he was screaming at the top of his lungs, shouting that line about rock and roll. And every time he did, I remember thinking, 'This song is the most mediocre song I've ever heard in my life.'" And that just made me sad. About life, about the world. It was horribly depressing."

"I guess that's why Louie ran away," Oleen said, frowning.

"Mom, were you even singing?" asked Jenny.

"No," Oleen said. "When I started to sing, Ida pointed at you all and told me to be quiet, so I just mouthed the words. I think Louie has cat telepathy."

"Or that song is just so bad that even though you didn't sing it out loud, it hornswaggled his brain somehow," said Ida.

Jenny giggled. "Hornswaggled his brain?"

"You know," Ida said, gesturing toward Oleen's head with her hands, "Messed it up. Fried it."

"I think that is very possible, Mom," said Scott.

"I want to see your ring, dear," Ida called to Lauren. Ida

started to stand up, but Lauren motioned to her to stay on the sofa.

Lauren walked across the room, and Oleen patted the sofa for Lauren to sit. Ida and Oleen both scooted in next to Lauren, who held her hand up in front of her so both could admire her ring.

"Wow!" Ida said. "That's a beautiful ring."

Oleen took Lauren's hand.

"It sure is. Oh, Lauren," she said, wiping her eyes. "You and Mike are going to be so happy." Tears appeared on her cheeks.

"You're going to make me cry, Oleen," Lauren said.

Scott sat back down in his chair, followed by Steve, who sat next to him. Agnes took the chair by the window, and Mike squeezed himself onto the end of the couch next to his mother. He put his arm around Oleen and pulled her to his shoulder. With no open furniture left, Jenny sat on the floor next to Agnes.

"So, do you guys have a date in mind yet?" asked Jenny.

"No," said Lauren, "But it's going to have to be in January. My sister is leaving in early February to teach English in China, and she'll be gone for a year, at least. We wanted to make sure she could come without having to spend the money on a plane ticket to fly back in the summer. I think we're going to do it this coming January, so it will be a short engagement. In fact, that only gives us about seven months to plan the wedding, but why wait?"

"Will that work out okay with your job?" said Jenny.

"Well, the school might *prefer* that all teachers get married in the summer, but that's not practical," Lauren said. "I know Janie got married in the summer, which was nice because she didn't have to go back to work right after the honeymoon. And also because that's how I met this guy," she said, reaching behind Oleen to pat Mike on the shoulder. He squeezed her hand.

"Janie promised to pop in every day to be mean to my class while I'm out. That way if the substitute is too lax, then at least they'll get five minutes a day of discipline."

"I think the only way to get large groups of seventh graders to all be quiet at once is with a taser," said Jenny. "At Starbucks we were near a middle school, and those kids came in *every* weekday. I always felt like I needed to drink after they left. I mean, it's not like I ever drank at the store or anything, but I sure did feel like it."

"They were incredibly loud," Steve agreed. "And January is a great time to get married. My *Farmer's Almanac* day-by-day calendar had a page that said, "Marry when the year is new, he'll be loving, kind and true. I just love weddings." Steve wiped his eyes.

Scott put his hand to the side of his mouth as though to block Steve from hearing what he was about to say.

In a whisper, the volume of most people's normal speaking voices, Scott said, "Steve's obsessed with the *Farmer's Almanac.*"

"I heard that, Scott," Steve said. "You can't whisper. I don't know why you think you can whisper. And yes, I am. It has lots of wisdom and handy hints."

Scott stifled a laugh. "Handy hints?"

"Maybe they'll have some hints about how to whisper. You still can't whisper," said Mike.

Ida looked at Scott.

"You never could whisper, dear. And those words of wisdom make sense. Delbert and I got married in July, and Oleen and Gary got married in October. I'd say Delbert and Gary have been loving and kind, but I don't know about true."

Mike looked at Ida, who looked back at him and said, "It's a long story, dear. We'll tell you later."

Mike turned back toward the group.

"When we were kids, Scott had such a loud whisper that we called him 'The Scott Heard Round the World.'"

"Mike's very proud of coming up with that name," said Jenny.

"And coming up with that nickname is Mike's crowning achievement," Scott said to Lauren. "It was all downhill from there until he met you. You are definitely his better half, Lauren."

Mike threw a pillow at Scott, which bounced off Scott's head and landed at his feet.

Scott picked the pillow up off the floor and said, "We should take this home to Gary. He's gonna need it."

"Huh?" said Mike.

"We've had an issue while you were away on your trip," Agnes said. "No one is hurt, but Gary has been crying a lot. Into pillows and towels and things. I'm trying to think of how to explain it."

"Maureen caught Delbert and Gary making out up against Delbert's truck," said Scott. "They're gay. With each other."

"Oh, that," said Mike. "Yeah, I know."

30

MONDAY

The room went silent.

"You, you KNOW?" asked Oleen.

"Yeah," said Mike, "I thought you and Ida knew too. I thought all of you had some kind of arrangement or something. You know, because you've been married so long it was easier just to stay together and all."

"We most certainly don't have an arrangement!" Oleen said, putting her hand over her heart. "Your father's not gay, Mike."

"Yeah, Mom, he is. I caught him kissing some random guy once. They were out in the backyard one night sitting in lawn chairs, and I looked out my bedroom window and saw them kissing. To be honest, I wasn't too shocked. I had always thought Dad seemed kind of, uh, not masculine."

"You knew this when you still lived AT HOME?" Oleen said.

"Yeah." Mike shrugged. "It was when I was fifteen. It was around this time of year, I think, because Jenny was going to start college in the fall. I confronted Dad about it the next day. I couldn't see who the guy was, but when I asked him Dad started crying and told me it was Uncle Delbert. That didn't surprise me like you'd think it would, either. I always thought they acted weird sometimes. You know, all touchy-feely and stuff. I told Dad I'd keep quiet about it. He said you didn't know, Mom, but I didn't believe him. I figured you must have found out after Jenny and I were born and then felt like it was too late to do anything about it, and so you had some kind of arrangement where they saw each other and maybe you and Aunt Ida quietly dated other men if you felt like it."

Agnes rubbed her head and wondered if she should take a poll to see how many people on Gardenia Lane knew that Delbert and Gary had been sneaking around together.

"You thought I knew?" Oleen said. "I most certainly did not know!" Oleen crossed her arms and gritted her teeth. "And I would never have an 'arrangement' with your father, or whatever it is you call it!"

"Oh my god, Mike! How did you not tell me this when it happened?" said Scott.

"What was I gonna say?" Mike asked. "Hey, Scott, did you know our dads are gay?"

"Uh, YEAH!" said Scott. "I found out when I was eleven."

"You did?" asked Mike. "That does make sense. That was around the time Uncle Delbert stopped hassling you. You must have caught them or something, right? And since Uncle Delbert knew you knew, he quit hassling you?"

No," said Scott. "He didn't know I saw. Neither did your dad. I just felt better after that and started ignoring Dad when he acted like a dick."

"Scott!" said Ida. "Language!

"Mom, you know Dad acted like a dick," said Scott.

"Well, I would have chosen a different word. Maybe buffoon."

"Buffoon?" Scott laughed.

Jenny looked at Lauren. "So I'm guessing Mike must have told you this story, then. You don't look surprised."

"He did," said Lauren. "Mike told me he thought all of your

parents had some kind of arrangement worked out where they stayed married, but your dads were, uh, together."

"Well, then I wish I'd brought George Clooney home back when he played that handsome doctor on *ER*," said Ida, "Because I've missed years of his company."

Everyone was quiet for a minute. Oleen sat with her elbows on her knees and her head in her hands.

"I'm going to kill that man!" said Oleen. "With his nightshirts, and those stupid crewneck sweaters that look like they're from 1992. With that mustache and those sweaters he looks like that neighbor man on *The Simpsons*."

"Ned Flanders," Scott said. "I never thought about it, but you're right," he said. Uncle Gary does look like Ned Flanders. Good call, Oleen."

Oleen balled her hands into fists.

"Calm down, dear," said Ida, looking at her sister. You can't try to kill Gary, it wouldn't be a fair fight. He'd either cry or run away."

"Or both," said Scott.

"So," said Agnes, counting out on her fingers, "Maureen caught them yesterday. I knew, Jenny knew, Scott and Steve knew. And now Mike too? This is crazy. Besides being gay, they were also stupid, and I don't believe the two have any correlation."

"I've always wondered if Dad might have wanted to get caught," said Mike. "After that night, I caught him coming home late a few more times that summer, after everyone else was asleep. Dad said he and Delbert had lost track of time doing car stuff, but I didn't believe him."

"They were working on a lot more than just cars," Scott said. "Maybe that's why Dad has that amazing chair in the garage. Eww."

"I think we need to go back to the Silver Kettle for dinner," said Oleen.

"You don't need to drink your dinner," said Ida.

"Oh, Ida, Oleen," said Steve, "Before I forget, I have four free tickets to that French-Canadian circus—I can't remember the name."

"Circus Nom de Plume," said Scott. "I'm fluent in French."

"You don't have to be fluent in French to know that phrase. And that's not even what that circus is called," said Mike.

Scott shrugged.

"How did you get free tickets to that?" asked Jenny.

"Mr. McGruder comes into the gallery a lot, and he gave them to me," said Steve.

"Mr. McGruder?" asked Mike. "How in the world do you know Mr. McGruder? Other than through Scott's 'shapely buttocks' story.'"

"He works at the civic center now and he's, I think, the Executive Director of Event Programming there," Steve said. "He's not in charge of any of the programming that goes on in the center itself, but he's in charge of the special events, like when a speaker comes in, or there are dinners there, stuff like that; he works out the logistics. The circus isn't part of the regular programming in the center, it's held in an old-timey circus tent that's been put up in the parking lot. Well, Mr. McGruder worked with them to get everything planned out, so he can go watch it anytime he wants and he gets free tickets. We've talked a lot at the gallery, and he's bought some art from me, and he just gave me the tickets last week."

"That is so random," said Jenny.

"Didn't he used to do something boring for that big chemical company?" asked Oleen. "How did he end up in charge of event planning at the civic center?"

"He did supply-chain management for the chemical company," Steve said. "It's a lot of logistical stuff. I guess maybe it translated to this new job or something."

"And his wife's best friend is the Director of Annual Giving there," Scott said. "That might have had just a teensy bit to do with it. I think her name is Rose or something."

"Well," said Oleen, "Bill McGruder should enjoy the circus. All those scantily clad butts for him to look at."

"That's true," said Ida. "He should love that. Sounds like the perfect job for him."

"Ida, Oleen, the circus is tonight. It's opening night," said Steve. "Maureen and Alex were supposed to go with us, but Alex called this morning and Maureen and all three kids came down with some stomach bug, and Alex is looking after all of them, so they can't go. We want you guys to come."

"I think it's a good idea," Ida said to Oleen. "I'm afraid if we let you stay home tonight we're going to see you on *Inside Edition* tomorrow night because you killed Gary."

"*Inside Edition*. Is that show even on anymore?" said Lauren.

"I don't know, dear, but it seems like something that would end up on that show," said Ida.

"This situation seems more like something that should be on Maury Povich," said Oleen. "That show where he tells men if they're the father or not."

"They're always the father," said Jenny.

"Or the *Jerry Springer Show*," said Oleen. "Where sometimes people hit each other with chairs. I'd like to hit your father with a chair, now that I think about it."

"Please don't kill or maim Dad, Mom," said Mike. "I'd like you both alive for the wedding."

"And I don't think you'd like jail very much, honey," said Agnes. "Your mom told me you never did like being stuck in small spaces. She said one time when she took you two to that old downtown Macy's, way back before it closed, that she had you in the elevator to go down into the fur vault—you liked to go touch all the coats—and as soon as the doors closed, you started screaming and then you said your stomach hurt and you threw up into the cuffs of a man's pants."

"Your stomach always hurts when you're stressed," Ida said to Oleen. "I don't remember that, though. We must have been little. Also, that's pretty disgusting."

"Caroline said you were about four or five," Agnes said.

"Gee, thanks for sharing that story, Agnes," said Oleen.

"So, do you guys want to go with us?" Steve interrupted.

"They've got liquor!" Scott said.

"We'll go," said Ida.

PART III

31

MONDAY

G ary sat on the front porch in a red rocking chair thinking about his situation. He sat so he had a good view of Ida and Delbert's house, though he hadn't seen anyone enter or exit the house since Mike and Lauren had left earlier. After Delbert had slammed the door in his face, Gary had tried knocking on the door several more times, and even calling Delbert on his cell phone, but Delbert had chosen not to respond to either. Gary couldn't believe it. Well, he could, but he didn't want to. Ida was right about Delbert avoiding confrontation.

As Gary sat, rocking back and forth, hoping if he rocked fast enough, he might be launched into outer space, he saw Ida's car pull into the driveway next door. Agnes got out of the front seat on the driver's side, while Ida got out of the passenger seat. He didn't see Oleen exit the car, but he saw her as she followed Ida and Agnes into Ida's house. No one waved at him, even though he was pretty sure his mom had seen him sitting there. Now even his own mother hated him. Just add her to the growing list.

Though he had no idea where the thought came from, Gary

remembered that time Oleen had taken Ambien and eaten an entire box of Ho Hos without knowing how it had happened. Both Gary and Oleen loved Ho Hos, and they were hard to find in stores, so he ordered them online from Amazon.com. You could get anything from Amazon. Hell, he bet you could even buy nuclear weapons there. Hoping Oleen hadn't found the secret stash of Ho Hos he kept hidden in a box in the top of the hall closet, Gary headed into the house.

Oleen stood inside Ida's closet, looking for something to wear. Ida's and Oleen's houses had identical floor plans, and only looked different on the outside. When they had the homes built all those years ago, it had been easier and less expensive that way. Standing in Ida's walk-in closet, it was easy for Oleen to forget she wasn't in her own house. Ida's clothing and shoes took up most of the closet, while Delbert's attire appeared to be relegated to the back right corner. Delbert and Gary wore about five things each, all the time, and rotated those five items. If they were gay, well, they certainly weren't fashion-conscious.

Oleen stood in front of Delbert's things. There was a column of mesh drawers, each sporting a printed label to indi-cate what was inside. Ida had the closet renovated several years ago, and it looked like the Container Store had exploded inside it. Ida had bought a label maker when she had redone the closet and had gone crazy, labeling just about every item in the house. She had even come over to try to label Oleen's things, which Oleen had declined, as her own organizational skills were lacking to the point that she wasn't even sure which drawers contained which clothing.

Oleen opened the drawer that said "pajamas," which, presumably, contained Delbert's pajamas, and noticed two pairs of plaid pajama pants and several white t-shirts. There was a distinctive lack of nightshirts in Delbert's pajama drawer, but she supposed that would be true for most men who weren't Gary. Unless Delbert hid his nightshirts from Ida the way Gary hid his secret stash of Ho Hos from Oleen in a box in the top of the hall closet, though somehow she doubted it. She shook her head.

Oleen moved back to Ida's section of the closet and selected a pair of jeans from one of Ida's mesh drawers, which was helpfully labeled, "jeans." Then she chose a blue button-down shirt from one of the many racks of Ida's shirts, dresses, and dress pants. The blue matched Oleen's eyes, which made her feel a little better. She got dressed in the closet, surprised to find that Ida's jeans fit, as she really needed to lay off on the Ho Hos. Oleen exited the closet to find Ida, who had dressed in the bathroom, sitting on the edge of the bed touching up her makeup. Oleen took her own makeup bag out of her purse, sat down next to her sister, and began doing the same thing.

Agnes sat in a chair by the window, and Ida and Oleen were afforded a clear view of both Agnes, and of Oleen's house from their perch on the side of the bed.

"I could have gone home, you know," Oleen said, using that distinctive, sad voice both Ida and Agnes knew so well.

"Honey," said Agnes, reaching out to pat Oleen's leg, "I don't think that would have been a good idea."

"That's the voice you always get right before you do something you regret later," Ida said. "Like in eighth grade, when you kicked Bobby Sanders in the groin because he told you your barrettes were ugly. I still think it was because he had a crush on you. Or that time Gary dried that beautiful pink sundress you got at the thrift shop, remember that?"

Oleen nodded.

"He dried it on high, and it shrunk to the point where you gave it to Maureen—she was the only one small enough to wear it. I think it was that spring right after she found out Santa Claus wasn't real because I remember she was kind of angry about the whole Santa Claus thing for about six months, and she seemed to feel better after you gave her that dress."

"That was very unlike Maureen," Agnes said. "I think she was twelve or thirteen, right?"

"Yes," said Ida. "Maureen turned thirteen just after she found out Santa Claus wasn't real. The sundress incident—I think that was the time you threw a pillow at Gary, and he tripped and broke his finger trying to stop his fall, wasn't it?"

Oleen nodded again.

"Well," said Ida, "This is much worse than having ugly barrettes or a shrunken dress, so I don't think you need to be anywhere near Gary until you've had a few days to calm down."

"I don't think I'll ever calm down," Oleen said, finishing her makeup and putting a tube of lipstick back into her makeup bag. Ida, who had always had a penchant for expensive makeup, and for applying it with great care, hadn't even finished her eyeliner.

"Even though I don't believe Gary's gay, of course," Oleen said.

"You'll calm down, honey," said Agnes. "You always do."

"I guess so," Oleen said. "I'll be right back." She hurried toward the bathroom.

"Do you think she's still in denial?" Agnes asked Ida once Oleen was out of earshot.

"No," Ida said, "This is what happens when she knows something is true, and she doesn't want it to be true. She tries to convince herself it isn't. Just give her a few days, and she'll come around. I'm only calm myself because I think somewhere in my mind I knew. That's the only way I can explain it."

"You're always calm, honey," Agnes said, patting Ida's leg. "Except when you're drunk."

Once Oleen had returned, she and Ida each slipped on a

pair of black ballet flats— why Ida had two identical pairs of black ballet flats, neither of which looked like they had ever been worn, Oleen had no idea. Oleen and Ida walked down the stairs, followed closely by Agnes. Once they had walked through the kitchen and living room, and Agnes had opened the front door, Ida said, "Wait, I want to get my perfume. Perfume always makes me feel better."

Agnes closed the door, and Ida dashed across the living room and into the bathroom off the kitchen.

"Now where is that damn thing?" Oleen and Agnes heard Ida call, her voice muffled by the distance. After a minute or two, Ida returned to the living room.

"I couldn't find it," she said. "I keep an atomizer of it in that bathroom because I forget all the time to put the perfume on when I'm upstairs. It's that Poison kind of perfume, Oleen. That one I got because the name sounded dangerous. I could have sworn I put it back in the bathroom after I refilled it, but I guess maybe it's upstairs. I'll find it later."

All three women turned around as they heard the sound of a door opening. Delbert stood behind them in the doorway that led from the garage into the kitchen, poking his head around the door as though checking to make sure no one was in the house. When his eyes fell upon Ida, they widened, and he quickly retreated into the garage, the door slamming with a thud.

"I suppose he'll stop doing that someday," Ida said. "He'll have to come out of the garage eventually."

Ida, Oleen, and Agnes exited the house through the front door and climbed into Ida's car.

32

MONDAY

After taking Agnes home, Ida navigated her Ford Expedition into the city to Scott and Steve's town-house. Scott and Steve didn't live in the heart of Midtown, the way Jenny did, but a few miles away from the middle of the city. They were still close to almost anywhere they wanted to go, but far enough away to escape the noise.

The townhouse sat inside a small, gated community of three-story brick townhomes, each with a garage underneath, elevated decks on the second and third stories, and a small garden and patio area out back. Ida pulled into the driveway, which was, in her opinion, way too short. Her car barely fit without hanging out over the back edge. Of course, when Ida had mentioned the size of the driveway to Scott, he had told her that, because her car was the size of a small tank, she might be better off parking it at an army base than in his driveway.

Ida and Oleen climbed the steep front steps to the front porch, on which sat the most beautiful patio furniture Ida had ever seen. It was even nicer than her own living room furniture, and just about as amazing as that lounge chair Delbert kept in the garage. Oleen rang the doorbell and Steve opened the door almost immediately.

"Hi, Ida, hi, Oleen," he said. "Come on in. I'm ready, but I don't know when Scott will be done putting 'product' in his hair."

"You look nice, Steve!" Oleen said. "I'm not used to seeing you dressed up."

"Thank you," Steve said, gesturing at his button-down shirt, tie, and dress pants. "I only wear this stuff to work, because people who visit an art gallery aren't too pleased when you wear jeans and ironic 80s t-shirts. Some of them are a bit, uh, I guess the word would be snooty."

"Well, then they wouldn't like me either," said Oleen, motioning to her own jeans and button-down shirt. "This is about as dressed up as I get."

"Why don't you two come in," said Steve. "It's too hot to stand out here on the porch."

"Thank you, dear," said Ida, as she and Oleen walked past him and into the living room.

The inside of Scott and Steve's house was fancier and more spacious than the insides of either Ida's or Oleen's houses.

Ida and Oleen took seats on one of the living room sofas. Steve pulled his phone out of his pocket and looked at the screen.

"It's 6:00," he said. "I better start checking on Scott now. We need to leave by 6:30, and it takes at least twenty minutes after I start telling him we're going to be late for him to get down the stairs and out the door, so I start telling him we're going to be late about half an hour before we need to leave. He's never noticed I'm telling him we're going to be late when it's way before the time we need to leave because he's too engrossed in his hair."

"He's always been like that, dear," said Ida. "I remember when Maureen graduated from college—Scott was twelve at the time—and it was about this time of year, you know almost summer. Scott had gotten ahold of some Sun-In somehow, and he started applying it right before we were supposed to leave. I have no idea why Scott thought that was a good time to do that."

"Oh, I remember that," said Oleen. "I think he said he had to get it in his hair before the graduation because the ceremony was outside and he had to "let the sun do the work." I'm pretty sure he read that in the instructions."

Steve laughed.

"He never told me that story, but it doesn't surprise me. That man is so obsessed with his hair. I bet he'd have it insured if he could. To be fair, though, Scott does have majestic hair."

Ida smiled.

"Well, go see if you can drag him down here," she said.

Steve went upstairs, and Ida and Oleen heard a muffled voice and then a loud reply.

"Come ON, Steve, I told you the other day how long it can take to get the product right. You just don't understand good hair."

Ida and Oleen heard muffled speaking again, and then, as Steve descended the stairs, they heard Scott yell, "Five minutes!"

Ida, Oleen, and Steve had been sitting in the living room chatting for about twenty-five minutes when they heard foot-steps on the stairs. They all turned to look as Scott swept down the stairs like Gloria Swanson's character in *Sunset Boulevard*, which happened to be one of Scott's favorite movies.

"The prodigal Scott returns!" Scott said. "With near-perfect hair."

Scott, like Steve, also wore dress pants, a button-down shirt, and a tie, though Scott's tie was a bow tie and not a regular tie, like Steve's. Oleen looked at Scott and rolled her eyes at Ida. Oleen noticed that, while Scott had on what he called his "fancy court shoes," Steve had on a pair of nearly new low-top black Converse.

"Scott, Steve," said Ida. "I hate driving Downtown, would one of you drive my car?"

"We can just take mine," said Scott. "Mom, are you sure this isn't because you need a designated driver?"

"I don't think I need any more to drink today, dear."

"Scott, just drive Ida's car," said Steve. "Your car is too small, and it's not comfortable, especially not when you have to sit in the back."

"I can't drive an aircraft carrier," Scott replied.

"Okay, Scott," Steve said, in the kind of slow, calm voice one might use to coax an upset toddler away from the candy aisle at the grocery store. "I can drive the car. You can sit in the back."

"It's okay," Oleen said, gesturing at herself and Ida, "We can sit in the back. I get carsick in the front. I know that's weird because most people get carsick in the back, but as I've gotten older, it's gotten worse."

Scott grinned.

"Now he can touch up his hair in the mirror on the way," Steve said to Ida and Oleen. "The hairstyling lasts all the way until we reach our destination. That's why he's so happy."

"Do you think your dad and Gary will get Mini Coopers now?" Ida asked, looking at Scott. "Not red, like yours, because that would be too flashy for your father. But maybe gray, or brown, even though brown cars tend to be quite ugly."

"Mom, just because it made gaywheels.com's list of the top ten most-researched cars last year doesn't mean only gay people drive it."

"Gaywheels.com?" Steve laughed.

"It's a gay-friendly automotive resource," Scott said, tossing his head so a piece of hair fell over his left eye. He brushed it back with his fingers.

"Why does there need to be a special car website for gay people?" asked Steve. "It's a car. A car is a car."

"Said the man who drives a ten-year-old Toyota Camry with a stick shift," Scott said.

"I love my car," said Steve. "It drives well, and it's perfectly nice."

"You just don't understand nice cars, Steve," Scott said, running his hand over the top of his head to show off his hair. "Just like you don't understand product."

"I'm glad I don't understand product," Steve said. "Or gaywheels.com."

"Maybe your father would enjoy gaywheels.com, dear. Now that he and Gary are gay," Ida said.

"I hate to tell you this, Mom, but Delbert and Gary have always been gay," said Scott. "It's not just something you come down with one day, like the flu, or a sudden love for beets, the way Janie did that one time."

"Oh, yeah," Ida said. "She was away at college, though, so I had no idea she was eating only beets for a while. Not until she called because, well, because when she went to the bathroom, it was pink. And neither of us knew that could happen when you eat too many beets, so she went to the student health center, and they told her that was what it was. She was so scared."

"That was because she'd just met Jason and was afraid he'd given her a disease," said Scott. "Which one might expect from Jason. I know because Maureen told me."

"Let's change the subject," said Oleen.

"Let's get in the car," said Steve, checking his phone. "We're going to be late."

33

MONDAY

The dashboard clock in Ida's car read 6:50, which Steve did not like one bit.

"We're going to be late," he said, "and I need to find Mr. McGruder before the show and thank him again for these tickets."

"We're not going to be late, Steve," said Scott, taking one last look in the mirror and flipping up the sun visor. "You always say we're gonna be late, and are we ever late? Uh, no."

"You're just late when you're by yourself, Scott," Steve said.

"Maybe it's not that I'm late, but that you're always early to the point where you think on time is late," said Scott.

"You should spend some time with Grace McGruder, Steve," said Oleen. "She's always early, even to parties!"

"I'm not that bad," Steve said. "Even I know no one wants you to be early for a party. When we go to parties Scott's in charge of time."

"Just call me Captain Time," said Scott, in what he thought sounded like a superhero voice, but which sounded like a regular person yelling.

"It only takes ten minutes to drive to the civic center from our house," said Steve. "I wonder why traffic is so bad."

"You know how it is in this city," Ida said, "Rush hour starts at four and ends at eight. But today is a holiday, so who knows. And we aren't on the highway. So, never mind."

The traffic inched forward and, by the time Steve had turned into the civic center driveway and parked the car in the parking deck, the dashboard clock read 7:05.

"I guess I will have time to find Mr. McGruder after all," said Steve. "Don't say it, Scott. I know you can't resist, but don't say it."

"I..." said Scott, sticking his face almost right in Steve's and widening his eyes, "Told you so."

Both Scott and Steve burst out laughing.

"You won't be telling me so for long if we don't get out of this car," Steve said.

Scott, Ida, and Oleen followed Steve across the parking deck, over a bridge, and down some stairs to the main civic center parking lot. The civic center was an enormous modern building with many, many windows. The first floor was entirely surrounded by floor-to-ceiling windows, and the five floors above were no slouches in the window department either. The public parking was all in a deck to the left of the building, and the deck extended from two stories underground to the top of the building and covered almost as much ground as the building itself did.

Stretching into the sky from the two front corners of the civic center building were two castle-like turrets. Why the civic center had turrets on it when it looked nothing like a castle no one knew, and how this had happened on a modern building was even more baffling. Still, somehow it managed not to look too tacky. Steve liked to refer to it as "easily recognizable."

The parking lot around the building was relatively large but not as large as one would expect for such a colossal structure.

The lot at the level of the building wasn't for general parking. It held the center's handicapped parking spaces, as well as many spots for drivers who were making deliveries. The majority of the parking lot was off to the side of the building and stretched around behind it. It was cordoned off from the rest of the lot by a mechanized parking arm so no cars could get through unless they were authorized. This part of the parking lot was used for special events, like festivals and the circus.

"I had no idea there would be so many people here," said Ida. "Thank you all for inviting us."

"Yeah, thank you," Oleen said. "Though I don't see how that tent is going to hold all these people."

"It's bigger than it looks," said Scott. "Steve and I have been to Circus Nom de Plume here three times. It comes every other year, and you'd be surprised how many people they can cram in there."

"That's not the name, Scott," said Steve.

"That's what I like to call it," Scott said, taking Steve's hand. "And you know you like it too."

Steve shook his head but allowed Scott to lead him toward the tent.

The tent was covered with black-and-white stripes, and had a large red flag waving from the top.

"I like the stripes," Oleen said. "They kind of make your eyes feel funny. Like they're moving. Or like you're drunk."

"The tent is always striped," said Scott. A couple of years ago the stripes were red."

"Scott was excited because the stripes matched his car. His car was brand new then," said Steve.

"I remember when you got that car, dear," Ida said. "It was the main thing you talked about for three weeks. I think that was hard on Steve, Scott. I thought he was going to need counseling."

"Gee, Mom, thanks," Scott said.

"It was hard," Steve said. "But I found a trick in the *Farmer's Almanac* that worked. It said to rub lavender oil on your temples to relieve stress, so I got a little bottle of it on Amazon, and whenever Scott was going on about his car I'd rub some on my head. Scott never noticed because, well, you remember how he got talking about his car."

"I remember," said Oleen. "His eyes looked sort of wild like he'd just escaped from an institution or something."

"Hello!" Scott said. "I'm right here. Why are we talking about me like I'm not here?"

"I'm sorry, dear," Ida said. "Lavender does smell wonderful, though."

"I wondered why you smelled like flowers back then," Scott said. "I thought it was from some air freshener you used in your car or something."

"Nope," said Steve. "Lavender oil, and it helped."

They proceeded into the tent, and Steve handed the usher four tickets.

"Can you tell me where I can find Bill McGruder?"

"I dunno," the man replied, gesturing to a small table at the far end of the tent with a sign over it that read "Information." "I don't know who that is. You'll have to ask over there at the information booth."

"That," said Scott, turning away from the usher and toward Steve, Ida, and Oleen, "is not a booth. That is a table with a sign over it. You can put lipstick on a pig but, at the end of the day, it's still a pig. And, at the end of the day, that," he said, gesturing toward the table, "will still be a table with a sign over it."

Steve shook his head and motioned for Scott, Ida, and Oleen to follow him to the information booth.

The woman who sat behind the table was wearing a black shirt and a black-and-white-striped top hat that matched the outside of the tent. A small red flag poked up from the top of the hat, which matched the red flag protruding from the top of the tent.

"May I help you?" the woman asked in a voice that sounded like she had spent the last three hours with her mouth over the valve of a helium tank.

"Uh, yeah," said Steve, "I'm looking for Bill McGruder."

"I think he's in there," the woman said, gesturing toward the door that led to the seats. Last time I saw him, he said something about going backstage to talk to someone."

"Thanks," Steve said.

Steve took Scott's hand and walked through the door into the— What would you call it? An arena? An auditorium? Steve wasn't sure what to call it, so he didn't call it anything.

Ida and Oleen walked several feet behind them, gawking at everything in the tent like they were tourists in New York City.

"Look up there." Oleen grabbed Ida's arm and pointed toward the stage. "Why is there a giant hamster ball up there?"

"Who knows?" Ida said. "I hear they do all kinds of things in this show. Like put their legs over their heads and play their backsides like drums. Maybe they're going to do that in that ball, and that will make it go. Let's just hope there's not a giant hamster in the show."

Steve stopped at the front row of seats and waited for Ida and Oleen to catch up.

"Scott, dear," Ida said. "Do they ever play their backsides like drums?"

"Do you have a flask in your purse or something, Mom? Because I didn't see you get a drink. No, they don't play their 'backsides' like drums."

"If you two want to go ahead and find our seats, Scott and I can see if Mr. McGruder is back there," Steve said.

Steve gave Ida and Oleen their tickets and showed them to an usher positioned halfway down the aisle. Steve and Scott walked to the side of the stage where an armed security guard stood next to a tall thin man in a suit. The two men had their backs to the seating area, but Steve recognized Mr. McGruder by his salt and pepper hair.

Stopping a few feet from the two men, Steve said, "Excuse me, Mr. McGruder?"

The tall man turned around, and visibly perked up when he saw Steve.

"Why hello, Steve!" he said, extending his hand to Steve, who offered his in return. Shaking hands with Mr. McGruder was like having a shark latch onto your hand and attempt to drag you into the sea. Steve pulled his hand away and tried to shake some feeling back into it.

"And this must be Scott!" said Mr. McGruder. "It's been so long since I've seen you. Too long. I think the last time was at one of our Memorial Day barbecues. I believe you were a teenager."

"I was fifteen," Scott said, raising his eyebrows. "That was the year I helped you bring all that food in from the pantry."

"I don't remember," Mr. McGruder said, staring into the distance.

Scott elbowed Steve in the ribs, and Steve stepped on Scott's foot.

Mr. McGruder offered his hand to Scott, who shook it while trying to hide his wincing.

"It's so good to see you, Scott. You've done real well for yourself with this young man here," he said, nodding his head toward Steve.

"Yes, I have," Scott said, touching Steve's arm.

"Well, let me show you to your seats," Mr. McGruder said. "Follow me. I think you'll be in for a big surprise."

34

MONDAY

M r. McGruder led Steve and Scott around and to the right side of the stage, where Ida and Oleen were seated in the front row.

"Surprise!" Mr. McGruder said. "Front-row seats!"

"Wow," said Steve. "Thank you so much."

"These *are* amazing seats," said Scott.

Ida and Oleen, who seemed to be bickering about something, stood when Mr. McGruder appeared before them.

"Ida!" he said. "Oleen! What a pleasure. It's been so long."

"Yes, it has," said Ida, stepping forward and hugging Mr. McGruder. "It's good to see you, Bill."

Oleen stepped forward and hugged Mr. McGruder loosely, patting him on the back as though clapping for a performance she hadn't particularly enjoyed.

"Nice to see you, Bill," she said. "Thank you for the tickets."

"Yes, thank you so much, Bill, dear," Ida said.

"Well, I'm happy to do it," Mr. McGruder responded in a voice so loud and jovial that he could very well have been a mall Santa Claus if he weren't so thin.

"I frequently visit Steve's gallery, and he's a wonderful

young man." Mr. McGruder patted Steve on the back. "I'm all too glad to have you here tonight."

Mr. McGruder pointed to the seats to the right of Oleen and Ida.

"I believe those are your seats," he said to Steve and Scott. "I have to check on some last-minute things before the show starts since this happens to be opening night, but I'll catch you afterward. Grace is here. She's backstage right now. You know, there's a lot of comfy seating back there. Be sure to come back-stage after the show, and you can meet some of the performers and say hi to Grace. I'll let the security guard know so he'll allow you back there."

"Thanks again," said Steve as he waved to Mr. McGruder, who had already turned and hurried around the stage and past the security guard, disappearing into the shadows. Scott walked around Oleen and Ida and took the seat to the right of his mother. Steve sat next to Scott on the far right end.

"Scott, would you be a dear and switch seats with Steve?" Ida asked. "I want to ask him a few things about the gallery."

"Mom, you've been to the gallery like ten times. What could you possibly need to ask Steve right now?" asked Scott.

"I just have a few questions about a painting I saw there last time we went. I'll forget if I don't ask him now. You know how my memory can be," said Ida.

"You have a great memory, Mom, except about movies and TV shows, but whatever." Scott stood up.

"She wants us to switch seats," he said to Steve as he motioned toward Ida. Steve looked puzzled, but stood up and moved over.

"Hey, Ida," Steve said once he was seated. "What's up?"

Ida whispered into Steve's left ear, "I told him I had some questions for you about a painting, but really I don't like to sit next to Scott at any kind of performance. Or at the movies. He talks to me the whole time, and he keeps asking me what's going to happen next, and I don't know what's going to happen next. I didn't write the show!"

"I know what you mean, Ida," said Steve. "He used to do that to me too, but I talked to him about it, and we worked out a signal I give him if I need him to be quiet."

"I'm impressed, Steve," Ida said. "I've tried for years to get Scott to stop talking at shows. But I'm his mother, so I suppose he wouldn't listen to me."

"Why do you two need to whisper about a painting RIGHT NOW?" Scott called from the end of the row. "You're not talking about art, are you?" Scott crossed his arms, his lower lip jutting out slightly.

"We are," said Steve. "Oh, look! I think the show might be starting."

Steve pointed to the left where two men in fancy costumes were walking through the audience. Each was dressed as a clown, in black-and-white striped jumpsuits and matching cone-shaped hats, their faces painted white. To Scott's relief, they weren't wearing those horrible red clown noses. Scott had always thought those noses were creepy.

The two sort-of clowns, if you could call them that, moved quickly through the audience, rubbing some people on the head and taking popcorn from others and tossing it out of the container and into the air. One of the clowns approached from Oleen's left. The clown took the popcorn container from the man next to Oleen and dumped the popcorn over the man's head.

"I hope they're going to replace that popcorn," Steve said to Ida.

Before Ida could respond, the clown moved past Oleen and Ida. He rubbed Steve on the head and stopped in front of Scott. The clown reached both hands out and adjusted each side of Scott's bowtie. He looked over at his compatriot clown, who nodded back at him. The clown who had adjusted Scott's bowtie grabbed Scott's hand and pulled him up out of his seat. Scott looked at Steve, who nodded at him and smiled. Scott ran his free hand through his hair and grinned.

The clown pulled Scott to the right edge of the stage, then up some steps and into the spotlights. The faces of hundreds of people stared at him, and Scott began doing his Miss America wave, his hand slightly cupped and moving from side-to-side like an animatronic character, a broad smile on his face. Laughter erupted from the audience.

"This will only encourage him," Oleen whispered to Ida.

With little warning, save for a muffled clanking noise, a hole opened in the floor about ten feet in front of Scott, and the large hamster ball that had been sitting on the stage when he, Steve, Ida, and Oleen had entered the auditorium rolled into it. Then a third clown rose up out of the hole and onto the stage. He stepped forward, and the hole closed behind him. This clown wore a yellow-and-white striped jumpsuit, a matching cone-shaped hat, and a large round red nose. Scott tried to hide his shudder from the audience.

The clown also held a giant red ball, which appeared to be inflatable. Scott stopped waving at the audience and stared at the clown, his smile now less genuine, pasted on his face so he resembled his mother and Oleen whenever they found them-selves in stressful situations.

The clown threw the ball at Scott, who caught it and threw it back. It was too heavy to be inflatable, but not quite as awful as one of those red rubber dodgeballs Scott remembered being hit with in elementary school.

The clown in the yellow-and-white-striped jumpsuit began to run, holding the giant red ball over his head. The two orig-inal clowns in the black-and-white-striped jumpsuits appeared on the stage out of nowhere, running and making high-pitched noises that, to Scott, sounded barely human. All three clowns ran in a large circle around Scott, making whooping noises and tossing the big red ball back and forth over Scott's head. The clown in yellow did a series of backflips around Scott, a move which was quite impressive, stopping abruptly in a perfect handstand, catching the big red ball with his feet as one of the black-and-white clowns threw it to him.

Despite his horror at the big red ball and the yellow clown's big red nose, Scott clapped along with the rest of the audience.

The yellow clown pushed off the stage with his hands, propelling the ball in an arc toward one of the black-and-white clowns, who caught it. The yellow clown landed on his feet, and the black-and-white clown who was now holding the big red ball tossed the ball back to the yellow clown.

The yellow clown threw the ball at Scott, harder than was necessary. Scott missed the ball as it came at him from high above, and in a downward arc. The ball careened toward Scott's face, which he tried to cover with his arm. The ball hit him right on the top of the head. The audience laughed and Scott stood upright, his hands going to his hair. Scott's hair was now full of static and sticking to his fingers, his forty-five minutes of styling with product ruined. Then the yellow clown ran straight at Scott, his big red nose nearly hitting Scott in the face.

"Aah! Aah!" Scott screamed, retreating backward and away from the clown, tripping over the big red ball in his haste to escape.

Scott's knees buckled over the ball, which was now underneath him, and he landed with a thud on his rear end.

Scott smoothed his hair, which still wouldn't lie flat, and stood up. His whole face was bright red, and his eyes darted wildly from clown to clown. Scott picked up the big red ball. Steve started to stand, but Ida put out a hand to stop him.

"You!" Scott yelled, pointing at the yellow clown. "You! You ruined my hair!"

Then Scott ran toward the yellow clown, holding the big red ball in front of him. Scott barreled into the clown, the big red ball hitting the clown in the stomach and knocking him onto his back in the middle of the stage. Scott landed sitting on the yellow clown's chest and began hitting the clown in the head with the big red ball.

"Big red noses!"

Whack.

"Creepy-hand pillows!"

Whack.

"Everything is creepy!"

Whack.

"And now you messed up my hair!"

Whack.

Scott raised the ball up to hit the clown in the head again, when the two black-and-white clowns, one on each side of Scott, lifted Scott up from under the arms. Scott dropped the ball, and the black-and-white clowns ran with him toward the back of the stage taking Scott, who was facing the audience and now kicking his feet and yelling, "You haven't heard the last of me, clown!" with them into the darkness.

35

MONDAY

Oleen and Ida stared at the stage where Scott had just been, mouths open, eyes wide.

"Now that was weird," Steve said. "I've never seen Scott get like that before."

Ida tore her gaze away from the stage, which now featured the yellow clown juggling three identical big red balls.

"Well, the audience seemed to love it," she said. "I think they thought it was a planned part of the show."

"I think they did too," said Steve. "I'm just hoping Scott isn't going to be in some kind of legal trouble or something. I know he's a lawyer, but I'm not sure he'd be able to follow his own advice and stay quiet if someone started asking him questions. I'm going to go see what's going on back there."

Steve hurried down the row in front of Ida and Oleen. He reached the place where the security guard still stood. The guard was typing on his phone.

"Uh, hi, sir, I need to check on my husband back there. He was just on the stage. I'm not sure where they took him."

The security guard looked up from his phone, shaking his head and chuckling "Now that," the security guard said, "was the best thing I've seen in a long time. I'll have to get someone to escort you out back."

The security guard spoke into his walkie-talkie and, a moment later, Mr. McGruder appeared.

"Is he okay?" Steve asked, his brow furrowed.

"Come on back, Steve, and you can talk to him."

"Is he in trouble?" Steve asked.

"No, the audience seemed to love it and no one was hurt, so we'll let it go. He may not want to come backstage later, though. There are about a dozen clowns—well, sort-of clowns—in the show. He kept telling me he hates clowns. You might want to get him a stiff drink from one of the concession booths."

Mr. McGruder reached into his pocket and pulled out two red tickets that looked like the kind you got when you bought into a raffle.

"Here," he said. "Good for two free beverages of your choice."

"Thanks, Mr. McGruder," said Steve, putting the tickets into the pocket of his pants.

"He's over here," Mr. McGruder said, leading Steve around a corner to a big blue sofa, which was adorned with many throw pillows.

Scott sat nestled amongst the pillows, drinking a bottle of water and talking quietly with Grace McGruder, who sat next to him.

"I'll let you take him to your seats. You can go back out the way we came in."

Mr. McGruder had turned to leave when a short young woman with flaming red hair approached the couch from the left. The room she came from appeared to be a dressing area of some sort with large, opaque screens surrounding it. The woman wore a very skimpy, very spangly black leotard, and her red ringlets streamed around her face like dozens of waterfalls.

She and Mr. McGruder stood way closer to one another

than a young woman in a tiny outfit and a married man more than thirty years her senior should stand.

"Hi, Bill," the woman said in a strong Russian accent.

She smiled and touched Mr. McGruder's arm. Then she leaned toward him and said something into his ear. He laughed.

"Well, I better let Sarah finish my hair now," she said, pulling her mouth away from Mr. McGruder's ear and returning to the dressing room.

As the woman walked away, Mr. McGruder's eyes latched onto her backside like a sea lamprey attaching itself to a passing whale. Mrs. McGruder stared at her husband, then turned to stare at the woman's retreating back. When she turned her head back around to stare at Mr. McGruder, Steve said, "We better get back out there, Scott. We don't want to miss the rest of the clowns."

Scott stood up, and he and Steve started back toward the door to the auditorium. As the security guard came into view, they heard Mrs. McGruder say, "I told you already, Bill, this has to stop. What the hell is wrong with you?"

The McGruders' voices became muffled as Scott and Steve passed the security guard and found themselves back amongst the rows of seats.

As soon as they got out of earshot of the security guard, Scott said, "Oh. My. God! Did you *see* how he was looking at that girl? It was like how Jason was looking at that waitress at the barbecue place, only ten times worse. Never mind, you weren't there. And did you *see* his wife looking at him? I was waiting for tiny daggers to shoot out of her eyes and stab him in the neck!"

"Well, you said he likes shapely buttocks, Scott, so I guess that's not too much of a surprise," Steve said. "But seriously, Scott, he's a dirty old man. You even confirmed that yourself with that story about him cornering you in the pantry. Even though I know you made that up. Anytime his name comes up, everyone in your family talks about him trying to feel up their butts. So, that's an old topic. A current topic is, what is going on with you? Are you okay? That was crazy!"

"I hate clowns," Scott said.

"You hate that he messed up your hair," said Steve. "Or maybe you hate what's going on with your dad."

"Okay, okay," Scott replied. "I don't know what happened. I was fine, and then I just snapped. Not about my hair or clowns, even though I do hate clowns. And having my hair messed up. Don't tell anyone, Steve, since I have an image to keep up, but I think the stress of the past two days might be getting to me. I'm just as shocked as you are that I did this." Scott waved his hand toward the stage. "This never happens; me getting out of control, I mean. And I think you may be right about my dad."

"It never happens," Steve agreed. "I was worried because I've never seen you get mad like that or snap like that. When you're mad, you just make snarky comments and roll your eyes. It kind of scared me."

"I'm okay," Scott said as they approached their seats. "Just pray the actual show starts soon, so I don't have to talk about it right now with Ida and Oleen. Mr. McGruder told me the audience thought it was part of the show, which means none of those creepy clowns is going to accuse me of assault or anything."

Scott stopped at the end of the row and took Steve's hands. "I'm sorry for scaring you like that. I just need to go run around the neighborhood a few times when we get home. You know, get the stress out."

"It's okay, Scott," Steve said. "I'm just glad you're okay, and nothing's wrong with you. Except for the stuff we already know is wrong with you."

Steve kissed Scott quickly on the lips, and they walked past Oleen and Ida to their seats.

"Is he okay?" Ida said to Steve before he even had a chance to sit down. "That was very, very strange. I've never seen him get mad like that. When he gets mad, he just sulks and rolls his eyes a lot."

As Steve started to answer, the lights went down and three very young-looking Asian girls in skintight red bodysuits rolled out from backstage all in a row, each atop a giant black-and-white-striped ball. Each girl stayed upright by running on top of her ball and making it roll forward, the rolling stripes causing Oleen to feel dizzy just like the tent had earlier. The two girls on either side of the girl in the center grabbed onto yellow cords that hung from somewhere in the rafters and were lifted up into the air, the balls they had rolled in on falling into a hole that had appeared in the floor. The girls floated through the air as though propelled by the wind, rather than by wires and two thick yellow ropes. Still holding on to the cords, the two girls dropped back down, one on each side of the girl who had been in the middle, each taking one of her hands and lifting her up off the ball atop which she was still running. A large set of sparkly yellow wings unfolded from the back of the center girl's costume. Her ball rolled forward and fell into the hole in the stage.

"They look about twelve years old," Oleen whispered to Ida, as all three girls landed on the stage, each climbing atop one of three small podiums, which had risen up out of the floor.

The girls took up identical poses on their podiums. All three reached behind their right shoulders and took ahold of their left feet, then pulled their feet up and bent their heads back until each girl's body formed a circle that looked like a snake trying to swallow itself.

"I've never seen a real-live contortionist!" Ida whispered to Oleen. "I thought they only had those in other countries, or in those massage parlors I mentioned to Scott once. He told me not to go there unless I wanted a happy ending. I told him: of course I want a happy ending; who doesn't want a happy ending? That's why romantic comedies are so popular. He told me you have to be very flexible to work there, almost as flexible as a contortionist. I told him of course you do because dealing with the public is very difficult. Oh, that man next to you is glaring at me, Oleen, so I'd better shut up."

By the time the last act before the intermission had begun, Ida had rested her head against the back of her chair and was snoring softly. The lights went down, obscuring the stage in shadows, and the stage crew ran out, barely visible in their all-black outfits, and set up a large, tall contraption that appeared to involve ladders. When the spotlights came back on, there was what looked to be the set for a trapeze act sitting on the stage. There were two tall towers with ladders leading all the way up them. Each tower had a small platform sticking out from the very top. The towers were about the same distance apart as the opposite walls of Scott and Steve's spacious living room. Two trapezes hung from the ceiling between the towers. A large net sat underneath the entire apparatus, a backup should one of the performers happen to fall.

Six figures, three male and three female, dropped from the ceiling like a sudden downpour. They plummeted into the net, where they bounced up and down, rockets launching into the glare of the spotlights, then falling back to earth. Each of the women was about the same height, which was relatively short, and each was wearing a skimpy, spangly black leotard. The first woman had straight blonde hair that was gathered in a knot atop her head. The second had dark, almost blue-black hair that was cut in an asymmetrical bob, and the third had fiery-red ringlets that cascaded around her face.

The three men looked almost identical to one another. They were all of about the same height and weight, and each towered above the women at about the same distance. Each man wore a pair of tight white pants, and a tight black shirt with red accent buttons at the wrists. Each also had his face painted white and wore what looked like a white swim cap over his hair. It was hard to tell them apart.

After the women finished jumping and flipping on the net, the men took their positions, two on one tower, and one on the other. Each of the women bounced upward from the net, grabbed one of the trapezes, and swung to one of the towers. The men helped the women grab onto the trapezes again, and much swinging, jumping, flipping, and flying around occurred. One of the men let go of the trapeze as he swung towards the audience, bouncing on the net and catching one of the girls, who had dropped from one of the towers.

Scott and Steve stared at the performers, mesmerized by their jumping ability. Ida snored softly. Oleen nudged Ida to try to wake her. And then, without warning, everything changed.

36

MONDAY

Ida was still asleep when the man landed on her. She was awakened by a thud and a whack on her legs, and when she opened her eyes all she could see was a field of white, and all she could feel was something poking her in the face. She opened her mouth and screamed, turning her head to one side to avoid having her eyes gouged out by whatever was poking her. She might be dead, she thought, though she doubted she was in either Heaven or Hell. An open field of white seemed more like what you'd find in Purgatory. And, if she were in Hell, at least a Hell personalized for her, there would doubtless be cucumbers. Ida couldn't stand cucumbers.

Oleen, who had been nudging Ida, felt a thud on her lap and saw her sister turn her head to the right. She heard Ida screaming and noticed that her own left wrist burned as though someone had held one of those long lighters you use to get kindling going in a fireplace to it. Oleen closed her eyes and screamed along with her sister, from surprise as much as from the pain in her wrist.

Steve, who had been so enraptured by the trapeze act that he didn't even remember he was at a circus in the first place, felt something hit the arms of his seat and roll toward him, pinning him against the back of his chair and blocking him from seeing anything but pitch black in front of his eyes. Steve froze where he sat, and couldn't figure out how to move, much less how to scream. Was he dying? Steve had no idea what was going on.

Scott, who had been staring at the trapeze act onstage, but who had been lost in his head thinking about his earlier antics, felt a thud and was jolted back to the present. He felt something pull his hair and he screamed as the wide, staring eyes and tight jaw of a man in white face paint and a white swim cap landed not two inches from his face. Scott couldn't move his head away from the man's face, because every time he tried, whatever was pulling his hair would yank his face back down until he was nose-to-nose with the man with the blank, lifeless, red, veiny eyes.

A deep voice boomed from the auditorium's speakers, "Ladies and gentlemen, we will now have a brief intermission. Please exit the auditorium through the doors in the back."

Oleen, Ida, and Scott continued screaming as the rest of the audience filed out the back of the tent. Some of the exiting crowd was snapping photos and taking videos, as the bevy of flashes and murmuring indicated. One man, in particular, must have been filming the scene, as suggested by his proximity to the disaster that was the front row at the French—Canadian circus. And also by the fact that he said, "Dude! We gotta get this on video!"

"Whoa, dude!" Ida heard the man say. He spoke in a voice like those men did in that movie about Ted and Bill, though she couldn't remember the name of the movie at the moment. She decided the man must be of high school or college age, because how could a successful adult talk like that and expect to be taken seriously as a contributing member of society?

"Oh my god!" his friend said in a similar voice, trailing the words together into one run-on phrase that sounded like "omagod."

Ida guessed there were only two of them, as she didn't hear anyone else saying anything. They were hard to hear over Scott's screaming. Ida had managed to stop screaming.

"Oh my god! Do you SEE that dude's leg? And look at his arms!"

"I know, dude!" The first man, or maybe boy, said. "Look, they're all messed up!"

"Oh shit!" said the second man/boy, "That dude on the end is stuck to his wrist. Look! His hair is stuck to his wrist button!"

"Dude!" the first man/boy responded. "Look! Dude in the seat keeps trying to sit up, and dead dude's wrist keeps pulling him down into his face. Oh, man, that would suuuck!" he said, dragging the word out so it took him approximately twenty-five minutes to say.

"Make sure you go around back and get a shot of dead dude's eyes, and of dude in the seat trying to pull his head away. This is gonna be so awesome on our YouTube channel!" the second man/boy said.

Scott could hear footsteps and felt the presence of one of the two "dudes" behind him. He couldn't tell how old they were from their voices, though they couldn't be adults, so he decided just to label them "dudes."

"Dude! This must suck for you!" said one of them, though Scott had no idea which one since they both sounded exactly like Keanu Reeves did in *Bill and Ted's Excellent Adventure.*

"Did the screaming tip you off?" Scott yelled between screams. He tried to swat the "dudes" away with his right hand, but missed. Mr. McGruder's shouts brought a quick end, both to the dudes' filming and to Scott's swatting.

"You!" Scott heard Mr. McGruder yell, his footsteps thudding toward the row of seats atop which the dead man lay. "You two! Get out of here and stop filming! Give me that phone!"

Scott heard the two dudes running away, not giving "that phone" to Mr. McGruder.

"Oh my god!" Mr. McGruder yelled. "Sarah! Grace! Someone call 911!"

Then he shouted, panic in his voice, "Is everyone okay?"

"Not really," said Scott, who had managed to stop screaming.

Scott had discovered the optimum distance from the dead man's face at which he needed to hold his head to avoid having to look right into those horrible, lifeless, staring eyes with all the red blood vessels in them. He tried to keep his eyes closed, but he couldn't stop peeking between his eyelids, like he was rubbernecking at a car accident, or watching an episode of that horrible show, *Mama's Family*. He didn't know how much longer he could hold his neck in that position, though, as he was starting to get a horrible neck cramp.

"I'm okay," Steve said, not needing to calm down as he had never screamed in the first place. He decided he must not be dead since he could hear Mr. McGruder talking. Unless Mr. McGruder was dead too, which didn't seem possible since Mr. McGruder had been backstage when whatever had just happened, happened.

Ida's voice was muffled on account of Steve's left shoulder, which she bumped into any time she turned her head to the right, and the fabric of the dead man's pants, which got in her mouth anytime she turned her head to the front. She couldn't even look to the left on account of the thing that was poking her in the face being in the way. So, Ida chose to get knocked in the mouth by Steve's shoulder, her teeth repeatedly slamming into her gums. She could feel the blood running out of her mouth. She hoped it wasn't ruining her blouse, which she'd gotten on sale at Nordstrom Rack, and which she knew she'd never find again at such a discounted price.

"I'm okay, but my wrist hurts," said Oleen, who had stopped screaming pretty quickly after the initial thud.

She was the only one of the four of them who could see what was going on. Being able to see what had landed on them, and so not thinking she was dying, had given her a leg up in the ability-to-stop-screaming department.

"Thank god none of you is hurt!" said Mr. McGruder. "Someone could have been killed!"

"It looks like someone was," Oleen responded.

37

MONDAY

I da heard light footsteps approaching, maybe running, toward the seats.

"Oh, oh, oh, Bill!" said the panicked voice of a woman. The woman had a thick accent that sounded Russian, or maybe German.

"Oh god, Bill!" The woman said. "Oh no, is that...Sergei?"

"I don't know, Katerina," Mr. McGruder answered. "I'm not sure who it is."

"We couldn't find Sergei when it was time to go out. Nobody knew where he was. Oh no, oh god. Please don't let that be him."

Then Ida heard heavier, faster footsteps and another thud as the seats were jolted. The dead man's body rolled toward her face, pinning her head against the seat. The thing that had been poking her was now stuck to the left side of her face.

"Oh hell, no!" she heard Scott yell.

"Watch where you're going, Fernando!" shouted Mr. McGruder. "You're going to destroy the evidence."

"Your wife called the police," the voice that belonged to Fernando said. "They should be here in five to ten minutes."

"Get this thing off me!" Ida heard Scott yell.

"Is it? Is it my Sergei?" said the woman with the Russian accent. Katia? Katrina? Ida couldn't remember what Mr. McGruder had called her.

Scott heard more footsteps, and then the woman with the Russian accent asked, "Is it Sergei?"

She must have been talking to Scott because he could feel her presence right in front of him, the way you can tell without looking that a TV is on, even when the sound is turned down.

"How would I know?" asked Scott. "I don't know who the hell this is, just get him out of my face."

"You can't move him, dear!" Ida shouted from down the row. "I've watched that *CSI* and that *Law and Order* show and you can't disturb the evidence."

"I don't care what those shows say, Mom!" Scott yelled. "Get him out of my face. My neck hurts, and if no one moves him, I'm gonna throw up on him. How's that for destroying evidence?"

Scott heard the light, retreating footsteps of, he assumed, the woman with the Russian accent.

"Bill! Bill!" the woman sobbed. "You have to see if it's Sergei!"

"Okay, Katerina. Fernando, help me roll him over."

"I don't think we should do that," said Fernando.

"I don't care what you think. Now help me roll him over," said Mr. McGruder.

Ida felt a whack on the arms of her seat, and suddenly she could breathe.

Scott began screaming again.

"Ow! Ow! What the hell are you doing! My hair! Aaaaaaah!"

Ida could see that Scott's head was bent over the dead man's face, and Scott's hair appeared to somehow be stuck to the dead man's wrist.

"His hair! Get his hair!" Ida shouted.

Fernando, who was dressed in the same costume as was the dead man, ran to Scott and fiddled with his hair, detaching it from the dead man's wrist

"It was caught on a button," Fernando said to Scott. "Sorry, I think I ripped out some of your hair."

"Um, ya think?" Scott said, staring at Fernando and wishing him a painful and protracted death.

Scott sat upright, moving his head back and managing to extract his arms from beneath the corpse. He held his hands up carefully to avoid touching it. Scott rubbed his neck with his right hand and covered his eyes with his left forearm.

"I am not looking down. Someone tell me when that thing is gone. I'm not doing anything until that thing is gone," Scott said.

Ida, whose hands were still resting on her lap beneath the corpse, turned her head from side to side trying to get rid of her neck pain. She could feel the blood running down her face, and she looked down to see that the front of her blouse was, indeed, covered in blood. She'd never get that out. Those laundry detergent commercials that claimed their product could get out bloodstains and grass stains were a lie. Janie had played soccer long enough that Ida had come to know this as a fact.

When Ida looked down at her shirt, she also glanced at the dead man, having forgotten entirely that something had been poking her in the face, and wondering what it was. Surely those tight pants she'd seen the trapeze men wearing didn't have pockets and, even if they did, who would do aerial stunts with a wallet and keys in their pocket? They'd fall out, just like Delbert's wallet had fallen out that time they rode the upside-down roller coaster at Six Flags.

Ida looked at the man's pants and noticed a large bulge in the front—a bulge that appeared to have been the reason Ida had nearly had her eyes gouged out.

With a shudder, Ida said, "Is that— That can't be—"

"It is," Oleen said, patting her sister on the shoulder.

"Oh my god! Oh my god!" Ida shouted, pulling her right arm from beneath the body and rubbing her mouth with her forearm. "Oh god, get it off! Get it off!"

Ida heard Scott laugh, but not as though anything was funny.

"Man, Mom, that may be the last dick you see for a while, considering the circumstances."

"Shut up, Scott!" Oleen and Steve said at the same time.

"Language!" said Ida.

Ida continued to rub her mouth and make spitting noises.

"If I never have another penis in my face again, that will be too soon!" she said.

"Please don't tell us about having penises in your face, Mom!" said Scott. "I'm traumatized enough as it is."

The woman with the Russian accent, who Ida could now see had flaming red curls and blue eyes, and who was quite beautiful, rushed toward Scott's seat. She fell to her knees, sobbing, one hand on the dead man's right cheek.

"Sergei, oh, Sergei, no!" she wept.

"Oh, man," said Fernando, who was large and tall with coal-black hair and olive skin. "It's Sergei alright. I hadn't seen him all day, but he didn't feel well last night, so I just assumed..." Fernando's voice trailed off as he looked at the dead man's— Sergei's— face.

"I assumed he was sick and wasn't performing or something," Fernando finished.

"I know you're not supposed to move a body and all," Scott said, "But get this damn thing off me. You already rolled him over. It can't hurt anything to put him on the floor."

"Fine," said Mr. McGruder. "Fernando, get his head. I'll get his feet."

Fernando, looking a little green and uncertain, walked to Sergei's head and put his hands under the dead man's arms.

"On three," said Mr. McGruder. "One, two, three!"

Mr. McGruder and Fernando lifted Sergei up and moved him over to set him on the floor.

"He's so heavy!" Fernando said, sliding his arms forward to better hold on. As he did this, the corpse's left arm shot up into the air.

Everyone, including the two circus performers, and Mr. McGruder screamed.

Fernando, who had almost set Sergei's body on the floor, dropped it the last few inches, and there was a thud as the head hit the ground. Hearing the thud, Mr. McGruder dropped the feet. The body lay on the floor, the right arm and right leg gnarled and twisted at angles one wouldn't see outside of a cartoon.

"That," said Oleen, "is disgusting."

Ida and Scott, both with closed eyes and both breathing heavily, each opened their eyes long enough to see the body.

"Oh, Christ," said Scott, laying his head back on the headrest and covering his eyes with his forearm again.

Uniformed patrol officers began to appear from several directions, cordoning off the area in which Oleen, Ida, Steve, and Scott sat from the rest of the seats. Yellow crime scene tape stretched behind the seats and around the body to the stage.

"You all stay here," said one of the patrol officers, pointing at them. "You can't move until the detectives and CSTs get a look."

"Fantastic," said Scott.

Steve, who still hadn't spoken, squeezed Scott's left hand, which Scott had rested on the arm of the chair. Scott squeezed Steve's hand back.

The red-haired woman continued to sob, now sitting cross-legged on the floor next to the body, a curtain of fiery ringlets shielding her face from view. Fernando knelt down next to her and patted her on the back, quietly murmuring something in her ear.

Mr. McGruder glared at them.

"Leave her alone, Fernando," he said. "Give her some air."

Fernando glared back at Mr. McGruder, but stood up and backed away from the woman. One of the patrol officers approached her.

"Ma'am," the officer said.

The woman didn't look up and continued weeping into her hands.

"Ma'am," the officer said again, a little louder.

The red-haired woman looked up then, black makeup smeared around her eyes creating dark trails, which marred her otherwise perfect white cheeks.

"Ma'am, did you know the victim?"

The woman nodded.

"It's my boyfriend," she said. "It's my Sergei."

38

MONDAY

The patrolman was writing in a small notebook, and the red-haired woman had stopped crying when Scott opened his eyes. He leaned toward Steve and whispered in Steve's ear,

"Oh my god, she must get around. So that was her boyfriend, *and* there's something going on there with Mr. McGruder, *and* did you *see* that Fernando guy? He was all patting her back and whispering to her, and he looked pretty pissed off when Mr. McGruder told him to get away from her."

"How do you even know this?" Steve asked Scott. "You've had your eyes closed this whole time."

"I was squinting and peeking under my eyelids. That way, if I somehow happened to glance at that thing down there," Scott said, gesturing toward Sergei's body, but not looking at it, "then it would just be blurry, and I could pretend it was part of some Impressionist painting where you can't tell what it is when you're close to it."

"Well, yeah, there might be something going on with Mr. McGruder," Steve said, "but maybe that woman just likes flirting with men, and we've established that Mr. McGruder pretty much likes anything female that's living and breathing. According to you, even fifteen-year-old boys he corners in pantries. So that doesn't mean anything."

The woman was rocking herself back and forth, her head resting on her knees. She was looking at the floor.

"Well, what about that Fernando guy?" Scott said. "Didn't you see how he was glaring at Mr. McGruder?"

"It looked more to me like that Fernando guy was trying to comfort the woman," Steve said. "They work closely together, so that makes sense. I noticed Mr. McGruder looking angry with that Fernando guy, though. Maybe Fernando just glared at Mr. McGruder because he thought Mr. McGruder was being a jackass. Mr. McGruder did act pretty angry with everyone, so I can see why that Fernando guy would be annoyed."

"Well, either way, there's something rotten in the state of Denmark," Scott said.

Steve rolled his eyes.

A large, tall man in a suit approached the seats from backstage. He must have been at least six foot five, and his short black hair sat on his head in a way that looked natural, but which could also have been the result of hours of styling with "product." Scott had managed to achieve that natural look only a handful of times since his first memory of becoming a hairstyling enthusiast.

Scott was fifteen when he had decided to apply Sun-In to his hair just as everyone was trying to leave the house for Maureen's college graduation. He now recognized that his timing had been unfortunate. However, he had been delighted with the results he had achieved after the sun at the outdoor ceremony had "toasted his locks," which is what Scott had always called the being-in-the-sun part of the Sun-In styling process. After that, he had become even more enthralled with haircare products, and had found many videos online that had helped him learn proper styling techniques.

Scott guessed this man had never touched any mousse, gel, or styling cream in his life. He looked way too masculine to have given "product" the time of day. No doubt he achieved that majestic hairstyle by doing nothing more than showering and running his fingers through his hair while looking in a mirror. Life was so unfair sometimes. Scott had to hand it to him, though. He was a good-looking guy, in his dark suit and red tie — though who wore a red tie with a dark suit these days? Mainly men who had no fashion sense, which supported Scott's assertion that the man didn't care about styling his hair either.

Mr. McGruder, who had been corralled into a seat by one of the patrol officers, tried to stand, but the patrol officer motioned for him to sit. The patrol officer tapped Katerina on the shoulder and motioned for her to sit in the row with Mr. McGruder. Mr. McGruder, Katerina, and Fernando sat in the row, though they each had two empty seats between them.

The tall man in the dark suit with the perfect hair walked across the stage and approached the front row. Just before he reached the edge of the stage, he squatted so he wasn't towering over the seats.

"I'm Detective James Beauregard," he said. "I'm the lead detective investigating this case. My partner, Detective Will Brennan, will be here shortly. Before we take a look at what's going on here, I need to get each of your names and contact information."

"Detective Beauregard, dear, I'm sure you have to follow a procedure for these things, but is there any possibility you could take that man away?" said Ida, gesturing to Sergei's body. She slurred her words on account of the blood dripping out of her mouth. "It's very disturbing. We'd love to help you, but it will be easier if we aren't all trying not to look at that man."

"I understand, Mrs.—?"

"McNair," Ida said. "Ida McNair."

"I understand how you feel, Mrs. McNair," said Detective Beauregard, "And I assure you we will move the deceased just as soon as the CSTs have a chance to take some photos of the scene and collect some evidence. Are you hurt, ma'am? What happened to your mouth."

"I'm okay," Ida said, noticing again, to her chagrin, that her blouse was likely beyond redemption. "It's from my teeth, I think. Knocking into Steve's shoulder. Steve, have I still got all my teeth?" Ida turned toward Steve and clenched her teeth together, opening her mouth wide. She looked like a kid who had just drunk large amounts of cherry Kool-Aid, which had stained her teeth a bright crimson.

"I'm so sorry, Ida!" said Steve. "I had no idea my shoulder did that to you. And, yes, you have all your teeth. Can you tell if any of them is loose?"

Ida poked around her mouth with her tongue. "No, I don't think so. Detective Beauregard?" Ida said. "Is it possible I could clean my mouth up and get another shirt? I'd like to start soaking this one in cold water. If I want to get the stains out, I can't let the blood dry. Then it will just be impossible."

Detective Beauregard nodded.

"Yes, ma'am. I'll see if they have a souvenir t-shirt you can put on. But that will have to be after the CSTs process the scene. We can get your mouth cleaned up, though. And we can see if you need any stitches and make sure all your teeth are okay."

"Thank you," Ida said, resigning herself to losing the blouse.

"Well, can we move, then?" asked Oleen.

"I wish you could, Ms.—?"

"Mrs. Johnson," Oleen said, with great emphasis on the Mrs. "My name is *Mrs.* Gary Johnson."

Ida looked at Oleen with narrow, puzzled eyes and that plastered-on smile she got during times of stress, though with the dripping blood she resembled a demonic clown. It was best if she didn't look in Scott's direction while he had his eyes open, as she didn't want to set him off on another maniacal clown assault.

"Ma'am," said Detective Beauregard to Oleen, "I'm going to need your first name too."

"It's Oleen," Oleen said. "And my left wrist is hurt. Do you have a Tylenol? Or maybe some ibuprofen?"

Detective Beauregard walked several feet in Oleen's direction until he was at the edge of the crime scene tape, then lowered himself off the stage. He squatted outside the crime scene tape next to Oleen's seat, looking at her left wrist.

"It's swollen," he said.

He reached past the crime scene tape and carefully lifted her wrist off the armrest, being careful not to touch the chair.

"Ow! Ow! Ow!" Oleen yelled.

"I think it may be broken," said Detective Beauregard. "I'll have someone take a look at it. We can at least get it stabilized in a bandage and sling. I understand this situation is uncomfortable for all of you, and I do apologize. And, Mrs. Johnson, I know you're hurt, but you are now part of a crime scene. If there has been a crime committed here, that is. So far no one has been able to tell us what happened. Once we've taken stock of the scene and collected evidence from you all, you will be allowed to leave your seats. Then we're going to want to question each of you. Mrs. Johnson, I'll have someone stabilize your wrist while you wait. It's not ideal, but it will have to do."

"And my sister," said Oleen. "You'll take care of her too?"

"We will," said Detective Beauregard.

"Sanders!" Detective Beauregard barked at an officer who stood right next to the stage, nursing a water bottle and staring into the distance.

The officer jumped, spilling water on his shoes. Officer

Sanders hurried to Oleen's seat, just outside of the crime scene tape. He stopped behind Detective Beauregard.

"Sanders," said Detective Beauregard, turning around, "Get some EMTs in here to look at these ladies and get them patched up. One may have a broken wrist, the other has mouth lacerations. They can't leave their seats right now, so this will have to be done without disturbing the scene. And they'll need some Advil or Tylenol or something. And find a t-shirt for this lady with the mouth lacerations," he said, gesturing behind him toward Ida. "She can't change yet, but get it ready so she can put it on as soon as we're done."

"Okay," said Sanders. "Ma'am," he called to Ida, "what size shirt would you like?"

"An extra-large," Ida said. "It will be too big, but I'm not aiming to be in a fashion show here. I want to be comfortable. And, Oleen, maybe later you can give the shirt to Gary to wear as a nightshirt," she said, looking at her sister.

Oleen scowled.

"Sure thing, ma'am," Sanders said, walking toward the stairs at the back of the tent.

"And your names?" Detective Beauregard asked as he moved down the row and stopped behind Steve and Scott.

"Steve Strickland," said Steve. "Well, Stephen. With a ph, not a v. People always get that wrong." He leaned his head back to look up at Detective Beauregard.

"Thank you, Stephen, with a ph," Detective Beauregard said in a voice that made Steve wonder why he'd bothered talking about the spelling of a first name he barely used.

Detective Beauregard moved next to the right side of Scott's seat, being careful not to disturb the crime scene tape. He looked at Scott, who had closed his eyes again.

"Your name, sir?" Detective Beauregard asked. Scott didn't reply.

Steve nudged Scott with his elbow, and Scott opened his eyes, looked up at the detective, then closed his eyes again.

"My name is Scott McNair," said Scott, "And you might want to get me a trash can, because I think the throwing up is going to start soon."

Detective Beauregard motioned to one of the patrol officers and quietly said something. The patrol officer hurried toward the backstage entrance and returned a moment later with a small trash can, which he set down on Scott's knees. Scott grabbed the trash can with one hand on each side.

"Please sit tight here while the CSTs photograph and collect evidence," said Detective Beauregard. "I'm going to ask each of you to write down your contact information underneath where I've written your name. Best phone number to reach you, and email if you have it, though we'll call if we need anything. In the meantime, I'll have a couple of patrol officers stay here with you. Please do not discuss what you observed until we've had a chance to speak with each of you individually. "And, sir," he said, looking at Scott.

"Yes?" Scott said.

"If you do throw up, please try to keep it in the trash can."

Detective Beauregard walked away toward the seats where Mr. McGruder, Katerina, and Fernando sat, presumably to give them the same speech.

"Lopez!" Detective Beauregard yelled at a dark-haired patrol officer with light brown skin.

The officer looked up from the ground, where he had been looking for evidence that might pertain to what had happened.

"Lopez," Detective Beauregard repeated, gesturing toward the area at the back of the auditorium. "Go help out there. They've detained the audience in the lobby, and we need to start debriefing them. Oglesby and Griffin are on it."

Lopez hurried toward the back of the tent.

"Scott," Ida called, sounding like she had after she'd had all the margaritas at the Silver Kettle earlier in the afternoon. "Do they think we had something to do with this?"

"No, Mom, I don't see how they could. This is pretty standard. I know it's kind of scary to be told you have to be questioned, but it will be okay." Scott reached behind Steve and squeezed Ida's hand.

Scott whispered loudly into Steve's ear, "Beauregard? What kind of a name is that?"

"A Southern one," Steve replied, not bothering to whisper.

"He sure is gruff," said Scott. "I guess he likes being in charge."

Steve closed his eyes and waved Scott away.

"Well, maybe he wants to use this case to make a name for himself," said Scott, "I guess the South shall rise again after all."

39

MONDAY

T wo EMTs attended to Ida and Oleen.

"It looks broken, ma'am," the male EMT said as he examined Oleen's left wrist. "I'm going to bandage it the best I can and set it, so it's stable. Then we'll take you to the hospital when all this is over, and they can decide what you need. It may hurt a little while I do this." The man handed Oleen two Advil, which she took with her right hand. He unscrewed the cap of a water bottle he had set on the stage. "You can use this to take it," he said, holding the water bottle out to her.

Oleen popped the Advil in her mouth and took a swig from the water bottle.

The female EMT crouched behind Ida's seat and asked Ida to open her mouth. Ida showed her stained teeth to the EMT, who, with a gloved hand, felt her front teeth.

"None is loose," she said. "I'm going to look at your lip now."

The woman carefully pulled out Ida's lower lip to determine the extent of her cuts.

"Ow!" Ida yelled, causing the female EMT to jerk backward,

and Ida to cry out in pain.

"I'm so sorry," the EMT said.

"Are you okay?" Oleen called out to her sister, who she couldn't see.

"Never been better!" Ida called back with some effort.

"Let's try this again," the EMT said to Ida. The woman examined Ida's lip and said, "You have several rather large lacerations, but I don't think you need any stitches. I'm going to place some rolled-up gauze between your lip and your bottom teeth. You'll need to hold that there for at least twenty minutes. Then we can see if the bleeding has stopped. First, though, here's some ibuprofen."

The woman handed Ida two Advil and an open water bottle. Ida turned her head back to its normal position, wondering if there was anyone here who wouldn't have some sort of neck pain tomorrow. She swallowed the tablets with a sip of water. Then the EMT pulled Ida's lip out gently and patted it dry with a gauze pad. The EMT placed some rolled-up gauze between Ida's lower lip and her teeth.

"Let's get you cleaned up now," the woman said, pulling several packages of large, sterile wipes from the pocket of the blue windbreaker she wore.

"I can do it," Ida said, sounding like Janie had the day she'd had her braces put on.

The EMT looked at Ida, not understanding.

"I think she wants to do it herself," Steve said from Ida's right.

"Oh, okay," said the EMT. "But I'll need to hand you the wipes, and you'll have to hand them back to me. And do your best not to touch your clothing with your hands or with the wipes."

After several minutes of additional medical attention, Oleen's wrist was bandaged and in a sling, and Ida's face was free of blood, her lower lip bulging with rolled-up gauze. Each woman sported a bag of ice, courtesy of the EMTs. Oleen's bag sat inside the sling on top of her wrist, and Ida held her bag to her mouth.

Hearing footsteps, Oleen looked up from her wrist and spotted a familiar figure walking toward the front row from backstage. The figure was of medium height and medium build, with a thick head of wavy blonde hair and piercing light-blue eyes. He wore a light-gray suit with a light-blue tie. The man waved at Oleen, smiling grimly. Then he stopped just to the left of the crime scene tape, next to Oleen's seat.

"Why hello, Will!" Oleen said. "Oh! I didn't put it together. I guess I'm in shock. Lots of shocks the past few days. Will Brennan! That's you."

"That's me," Will said.

"Well, I guess this is a weird time to introduce you, but oh well. You know Ida, and that's Steve—he's Scott's husband—and then I can't remember if you've met Scott. That's Scott on the end, there. And we're told that guy down there is named Sergei," Oleen said, gesturing to the body on the floor. "We're trying not to look at him."

"Hi," Will said, waving. Ida, Steve, and Scott waved back. "I'm so sorry you're in this situation. I'll try to hurry it up so we can get you out of these seats."

"Well, we've been sitting here for so long some of the horror has worn off," said Oleen. "Now he just seems like some drunk guy who passed out on the floor."

"What happened to you two?" Will asked, nodding toward Oleen and Ida.

"I think I have a broken wrist and Ida's mouth is all cut up from hitting Steve's shoulder," Oleen said. "I'll have to get my wrist set properly when we're done here. It hurts, but not like it did before."

"I'm sorry. Is your wrist hurt from, uh, him?" Will asked, gesturing toward the body on the floor.

"Yes," Oleen said. "That man down there landed on it. Sergei, I mean."

"Hey, I think we did meet once, Will," Scott said. "You guys were already out of college. Well, not Jenny. It was her last year because she was on the five-year plan, but I was in my last year of high school. Jenny came home over spring break, and you and Leah came with her, back before you lived here. Didn't you all stay at Maureen's? I think that was that one year Alex went out to California to work for Apple, and Maureen lived with that girl, I forgot her name. We all went to some club; Oxygen, I think it was called. That place closed a long time ago. I was surprised Maureen even came."

"I do remember that," Will said, grinning. "And we did stay with Maureen. She had that weird roommate at the time, and she and Alex weren't married yet because he took that job and Maureen was irritable the whole time. I had never heard her curse at all, but she sure did curse a lot while we were there. And it was always about Alex or when she was on the phone with him. Anyway, her roommate was very strange."

"That's right!" Scott said. "Her roommate was a weirdo. She was always making those ugly macramé wall hangings."

"Yeah," said Will. "She gave Maureen one when Maureen moved out. That's what Jenny told us, and we all had a good laugh about it."

"She did!" Scott said. "Maureen found that thing in the attic last year. Never hung it on the wall. Then her cat, Gordon, peed on it. She'd always wanted to throw it away, but couldn't bring herself to, so she was pretty pleased with Gordon."

"I think that was the night Jenny ruined that French tycoon's shoes," Will said. "I didn't get why a guy like that would hang out at that club, but I guess getting your shoes thrown up on is a good reason not to go back. And that's when you were with that guy, Jackson. He was pretty weird too, as I remember. Didn't he always wear mesh shirts? And weren't they mostly neon? But he wasn't as weird as Maureen's roommate, on account of him having never given you a macramé wall hanging."

"Let's never speak of Jackson again, please," Scott said, wincing. "I think that French guy liked very young women. After all, I think that place's slogan was '18 to party, 21 to drink,' and that guy seemed old as dirt even though he was about the same age I am now. He was the only person in there who appeared to have already graduated from college. And once I discovered you could buy stuff you couldn't afford with credit cards I decided he probably wasn't a tycoon either, like we thought, but that he probably was a douche."

"You're right! I forgot about Jenny throwing up on that guy's shoes." Will shook his head.

"Jenny's out in the car right now," Will said.

"Why in the world did you bring Jenny here?" Oleen asked.

"I don't know if she's told you, but I've been taking her to the shooting range with me sometimes. She says it helps her relieve stress, and she's a damn good shot," Will said.

"Jenny goes to a shooting range?" Scott asked, eyes wide, sounding impressed.

"Yeah, we just started a month or two back. She comes over a few nights a week for dinner. You know how Leah has always loved to cook. Jenny eats with us and she plays with Rachel, which is great because it gives Leah and me a chance to sit on the couch and relax for a few minutes. About once a week we go to the range. Leah's never had any interest, so when Jenny asked me to take her, I was happy. It's fun to teach someone how to shoot. Jenny's only gone with me three or four times, but she's a natural. We were there when I got this call, and the range is closer to here than it is to her place. Since she knew you all were here, she asked to come. I told her as long as she stayed in the car it was fine."

Will noticed the perplexed look on Steve's face.

"Sorry, man," he said to Steve, "I guess you don't know how I know Jenny. I'm married to her friend Leah. We've all known each other since freshman year of college."

"Oh yeah," Steve said. "Jenny's mentioned you. I just didn't put it together that you were the same Will. I have no idea how we've managed to never meet after all these years."

"Yeah," said Will, "me neither." He shrugged. "Jenny talks about you a lot, though. You and Scott. You two have been a godsend for her over the past six months."

"Me?" Scott asked. "Steve I understand. I wouldn't think Jenny would consider me helpful. Are you sure you didn't hear her wrong?"

"Yeah, she mentioned both of you," said Will.

Scott shrugged.

"We just go to brunch with her on the weekends," said Scott. "And sometimes she hangs out with us on weeknights. She and Steve both like those awful Hallmark channel movies, and sometimes those awful Lifetime movies—those are way worse than the Hallmark ones. They're about some cheerleader's mom who hired someone to kill another cheerleader so her daughter could be the squad captain or something."

"Don't knock it, Scott," Steve said. "Don't think I didn't notice the day you were watching that movie I DVRed: *Co-Ed Call Girl*."

"But it's got Tori Spelling," said Scott, "So it doesn't count. Everything she's ever been in could air as a Lifetime movie."

"Well, I guess it's not good to chitchat at the scene of a death," Will said. "Steve, in case you don't know, I'm the lead detective assigned to this case."

"That other guy said he was the lead detective," said Steve.

"Oh, Beaureguard?"

Steve nodded.

Will sighed.

"He's not. He's only been my partner for two weeks. I don't know why he said that. He just passed the detectives' exam the week before he was assigned as my partner. I don't know him very well," Will said. "He just moved here from Dallas, I think."

"It sounds like he's getting too big for his britches," said Ida, though no one could understand what she said.

"I think she said 'It sounds like he's getting too big for his britches,'" Steve said.

Ida nodded.

Will laughed at the word britches.

"Maybe so, Ida," he said. "Well, now I've got to start doing my job. I'm going to have the CSTs come over here and take some pictures and collect evidence. Once they're done, a patrol officer will walk you upstairs where my partner will ask you some questions. I'm going to have to recuse myself from investigating this case since I know all of you. If it turns out to be a murder, especially, there's no way I can be in charge of it or even peripherally involved. Right now it's just a suspicious death. I shouldn't have told you that, so don't say anything."

"Okay, dear," said Ida, her words still garbled. "We won't."

"She said we won't," Steve translated.

"I have to go back to my car now and call the captain and get another detective out here," Will said. "I shouldn't be at this scene at all. I need to get Jenny home too."

"Take her to our place, would you?" said Steve. "It's not too far from here, and she can give you the address."

"Sure thing," Will said.

"Just let her know we want to tell her what's going on when we get back. She's stayed over a bunch, so she'll be right at home."

Steve handed Will his keys, as a man wearing shoe covers on his feet began to take photos of the body. Will pocketed the keys, gave a small wave, then walked toward the back of the tent and disappeared up the steps and out of sight.

40

MONDAY

B y the time Oleen, Ida, Steve, and Scott had followed
the patrol officer out of the tent, Mr. McGruder, Katerina, and Fernando were gone. The audience, which
had been held for debriefing, was gone too. Steve looked at his
watch. It was nearly 10 p.m. Steve was happy the gallery didn't
open until 11 a.m. the next day, because he doubted they'd be
home anytime soon, and doubted even more that he'd sleep
much tonight. Scott was doing research on a case and would be
working from home tomorrow, so at least they didn't have to be
too concerned about what time this debacle would be over.

The patrol officer led them across the parking lot and
through the unlocked front doors of the civic center. Another
officer was posted at the doors and nodded to them as they
passed. They followed the patrol officer up a set of stairs and
down a hallway, which had benches on each side. The benches
were padded, unlike those uncomfortable chairs in the
auditorium.

The patrol officer gestured for everyone to sit on the
benches.

"I don't think we should sit in the same order," said Ida,

who had removed the gauze from her mouth and thrown it away, since the bleeding had stopped. "I think that order might be bad luck."

Scott sat down first, and Ida took a seat next to him. Steve sat next to Ida on the adjacent bench, and Oleen sat on the end of the bench next to Steve.

"This bench isn't very big," said Oleen. "That door is to Mr. McGruder's office," she said, gesturing to a door in front of the bench with a nameplate outside that read "Bill McGruder." "It makes sense this bench is tiny because I bet he only wants young girls with tiny perky butts sitting outside his office."

"Oleen!" Ida hissed. "Not now! We're about to be questioned by the police, for heaven's sake."

"Okay, okay," said Oleen.

"That joke is getting pretty old, Aunt Oleen," Scott called from the opposite end of the bench. "You need to find some fresh material."

Oleen crossed her arms as much as one can with a sling on one's left shoulder, and turned away from the group.

A moment later, the door next to Mr. McGruder's office opened, and Mr. McGruder stormed out. He flew by the benches and stomped to the end of the hall and down the steps.

"Well, then," said Ida. "I suppose this has all been very upsetting to him."

Scott opened his mouth to speak, but then closed it again, remembering they'd been told not to discuss the evening's events, and sure that if he did, the patrol officer would rebuke him.

Detective Beauregard appeared in the doorway of the office Mr. McGruder had just exited. He stood before the two benches, surveying the four people in front of him. Detective Beauregard pointed at Scott. "I guess we'll just start here and go down the row," he said.

Detective Beauregard motioned Scott into the office. Scott stood up and looked down the bench at Steve, who nodded at him, and Scott followed the detective into the office. The door on the other side of Mr. McGruder's office opened, and Grace McGruder burst out, fists clenched, and a murderous look on her face.

Oleen, who noticed Grace's anger, but who very much needed a bathroom, called out, "Grace, do you know where the bathroom is?"

Grace looked around and realized her exit from the office had an audience. The anger drained from her face, and she managed a slight smile. "I'm sorry," she said. "This is all just so upsetting. I saw the body. I mean, uh, Sergei, when I came out from backstage to see what was going on. As soon as I caught sight of it, er him, I ran backstage and didn't come out until an officer came and got me."

"We understand, dear," said Ida. "We were sitting there with him for a long time."

"That's ghastly!" Grace said, with wide eyes.

"We kind of got used to him," said Oleen. "He just seemed like a guy passed out on the floor after a while. Like how it was at those fraternity parties Ida and I used to go to in college. With Gary and Delbert, I mean. But, Grace, I need a bathroom. Do you know where one is?"

Grace took a breath and smoothed out her blouse and her black dress pants. "I'm on my way there now, so you can come with me. There's not one on this level, which makes no sense because most of the offices are on this floor. There are bathrooms on every other level, but they're all the way on the other side of the building. It's easier to go all the way up the stairs to the top floor. There's a bathroom right next to the stairs up there."

"Okay," Oleen said, standing and following Grace toward the stairwell.

The two women climbed four flights of stairs, and Oleen wondered why in the world it was easier to do this than to just climb up one flight and traverse the flat ground to the other side of the building. It was hard maneuvering upstairs with her left arm in a sling, and Oleen had to grab the railing on the right side of the stairwell and navigate each step as though walking across an icy pond. No way did she want to further injure her already mangled wrist. But they were almost to the top, and Oleen's stomach told her she didn't have much time, so she kept these thoughts to herself.

At the top of the stairwell was a massive locked door. It was a different kind of door than the other doors she'd seen in the building. It looked like the door to that panic closet in that movie with Jodi Foster where she had to hide from the home invaders. Boy, that movie came out a long time ago. She'd have to see if Scott knew the right name. She had never been good with names, of either people or of movies, even though she was way better than Ida about the names of movies and TV shows. Grace opened the reinforced door by swiping a keycard. Oleen wondered what could possibly be so secret up here that you'd need a keycard to get in.

The sixth floor of the civic center was different from the other floors. Well, Oleen had only seen the second floor and the lobby, and it was different from those. There was a long hallway right outside the stairwell, with a women's restroom just to the right of the stairwell exit. Instead of offices, there was a wall across the small corridor with windows covering the entire top half. The stairwell exit was a little to the right of the middle of the hallway, and Oleen could see that the windows in the wall in front of her stretched from one side of the floor to the other. She supposed the stairwell exit was closer to the middle of the hallway than to the end on this floor because of the large turrets that sat at each corner of the building.

Through the windows in the wall, Oleen saw a vast, open

expanse of space that contained artwork, lots of artwork. From statues to paintings to marble busts—there was every type of art imaginable. There was even a podium with a video monitor behind it. Oleen wondered if that was for some weird performance art show where people wore skimpy clothes and chanted strange things. She'd seen something on TV about those once, and that's what happened in the one she saw on *60 Minutes*.

Oleen's stomach indicated that she'd better stop staring at the artwork and get into the bathroom as soon as possible. She followed Grace's disappearing figure through the door marked "Women."

After Oleen had done what she needed to do and was washing her hands, she heard Grace crying inside a stall. Oleen wondered if she should check on Grace or give her some privacy. She decided on the latter. Besides, she could use this time to peek at the artwork.

Oleen exited the bathroom and looked through the windows again, admiring a beautiful landscape of haystacks and a colorful sky with a rising sun. The painting was surrounded by an ornate gold frame, which seemed gaudy to Oleen, but she supposed she wasn't trained in art. Maybe the frame was beautiful, and she just couldn't see it.

The painting looked like one of those Impressionist paintings she'd seen at the art museum last fall. Mostly there were paintings by Monet in that exhibit, and he only seemed to paint lily pads and flowers, so it must be by some other artist. That was a traveling show, and she and Jenny had gone one Sunday afternoon. Even though Jenny had an excellent head for numbers, she had always enjoyed crafts, and as a child had won several drawing contests at her elementary school.

Oleen and Jenny had loved the exhibit so much they had invited Ida and Agnes to go back with them the following weekend. But, when Oleen had gone on to the museum's website to buy tickets, she had seen that the exhibit had closed at the end of the prior Sunday, the day she and Jenny had visited. They'd been too caught up in the paintings to notice. The exhibit had moved on to the museum in Birmingham, so Ida and Agnes had missed out.

Oleen had seen on the museum's website that a new temporary exhibit would be opening on the upcoming Friday, but all it had in it was the art of that awful Andy Warhol man. If Oleen wanted to look at soup cans, she could just open her kitchen cabinets. Oleen briefly considered what a mountain of artwork was doing on the top floor of the civic center, but then the sound of muffled voices interrupted her reverie. The voices sounded like they were coming from her left. Without thinking about it, Oleen walked in the direction of the voices. As she proceeded down the hallway, the voices became louder. The voices sounded like they were arguing. Oleen reached the end of the hallway and realized she was standing by one of the two castle-like turrets that adorned the front two corners of the civic center.

Oleen couldn't see around the open doorway from where she stood on the left side of the hallway, but she noticed a large potted tree on the right side that she could use as cover while she figured out what was going on. She looked left and right and then darted across the hall and behind the tree. From this vantage point, she could see into the area inside the turret. It was a circular space with a bench stretching all the way around it. There were windows around the top half of the turret, through which Oleen had a lovely view of the twinkling lights of the city skyline. There wasn't a door leading into the turret, the area was just open, so she could easily see the two figures inside by peeking through the leaves of the tree.

The two people in the turret appeared to be having a disagreement. One of the figures was tall and olive-skinned with a thick head of blue-black hair. He wore jeans and a t-shirt, and remnants of white face paint peeked out of the shirt's rounded neckline. The other figure, a woman, was dressed in tight jeans and a low-cut purple V-neck T-shirt. The woman only came up to the man's chin, and Oleen wasn't sure if the man was very tall or if the woman was very short. Flaming red curls framed the woman's face.

"No one can know!" the woman said in an urgent whisper. "Especially not Bill. I'll get fired."

"No you won't!" The man said. "You were dating Sergei, and that didn't matter to him."

"This is different," the woman said. "Bill will be mad. He might do something. He might tell someone."

"We have to tell the police," said the man. "I'm pretty sure Bill's wife knows. No doubt she'll tell the police. Or Bill. I'm sure she's furious. You can't act like that with him when she's around, you know. You need to stop doing that. And we need to be honest."

Oleen leaned further into the potted tree, as the voices became more muted. She found she could hear a little better by bending her ear into the leaves and steadying herself by propping one foot up on the rim of the reddish-brown clay pot the tree grew from.

"Bill's wife...may be...the one." Oleen heard the man's broken sentence, though many of the words were too faint for her to make out.

Oleen felt a presence behind her, then heard her name.

"Oleen?"

Oleen screamed. Behind her, Grace McGruder screamed. Grace's sudden appearance caused Oleen to jump, and she lost purchase on the pot, riding the tree down toward the turret like it was one of those Styrofoam surfboards Mike and Jenny had loved playing on many years ago during family trips to Jekyll Island. A boogie board, that's what they were called.

Oleen hit the ground with a crash, causing the man and the

woman who had been whispering inside the turret to scream almost as loudly as Oleen had. The pot broke into pieces, and dirt flew everywhere. Oleen had wondered whether or not the tree was real because some fake plants looked so real these days. The soil that was seeping into her left shoe was all the answer she needed.

Grace spotted the two figures inside the turret.

"Katerina! Fernando! How did you get up here?" she asked in a choked voice.

Oleen noticed Grace's clenched fists as she spoke to Katerina and Fernando. Then she stopped noticing as a wave of pain shot through her right wrist when she struggled to push herself up.

"Shit on a shingle!" Oleen cried.

Grace unclenched her fists and bent down toward Oleen. "What's wrong?"

"I think I broke the other one too," Oleen said, holding up her right wrist. Then she laid her head back down on top of the tree and curled into a fetal position.

41

MONDAY

Grace knelt on the floor next to Oleen.

"Let me look at it," she said. Grace took Oleen's right wrist in her hands and examined it. "I don't think it's broken, Oleen," Grace said. "I'm pretty sure it's just sprained, though you could have injured a tendon or torn something. You should have both wrists looked at as soon as possible. You don't need to be sitting around down there waiting to talk to the police. They can just go with you to the hospital if they're that concerned."

"Ow!" Oleen yelled as Katerina and Fernando hurried by, one of them stepping on the toes of her now bare left foot as they walked past. She'd slipped off her left shoe on account of it being filled with dirt.

Oleen looked at Grace, who stared with narrowed eyes at Katerina and Fernando as they hurried down the hallway and out of the locked door that led to the stairwell. The door swung shut behind them.

"I have no idea how they got up here," Grace said to Oleen. "And what in the world were you doing?"

"Grace?" Oleen interrupted. "Can you call Ida and maybe have someone come up here and help get me down? I don't need a stretcher or anything, but I don't think I can walk down without help because I'll fall and break both ankles and crack open my head. I left my phone downstairs in my purse, though."

Grace plopped down on the ground next to Oleen and rummaged around in her purse until she found her cell phone.

"She still has the same number she's had since 1996," said Oleen. "I bet you've got it in your phone."

Grace scrolled down her phone's screen to Ida's name and showed the number listed to Oleen.

"That's it," Oleen said.

Grace hit a button on her phone. "Hi, Ida, it's Grace. Yes, everything's okay. But Oleen fell, and I think she's sprained her other wrist. We're up here on the sixth floor, but she can't get down all the steps without some help. No, she'll be okay. No, she just needs to get them both looked at. OK, thanks."

"Ida's asking two of the patrol officers to come up here. She said she'd come herself, but they won't let her leave. I better go meet them at the door, since they won't be able to get in," said Grace. She hurried away, stopping at the door to the stairwell.

Oleen lay amongst the tree branches and leaves. She tried to decide what type of tree she had toppled, but she didn't possess Agnes's powers of plant identification. Agnes had an encyclopedic knowledge of plants and flowers. Oleen wouldn't be surprised if Agnes could identify some ancient fern from the Cretaceous period just by looking at an imprint fossil some paleontologist had discovered in a big canyon in Nevada.

She looked around the hallway. Well, around the part of the hallway she could see, considering she was lying on her side atop an upended potted tree, and she could turn her head in a limited arc before she ran into a branch or got poked in the eye by a leaf. Oleen looked in front of her into the turret and noticed again how beautiful the view of the skyline was. She could only see the very tops of a few buildings from her prone position, and she could see how the gathering clouds in the sky swirled like ink that had just been dropped into a bowl of water. It looked like a storm was coming. Oleen loved summer storms.

She examined the benches, which sat atop wooden cabinets with curved fronts. The cabinets stretched all the way around the turret just like the benches did, and she wondered if there was room inside them to store anything, or if the cabinet doors were only there for show.

Oleen imagined the turret would be a romantic place to sit and watch a thunderstorm. Then Oleen remembered that Gary and Delbert were supposed to be gay. She tried to imagine the two of them sharing a romantic tryst in that turret, rain beating down the windows around them, and lightning illuminating their clasped hands. Oleen almost chuckled. Would Delbert wear the oil-stained, denim overalls he wore every day to the auto repair shop? Because overalls were not in any way romantic. Maybe Gary would wear one of his ugly sweaters, possibly with sweatpants underneath. Oleen didn't know whether to laugh at the absurdity of the thought, to cringe at the two men's atrocious senses of fashion, or to cry because she feared she'd never again share a romantic moment with her husband.

As she tore her eyes from the benches, and from the spectacular view of the sky, Oleen noticed that the floor around her was made of a white tile similar to what one might find on the floor of an elementary school classroom. The floor of the turret was covered with a light gray, industrial-grade, non-fluffy kind of carpet. Oleen remembered the rug burn Mike had gotten that time Jenny had dragged him across a similar rug in their living room. That was so long ago, and she and Gary didn't even have that carpet anymore. Still, thinking about the kind of rug burn industrial carpet could give you caused Oleen to shudder.

Oleen saw something white at the base of one of the under-bench cabinets. It was almost in the corner of the right side of the turret. She squinted at it and wished she had her glasses, but she'd left them downstairs in her purse. She turned her head to the left until she could see Grace out of the corner of her eye. There weren't any police officers there yet, so Oleen scooted herself toward the turret. She was only about two or three feet from where the tile changed to carpet, so she lifted herself up on her forearms, and inched forward, alternating her weight from her left forearm to her right one. With effort and not a little pain, she dragged herself forward until she reached the place where the tile floor of the hallway met the carpet of the turret. Oleen looked back down the hall toward Grace, who still stood by the stairwell door. Grace had the door open a crack so she could see the police officers when they showed up, which made sense, as the door was completely solid and lacked a window.

Turning her head back toward the turret, Oleen scooted herself right up to the bench until her nose almost touched it. Then she looked down and saw the curved corner of the white piece of plastic poking out from under the cabinet. Oleen tried to use the fingers of her right hand to slide the plastic out. Her wrist throbbed, but she seemed to have dislodged the piece of plastic from where it had been stuck. It had edged out enough that she could see a bit of color on the front. She couldn't pull it out, though, because her wrist hurt too much. Oleen turned her nose down to the carpet, moving her face toward the bench, and set the tip of her nose down on top of the part of the piece of plastic that was now visible. She tried to scoot the plastic out with the tip of her nose, but it wouldn't budge. She turned her head to the side, positioning her chin right up against the bench and on top of the piece of plastic. She pressed her chin down with the collective force of the entire stable of wrestlers from that *Wrestlemania* show Mike and Scott had watched when they were kids. She pressed down and pulled her head away from the bench. The plastic popped loose, and Oleen's chin throbbed from the rug burn she had only moments before imagined the industrial carpet might inflict. Oleen rested the right side of her face on the ground next to the piece of plastic.

The piece of plastic was small and rectangular, with rounded corners. There was someone's picture on the left side and, on the right side, there were words. Oleen's eyes were too close to make out what it said. She could see down the hall to where Grace was ushering two patrol officers through the stair-well door. Oleen lifted her head and looked down at the piece of plastic. On the left side was the smiling face of an attractive young man with light-brown hair. On the right was some typed information. It was a driver's license, and the name on the license read "Sergei Petrovsky." Oleen grabbed the license with the fingers of her right hand. Her wrist throbbed in agony as she thrust the hand holding the driver's license down the front of her shirt, and wedged the license into the left side of her bra. Her chest would look weird, as the outer left side of her bra now sported a flattened, rectangular area. Oleen silently thanked the universe that hardly anyone would be looking at the boobs of a sixty-something-year-old woman. She removed her hand from her shirt just as Grace arrived. Grace looked down at her with an expression that suggested Oleen had sprouted a third wrist out of her forehead—a wrist she would no doubt soon injure in some way.

Grace was undoubtedly trying to figure out why Oleen was lying on her stomach with her nose up against the cabinet underneath the bench in the turret. Even Oleen wasn't sure why. She wondered if she was sliding off the rails and would soon end up on that *Intervention* show, if that show was even on anymore.

"Beautiful sky," Oleen said. "Just wanted to get a closer look. Now I'm so tired."

Oleen laid the right side of her face back down on the carpet as two patrol officers knelt down and helped her up.

42

MONDAY

"Ow! Dammit!" Oleen cried, as one of the patrol officers missed a step, knocking her into the handrail attached to the right side of the stairwell. Her right hand whacked the wall, sending a jolt of pain through her wrist.

"I'm so sorry, ma'am," the officer to her right said.

Oleen recognized him as Officer Lopez, one of the officers Detective Beauregard had been ordering around earlier. Oleen observed his deep-brown eyes and thick, luxurious eyelashes. She'd been trying for over fifty years to get her own eyelashes to look that way, and this young man didn't even have to make an effort. Oleen sighed inwardly at the unfairness of life. Youth was wasted on the young, and eyelashes were wasted on the men.

The officer to Oleen's left was another one Detective Beauregard had yelled at. Sanders, she thought his name was. He had a fluorescent-pink t-shirt tucked into the back of his pants, and it billowed out like a cape anytime he walked quickly. Oleen guessed it was the new shirt Detective Beauregard had promised Ida, but which had never shown up earlier when they were allowed to leave their seats in front of the stage.

Grace followed behind the group, her wedge-heeled sandals clomping on each step on the way down. Oleen often wondered how women managed to walk so easily in heels. Oleen herself had worn heels once, back in the early days of her CPA career, but walking in such tall shoes had always been an effort for her. Oleen had only worn heels back then because she'd wanted to look terrifying in an office full of men. She had worn severe black suits, high black pumps, and had pulled her then strawberry-blonde hair back into a rigid bun. For a time she had even worn black-rimmed eyeglasses, though they had contained only plain plastic lenses with no prescription whatsoever. Oleen had never been harassed or belittled because the men were afraid of her.

She had become a partner in her firm within her first five years of working there. She had, in fact, been one of the youngest associates ever to make partner in the firm of Norman, Peters, and Harry—well, aside from Delbert, of course. Oleen had been only too happy to hang up the work costume when she had retired ten years ago, and she loved her current job as the part-time bookkeeper for Delbert's auto shop. In her current position, she worked from home and didn't even have to put on pants if she didn't feel like it, even though she always did, as she didn't want to look like Gary in one of his nightshirts.

Still, Oleen's work persona and her actual self were nothing alike. Back when she'd worked at the firm, she had taken off her fussy attire the moment she walked through the front door of her house. She would remove her too-tight pumps, take off her pantyhose, and unhook her bra, all of which gave her a sense of freedom akin to what she imagined convicts felt on their first day of release from prison. The moment Oleen arrived home from work she would don a pair of sweatpants or shorts and an old t-shirt, her favorite being a shirt she'd found at a thrift shop that said: "Do it with a screamer." It had a picture of a power drill on the front. Oleen figured the shirt must have been a promotional t-shirt for a tool company, as she couldn't imagine what other reason it would have had for existing. That shirt had also been a fantastic tool (no pun intended) for getting Jenny and Mike to behave during their preteen years, as all she had to do was threaten to wear it in public, and they would suddenly become obedient, angel children.

Oleen's trip down memory lane was interrupted by another near trip down the stairs, as Sanders stopped suddenly without warning Lopez he was doing so. Lopez pulled Oleen down to the right as Sanders rooted her left arm firmly in place a couple of stairs back.

"Shit!" Oleen called, as her left wrist, which was still rigged up in the sling, was pulled away from her body by Sanders's sudden stop, then snapped back to her side like a rubber band.

"Officer, I've got it," Grace said, bending down to pick up the pink t-shirt that must have slipped from the waistband of Sanders' pants when the two men had almost snapped Oleen like a wishbone a moment before.

Oleen marveled at Grace's ability to bend down and pick up dropped items while wearing three-inch wedge heels and form-fitting pants, all while standing on uncarpeted stairs, and without slipping and cracking her head open. Oleen and the two officers made slow progress down the stairs. Grace trailed behind them, the clip-clopping of her shoes reminding Oleen of that man driven to madness in that Edgar Alan Poe story about the weird, scary beating heart. By the time Officer Sanders pushed open the door to the second floor, Oleen had made a game in her head of figuring out all the ways the officers could cause her more bodily injury on the way back down to her family.

During the rocky trek, which had brought to mind a book

she'd once read about the Donner Party, Oleen had decided that, if given the opportunity to kill one of the two patrol officers, she might never be able to make a decision. In all likelihood, each officer would have died of old age before Oleen had made up her mind. Then Oleen realized that she'd be dead long before either of the officers even reached the age she was now, a sad fact which she shelved in her mind next to all the other sad facts she had learned in her life. For example, that men always got the good eyelashes, and that your driver's license photo would always look like a mug shot that was taken of you right after you'd been on an all-night drinking binge and gotten arrested for shoplifting from a Walmart.

Officer Lopez opened the door from the stairwell to the second floor, to Oleen's delight, and she stumbled into the hallway, walked a few feet to her right, knocked into the bench, fell over Scott's knees, and landed face-first in Ida's lap. Oleen tried to push herself up, her two bum wrists being of no help.

"Come on, Oleen," Scott said, trying to lift her off him. "Let's get you up. Are you drunk again?"

Oleen, who didn't realize that Ida had lowered her head down to say something to her, lifted her head to tell Scott that, no, she was not, in fact, drunk, and in the process knocked the back of her head into Ida's chin.

"Shit!" Ida said as blood began to trickle out of her mouth and into Oleen's hair.

"Language, Mom!" Scott said.

Grace rushed to Ida, stopping in front of her and pulling a packet of tissues from her pants pocket. Grace yanked some tissues free from the plastic wrapper and handed a wad of them to Ida. Ida rolled two tissues up and stuffed them between her lip and her teeth. She used the rest of the tissues to mop the droplets of blood from Oleen's hair.

Oleen felt arms lifting her up and setting her down on the bench next to Ida. Scott and Steve stood in front of her, having just deposited her next to her sister. Behind them, a door opened, and there stood Detective Beauregard and another man in a suit whom Oleen did not recognize. Oleen noticed that this new man had black hair and stunning emerald-green eyes. Like Officer Lopez, the new man also had spectacular eyelashes. Maybe there was something in the water here at the civic center.

"What's going on?" Oleen asked, looking from Grace to Scott to Steve, to the two detectives, and finally to her sister. The two patrol officers stood off to the right, a fair distance away from the group, which was fine with Oleen.

"Well, dear," Ida said, "Scott and Steve are free to go. Detective Beauregard just finished talking to Steve, and this young man here," she said, gesturing to the man with the bright-green eyes and enviable eyelashes. "He wanted me to go into the office and talk to him, and I said I couldn't until you came back because you need to go to the hospital and I'm going with you."

"I want Ida to come with me," Oleen said. "And she needs that shirt." Oleen pointed at Sanders, who now had the fluorescent-pink shirt draped around the back of his neck like Rocky Balboa preparing to face an opponent in a boxing ring at the Barbie Dream House.

"Please give my sister that shirt," Oleen said to Sanders.

Sanders looked around, realized he had the shirt draped across him, removed it from his neck, and tossed it to Ida.

Ida stood up, taking the pink shirt with her, and walked past the green-eyed man into the office.

"You just stay there, dear," Ida said, pointing at the man, "And then you can take Oleen and me to the hospital, and you can question us while we wait for a doctor to see her. We don't need an ambulance."

Ida closed the door behind her.

"Well then," said the detective, his eyes dancing with amusement. "I guess that's what we'll do."

Ida emerged a moment later wearing the fluorescent-pink t-shirt, which was so large and flowed so voluminously over her now barely visible jeans that she looked like an ancient, though flamboyant, druid about to conduct a ceremony on a hilltop. Noticing her sister's new outfit, Oleen shook her head in dismay, realizing that the pink souvenir t-shirt was the perfect size for Gary to wear as a nightshirt.

"I'll need that other shirt," Detective Beauregard said to Ida, pointing at the bloody blouse she held in her right hand. He held a large plastic bag out to her, and Ida dropped the blouse in.

"If the stains happen to come out, please let me know," Ida said. "That blouse was Michael Kors, and I got it at seventy percent off."

"That shirt is huge," Oleen said, gesturing to the flowing fluorescent-pink tent that covered three-quarters of Ida's body.

"They only had a double extra-large," Sanders called from several feet away.

"In pink?" Scott asked.

Sanders shrugged.

"At least she won't get run over on the way to the car," said Scott.

43

MONDAY

To Oleen's relief, the detective with the green eyes—she still didn't know his name—didn't drive a police car. She guessed that made sense because on TV shows detectives never seemed to drive police cars. Their vehicles were ugly, though, and had probably never made gaywheels.com's annual list of the twenty most popular cars. The detective drove a silver Ford Explorer which was not new, but which was, perhaps, not so old that it took three tries to pass its emissions inspection either.

His car was parked in the roundabout right in front of the doors to the civic center. While the car was unmarked, Oleen saw a sign on the front dashboard that was there to keep it from getting towed. Ida, Oleen, Scott, Steve, and the detective stood under the overhang just outside the civic center doors, trying not to get pelted by the steady downpour that had begun since they had first entered the civic center an hour ago. Thunder rumbled in the distance, but there was no lightning yet. The rain had diluted the hot, humid air, and Oleen shivered even though the temperature had only fallen, in Oleen's estimation, into the mid-seventies.

Oleen's left wrist was still held against her body by the sling, and her right wrist had been stabilized in a makeshift sling Steve had created from another double-extra- large, fluorescent-pink souvenir t-shirt Detective Beauregard had found on a chair in Mr. McGruder's office. Steve had stretched the shirt out by pulling on the left sleeve and the bottom right corner, placing Oleen's arm in the fabric in between, and then tying the two ends tightly together around her neck. The t-shirt was thick, and the knot Steve had tied pushed uncomfortably into the base of Oleen's vertebra. It was like she had a goiter, only on the wrong side of her neck.

Ida, in her voluminous, flowing pink top, which in the future she might be able to use as a Snuggie, and Oleen, with her rosy Day-Glo sling, looked right at home standing across the parking lot from a circus tent. Ida remembered the time when Scott was nine and had taught himself magic tricks from a kit he had received as a birthday gift. For some reason, the kit had also included three hacky sacks and instructions for learning how to juggle, though Ida didn't consider juggling magic. Still, she had fun learning how to juggle the hacky sacks with Scott, and he had eventually added a tennis ball to the mix. Within two weeks, Ida could competently juggle four objects at one time. She had drawn the line when Scott had suggested she juggle knives, though. She still juggled tennis balls sometimes when she was stressed, but no one except Delbert even knew this fun fact. Ida figured that, in her current outfit, her juggling knives, or even juggling knives while riding a unicycle would appear perfectly reasonable.

Scott's loud voice cut through both the pounding rain, and Ida's thoughts. "We'll meet you at the hospital, Mom. You and Oleen don't need to be traipsing around town at almost midnight in the rain."

"Traipsing?" Steve laughed.

"Oh, Scott," said Ida. "Go home. We don't need you with us.

Oleen is going to be fine. We might want to rest in the waiting room, and you'll just talk the whole time. And we'll be perfectly safe. We'll have this fine young man there to protect us and he also carries a gun." Ida giggled.

"I do," the detective said.

Oleen, Scott, and Steve looked at each other.

"I'm sorry, dear," Ida said to the detective, "But can you tell me your name again? The first time you told me was just as my sister came galloping down the stairs and fell right on top of Scott and me, and I think I missed it."

The detective smiled.

"Andrew," he said. "Andrew Davenport. But you can call me Drew."

Drew smiled, and his bright-green eyes crinkled. He had actual dimples. Ida, Oleen, Scott, and Steve all stared at him the way teenage girls used to stare at magazine photos of Erik Estrada in 1982. Drew, thought Ida, was one of those men who was so good-looking that just being in a room with him made you blush. Even when you were sixty-five years old and happily married. Hell, even when you were sixty-five years old and married to a man who had been having a secret love affair with your identical twin sister's husband for the past forty-five years. The fact that Drew carried a gun only added to his appeal. And Ida really, really disapproved of guns.

With effort, Steve tore his eyes away from Detective Drew Davenport to face Scott.

"Scott, they'll be fine. And I'm sure they won't be traipsing around in the rain, and they won't be frolicking anywhere either. I know your mom will text us and keep us updated, and we can call your dad, and he and Gary can meet them at the hospital. I'm sure they'll want to do that anyway."

"Um," said Ida, "I'm not sure calling Delbert and Gary is the best idea, Steve, dear."

"Ida, I know things aren't great now, but you can't keep all this from them. They could even have seen a story about what happened on the news by now. Didn't you see all the news vans here earlier? They were just leaving when we came outside. There are even some parked across the street right now, see?" Steve pointed across the street to where three white news vans sat parked on the sidewalk in front of a large block of apartment buildings. He figured it was illegal to park like that, but since the whole police force seemed to be here and no one had said anything, he guessed it must not be that big a deal.

"Gary will be asleep on the couch snoring," said Oleen. "In his pajamas and a pair of black socks. Er, not pajamas. Sweatpants, you know. And a big shirt. He falls asleep by nine with a bowl of dry Rice Chex in his lap. That's his evening snack, but almost every night he just falls asleep and dumps the bowl on himself. After a while, I told him he had to stop pouring milk on them because the sofa started to smell like the old sofa did when Mike and Jenny were babies, and they spit up milk on it all the time."

"And Delbert lives in the garage now," Ida said. "Sometimes he takes his laptop out there, but all he'd be watching is either ESPN or reruns of the Andy Griffith show. I don't think they show news on those channels."

Drew looked from Ida to Oleen, but didn't say anything.

"Well, we need to go tell Jenny what's going on," Scott said. "I'm sure she's worried. Steve's texted her, but this story is way too long to tell in a text. I'll call Dad, and he and Gary will meet you at the hospital. And I'll text Agnes too, since she never sleeps and will want to know."

Both Ida and Oleen glared at Scott.

"Are you ready, ladies?" Drew Davenport asked.

The three dashed across the parking lot in the pouring rain, Ida and Drew on each side of Oleen to make sure she didn't fall. By the time they reached the car, all three of them, had wet, dripping hair and damp clothing.

Drew opened the rear driver's side door, and Ida and Oleen climbed into the Explorer. Then he jumped in the front and started the car.

Once the Explorer's lights faded as it left the parking lot, Steve asked Scott, "I wonder why neither of them tried to sit in the front."

"Well," said Scott, "Oleen gets carsick in the front and Mom, well, did you *see* how she was acting with that detective? All giggly and flirty?"

"No she wasn't, Scott," Steve said. "I did notice her blushing, though."

"Yeah," Scott said. "He's got the kind of looks that make you feel self-conscious and embarrassed when you stand within five feet of him. And Mom wouldn't be able to deal with sitting next to him in the front of the car. I mean, who could?"

Steve nodded. "I know what you mean."

44

MONDAY

A fter Ida, Oleen, and Detective Studmuffin, as Scott had started calling him, had driven away in the silver Ford Explorer, Scott and Steve were left standing under the overhang in front of the civic center.

"Why do you insist on calling him that, Scott?" Steve asked.

"Because it can be his code name," Scott said. "And Detective Studmuffin has a nice ring to it, don't you think?"

"No, I don't think. It just sounds cheesy and stupid," Steve said. "I am never going to call him that. Not even as a codename. Besides, why do we need a codename for him?"

"Because it's fun," Scott said.

"Try it with your mom and Oleen, then," Steve said. "It's clear you think he's all attractive and stuff, Scott. And I'll give you that, he is. But why do you have to be all inappropriate telling me about how hot the detective is? You're tacky sometimes, but you don't have to be THAT tacky."

"Huh?" Scott said.

"I mean, what would you say if Jason told Janie all about how 'hot' some other woman was?"

"I wouldn't say anything," Scott said. "I'd just kick him in the groin with a pair of steel-toed boots."

"Well, Scott," Steve said, "Aside from the fact that you wouldn't be caught dead in a pair of steel-toed boots, I think you've got some pot and kettle stuff going on here."

"Huh?" Scott said again.

"You know, the pot calling the kettle black?" said Steve. "Janie is Jason's wife, and you don't think he should be saying other women are hot right in front of her face. I'm your husband, so don't you think you shouldn't be saying some other man is hot right in front of my face?"

"Well, he's obviously not gay," Scott said, "So there's no reason to feel threatened."

"I don't feel threatened, Scott. I know no man on earth could ever be as patient as I am with your excessive grooming rituals. But it's just tacky, and I don't like how it makes me feel. I'm sure your mom and your aunt will be more than happy to 'dish'—isn't that what you call it?—with you about Detective Davenport later."

"Fine," said Scott. "You're no fun."

"I'm a lot of fun," Steve said, kissing Scott on the cheek, "And that's why you love me."

Scott smiled and shook his head.

"It's raining so hard," said Scott. "We are gonna get so drenched getting over to the parking deck."

"Maybe we can go back into the building," Steve said. "Then we can go under the walkway."

"Leaving that door unlocked with no officer guarding it seems like terrible crime scene security," Scott said. "But you never know. This place is a circus already."

Steve rolled his eyes. Then he turned around and pushed the bar on the door to the civic center. It didn't budge. "Guess we'll have to stay under the overhang and walk behind these bushes," Steve said.

"My shoes are gonna be ruined," Scott said. "And they cost $250 on sale. They're my best court shoes."

"That's why you need to be more practical, Scott," Steve said, lifting up his right pant leg to reveal one black low-top Chuck Taylor tennis shoe. "If I ruin these, I can put them in the washing machine and they're good as new."

"I'd never wear those, Steve. I bet you have one of those pairs from the 80s with the fold-over high-tops in fluorescent colors, too."

"They're green and blue," Steve mumbled. "But they're at my parents' house, so that doesn't count."

"I can't ruin these," Scott said.

"Well, take them off, then."

"Um, okay. But you have to help me. Let me put my arm around your shoulder so I can get my shoes and socks off. These socks cost like $50, so I can't mess them up, either."

Steve sighed. "Okay, studmuffin," he said. "Do your foot striptease and let's go. I'm starting to get rained on here."

Scott put his arm around Steve's shoulder and Steve held Scott up as Scott removed his shoes and socks, being careful not to slip. He let go of Steve's shoulder and, standing barefoot on the wet ground, shoved each sock deep into the toe of each shoe. Then he tied the shoe's laces together and draped them around his neck. He also rolled his pant legs up almost to his knees.

"All you need is a straw hat," Steve said. "You look like Huckleberry Finn."

"If I had one my hair would be dry," Scott replied.

Scott and Steve slowly inched their way against the side of the building and under the overhang toward the parking deck. Scott could feel the damp earth squishing between his toes. He wondered if the mud on his feet would function as a skin treatment and soften his heels. They always seemed to get dry and cracked.

When they reached the corner of the building that led into the parking deck, Steve threw his hand out in front of Scott, interrupting Scott's contemplation of the hydrating properties of mud.

"What the hell?" Scott yelled, though the pelting rain drowned out his voice. Scott knocked into Steve's arm, careened backward, and fell flat on his butt in the mud. "Oh my god, Steve!" Scott cried. "I'll be at the dry cleaner's for six hours tomorrow! I sure hope you did that for a good reason."

Steve turned his head and looked down at Scott.

"Shh!" Steve hissed. "I think I see something."

Scott scrambled to his feet, nearly sliding to the ground again.

"Be very quiet," Steve told Scott and ushered him toward the corner of the building.

Both men peered around the brick building and into the parking deck. About halfway across the first level, they could see a woman's back. The woman was leaning down into a car window, and she appeared to be yelling.

"I think that's the employee parking area," Steve said, pointing to a sign that said, "Employees Only, visitor parking levels 2—6."

"Who is that woman?" Scott asked. "And what kind of car is that?"

"It looks like one of those Smart car things. Maybe blue or something. It's so tiny. It's even worse than your car, Scott."

"I can't see!" Scott whispered in a loud speaking voice.

"Shh! They'll hear you."

The woman's yelling became loud enough to break through the blanket of rain. A loud clap of thunder boomed, and a streak of lightning turned night into day.

"That looks like Mrs. McGruder!" Steve said. "She's yelling into the car window."

Mrs. McGruder's voice became audible.

"How could you do that, you little bitch! You knew what I'd do. I told you. Bet you're not surprised now, huh? And you can't tell anyone either, or it will be back to auditioning for the Russian State Circus for you. Don't think I didn't look you up!"

A screech of tires sounded as the blue Smart car rocketed backward out of the parking space. Mrs. McGruder jumped back from the window, and the car barreled toward the exit. It was a good thing the parking deck had no arms that raised or lowered, as either the arm or the car would have been summarily destroyed.

Scott and Steve tried to duck behind the bushes as the car flew by them, but they were not fast enough. The driver had to slow down to traverse the small speed bump at the deck's exit and, as she did so, she looked to her left, right at the corner of the building where Scott and Steve stood frozen in place. It was Katerina, the red-haired trapeze artist, and she was glaring at them out of the window of her car. Then she faced forward, and peeled out of the lot and onto the street.

45

MONDAY

"Scott! What the hell are you doing!" Steve exclaimed as he navigated Ida's Ford Expedition around the tight curve and down the ramp from the second level of the parking deck to the first.

"Wow, you must be pretty upset. You said hell," Scott replied, as he undid his belt, lifted his butt off the passenger seat, and pulled down his pants.

"Seriously, Scott! We are not going to drive around with you not wearing pants! What if we get pulled over? If you needed to pee that badly, you should have done it in the bushes."

"Relax, Pants Police," said Scott. "It's not like I'm not wearing boxer shorts. And I have to start getting the mud off the butt of these pants. If I let it set it will never come out. All those detergent commercials that say any stain will come out are full of lies." Scott still had his shoes tied around his neck, socks stuffed inside, so the legs of his pants slipped easily over his ankles and off his feet.

"Well, at least put your seatbelt on," Steve said as they hit the speed bump at the parking deck's exit.

"Okay," Scott said, complying.

They turned out of the civic center parking lot and reached a stoplight. Steve looked around the backseat until he spotted a blanket, which he grabbed and tossed on to Scott's lap.

"And cover yourself. What if we drive by a big truck? They'll see you don't have pants on!" Steve said.

"And it will make their night," said Scott, raising his eyebrows. "My mom is always prepared for emergencies, including those of the stain-removal variety. You saw how she has a blanket in the backseat. I bet she has some of those new detergent wipe thingies in the glove compartment." Scott opened the glove compartment with his right hand and grabbed randomly at things until he pulled out a flat red package.

"A-ha! I was right!" he said, yanking up the adhesive tab on the top of the package and removing what looked like a baby wipe.

Scott patted the wipe onto the rear end of his pants, which he now had draped across the blanket on his lap.

"Do you think this will mess up my pants, Steve?" Scott asked. "These wipes can't be meant for dry-clean-only clothes, but they're all I've got."

"I have no clue," Steve said. "Aside from the ugly suit my mom made me wear to First Communion when I was, like, eight, I've never owned anything dry-clean-only in my life.

Aren't you supposed to call your dad and Agnes?"

"I can't now. Gotta fix the pants."

"Fine," Steve said, pulling into the parking lot of a Waffle House. "I'll do it. You're gonna be obsessed with that til you're done."

"You could just call while we drive, you know," Scott said.

"Yeah, but I don't have my headphones, and I don't want to get in a wreck with you not wearing pants. You know there's that old wisdom about always wearing clean underwear in case you get in an accident. It means you should wear pants too."

"Who said you should wear clean underwear in case you get in an accident? The last thing I care about if I'm in an accident is how my underwear looks. Unless one of the paramedics is Sam Elliot. That man never ages." Scott sighed.

Steve rolled his eyes.

"It's old wisdom from way before you, or I, or even Sam Elliot was born. I read it in the *Farmer's Almanac*."

"You say I have excessive grooming rituals, Steve. Which is weirder, wanting to have good hair or constantly reading the *Farmer's Almanac*? Soon you'll be wanting to plant yams in our garden."

Shaking his head, Steve pulled his phone from his pocket, scrolled through some numbers and hit the call button. After about five rings, Delbert answered.

"Hi, Delbert, it's Steve. Scott would call you, but he's busy wiping his butt in the car. No, he can explain that to you later."

Scott scowled at Steve.

"It's a long story, but some stuff happened at the circus and Ida and Oleen are at the hospital with a detective. We told them you and Gary would meet them there. We have to go home because Jenny's at our house and she'll be worried. She was there earlier.

"No, at the circus. With another detective. It's a long story. Just call or text Ida and she can tell you which hospital to go to. Oleen may have two broken wrists. They'll have to explain when you get there. Yeah, you need to take Gary too. And Agnes. You should call her because she'll want to go to the hospital with you. No, of course it's not too late. You know Agnes never sleeps."

Steve hung up. As Steve turned into the enclave of townhouses in which he and Scott lived, Scott's phone pinged with a text.

"It's your phone, Scott. It's in your pants. Maybe it's Sam Elliot."

"I'll look at it in the house," said Scott.

After much arguing, Scott agreed to pull his Mini Cooper out of the townhouse's garage so Steve could pull Ida's Expedition in.

"The neighbors don't want a car hanging out into the street, Scott," Steve said, "And our driveway is so tiny that your car is, like, the only car in the world that won't hang over the edge. Your mom's car will fit just fine in the garage next to mine."

"You forgot the Smart car," Scott said, having stopped wiping the butt of his pants.

"Huh?"

"The car that crazy red-haired woman was driving when she gave us the stare of death."

"Oh yeah," said Steve. "That would fit too, but I'm not too inclined to invite her over. She seems like someone who'd kill you while you were in the shower like in that scene in *Psycho*."

"That, my dear, we can agree on!" Scott said.

Scott handed Steve his pants and picked up the red plaid blanket Steve had found on Ida's backseat. Scott lifted his butt off the seat and wrapped the blanket around his waist like a towel. It fell nearly to his ankles.

"That's really attractive," Steve said. "You should wear it to court."

"Just open the garage," said Scott.

Steve fumbled in his pocket for the garage remote, raising the door for Scott. A few minutes later, Ida's car sat in the garage next to Steve's Toyota Camry, and Scott's Mini Cooper sat outside the closed garage door in the driveway, not hanging out into the street.

"We should have gone in through the door in the garage," Scott said, gesturing to the steep front steps. "How am I gonna climb all those steps in my skirt?"

"Women do it all the time in skirts *and* heels," Steve said. "I even saw Jenny do it once. Buck up, Scott."

Scott held onto the porch railing, pulling himself up as though fighting his way to the top of a hill in the midst of a monsoon. He could only move each leg forward a little bit at a time or the blanket was likely to come undone at the waist and fall off, exposing his boxer shorts to all the nonexistent people standing on the dark, empty street. Scott didn't particularly care if this happened, but he was sure Steve would, so he shuffled and pulled himself up the steps like he was 106 years old.

When he and Steve reached the front door, Scott fumbled in the pocket of his pants for his phone. It was much harder to find your phone in the pocket of your pants when you weren't wearing said pants, Scott thought as Steve held his pants out to him. Scott removed the phone from the pocket and touched the screen several times.

"It's Agnes," he said. "Delbert and Gary are going to pick her up and take her to the hospital with them. That's good because they could use a chaperone."

Scott rummaged in his pants' pocket for his keys but, before he could grab them, the door opened and an excited female voice said,

"There you are! I was wondering what was taking so long. I'm so glad you're not dead! I made some pasta! Come in!"

Scott stumbled through the door, nearly tripping on the bottom of his skirt. He collapsed on the sofa.

"Thanks, Jenny!" Steve said. "I'm starving. Even though I shouldn't be hungry after sitting under a dead body for over an hour."

Jenny stared at him with wide eyes.

"I hope the dead body and the fact that you're holding Scott's pants aren't related."

"Shut up, Jenny!" Scott called.

Scott stood up from the couch and walked toward the kitchen.

"Nice skirt," Jenny said.

"I gotta take a shower," said Scott. "Gotta wash the dead guy outta my hair."

Scott pulled himself up the stairs holding onto the railing. Once Scott reached the top of the stairs, Steve and Jenny heard a thud.

"Ow!" yelled Scott. "I'm never wearing a skirt again."

"I'll explain," Steve said, ignoring Scott's cry. "Let's get some food and sit on the couch. I can't spend any more time in a hard chair, and I can't do anything until I eat something, either."

"You sit, I'll get it," Jenny said, going to the kitchen and heaping the vegetarian pasta from the pot on the stove into two bowls, handing one to Steve as she sat down next to him on the sofa.

"Tell me what happened," she said.

PART IV

46

MONDAY

Delbert sat in the lounge chair in the garage trying to muster up the energy to stand. He'd been sleeping like a dead person until Steve called to tell him that Ida and Oleen were at the hospital. He had no idea what could have happened that Oleen had broken wrists and that Ida and Oleen were with a police detective, but it couldn't be anything crappier than what had happened during the rest of this weekend. Delbert had called Gary to tell him. He would have just texted, but Gary might have been asleep, and if he didn't show up at the hospital with Gary in tow he was sure he'd be in big trouble with everyone.

Delbert knew he shouldn't be annoyed he had to go to the hospital to check on his wife and her sister. He wasn't upset that they'd gotten themselves into a mess or anything. He wasn't even bothered that it was late as hell, nor that he was supposed to be up early the next morning. He was mostly aggravated that he had to pick up Gary and drive him to the hospital too. Agnes he didn't mind driving, it was Gary he was dreading, and since Gary was weird about paying parking fees, there was no way Gary would agree to drive separately.

Delbert remembered the time he and Gary had taken Jenny and Janie to the art museum. The girls must have been teenagers then, and both had wanted to see some art exhibit, probably because it had some paintings of naked men in it. It had been raining that day, but there was parking right on the street in front of the museum, which was just about as close to a miraculous occurrence as Delbert had ever seen. There had been a parking guy down on the street, collecting money because the fee was so high there was no way anyone would have had that much change to put in the parking meter. Parking was $20, which Delbert was glad to fork over to avoid having to trudge around Downtown in the rain. Gary had pitched a fit about the cost, even though he wasn't the one paying. Delbert had paid the fee, and he and the girls had left Gary in the car. After a few minutes, Gary had appeared next to them inside the museum in the ticket line, arms crossed over his chest. Delbert just couldn't deal with that today.

Delbert managed to drag himself into the house to throw on some jeans and a t-shirt over his boxer shorts. It was so hot in the garage with the door closed that he hadn't even been wearing a shirt. He bet he smelled bad, but he doubted he'd smell any worse than some of the patients at the hospital, and at least no one would be forced to give him a sponge bath to get rid of the stench.

Delbert put on a pair of tennis shoes and added a black sweat jacket with a hood to his ensemble since it was raining and he didn't want to get wet. He texted Gary to let him know to be outside in the next five minutes and ready to leave. Gary responded with a thumbs up, the stupidest emoji in existence in the world of incredibly stupid emojis that were available to Delbert on his phone. Gary hadn't even bothered to select a skin tone for the thumb. It was just yellow. What an idiot.

Delbert returned to the garage, opening the garage door and starting his truck. It was a good thing his enormous truck had two rows of seats so Agnes could come with them. No way did Delbert want to be stuck alone with Gary for a thirty-minute drive. Gary might cry the whole time and accuse Delbert of "denying their love," and Delbert didn't have any pillows in the backseat for Gary to cry into. Delbert supposed that, maybe, in the back of his mind, he did have an inkling that denying their love was exactly what he was doing, but ignoring that inkling was working quite well for him for the time being.

Delbert backed the car out of the garage, and down the driveway. The garage door whirred shut as the truck moved away from it. He pulled the truck onto the street and then up into Gary and Oleen's driveway. Gary wouldn't be coming anywhere near his garage if Delbert could help it. Delbert waited a couple of minutes and, not seeing Gary on the porch, he honked his horn twice. Gary opened the front door of the house and hurried down the steps through the rain. He opened the front passenger door of the truck and started to climb in. Delbert noticed that Gary too was wearing a black sweat jacket.

"Get in the back," Delbert growled, in the manner of a surly bridge-guarding troll.

"Huh?" said Gary.

"Get in the back. We're picking your mom up, and she gets to ride in the front. She's only a few blocks away."

"But Mom doesn't even like to ride in the front," said Gary.

"She does tonight," Delbert said. "It's Ladies' Night in the truck tonight."

Gary climbed into the backseat, scooting over until he was right behind Delbert.

"Don't sit right behind me, Gary. It's creepy. Like you're the man with that hook for a hand from that old urban legend. And in that story it was raining like it is tonight."

Gary reached around the seat and touched Delbert's arm.

"Jeez, Gary!" Delbert said.

Having his arm grabbed and then looking in the rearview mirror and not seeing anyone made Delbert jumpy.

"We have to talk about this sometime, Delbert," said Gary. "You can't deny it forever."

Delbert threw the truck into reverse and peeled down the driveway like someone from one of the Fast & Furious movies. *The Tokyo Drift* one, he decided. The night he had seen that movie had not been a fun night. He'd convinced Ida to go with him. She was so out of it as far as the names of TV shows and movies were concerned that she'd missed the first part of the title altogether. She'd thought the movie was just called "Tokyo Drift," and had agreed to see it because she had thought it was about the rise and fall of geisha culture in Japan. Delbert had failed to correct this assumption because he didn't want to go to the movie alone, Gary was out of town for work, and Scott would never want to see a movie like that. He should have asked Mike, he guessed, but hindsight always seemed to be 20/20. Delbert had done a lot of yard work that weekend and if he remembered correctly, he had even folded all the laundry.

"Jesus, Gary! Just move over so I can at least see you," Delbert said.

Gary scooted over to the passenger side and put on his seatbelt.

"You don't have to drive like a maniac, Delbert! You may slam my head into the window and knock me unconscious, but that isn't going to make me forget the feelings we have between us!"

Sometimes it was very easy to see how Gary's dad could have been crazy, Delbert thought. Jenny had issues, sure, and they probably came from Gary's dad, but at least she was dealing with them. And everyone had always known something was off with Jenny. It had always been obvious she didn't act the way she did on purpose. She just hadn't ever seemed to be able to help it, at least not until the past half year. But Gary... Sometimes Gary acted as nuts as a three-dollar bill, and it was clearly by choice.

Delbert answered Gary's assertion about the feelings between them by gripping the steering wheel as though he were hanging from a rafter one hundred stories above New York City like in one of those old photos from when the Empire State Building was being built. Delbert could see Gary in the rearview mirror, and Gary was staring out the window with an angry intensity that was greater than or equal to the anger he had exhibited during the visit to the art museum all those years ago.

"Just go get Mom," Gary spat.

"I think I will," said Delbert, shifting the truck into drive and screeching off down the street.

47

MONDAY

"Come on!" Agnes said to the dark-skinned woman at the check-in window of the emergency room. "Why can't all three of us go back there?"

Agnes gestured to Gary and Delbert, who stood behind her in their matching black sweat jackets and matching expressions of general disagreeableness.

"Ma'am, she's just having her vital signs checked right now, her twin is back there, and that detective. Between you and me, that detective is looking like a snack, but there isn't room for anyone else."

Agnes raised her eyebrows, filing away the phrase "looking like a snack" for future use. She'd have to remember to ask Scott about it.

"Well," Agnes said, "Isn't that all the more reason to let us back there? Those two are gay you know." Agnes gestured to Delbert and Gary again. "And I'm never too old to appreciate a nice-looking man. We'll all enjoy it."

The woman at the window paused for a moment, looking down at some papers. She looked up at Agnes.

"Let me see if I can have her moved to an exam room. We

don't often do this, but you all are an interesting group. It might make a good show for all of us here. Night shifts are either really interesting or horribly boring. You got us on a boring night." The check-in woman lowered her voice to a whisper, "And just who ARE those two?" she asked. "Are they the twins' brothers?"

Agnes cupped her hand over her mouth to speak toward the check-in woman's ear.

"No," she said. "Those two are the twins' *husbands!*"

"Oh well then, I'm sure we can make arrangements. Between this situation and that fine-looking man back there, you all just got priority seating."

The woman walked out from behind the check-in station and down the hall to a curtained area. Agnes heard murmuring and saw a blonde-haired nurse wearing pink scrubs covered in cats move out from behind the curtain. Behind the nurse came Oleen, and then Ida. Ida was dressed in some bright-pink flowing outfit that likely glowed in the dark. Behind Ida was the police detective that, Agnes had to admit, looked how movie stars used to look in the 1930s and 40s before they started doing cocaine and throwing telephones at people in hotel rooms.

The woman from the check-in desk motioned for Agnes to follow, and she, Delbert, and Gary did.

The check-in desk woman led them to an exam room, then left to return to her post at the check-in station. This exam room was much larger than any emergency room exam room Agnes had ever seen. It looked like two rooms joined together to make one.

The blonde-haired nurse noticed Agnes staring around the room and said, "This is where we bring VIP patients. You know, pro baseball and football players, and stars who are here filming movies. It keeps them away from the nosy folks in the waiting room."

Agnes wasn't sure being VIPs in the emergency room was such a good thing.

Ida helped Oleen onto the exam table, then climbed up and sat next to her sister. A huge fluorescent-pink t-shirt, identical to the one Ida had on was tied into a makeshift sling around Oleen's neck, holding up her right wrist. Her left wrist was bandaged and held up by a real sling. Agnes looked from Oleen's sling to Ida's shirt. The shirt was so ill-fitting that it billowed around Ida like an open parachute as it reached terminal velocity during a skydive.

Gary and Delbert, in their jeans, tennis shoes, and matching black sweat jackets, looked like they were ready to put on ski masks and rob a bank. Agnes, carrying a large white leather tote, and wearing white Capri pants, blue ballet flats, and a matching blue-flowered sweater set looked like she was on her way to attend the Annual Easter Egg Roll on the White House lawn. She could see why they all needed to be hidden back here in this VIP room. Except for the detective. He should be on view for all to see.

His shiny black hair fell just above his ears, and his bright-green eyes made her think of one of those elf people in the *Lord of the Rings* movies. His shirt and tie contrasted nicely against his tanned skin, and she could tell he was quite genetically blessed in all areas of his appearance, if his muscular forearms were any indication. Agnes noticed he had a gun strapped to his waist. Agnes would never, ever own a gun or even want to shoot one, but, for reasons of which she wasn't sure, that gun looked quite nice hitched to that detective's waistband.

Agnes reached into her purse and absently grabbed a piece of paper. She looked down to see that the paper was an ad for a local arborist service. She had removed that paper from her mailbox flag earlier that very day. The arborist service distributed these ads to every mailbox in the neighborhood at least three times a week. Using all that paper, they had to be killing more trees than they were saving.

Agnes folded the piece of paper in half and began to fan herself with it.

"There's not good air circulation in this room," she said. "It's getting hot in here."

The detective was the kind of man who sucked all the air from any room he entered. Agnes sort of wanted to run away from him because he was so attractive. She was sure it was evident from her pink cheeks and sudden need to fan herself that his looks had affected her. She felt like she was standing naked behind the podium at the monthly homeowners' meeting. Agnes looked around the room and noticed both Ida and Oleen playing with their wedding rings, and whispering to each other. Agnes wondered how Oleen, with two messed-up wrists, was even managing to play with her wedding ring. Then Agnes noticed the contorted expression on Oleen's face and Ida's bright-red cheeks and Agnes decided they must be using their rings as a way to keep themselves from looking at the gun attached to that detective's waistband.

Delbert shifted his weight from one foot to the other, looking anywhere but at the detective. Even the nurse became intent on searching through the cabinet for a box of rubber gloves.

But Gary, well, Gary sure was staring at the detective. He was staring at the man the way he looked at a full box of Ho Hos: with longing and also shame. In the case of the Ho Hos, the shame was because Gary knew he was going to eat the entire box in a single sitting. In the case of the detective, the shame was because Gary felt like everyone in the world now knew his secret.

"Gary!" Agnes called, as the detective took in Gary's mustache and wide, staring eyes.

"Huh?" Gary said, turning toward his mother.

"Let's see if we can find out what's going on with Oleen's wrists. I hope she won't need surgery like your Uncle David did that time he fell off that donkey."

"Why don't you all sit down," the blonde-haired nurse said, motioning to several mismatched chairs that sat against the wall of the room opposite the exam table.

Agnes, Gary, and Delbert all took seats.

"You too, detective," the nurse said, holding the box of rubber gloves she had liberated from the depths of the cabinet.

On the word detective, the nurse motioned to the chair next to Delbert with the hand that held the box of gloves, swinging the box in one fluid movement. Through the open top of the box, a cascade of rubber fingers and hands came flying out like bats tearing out of a cave at dusk.

"Oops," the nurse said.

"Here, I'll get them," said the detective.

He bent over, his backside facing the row of mismatched chairs, his rear end positioned right in front of Gary's face. Gary stared, mesmerized, and Agnes saw Oleen watching Gary as he gazed at the detective's butt.

As the detective stood up, tossing the last rubber glove into a small trash can the nurse was holding out to him, Agnes saw Oleen whisper something into Ida's ear, and both women glared at Gary as though if they stared hard enough and with enough hatred, Gary would suddenly burst into flames.

This was bad. This was very, very bad.

48

MONDAY

T he detective sat down in the chair to Delbert's left, then turned toward Delbert.

"Hi," he said. "My name's Andrew Davenport, but you can call me Drew. I'm the detective in charge of the case."

"He said we can call him Detective Drew," Ida said, giggling like a twelve-year-old girl staring at a photo of a young Scott Baio in *Tiger Beat* magazine.

"Detective Drew" held out his hand to Delbert, which Delbert shook harder than was necessary.

Delbert hoped the detective couldn't tell how sweaty his palms were.

"I'm Delbert," Delbert said. "Delbert McNair. I'm Ida's husband."

Then Detective Drew leaned across Delbert and repeated the introduction to Gary. Gary looked scared, but took Detective Drew's hand and, after making contact, pulled his hand away like he'd been given an electric shock. As Detective Drew encroached on Delbert's personal space, Delbert leaned as far back into his chair as possible, even tipping the chair's front legs off the floor in an effort not to make any bodily contact with the man.

"So, Gary," Detective Drew asked, "I'm guessing you're Oleen's husband?"

"Um, yes," Gary said.

"And you must be Agnes, Gary's mother," Detective Drew called down the row of chairs to Agnes. "Ida and Oleen have been telling me about you. All good things."

Agnes waved at the detective.

"I'd get up and shake your hand," she said, "but I'm not sure I'd make it back to my chair. It's so late, and I'm kind of tired. I might end up having to stay over there and sit in your lap."

Oh my god! Agnes felt her cheeks flaming. Why the hell had she said that? She tried to pretend she wasn't in the room anymore as Detective Drew laughed.

"I have bony knees," he said. "I doubt you'd be comfortable."

To Agnes's immense relief, right at that moment, a woman in a white lab coat walked in, calling the attention away from Agnes and the waterfall of shame that had overtaken her, and which she was sure was visible to others.

The woman, who had fair skin, dark auburn hair, brown eyes, and a dusting of freckles across her nose said, "Hi, I'm Doctor Delaney and I'm responsible for Mrs. Johnson's care this evening."

Agnes eyed the doctor. Dr. Delaney didn't look like she was any older than twenty-four, which couldn't be possible, could it? Was she some female version of Doogie Howser, M.D.? As this woman aged she would be the luckiest person in the world. Unless she started drinking heavily, or something like that. Then she'd begin to look haggard, but then she wouldn't be a doctor anymore, either. At least, Agnes hoped not.

"We need to take you away for some x-rays, Mrs. Johnson,"

Dr. Delaney said, breaking into Agnes's thoughts about the doctor's age.

Her attention brought back to the present, Agnes remembered the comment she had just made to Detective Drew and wished she could slide off her chair like one of those Salvador Dalí clocks, and then across the room and down into the heating and air return vent.

"Lisa," Dr. Delaney said to the blonde nurse, "would you please escort Mrs. Johnson down to Radiology? Take her in this wheelchair, please. I'm sure walking isn't easy with two injured and painful wrists."

On any other day, Oleen wouldn't have been caught dead in a wheelchair, or in any other type of wheeled contraption designed to transport old or sick people anywhere. Oleen went to the grocery store on Senior Wednesdays purely for the ten percent discount, and those old people in those motorized chairs always made her so mad. Half of them didn't even need the chairs and were just lazy, and all of them blocked the aisles like they thought they were ghosts other shoppers could pass right through. It made Oleen want to get into a motorized shopping cart herself and mow down anyone in her path in the food shopping equivalent of road rage. Or would you call that aisle rage?

Oleen sighed, too tired and in too much pain to care anymore. She sat down in the wheelchair without any fuss. She was glad the wheelchair wasn't motorized because, if it were, right now she would use it as a battering ram to slam her husband's chair against the wall of the exam room. Preferably with him still sitting in it. Then she would back over him a couple of times for good measure.

Lisa wheeled Oleen out of the room for x-rays, and Dr. Delaney left promising to be back in a few minutes.

Delbert asked, "So what happened here? Why does Oleen

having broken wrists require a detective as an escort to the hospital?"

"Well, dear," said Ida, "Oleen's left wrist was broken when the dead man landed on it."

"What?" Delbert, Gary, and Agnes all cried at the same time.

"Yes, his name was, uh, is, Sergei. The poor man fell on us during the trapeze act. I think he was already dead, though, so at least that's a positive."

Ida was still sitting on the exam table. Delbert, Gary, and Agnes all stared at her. Detective Drew did not stare. Instead, he stood up and walked the three or four feet from his chair to the exam table. He pulled a rolling stool out from under a small desk next to the table, sat down on it, and turned himself around to face the chairs against the wall.

"Ida," he said, looking at Delbert, Gary, and Agnes. "I'm going to ask you not to go into too much detail as I still have a couple of questions to ask you and your sister before you leave. If you don't mind, I'll give your family a condensed version of the story."

Detective Drew looked at Ida. She nodded.

"Ida, Oleen, Scott, and Steve were sitting in the front row of the French—Canadian circus. At the end of the trapeze act, a man suddenly fell, likely from the rafters, and landed across their four seats. He appeared to already be dead when he fell, though I don't know that for sure. We had to rule them all out as suspects, I mean, assuming foul play was involved, and we don't have any reason to believe that any of them were involved in this incident. Oleen's wrist was injured when the man landed on it."

Delbert and Gary stared at Ida, mouths opening and closing, trying and failing to form words.

"Why, that's horrible!" Agnes said.

"It was pretty horrible," Ida said. "But we sat there for so long we kind of got used to him lying across our laps. Like when Louie curls up in your lap, Agnes, and you forget he's there and you stand up and dump him off, and he runs away. Only Sergei was too heavy to dump off. And if he'd jumped down and run away, I'd be here in the morgue instead of in this room because I would have had a heart attack. You all know how I'm not fond of those zombie movies."

Detective Drew tried to cover his laugh by coughing.

"You were sitting under a dead person, Ida?" asked Delbert. "Are you okay? Do we need to get you someone to talk to?"

"I'm fine, dear," Ida said, waving her hand in dismissal of the question. "I don't need to talk to anyone, except this young man here when he asks us the rest of his questions."

Ida gestured toward Detective Drew and stared straight into Delbert's eyes.

"After all, lying under a dead person is only the SECOND worst thing to happen to me in the past couple of days."

49

MONDAY

W hen Lisa wheeled Oleen back into the exam room, Detective Drew was explaining that neither Scott nor Steve had been injured and that Ida's injuries had been minor.

It was too bad the same couldn't be said for Ida's blouse. She didn't even have it anymore. One of the CSTs had taken it away as evidence. Maybe crime labs had some special blood stain remover. Ida would have to remember to ask someone about that.

Oleen shimmied back onto the exam table with help from Lisa, and Lisa said, "Dr. Delaney will be back in a few minutes. She's consulting with the radiologist. I'll be back with her. I need to check on another patient right now."

After Lisa had exited the room, Ida noticed that Oleen's left wrist was no longer bandaged or in a sling, and that the pink t-shirt that had been holding up her right wrist was now draped over her left shoulder. Oleen carefully moved her right hand up to her left shoulder and grasped the shirt. With great effort, she tossed the shirt at Gary. It landed two feet in front of his chair.

"Ow! Ow! Ow!" Oleen cried.

"Why did you do that, Oleen?" Ida asked. "If that one wasn't broken it is now!"

"It hurts less than the left one!" Oleen said. "That one's broken, I think. I bet this one is just sprained."

"What do you want me to do with this shirt, Oleen?" asked Gary. He leaned forward and picked the huge, fluorescent pink t-shirt up off the floor.

Oleen narrowed her eyes at Gary.

"I thought you could sleep in it. You know, as a *nightshirt*."

Oleen looked straight at Detective Drew when she said nightshirt.

Looking back at Gary she said, "Maybe you can wear some sweatpants under it since that seems to be your new style. Or maybe some tights like that Rainbow Bright character wore. Jenny loved her, but god she was annoying. The shirt and the tights would be the perfect colors on you."

Gary coughed and pulled the sleeve of the pink shirt up to his eyes to wipe away the tears that had started to rush out of them.

Detective Drew looked around the room, but he was smart enough not to light a match while standing next to a powder keg.

Delbert grabbed a pamphlet out of an acrylic display container that hung on the wall just to the left of the chair Detective Drew had sat in earlier. The display held a variety of medical pamphlets. The front of the pamphlet Delbert grabbed said "Understanding Your Tracheotomy." Delbert opened the pamphlet and studied it the way Ida had often seen him study automotive manuals.

"Hand me one," Gary said to Delbert.

Without looking up from his pamphlet, Delbert grabbed another pamphlet from the wall and handed it to Gary. "Menopause and You," the front of the pamphlet said.

Looking over Gary's shoulder and reading the title of the

pamphlet, Agnes said, "Give that one to me, Gary. Oleen, Ida and I have been talking a lot about hot flashes lately. I want to see what it says."

Gary rolled his eyes and sighed, handing his mother the pamphlet.

Gary nudged Delbert with his elbow.

"Another one," he said.

"Here, I'm done with this one," Delbert said, handing "Understanding Your Tracheotomy" to Gary.

Delbert grabbed another pamphlet from the display and was settling in to read "Psoriasis: Fact and Fiction," when Dr. Delaney returned with Lisa. Lisa held a big manila envelope out of which she pulled a large x-ray film. She placed the film on the light board that was attached to the wall over the desk from under which Detective Drew had gotten his stool. Dr. Delaney turned the light board on, and a black-and-white image of a skeletal wrist appeared on the screen.

Delbert, Gary, and Agnes looked up from their pamphlets. Ida and Oleen turned toward the light board, and Detective Drew spun around on his stool to face the doctor.

"This," Dr. Delaney said, pointing to the light board, "Is Mrs. Johnson's right wrist. As you can see, there are no broken bones." Dr. Delaney gestured up and down the length of the image. This wrist just has a bad sprain and will need to be bandaged and possibly splinted for a short time. We'll see how it feels once it's wrapped up."

Dr. Delaney nodded at Lisa. Lisa put the first x-ray film back into the envelope and removed the second, placing it on the light board. Another image of a skeletal wrist appeared, although this one didn't look quite right.

"This is your left wrist, Mrs. Johnson," Dr. Delaney said, gesturing to the light board. "This wrist is broken. But I do have some good news. It's not a complicated fracture, and you won't need surgery. You've broken the larger of the two bones in your forearm, as you can see here. This type of fracture is the most common type of broken bone we see. It doesn't appear to be out of position so I won't have to reset it. We have to give anesthesia for that."

Oleen winced.

"Today we're going to put a splint on it, which you'll wear for about a week while we wait for the swelling to go down. Then we'll put on a cast, which you'll wear for about eight weeks while we wait for it to heal. I'm going to refer you to an orthopedist for follow-up visits. He can put on your cast and do additional x-rays when you go back. And if you start to have any other pain or more swelling he can also do an MRI if needed. Then you'll see him for the remainder of your treatment, and he may possibly refer you for physical therapy."

Eight weeks? Oleen wasn't too happy about spending eight weeks with a cast on one wrist and a splint on the other. Maybe she could use them to pummel Gary on the head.

"How long does she have to wear the splint for the sprain?" Ida asked.

"Maybe a week or two," said Dr. Delaney. "She'll need to ice it, rest it, elevate it—

I'll give you a full set of instructions. She may need some help with things like showering and putting on makeup for a while. Are you right or left-handed, Mrs. Johnson?" Dr. Delaney asked.

"Right," Oleen said.

"Well, that's fortunate. You may not need as much help then."

Ida and Agnes looked at each other.

"She'll be staying with me," Agnes said. "Oleen, Ida, and I will be staying at my house, and Ida and I will take good care of her."

Dr. Delaney, Lisa, and Detective Drew all eyed Delbert and Gary, but none of them said anything.

"Does anyone have any more questions before we fix Mrs. Johnson up?" asked Dr. Delaney.

"Yeah," said Gary. "I thought you showed all your x-rays on screens through computers now. That's how it looked in all the other rooms. I sort of peeked into some as we walked by."

"This room hasn't been updated yet," Lisa answered. "It's not used very often, so it's the last to get the upgrades."

"I have a question," said Delbert. "Oleen, if your left wrist is broken because the guy fell on it, is that what happened to your right wrist too?"

Ida answered for her sister. "No, dear, she sprained her right wrist because she was peeking at some people through a potted tree and it fell over with her on top of it."

"Wha—" Delbert started to say, but Detective Drew interrupted him.

"Let's get Oleen fixed up," he said to Dr. Delaney and Lisa, "If it's okay with you two, Ida and I will stay while you treat Oleen, and I'll ask Oleen and Ida my last couple of questions. They're not too personal or specific, so it should be fine. Maybe everyone else can wait out in the waiting room until we're done in here."

"Fine with me," said Dr. Delaney.

"They'll see you in a little bit, guys," Detective Drew said, motioning to Delbert, Gary, and Agnes.

The trio stood up and filed out of the exam room. The psoriasis pamphlet floated out of Delbert's hand and down to the floor, landing right next to Detective Drew's shoe.

50

MONDAY

Agnes stood outside the automatic doors to the emergency room. It was hot and muggy, as it usually was after a summer thunderstorm. Agnes fanned herself with the menopause pamphlet as she looked back into the waiting room where Gary and Delbert sat, each slumped down in chairs on opposite sides of the room. They were lucky the emergency room wasn't crowded, or they wouldn't have such an array of seating options.

Agnes looked at the clock on her phone. 2:45 a.m. Good god. Agnes never slept past 7 a.m., but she didn't see any way around sleeping late tomorrow unless she went to the gas station on the way home and got one of those Five-Hour energy drinks. Then she might be able to get up at 7 and stay awake all day long.

She had always assumed those drinks were some sort of sexual aid because of the way their packaging looked. Then, one day she had gone to the gas station with Scott to fill up that tiny car of his. As they had waited in line inside the gas station to buy Agnes a Diet Coke and Scott chocolate milk, Scott had noticed Agnes eyeing the Five-Hour Energy drink display.

"Those taste pretty bad," Scott had said. "I only use them when I have to drive long distances by myself. You know, to stay awake."

Not seeing how one could need a sexual aid while taking a road trip by himself, Agnes had discerned that the drinks simply contained massive quantities of caffeine, and were supposed to keep you from falling asleep. She had chuckled.

"I know," Scott had said to her, "I've always thought they looked like some weird sex thing too. Horrible, horrible packaging."

Agnes looked up at the sky, where the clouds were beginning to dissipate, and a few stars were now visible. Then she looked back through the emergency room doors. Ida, Oleen, and Detective Drew were approaching the exit. Oleen had matching splints on her wrists. She stepped outside and held them up for Agnes to see.

"Very fashionable, honey," said Agnes.

"Thank you for your help tonight, ladies," Detective Drew said, nodding at all three of them. "I'll be in touch."

He walked down the sidewalk to his Ford Explorer, got in, and drove out of the emergency room parking lot.

"I wouldn't mind if he kept in touch!" Oleen said, laughing and bumping her sister with her hip.

"Oh please, Oleen! That man is half your age!"

"Well, it appears I'm about to be single again," Oleen said. "And it could happen. I mean, look at Michael Douglas and Catherine Zeta-Jones. I'm pretty sure Catherine has to exhume him from a coffin every morning, and he still managed to snag a younger, very attractive partner."

"I'm not so sure she's all that young anymore, dear," Ida said. "He's just old as dirt. It's kind of like if Steve stood next to Shaquille O'Neal. Steve's, what? Six foot two? He's pretty tall. But next to someone over a foot taller, Steve would look like a midget. That's how it is with Michael and Catherine. Since he's about six hundred years old, he makes her look twenty-four."

Oleen stuck her tongue out at Ida, then looked back into the emergency room waiting area, where Delbert and Gary still sat in their opposing chairs. Gary now had his hood pulled over his head. He was crying. Maybe she had been too hard on him.

Oleen turned back to Ida and Agnes.

"What are we going to do?" she asked them.

"About what?" Agnes said.

"You said you rode over here with Delbert and Gary in Delbert's truck," Oleen said. "We don't have a car. We came here with the detective. Scott and Steve have Ida's car."

"That's right!" Ida said. "Well, that's inconvenient."

"It may be irritating for you two, but if Gary sits up front with Delbert, the three of us could squeeze into the back," said Agnes. "They can drop us off at my house."

"Or we could get one of those cars," Ida said. "What's it called? An Uzi?"

Oleen burst out laughing.

"An *Uber*, Ida. An Uzi is a gun. Are you going senile? I guess we could get one of those, though. I have the app on my phone. Mike put it on there in case I ever got stranded somewhere and couldn't reach anyone. He even signed me up and added my credit card and taught me how to use it."

"That was thoughtful of him," said Agnes.

Oleen nodded.

"We can try to ride with them," Ida said, gesturing toward the waiting area. "It's just a half hour. We don't have to talk to them."

Agnes looked inside and saw Delbert and Gary had noticed it was time to go. Each approached the automatic doors from opposite sides of the waiting room. They joined Ida, Oleen, and Agnes on the sidewalk.

"We'll ride with you," Agnes said. "The girls don't have a

car. They rode here with the detective. The three of us will sit in the back. You two can sit in the front. You can drop us off at my house."

Gary and Delbert glared at each other.

An ambulance pulled up and parked next to the entrance, though it didn't have its flashing lights on. A tall, muscular man wearing a tight white t-shirt and with a completely bald head emerged from the driver's side door. He noticed the group on the sidewalk and jumped slightly.

"Ohmygod!" The bald man said, in a voice three octaves higher than Oleen's. "Is that Delbert and Gary I see? Ohmygod! I was wondering if you two were ever going to come back after your trial week. You did so great in my classes those times you came!"

"Hi, Rick," Delbert mumbled.

"You're an EMT?" Gary asked.

"Well, yeah!" said Rick. "I'm an EMT full time, but I'm also a certified Pilates trainer. I teach classes at Gray's Gym and a couple of other places on my off days. You should totally come back to Gray's! We're about to start a men's rowing team. First, we're going to practice on rowing machines, and then we're actually going to do it in real boats and maybe even compete."

"Great," mumbled Delbert.

"Well, see you guys," said Rick. "I gotta go. Say hi to Scott for me. Tell him thanks for those pointers on my glute workout. Helps with the Pilates." Rick patted both sides of his butt with his hands.

He disappeared through the automatic doors, and Oleen pulled her phone out of her purse. She touched the icon for the Uber app and entered Agnes's address.

51

MONDAY

The Uber picked Agnes, Ida, and Oleen up, and Delbert and Gary were left standing on the sidewalk together.

"Damn that Rick!" said Delbert.

"Well, what did you expect him to do, Delbert?" Gary asked. "It's not like he knows we're married or that nobody knows we're gay."

"We're not gay," said Delbert.

"You need to stop denying it, Delbert, and be a proud gay man. I'm starting to embrace it. It's kind of a relief. Rick was just being friendly. He's very accepting, and you should be happy about that."

"Oh my god, Gary," Delbert said. "I am not gonna be, what did you call it? A proud gay man? Jesus. Next, you're gonna expect me to wave a rainbow flag and join the Village People."

"Well, I think it's quite liberating to stop living a lie."

"The only lie you've stopped living is thinking that night-shirts are ever okay for a man to wear, Gary. Thank god you started wearing sweatpants under them. I've always thought that was bizarre."

"Okay, whatever, Delbert," Gary said. "Just go get your truck so we can go home."

"Fine." Delbert huffed away toward the parking deck, then he turned around and stomped back toward Gary.

"I think you have the ticket," Delbert said.

"That's why you should have listened to me and parked on that side street where they don't charge for parking."

"Just give me the damn ticket," said Delbert.

Gary reached into the pocket of his jeans and extracted a white parking ticket. He handed it to Delbert, who shoved it in the pocket of his sweat jacket and stomped back toward the parking deck.

Gary stood on the sidewalk and looked up at the sky, and then at his phone. It was 3 a.m. He hadn't been up this late in he didn't know how long. Back when they were in college, Delbert and Gary used to stay up talking this late all the time, but he certainly wasn't going to remind Delbert of that.

After a length of time so drawn out that, had Gary been a woman, he could have gestated and birthed a baby, Delbert drove up to the sidewalk in his truck. Gary opened the passenger-side door.

"Get in the back," Delbert said.

Gary crossed his arms as he stood in the open passenger-side door of the truck. "I will not!" he said.

"Then you're not riding in this truck," said Delbert.

Gary climbed into the front seat of the truck and slammed the door.

"I most certainly will not sit in the back, Delbert McNair. I know you're going to keep trying to deny our love, but telling me I have to sit in the back—treating me like a second-class citizen—well, that's just plain mean."

Delbert tore out of the emergency room parking lot before Gary could even get his seatbelt fastened. The truck reached a stoplight, and Gary was able to fasten his seatbelt.

"Okay, okay," Delbert said. "I guess that was kind of mean, Gary. I won't make you ride in the back again."

Delbert patted Gary on the knee, then returned his hand to the steering wheel. "I'm sorry," Delbert said, with a huge sigh.

Gary smiled the rest of the way home.

After they had parked in Delbert's driveway, Delbert rushed from the truck as though fleeing a fast-approaching tsunami. Delbert had shut the front door of his house and turned out the porch light before Gary had even gotten all the way out of the truck. Smiling to himself, Gary walked across the damp grass of his front yard, sat down in the red rocking chair, and looked out at the neighborhood. He didn't feel tired anymore.

∼

Agnes, Ida, and Oleen climbed out of the Uber and stood in Agnes's driveway.

"Thank you!" Oleen called. "I'll leave you a tip."

The driver waved and pulled off down the street.

"How are you going to leave him a tip, Oleen? He's just left. Are you going to fold a ten-dollar bill into a paper airplane and hope it catches up to his car?"

"No, Ida. You can leave a tip in the app. Mike says nobody tips Uber drivers, but I'm going to tip that man. It's so late out it can't be safe. I'm sure his mother is worried about him."

"That man had a lot of tattoos, Oleen," Agnes said. "And he barely fit into the front seat of the car. I don't think his mother has a lot to worry about."

"Well, it's still nice to leave a tip in the app. Leave me alone," Oleen said.

Agnes pulled her keys from her purse and unlocked her front door. Louie greeted her with a loud meow.

"He acts like no one ever feeds him. He just ate before I left for the hospital. He tricked me into giving him a second dinner."

"How did he do that?" Ida asked.

"He wouldn't stop meowing, so I gave him another can of cat food. Then he stopped. You were hungry weren't you, little Louie?" Agnes said, bending toward the orange cat and holding out her hand.

Louie jumped up on his hind legs and rubbed his face on Agnes's fingers.

"I think he's manipulating you, Agnes," said Oleen. "Jenny used to do that when she was little. She'd finish almost all of an ice cream cone and then drop it on the ground, so dumb me would get her a second cone because if I didn't, she wouldn't stop crying. You don't want to go down that road. It took me forever to break her of that habit. She just wanted extra ice cream!"

"Well, he's my baby," Agnes said, sitting down in one of the living room chairs.

Louie jumped into her lap and started purring. Agnes bent her face down toward Louie's, and Louie licked her nose.

"I'm dead on my feet," Oleen said. "I'm going to go get into bed in one of the guest rooms. I don't care if I brush my teeth or even eat. Goodnight."

Oleen walked out of the living room, and Ida heard a door close. Ida sat down in the chair next to Agnes's.

"She must be exhausted," Ida said. "She didn't even turn on the light. She just opened the door and got into bed. I hope she took off her shoes."

"Well, I'm not sure I can sleep right now," Agnes said. "I feel wired and also hungry. Do you want anything to eat, Ida?"

"Yeah, I'm starving," Ida said. "Have you got Cocoa Puffs?"

"Of course," said Agnes. "You know they're my favorite, so I have two boxes. Will you get two of those giant mugs from the cabinet, Ida, and both boxes, and the milk, and some spoons?

Oh, and maybe some paper towels and a couple of bottles of water? I am just fine with eating all the Cocoa Puffs right now. I'm sorry to have you wait on me, but I don't think I can get up."

"Because if you did you'd have to sit in my lap?" Ida asked, laughing.

"I can't believe I said that!" Agnes said. "I wanted to hide behind the exam table."

"He was good-natured about it," said Ida. "I'm sure he gets that a lot, from women young and old. And probably from men like Delbert and Gary."

After making two trips, Ida had gathered the Cocoa Puffs boxes, milk, spoons, mugs, paper towels, and water bottles and set them on the table between the two chairs. She and Agnes each poured themselves some cereal and began eating.

"Okay, Ida, I want to hear all about what happened tonight. As I heard Scott say once, give me the deets."

52

TUESDAY, THE DAY AFTER MEMORIAL DAY

un was streaming through the curtains when Oleen woke up. She had to go to the bathroom. She had dreamed she was in the bathroom about to go, so it was a miracle she had woken up in time. One time she had a dream she was in the bathroom needing to go, and she had wet the bed. And she'd been fifty-five, not five!

Oleen tried to push herself up off the mattress and into a sitting position. The pain that shot through both her wrists when she did this caused the events of last night to come rushing back to her. She had a broken wrist and a sprained wrist, and she was wearing two splints. She looked down at her wrists. She looked like she had two flippers like a seal. Hell, maybe she'd spend the day out in front of her house clapping her splints together and barking. She'd do it right under the living room window so Gary wouldn't be able to watch *Sunday Morning* in peace.

Oh, wait, today was Tuesday. Had Sunday only been two days ago? Holiday weekends always messed her up. She guessed Gary would be going to work today. The man only missed work if he had an illness on par with the Ebola virus, or if there was a particularly exceptional car show in town. Oleen wasn't sure what qualified a car show as exceptional. A car was a car, in her opinion.

Since Oleen couldn't push herself up off the bed, she lay on her back with her legs over the side and her feet touching the floor. Then she slid to the ground as though she were boneless. She landed on her rear end, where she encountered the same problem of not being able to push herself up to a standing position as she had on the bed. Boy, did she have to pee! This wasn't going to be easy.

Oleen spotted the wooden chair behind the small desk across the room. She was only a few feet away. She turned her head toward the chair and lay down on her back with her knees bent. Then she used her feet to push herself backward and shimmy with her behind until her head hit one of the chair legs. The head bump knocked some of the grogginess out of her. She sat up in front of the chair, using only her stomach muscles for leverage, wishing she'd listened to that P90X man on TV all those times he'd urged her to order his Ab-Ripper DVD during late-night commercials.

Now that she was sitting with her back to the chair, Oleen inched around to face the chair. She draped the upper part of her body over the seat of the chair, going up on her knees, and pulling her knees in close to the chair legs. Her butt was sticking out, and she had her face on the chair seat when she heard the door open.

"What in the world? Are you okay, Oleen? I heard a commotion and thought you might have hurt yourself."

"I'm fine, Ida," Oleen said out of the right side of her mouth since the left side of her mouth was pushed up against the seat of the chair.

"What are you doing?" Ida asked.

"Trying to get up and sit in this chair so I can stand and go to the bathroom. I've got to pee so badly I'm about to pee on the floor. Just drag Louie's litter box in here. That will be easier."

"Oleen, why didn't you just sit on the edge of the bed and stand up using only your legs? It might have been hard, but doable."

Oleen considered this question for a moment. Rather than admitting that standing up from a sitting position on the bed would have, indeed, been the more sensible option, she said, "Please get me up and take me to the bathroom."

Ida stood behind Oleen and reached her arms around Oleen's waist.

"Sit up, okay?"

Oleen pulled her upper body back up, so she was now balanced on her knees. Ida put her arms under each of Oleen's arms and lifted.

"Stand up," Ida said.

Oleen was able to stand, and Ida helped her across the hall to the bathroom. Oleen used the bathroom, feeling a relief on par with the relief she had felt many years ago when she had awakened from a dream in which she'd been dancing naked on the stage at Mike and Jenny's high school.

"How are you doing in there, dear?" Ida called through the door.

"Much better!" Oleen called back.

"Do you need any help?" Ida asked.

Oleen was not letting anyone wipe her bottom like she was three years old. She'd just have to figure something else out. Maybe she could use the hairdryer, though she'd have to figure out how to plug it in. With any luck, in the next day or two, she could remove the heinous splint from her right wrist and resume normal bathroom activities. For now, she cleaned up as best as she could, then stood up and opened Agnes's bathroom closet.

Oleen was lucky Agnes had a weird bathroom closet. The

door had been removed, and a colorful curtain blocked the contents from view. It was actually quite an attractive decorative touch. Oleen was going on a hunch when she pushed the curtain back with her splinted right wrist and looked into the closet.

After a couple of seconds of scanning shelves with her eyes, she saw them in the back of the closet. "Incontinence Pads," the box read. Oleen knew it! Agnes was over eighty, after all. The box was already open, which eliminated a considerable obstacle for Oleen. She pulled one pad out. Now using the bathroom wouldn't be an issue. She'd just pee in her pants if it got really bad. Two minutes later, Oleen exited the bathroom feeling much better, and still wearing the nightgown she'd put on last night. It had been lying on the guest bed, and she had been too tired to bother asking if it was okay for her to wear it.

Ida was still standing outside the bathroom door when Oleen exited.

"What time is it?" Oleen asked, yawning.

"10:30," Ida said.

"Wow! I've slept more soundly and for much longer since I found out Gary was gay than I have for the past thirty years. Gary should decide to be gay more often. I don't know what I was doing in there," Oleen said, gesturing across the hall to the guest room. "I don't know why I didn't just stand up from the bed. I guess I wasn't awake yet. What are you wearing, Ida?"

Oleen noticed Ida's outfit, which consisted of the vast fluorescent-pink shirt from last night and a pair of long underwear.

"Isn't it kind of hot for those pants?" Oleen asked.

"It was all Agnes had," Ida said. "She doesn't have any sweatpants or yoga pants, or even leggings. I didn't want to wear those jeans anymore. I ate so many Cocoa Puffs last night I can't even button them. I don't know what Agnes wears for her power walks because she said she didn't have any athletic shorts, either. Maybe she wears Capri pants and a sweater."

Ida and Oleen both laughed.

"I have a pair for you on my bed, and Gary left your shirt on the chair in the exam room last night. I guess he didn't want a pink nightshirt. Let me get them for you. Or you just go in there and change."

Oleen went into Ida's room, and Ida closed the door for her. Oleen changed into the long underwear and the colossal fluorescent-pink t-shirt. She emerged into the living room, in an outfit that exactly matched her sister's. Agnes sat on the sofa in a pair of red Capri pants and a three-quarter-length shirt with red and white stripes. An image of a blue anchor decorated the front of the shirt. Agnes was watching CNN, which was airing coverage about the dead man from the circus, though she had the sound on the TV turned down.

"They say he was already dead and he was strangled," Agnes said. "I guess that can be a consolation to his family. He was Russian, you know. And they said he was probably killed sometime Sunday evening or early Monday morning."

A loud knock on the door, combined with a shouted, "Anybody home? We have alcohol!" caused all three women to look away from the television.

Oleen stood up to get the door, then remembered she wouldn't be able to turn the knob to open it and sat back down. Ida opened the door to find Scott, Jenny, and Janie on Agnes's doorstep. Jenny held two huge takeout bags from the breakfast place a few miles away, and Scott carried a big brown bag which had to have been from a liquor store. He also had a backpack slung over one shoulder.

"I got champagne at 10 a.m.! I'm so glad for capitalism," Scott said. "And it's not the kind that will give you a headache, either! The champagne, not the capitalism, though I guess it's possible to get a headache from either."

Scott pulled three huge bottles of champagne and two big containers of orange juice out of the paper bag and placed them on the dining room table. Then Jenny followed, setting down the takeout bags. Janie came in last and flopped down into a chair, her belly protruding.

Oleen looked at Janie. If Oleen and Janie tried to go out anywhere together, then they'd be entitled to a handicapped parking space. Oleen did need to go to Chico's again soon. Maybe Janie could go with her, and they could park right outside the door.

"Oh, Mom, we drove your car over since we took it home last night. Someone will have to take us home later, though, so please don't get too drunk," Scott said. "Now, everyone get some food and a mimosa, or orange juice if you're pregnant or on meds. We're going to list out the evidence and analyze this crime."

53

TUESDAY

"Well, this is a nice surprise," said Agnes, as she pulled six champagne flutes from one of her kitchen cabinets.

"Janie and Jenny can still have their orange juice in these," Agnes said.

"Someone is bringing me some adult beverages in the hospital as soon as this baby is out," Janie said, rubbing her belly. "That and a sub sandwich with every cold cut known to man."

"Classy," Scott said. "I'll make sure I'm the one to bring it so I can bring you some malt liquor that I'll buy at the gas station. I won't even take it out of the paper bag."

Scott passed mimosas to Agnes, Ida, and Oleen, and made one for himself. He handed Janie and Jenny champagne flutes full of orange juice.

"I thought you were working from home today, dear," Ida said. "Weren't you supposed to be researching a case?"

"Yeah," said Scott. "*This* case. I do have another case to research, but it's just a typical workplace discrimination case, and I had a similar one last month, so a lot of the legal research

I need to do is done. 'Work from home' can have many meanings, Mom. Sometimes it means sleep late and sit on the patio all day with food and beverages. And sometimes it means go to the gym and then sit with my laptop at the Starbucks around the corner and gossip for three hours with the barista about the guys at the gym while pretending to work. Gray's Gym is like its own little *Peyton Place*, you know."

"I never cared for that movie," Agnes said. "So much drama and upheaval."

"Exactly," said Scott, raising his champagne glass to Agnes, who clicked hers against it. "To drama and upheaval."

Agnes shook her head.

"You know, Scott, it's kind of surprising you and Steve ended up together. He's so calm and peaceful, and you're so, well, dramatic," Janie said.

"Steve keeps Scott in check," said Jenny. "I know because he told me. He said he's 'The Scott Whisperer.'"

"He told you that, did he?" asked Scott. "Well, I add excitement to his life. Without me, he'd be bored stiff."

"He told me that too," Jenny said.

Scott smiled and set his champagne glass down on the kitchen table. Then he picked up his bookbag and spirited it into the living room, setting it down on the floor by one of the sofas. Agnes's living room TV hung on the wall over the fireplace.

"Where's the remote?" he asked, pointing to the TV.

"It's in that drawer in the table between the two chairs," said Agnes.

Scott sat down on the sofa, unzipped his bag and pulled out a laptop, two cables, and an Apple TV.

"I have one of those, Scott," Agnes said, pointing to the Apple TV which sat on a shelf beneath her wall-mounted television.

"Really?" Scott asked. "And you know how to work it?"

"Of course I do," Agnes said. "Mike and Jenny went in together and gave it to me for my birthday last year so I can watch all my old movies on Netflix and through that iTunes Store thing. Jenny even programmed my phone to act as a remote control since that damn remote control is so tiny, and I lose it all the time. Mike and Jenny are so good with technology."

Jenny smiled and blushed.

"Well, you don't have *this* Apple TV," Scott said, standing up and unplugging the cables from the back of Agnes's Apple TV.

He moved Agnes's Apple TV into the drawer from which he'd gotten the remote.

"Don't want to get them confused," he said.

Then Scott put his Apple TV in the place where Agnes's had sat a moment ago. He plugged the two cables that Agnes had used on her own device into the back of his Apple TV.

"Guess I don't need my cables," he said. "I didn't expect you to have any."

Scott turned on the television with the remote control, setting the remote next to him on the sofa. The Apple logo appeared on the TV screen as the Apple TV powered on. Then Scott pulled out his laptop, detaching the screen from the keyboard. He pulled a small stylus from the bottom of the screen.

"What in the world is that?" Oleen asked, looking over Scott's shoulder.

"It's called a Surface," said Scott. "It's made by not Apple. You can use it as a tablet or a laptop. It's great for making presentations."

Jenny frowned.

Without looking up, Scott said, "I know, Jenny, I'm usually loyal to Apple, but it's just better than the iPad."

"I'm sorry you are delusional, Scott," said Jenny. "That must be so hard for Steve."

Ignoring Jenny's comment, Scott fiddled with the screen of the tablet.

"Now, usually only Apple products work with the Apple TV. You can project the screen of your phone or iPad, or your laptop up there and stuff," Scott said. "But this guy at the gym, he's in IT and also an excellent hacker. He hacked the OS of both my Apple TV and my Surface, so now I can use them together. Don't ask me how. He just did it for me, and I paid him $200. Took him, like, three minutes."

"That's not possi—" Jenny said, her sentence interrupted by the appearance of Scott's tablet screen on the television.

"Yes it is," Scott wrote with the stylus, and the large red handwritten words appeared on the television.

"The guy who did this for me—he's from Chicago—when he was fourteen, he hacked the city government website and replaced the homepage with New Kids on the Block videos that played on a loop. The city couldn't fix it for about six hours. Sounds hilarious to me, but apparently he ended up doing a lot of community service after that."

"Oh, Scott," Oleen said. "Speaking of that gym, Rick said to tell you thanks for the tips on his glute workout."

"I'm not even going to ask where you met Rick or why you all were talking about his butt," said Scott. "We have work to do right now, but I definitely want to hear later."

"Now, everyone, gather around, get some food and drinks. Sit down. Uncle Scotty has something to show you."

Janie wrinkled her nose at the phrase "Uncle Scotty." Oleen and Ida passed Scott and sat down together on one of the couches.

"What in the world are you two wearing?" asked Scott. "Do you want me to take you to REI for some snow boots and a parka?"

"It's hard to explain, dear," Ida said. "We'll tell you later. Janie, why are you here? Don't you have to work?"

"No, my principal had mercy on me and let me leave as soon as I turned everything in instead of holding me hostage all day. Being pregnant is the greatest get-out-of-jail-free card there is, aside from your kid being sick. I mean, at schools where everyone is sympathetic to that. I know they maybe aren't in other kinds of jobs," Janie said. "And now I don't have to go back until August, but I hope to have this baby the day before school starts and then I can miss the first three months of school for maternity leave."

"Glad you love your job so much, Jane," said Scott.

"You come do my job for one day, Scott," Janie replied. "You wouldn't last an hour."

"And Steve's working?" Agnes asked.

"Yes," said Scott, bouncing his knee up and down. "Now, everyone sit and listen so we can get started. We have a crime to solve here."

Agnes wondered how the group of them was going to solve this crime, but, intrigued, she sat down and remained quiet.

"First, we are going to look at the suspects. We'll make a diagram like they do at the police station. You've probably seen that on *Law and Order* or *CSI* or whatever."

Scott touched his tablet, and seven photos shot up from the bottom of the television screen, portraying Scott, Steve, Ida, Oleen, Agnes, Jenny, and Janie.

"Why do you have Jenny and Janie and me up there, Scott?" Agnes asked. "We weren't even there. And none of the rest of you is even a suspect."

"I didn't want you to feel left out," he answered. "And it was fun picking out pictures of everyone. It's FYE."

"FYE?" Agnes asked

"For your entertainment," Scott said.

"Scott, you are *so* dramatic," Janie said. "I hope one day Steve is canonized."

"Well, he did go to Catholic School, so maybe he will be.

Maybe if he levitates one of the paintings at the gallery or something."

"Sco-ott!" Jenny cried, drawing his name out into two syllables. "How did you even get that picture of me, and why would you use that?"

The picture to which Jenny was referring showed a woman in a black dress wearing a giant pink unicorn head with her ensemble. It looked like it came from a mascot costume. The woman appeared to be dancing.

"It doesn't even show my face!" she said.

"I'm Facebook friends with Leah," Scott said. "I went back a ways through her photos and found this. It's from a Halloween party."

"Yes," Jenny said, hanging her head. "I'm gonna kill Leah. I forgot she put that up there. That was, like, ten years ago! I hope she just forgot it was up there. She knows how anything that reminds me of when I used to drink embarrasses me."

"Well, Leah may have forgotten, but Facebook never forgets," said Scott.

"Scott," said Oleen, "Why are Ida and I eighteen in those photos? Those are our senior yearbook pictures. We have those awful smiles on our faces. We never were good at sitting for portraits."

"Because I went into the archive of that photo site Jenny used to share all those old photos she scanned a few years ago when she found that box in Agnes's attic. And I thought these were funny. That was nice of you, Jenny."

"I'm sure there are some nice ones of you in Zubaz pants, Scott," Jenny said. "I'll have to find them and go see that IT guy at your gym and have him put them on the city's homepage."

"I'm so glad to finally see the maniacal smiles in some old pictures," Janie said. "Good job, Scott."

"Well, I'm quite pleased with my photo," said Agnes, looking at the individual picture of herself on the screen.

It was from Janie's wedding when she'd had her makeup and hair professionally done.

"I like mine too," said Janie. Hers was an individual portrait, also from her wedding.

"I'm not gonna make fun of my grandma or a pregnant lady," Scott said. "I do have some sense of propriety. Maybe not much, I grant you, but some."

"Well, at least we know maybe you were only born out in a barnyard, and not in a barn," said Jenny.

"What is Steve wearing?" Ida asked, looking at the photo of Steve and turning her head to the side trying to figure it out.

"Oh, that's from the same Halloween party where that picture of Jenny was taken. I got it off Leah's Facebook page too. I think he's supposed to be Luigi. You know, from the Nintendo games."

"That's right!" Jenny said. "I remember his costume was a very poor approximation of Luigi. He refused to let me help him with it."

"That was nice of you, Scott," Janie said. "I'm sure he'll be delighted you showed everyone that picture."

"I showed this to him," Scott said, gesturing toward the television. "He thought it was all funny, but he told me not to use that picture of Jenny."

Jenny smiled.

Scott shrugged. He touched the screen again and the seven images faded to black. Then two large images shot up from the bottom of the screen, both surrounded by stars and rainbows.

"Wait!" said Scott, touching the screen of his tablet with the stylus and pausing the presentation. "There's no sound. We need sound."

"Oh sorry, honey," said Agnes. "I had the TV on mute. We've been watching the news this morning, but first I was doing a little housework, and then the girls and I were talking, so I put it on mute as soon as I turned it on, before anyone else woke up."

Jenny grabbed the remote control and hit the mute button, setting the remote down next to her, as Scott once again touched the stylus to the tablet's screen, unpausing the presentation.

As the pictures flew into position, the Village People's "YMCA" blared at top volume.

"Oh my god, turn that down!" Jenny said, snatching up the remote and quickly changing the television volume to a level that wouldn't induce immediate deafness in everyone who stood within fifty feet of the TV's speakers.

"Agnes," said Oleen. "Is your hearing okay? Why do you have your TV turned up so loud?"

"Oh, my hearing is fine, honey," Agnes answered. "I was in the kitchen cooking yesterday, and I turned it up so I could listen to CNN."

"You really do spend too much time on those news networks, Agnes," said Ida. "It isn't good for you."

"Well, it hasn't made me deaf, so I'm okay with it," Agnes said.

Looking back at the screen, and hearing the continued, though much quieter melody of YMCA, Agnes noticed the pictures that had just rocketed up from the bottom of the screen were separate photos of Delbert and Gary that had been taken at the McGruders' Memorial Day barbecue. Both men had on short shorts and tube socks with colored stripes around the top.

"I think that was 1984!" said Oleen. "I always hated those atrocious socks. Gary wore them with black tennis shoes. You can see those in the picture. Reeboks, I think. Eww."

"Uncle Delbert still wears those shoes!" Jenny said. "And is my dad wearing a sweatband around his head?"

"I think he is! And around his wrists! For once my dad did

better on the fashion front than yours," Janie said, laughing like a hyena.

"My dad isn't exactly fashionable," Jenny said, touching Janie's arm, "But your dad makes mine look like an Armani model in these photos. This is truly shocking."

Jenny and Janie continued to laugh.

"Who knew Uncle Gary would ever be dressed worse than my dad?" Janie said. "I think I'm gonna wet my pants, and I already do that sometimes. It will be nice that this time there's a reason."

"Was that really necessary, Scott?" Ida asked, as everyone else giggled.

"Yes, yes it was. Now, let's get down to business. I have some surprises in store."

54

TUESDAY

"**O**kay," Scott said, as the last notes of YMCA faded into the background. "That was just the warm-up. Now we get serious."

Janie wasn't sure Scott could get serious, except when it came to his personal grooming, but she kept this thought to herself.

Scott touched his tablet, and the television screen changed. At the top, in a large, bold and sinister font, the word "Suspects" loomed in red over the photos of four people. The photos were stacked down the left side of the screen, and the names of the people in the photos were listed on the right side of the TV screen, next to the pictures.

From top to bottom, the names read "Katerina Popov, Fernando O'Brien, Grace McGruder, and Bill McGruder."

"Fernando O'Brien?" Agnes said. "What an interesting name. What nationality is he? He looks Hispanic."

"Uh, we call it Latino today, Agnes, says the anti-discrimination lawyer," Scott said.

"And young Fernando does have quite an interesting background," Scott continued. "His mother is from Madrid, so you're right that he's part Spanish. High-five for not calling him Mexican, Agnes. And Fernando's father is from Dublin, but Fernando was born in Rapid City, South Dakota. Don't even ask me what there is in Rapid City, South Dakota, much less how or why people from two cool international cities would end up there. But I do think young Fernando had the right idea when he joined the circus and got out of there. By the way, his middle name is Seamus."

"How do you know all this, Scott?" Ida asked.

"Well, when we got home last night, I went upstairs immediately to wash that corpse right out of my hair. You know, like that old commercial said."

"I believe it was gray, not corpse," said Oleen. "And there's also some song, I think, about washing a man out of your hair, but I'd prefer a song about beating a man to death with a wrist splint."

"Yeah, whatever," Scott said. "I came downstairs from my shower and Jenny had made us veggie pasta. She even had some without broccoli for me in a separate bowl, which was very thoughtful, since broccoli is the Devil. Thank you, Jenny."

"Says the man who put up a photo of me wearing a unicorn head," Jenny responded.

"Those two things are not related," Scott said. "So I took my pasta over to a chair in the living room while Steve and Jenny were watching this hideous Hallmark Channel movie where Meredith Baxter was trying to locate her kidnapped granddaughter in the Catskills, and I knew I couldn't possibly deal with that , so I took my food upstairs and did a little research."

"That movie was good!" said Jenny. "Steve DVRed it so we could watch it."

"Uh-huh," said Scott. "Well, I found out all about Fernando and Katerina from the French—Canadian Circus website. That's where I got their pictures, too."

"Scott, why is Mike in that picture with Grace? And why is he, like, seventeen?" asked Agnes.

"Because young Mike has always thought Mrs. McGruder is a MILF," Scott said.

"What in the world is a MILF?" asked Ida.

"I'll tell you later, honey," said Agnes, patting Ida's shoulder.

In the photo, Grace McGruder wore tight Capri pants and a low-cut tank top. Agnes had to admit that Grace looked quite good in that photo; still did, for that matter.

"I'm loving Mike's sleeveless denim shirt," Jenny said, laughing.

"It was the early 2000s, Jenny," said Scott. "Give him a pass. We were all victims of denim back then."

"That's an interesting photo of Bill," said Ida. "That picture is pretty recent. Is that Julie Wellington next to him? They're standing close. You know, she and Thomas got divorced a couple of years ago. You don't think—"

"Oh my god!" Oleen said. "We'll have to investigate that further, Ida. Scott, how do you even have that photo?"

"Mr. McGruder's Facebook posts are all public," said Scott. "There are a whole bunch in which he's standing way too close to a number of women. I wouldn't assume he's the reason for the Wellington's divorce. But I wouldn't not assume it either. The man seems like a serial philanderer to me, even though I have no evidence. Then again, I think gossip, by definition, isn't supported by evidence."

"So Katerina, Fernando, and the McGruders? Those are the suspects?" asked Jenny. "Steve told me about it last night, so I've got a good idea of what happened, and Janie and I went for a walk early this morning, and I told her."

"It was more like a plod for me," said Janie.

Scott touched his tablet and it faded to a blank screen with the word "Evidence" at the top.

Scott wrote a number one.

"First," he said, "We all saw how Fernando was comforting Katerina when she found out Sergei was dead, and we all saw Mr. McGruder glaring at Fernando."

"I saw that!" Oleen said. "Bill sure did look angry. But Fernando was glaring right back at him. It was like when I saw Julie Wellington's two little chihuahuas fight over a plate of food that time I went by her house after her divorce. Don't know why I did that."

"And Fernando seemed a bit too—I don't know—maybe familiar? With Katerina, I mean," said Ida. "Like it was more than just that they performed together."

"Oh, I think they performed together, alright," Scott said. "On that couch backstage."

"Eww," said Oleen.

"Steve doesn't agree, but I think both Fernando and Mr. McGruder have something going on with the Russian devil," said Scott.

"*And* she was with that Sergei guy too?" asked Janie.

"Yep," said Scott.

"Boy, she seems to have gotten around," Agnes said. "Who has that much time or energy?"

Next to the number one Scott had written on his tablet, he wrote:

Love Triangle:

Katerina + Sergei

Katerina + Fernando

Katerina + Bill

"I think that might be a love quadrangle," said Scott.

"You know, I haven't had a chance to tell anyone this yet," said Oleen, "because last night the police wouldn't let us discuss things, and I didn't tell Agnes and Ida last night because I didn't want to talk about it in front of the Uber driver, and then I went to sleep as soon as we got home—"

"Spit it out, Oleen," said Scott.

"You took an Uber?" asked Jenny.

"We did," said Oleen. "Your brother put the app on my phone and taught me how to use it. Last night I saw Katerina and Fernando arguing when I went upstairs to the civic center bathroom. I heard them, and then I hid behind a potted tree to hear them better. That's how I sprained my right wrist. I fell over on the tree."

"I thought you just tripped over it," Janie said. "You were hiding behind it and spying? Oleen!"

"Well, I got some good intel. I could sort of hear them. They were arguing, I think. They were in one of those ugly turrets. It had seats around the edges. I was up there admiring the art while I waited for Grace to finish up in the bathroom. You can only get up there to the top floor using a keycard. That door is so thick you could use it in a bank vault. Or a panic closet."

"Panic room," Scott said, "That's what you call them. Not a closet. A room. Like that movie."

"Wait, the art? What art?" asked Ida.

"The whole top floor of the civic center is filled with all kinds of artwork," Oleen said. "I have no idea why it's there, but I could have spent hours up there looking through the glass at it. I want to ask Steve if he knows why it's there."

"The top floor of the civic center is where they store works from the art museum's permanent collection that aren't currently on display," Scott said. "You know, because they always have those temporary traveling exhibits coming through, so they can't always have everything in the permanent collection out. There's just not enough room. So that's where they keep it. There's some hidden freight elevator at the back of the floor that leads into a covered loading dock-garage thing in the back, so no one sees anyone coming and going with the art. You know, to prevent theft. Steve's mom told him. When she used to run the gallery, she toured it. She used to be a big deal, Steve's mom."

"Wow! I had no idea," Jenny said.

"Well, getting back to Katerina and Fernando... What happened, Oleen?" Scott asked.

"Well, they were arguing and Fernando—I think he said they had to tell the police. I don't know what. And Katerina said no one could know, especially not Bill, because she'd get fired. And Fernando told her she hadn't been fired for dating Sergei, so she wouldn't get fired now. And then she told him it was different because Bill would get mad and do something. That's when Fernando said they had to tell the police, I think. And he said they had to be honest. He said he's pretty sure Grace knows, and she'll tell the police. Or that she'd tell Bill and, either way, she's probably furious. And that's when they were whispering, and I leaned in and heard one of them say something like, "Bill's wife may be the one." And then I fell on the tree and landed at their feet."

Everyone was silent.

"I fell because Grace tapped me on the shoulder and scared me. I was already leaning forward with my foot on the edge of the pot. And then she yelled at Katerina and Fernando about why they were up there and how they got up there with no key card, and they walked past us and left. I have no idea how they could've gotten up there because that door was thick, and reinforced, and unless you were the Incredible Hulk in those tight purple pants, you'd never be able to bust it down. Then Grace called Ida on her phone and went to wait by the door to the stairwell for the police, and I saw something on the floor in the turret. I shimmied on over on my stomach and was able to pull the thing out and stick it inside my bra. It was that Sergei guy's driver's license! It's wrapped up in my bra in the guest bedroom right now. One of them must have dropped it up there."

"That's weird. Why would they have that?" Janie asked.

"You hid it in your bra? Good job, Mom," Jenny laughed.

"Don't you think you should give that to the police, dear?" said Ida. "The license, not your bra."

Oleen shrugged. "I'll give Detective Drew my bra," she said, waggling her eyebrows.

"I have to see what this guy looks like," said Janie, as Ida gave her sister a scornful look.

Scott wrote a number two on the screen of his laptop. Next to it, he wrote:

Love Triangle:

Grace? Bill? Jealousy

Is Grace THE ONE?

"It's like you're writing a movie script up there," Janie said.

"Steve and I saw some stuff too," Scott said. "After I beat up the clown and they dragged me backstage, Steve came to get me, and we were sitting on the couch. I'm gonna call it the sex couch because I'm betting that's where all the magic happens."

"Eww, Scott!" said Jenny, "And you beat up a clown? Steve didn't tell me that part. I cannot WAIT to hear that story. I hope there's video, and that I can post it on YouTube."

"There may be a video of my head stuck to the body's shirt cuff on YouTube. I can do without re-living that," said Scott.

"Oh, Steve told me that," said Jenny.

"Yeah, I bet he did," Scott said. "So Steve and I are sitting on the sex couch," said Scott. "And Katerina comes out from some dressing room and right in front of Mrs. McGruder she saunters on up to Mr. McGruder and gets all up on him in her tight little leotard and whispers in his ear, but it's more like she's trying to suck out his eardrum, she got that much all up on his ear."

"I was not aware you could get 'all up on someone's ear,'" Jenny said.

"If you'd seen it, you'd understand," Scott said. "And when Katerina walks away, Mr. McGruder's all looking at her butt and stuff, right in front of his wife! And then, when we get up off the sex couch and we're leaving, we hear Mrs. McGruder yelling at Mr. McGruder about how she told him it had to stop and what the hell is wrong with him."

Scott wrote a number three on the tablet and next to it:

Bill and Katerina—affair?

Grace angry

Fernando angry?

Bill = man-ho

Katerina = lady-ho

"And, finally," Scott said, like a newscaster about to end the 11:00 p.m. broadcast, "after you and Oleen left, Mom, Steve and I got locked out and had to get to the parking deck by going down the wall at the front of the building. It was raining hard. Almost ruined my shoes and my pants."

"Tragedy," said Ida. "I ruined my blouse. And you know how no detergent ever gets those tough stains out."

"I know," said Scott. "It's a lie. So, Steve and I get to the edge of the building and we're peeking around the corner into the deck because Steve hears voices. It's Mrs. McGruder yelling at Katerina. Katerina is already in her car, and Mrs. McGruder is bent down yelling through the window. She's like, 'You bitch! How could you do that?' and 'I bet you're not surprised. You knew what I'd do.' And then she's like, 'You're going back to the Russian State Circus. Don't think I didn't look you up.'"

"Really?" asked Ida. "I had no idea Grace had all these issues with anger. She's always seemed so polite!"

"She's mad because Bill is a man-whore, Ida," said Oleen. "Wouldn't you be if you knew Delbert was stepping out on—"

Oleen stopped when she noticed Ida's wide eyes and how her mouth had formed a perfect, round o.

"Never mind," she said.

"And *then*," Scott said, "Katerina screeches out of her parking space—I'm surprised she didn't run over Mrs. McGruder's foot, really—and when she leaves the parking deck, the Russian devil stares straight at us like her eyes can shoot nuclear rays that are gonna kill us. Oh and, Mom, her car is even smaller than mine."

Scott wrote a number four on the tablet and next to it:

Mrs. McGruder:

Mad as hell and not gonna take it anymore.

"Janie is right, Scott," said Agnes, "Your list certainly does look like a movie script."

"Now that the evidence is all out—does anyone have any more, by the way?" Scott said.

Everyone shook their heads.

"Well, now we need to talk about what it means."

Then the doorbell rang.

55

TUESDAY

I da got up to open the door. The bell rang two more times before she could answer it. Ida opened the door to find Piper, Matilda in tow, standing on Agnes's front porch. Piper was holding a cake plate with a dome over the top.

"You can't keep ringing the doorbell, Matilda," Piper was saying to her daughter. "Once is enough. Ringing it over and over is very rude."

Matilda rolled her eyes. Piper looked up when she heard the door open.

"Oh hi, Ida," she said, smiling. "I brought you all a little something. I know you went through a lot yesterday. I tried to take it over by your's and Oleen's houses, but Gary said you were all over here with Agnes."

Piper looked Ida's outfit up and down. "It's pretty warm today for those pants, but I do like the pink."

Freezing in place, as though she were being held up by a dangerous man with a knife, Ida plastered on her maniacal grin.

"Thank you so much, Piper. Come on in."

Hearing his mother say the name Piper, Scott used the television remote to switch the input back to the cable box. The Weather Channel appeared on the screen, and Jim Cantore was being whipped around by winds that seemed to have something to do with tornadoes in the Midwest.

Looking at the screen, Scott said, "We should just be glad we only had a body fall on us. When Jim Cantore rolls into town you know there's gonna be some destruction on a biblical scale."

Piper walked into the living room.

"Well, don't you have a crowd in here," she said.

Oleen looked at Piper, wondering why Piper always had on some sort of dress, with pearls. This dress was lavender, and she had on matching lavender sandals. It was bizarre.

"It's a good thing I brought a layer cake," Piper said. "Red velvet."

Oleen herself only baked when she had to, such as for baby showers and holidays. She had been so happy when both her children had moved on from elementary school to junior high school because then she no longer had to make cupcakes for them to take in on their birthdays. She always felt a slight disdain for people who baked willingly, and especially for people who baked willingly and enjoyed it. If someone she knew had a death in the family or a difficult event, Oleen headed straight for the freezer section at Costco.

"I love red velvet!" said Jenny. "Here, I'll take it to the table."

Jenny took the cake from Piper and set it down on the dining room table, wishing Piper would leave so she could have a giant piece. Jenny walked back to the living room and sat down on the sofa, eyeing the cake as Gary had eyed Detective Drew's backside the night before.

"I just wanted to say I'm sorry about what you all went through last night," Piper said. "Mom told me about it, and it sounds just awful."

"It wasn't fun," Scott said, using the remote control to mute the television. On the screen Jim Cantore took refuge under the awning of a Dairy Queen as one of the outdoor umbrellas blew away, swept into the sky by a fierce wind.

"Why don't you all sit down? Would you like some orange juice?" Agnes asked.

"Uh, sure," Piper said. "Do you want some, Matilda?"

Matilda nodded, then took her iPhone from her pocket and began scrolling down the screen. After the punch fiasco at the baby shower, Agnes knew better than to even mention there was champagne.

Piper led Matilda to the sofa opposite Scott and sat down, with Matilda in the middle and Oleen on the other end.

Agnes handed Piper and Matilda their glasses of juice; not in champagne flutes because she didn't want Matilda to get any ideas, and certainly not in plastic wine glasses. Piper took a sip of her orange juice, and Matilda set hers down on the coffee table.

Ida was thankful Agnes's coffee table had a glass top, and that there could be no rings produced by a lack of coasters.

"My, Matilda," Oleen said, "You smell very nice! You smell just like Ida's perfume. That Poison stuff."

"Oh, I have that perfume too, and Matilda is always getting into it," Piper said. "I keep telling her to stay out of it, but what are you gonna do?" Piper shrugged.

Janie looked at Matilda and patted her belly, hoping her unborn child could somehow sense Matilda's behavior and would know not to replicate it.

"You know, we were supposed to leave for the beach early this morning," Piper said, "But after hearing what happened at the circus last night, I felt like we should stay to be here for Mom and Dad. Originally we were going to leave Monday morning, but Andy didn't feel well all day Sunday, and even though he felt better Sunday night, he woke up on Monday with this horrible stomach virus. Sorry, too much information.

We were going to try again today, but then all this happened. Andy is feeling okay now, but we agreed to put off our trip for a week and reduce Matilda's summer camp by a week. Andy called the hospital and rescheduled his week off, so now we're going next week. He's already back at the hospital this morning. I didn't think he should go back until he's felt well for twenty-four hours, but he doesn't listen to me about health stuff, or about anything else."

Piper sighed and looked down at her hands. She twirled her wedding ring around her finger.

"Your parents must be shaken up, Your dad moved, uh, Sergei, you know," Oleen said, glancing at Matilda.

Matilda pulled a small glass bottle with a cork in the top from her pocket. She removed the cork and poured some of the liquid that was in the bottle onto her hand. Then she rubbed the liquid onto her neck and arms and recorked the bottle. A strong, sickly sweet odor washed over the room.

"Give me that," Piper said. Staring at her mom, Matilda handed over the bottle.

"Is this that bottle you got at the beach last summer, the one with the swirled sand in it?" Piper asked.

Matilda nodded.

"And you dumped the sand out and poured some of my perfume in?"

Matilda nodded again.

"You can't do that, Matilda!" Piper said. "You have to ask permission. If you'd like some perfume, we can go to Bath and Body Works and get you something more appropriate. My perfume is not appropriate for you. It's expensive, and you don't need actual perfume. We'll get you body spray or something."

"Well, perfume covers up the smell of dead bodies. They stink, you know," Matilda said.

Oleen and Ida exchanged glances.

"That's not a good thing to say, Matilda. It's disturbing," Piper said.

Matilda went back to her iPhone.

The conversation was cut short by the ringing of Ida's cellphone. A blaring rendition of "Yankee Doodle" erupted as though from a megaphone.

"Yankee Doodle? Really, Mom?" Scott said. "And you call yourself a Southerner." Scott shook his head.

Ida found her phone between the sofa cushions and noticed a number she didn't recognize was calling. Grateful for any excuse to get away from the overpowering scent of perfume, she hit the answer button on the phone and stepped back into the guest room.

"Hello," she said.

"Hello, Ida? This is Drew. Drew Davenport."

"Oh hi, Detective. How are you? I hope you got some sleep last night."

"I got a little," he said, yawning. "I'm calling because I'd like you to come down to the station and answer a few questions. Don't worry. You're not a suspect, and you didn't do anything. It's just— Well, we found something backstage, and it has your fingerprints on it. Yours and some others we can't identify. I just want to see if it belongs to you and if you have any idea how it could have gotten backstage since I know you weren't back there."

"Okay, Detective, I understand," said Ida, feeling a prickling at the back of her neck. "And thank you for reassuring me I'm not in trouble or suspected of anything. Getting called to the police station is kind of like getting called to the principal's office."

Detective Drew laughed.

"I understand," he said. "I used to get called to the principal's office a lot."

"Can you tell me what you found, though? I can't imagine

how anything of mine could have gotten backstage. Steve and Scott were back there, but I don't know what of mine they could have possibly dropped backstage. They didn't have anything of mine."

"I guess it won't hurt to tell you since you're not a suspect," said Detective Drew. "It's an atomizer. One of those things for perfume. And one of the CSTs even identified the scent because she thought she had recently smelled it at a department store. We don't know for certain if she's correct, but she said she thinks it's called Poison."

56

TUESDAY

I da hung up the phone. She walked back to the living room.

"Oleen," she said, "Would you come here a minute? I need some help."

Everyone watched Oleen exit the living room and disappear around the corner. Ida led Oleen into the guest room and closed the door behind them.

"I'll explain in a minute," said Ida, "But first, no one is hurt or dead. We just need to get Piper and Matilda out of here as fast as possible, okay? I'm going to say that it was Maureen on the phone. You know how they all had that stomach bug yesterday. I'm going to say that all five of them are sick now and we need to go look after them."

"But what about Scott, and Jenny, and Janie, and Agnes?" Oleen asked. "That's not very believable that it will take six of us, including a pregnant woman, to look after people who are throwing up and god knows what else. I have a better idea. Just stay quiet, and I'll handle it."

Oleen walked back into the living room. Ida followed, feeling uneasy but waiting to see what Oleen was about to say.

"Piper, we're all going to have to go now," said Oleen. "I'm so sorry to cut this visit short, but that was Gary who just called Ida. Delbert was out front trimming some bushes, and he cut himself pretty badly with the hedge clippers. It's so bad that Gary had to find the tip of Delbert's finger and keep it on ice in a cooler. We all have to go meet them at the hospital. I hope they can reattach Delbert's finger."

Ida stared, open-mouthed, at Oleen.

"Oh my god, Mom, is Dad okay?" Janie asked, getting to her feet and running to her mother.

"Wow, I am not a fast runner," Janie said.

"Uh," Ida said as Janie touched her arm, "Gary said he found the finger pretty quickly, so it seems likely Delbert won't lose it. And he's stopping the bleeding with a t-shirt."

"I drove your car over here, Mom," Scott said, jumping up and running to the front door. "I'll start it. Everyone come on."

"That's just horrible," Piper said, hurrying Matilda toward the front door. "Please let me know how Delbert is doing."

"I want to see the finger," said Matilda.

"Be quiet, Matilda!" Piper said, ushering Matilda toward the front door. She hurried Matilda down the front steps of the house and toward her black BMW sedan. Piper opened the front passenger door of the car for Matilda and slammed it shut behind her. Piper climbed into the driver's seat, started the car, backed out of the driveway, and drove off down the street.

Agnes stared at Oleen.

"Is it bad, honey?" Agnes asked Ida. They were still standing in the living room.

"Oh, Delbert's fine, Agnes," Oleen said as Scott honked the Expedition's horn. "Ida told me we needed to get rid of Piper and Matilda, and that's the first thing I came up with."

"Good god, Oleen!" said Ida. "Why did you tell her that? Delbert and Gary aren't even home today. They're at work."

"Well, Piper doesn't know that," said Oleen.

"Wait a minute, honey," Agnes said. "They must not be at work. Piper said she went to your houses and Gary said you were over here."

"Oh, right," said Oleen. "I wonder why they didn't go to work."

"They were probably too tired," Ida said. "We didn't leave the hospital until 3 a.m. They probably wanted to sleep; hopefully in separate houses."

"Eww, Ida!" Jenny said.

"Thank god Dad's okay!" said Janie.

"But what made Oleen have to make up that lie to get rid of Piper and that horrible daughter of hers?" asked Jenny. "I mean, aside from basic human instinct."

"The police want to question me," Ida said. "They found something of mine backstage."

"When did you go backstage?" Oleen asked. "Unless you turned invisible, I don't remember that happening."

"I didn't," said Ida. "And they know that. They don't think I did anything. They just want to know why it was back there. They said I may be able to help. Well, it was your love interest, Detective Drew, who said that, Oleen."

"Let me just get this stuff in the fridge," Agnes said, collecting the leftover breakfast foods, orange juice, and champagne.

Jenny and Janie picked up the used plates and glasses, dumped the remnants of food in the trash and the drinks into the sink, and stuck everything in the dishwasher. Agnes put a dishwashing tablet into the little compartment on the door of the dishwasher, shut the door, and set it to start washing.

"I hate walking in to a mess," Agnes said.

Jenny grabbed the domed cake plate.

"Good idea," said Janie, hurrying into the kitchen, opening a drawer, and grabbing a huge handful of forks.

"We'll need water," said Jenny.

"There's a case in the back of my car," Ida said. "Delbert never unloaded it the last time we went to Costco."

"And paper towels," said Janie.

"I've got some of those back there, too," Ida said.

Outside, Scott honked the horn three more times.

"He still thinks Delbert lost a finger," Jenny said with a giggle. "By the way, Mom, you're insane. But I was very impressed you told that story without that mental patient grin on your face like I would have expected."

Once Agnes had locked her front door, and everyone had piled into Ida's Expedition, Scott backed out of the driveway.

"Which hospital?" Scott asked. "And, Jenny, why did you bring a cake to the hospital?"

"Oh, none, dear," Ida said. "We're going to the police station. That wasn't Gary. It was that good-looking detective. They want to question me about something they found backstage."

"Good god, Mom! Why would you two make up that story, then? I thought Dad might die, or become an amputee."

"It was the quickest way to get rid of them," said Oleen.

"Well, I guess that's true, Mom, but what of yours could be backstage?" Scott asked.

"They found my atomizer in the couch back there," Ida said. "It's probably mine, because I couldn't find it the other day and Detective Drew said one of the technicians thought it smelled like a perfume she'd sniffed at a department store. She thought it was Poison, and that's the perfume I keep in my atomizer."

"They found it in the sex couch. Makes sense someone would be wearing a little perfume on the sex couch," said Scott, as he set the GPS for the police station.

"Oh my, god, Ida!" Oleen said, grabbing her sister's arm. "Oh my god!"

"What is it, Oleen?" Ida said.

"Matilda! It's Matilda!"

"Huh?" Ida said, looking at her sister.

"Your atomizer! You couldn't find it in the downstairs bathroom before we left for the circus. Remember how much time Matilda spent in that bathroom during the baby shower? And today she smelled like your perfume. It was Matilda! She stole your atomizer!"

"Is that true? Mom, do you think she took it?" Scott asked.

"Oh my god! I bet she did!" Janie said. "There's no other explanation. Unless Scott decided he liked the scent and took it backstage with him to sit on the sex couch."

"He wanted to entice one of the clowns he beat up!" Jenny said. "He didn't want them to sue."

"Shut up. I hate clowns," Scott said.

"That's the only explanation!" Janie said. "But that means Matilda was backstage between the baby shower and the Monday night circus performance. And Piper said they spent all day yesterday at home because her husband hadn't been feeling well, so when would Matilda have been there?"

"Sunday night, I guess," Scott said, shrugging.

"But that doesn't make any sense," Ida said.

"She could have seen something, Ida," said Oleen. "We should try to talk to Piper and see why Matilda was down there."

"*If* she was down there," Ida said.

"Scott, I want you to come in when they question me," Ida said. "They'll just think I'm a scared old lady, so they won't think I'm hiding anything if I bring a lawyer. They'll just think I don't know what to do. But I don't want to mention Matilda. I don't want to cause problems for Piper and her family if our theory is wrong. They're going through enough as it is."

"Okay, I guess you don't have to mention that yet. We can call Piper when we get home and see what we can find out and then decide if we should tell the police. Besides, that will be more fun," said Scott, smiling broadly.

"Only you, Scott," Jenny said, shaking her head.

Scott pulled into the parking lot of the police station and stopped the Expedition in a spot right next to the front door.

"I hope they don't mind having a tank parked in their lot," Scott said, looking at Ida. "Everyone but Mom and I has to stay in the car."

Oleen rolled down the driver's-side window on the second row of seats in the Expedition.

Scott and Ida climbed out of the car and stood, side-by-side, next to it. Oleen looked them over. Scott had on cargo shorts, a tank top, and flip-flops. Ida sported her voluminous pink t-shirt, thermal underwear pants, and ballet flats.

"You two look like you belong in the drunk tank," said Oleen.

"I haven't had a shower since Sunday morning, so you might be right," Ida said.

57

TUESDAY

Oleen got out of the car as soon as Ida and Scott had disappeared through the front door of the police station. She went to the back of the car and opened the double doors.

"Hey," Oleen called to Jenny, who was sitting in the back row of seats with Agnes, "I'm going to hand up water and paper towels, okay?"

Oleen handed four water bottles and a roll of paper towels to Jenny, who passed them out to Agnes, Janie, and herself, putting one on the seat in front of her for Oleen. Janie, who had been sitting in the front passenger seat, moved back into the seat Ida had vacated.

"Hey!" Oleen said from the back of the car. "I found binoculars! Who knows why Ida has these, but now we can see what's going on in there."

"It's a good thing all these seats are bucket seats now and not bench seats like in Ida's old car," said Jenny. "Now we can all just turn and eat the cake at the same time."

"Oleen?" Agnes asked.

"Yes?" came Oleen's muffled voice from the back of the car.

"Is there anything back there we can prop the cake up on so we can all eat off it at once?"

Oleen rummaged around in the back of the car.

"Wow!" she said. "I have no idea what Ida thinks might happen while she's driving, but she's got loads of stuff back here. Dust masks, water, paper towels, beef jerky, an umbrella, binoculars—and a tiny little step ladder. I thought Doomsday preppers stored their stuff in basements or weird shelters they dig out in their yards, but maybe not. When I ask her, she'll say Delbert never unloaded any of it after their last trip to Costco. Just you wait. Oh, and that little step ladder. That will work for the cake."

Oleen laid the step ladder flat on the ground and draped the strap of the binoculars around her neck. She closed the back doors of the car and picked up the ladder. Then she walked back to the second-row passenger-side door, opened it, and put the step ladder on the seat. Janie unfolded it and set it in the aisle between the second and third row of seats. Jenny, who had been holding the domed cake plate in her lap during the trip to the police station, set the plate on top of the step ladder. Janie reached into the front seat and took four forks from the handful she'd pulled from the drawer at Agnes's house.

"Sorry, but I kind of sat on these on the ride over," said Janie. "I threw them on the seat before I climbed in, and I could feel them poking me in the butt the whole way over, but it was too hard to lift myself up and get them out."

"I'm okay with your butt having been on my fork as long as I get to eat this cake," said Jenny.

Agnes removed the dome to expose the two-layer red velvet cake with white icing. Jenny stuck her fork in and sliced off a piece of red cake with a large amount of icing on top. She put it in her mouth.

"Mmm, cream cheese icing," she said. "It's so sweet, and

with the amount of icing Piper used I have no idea how she's so skinny. She must not eat it while she makes the cake, though. Unlike me. Does anyone else think it's weird that she wears dresses, like, all the time? And not comfy sundresses, but dresses you'd wear to some work function or to a funeral? Today she had on pearls!"

"I think it's weird, honey," said Agnes. "You know I like to look good, but there are limits to what I'll do. I'm not wearing a funeral dress the day after Memorial Day unless I'm going to a funeral."

"It was lavender. So maybe it's not good for a funeral," said Janie. "Maybe for the visitation the night before? Or at a wake! I hear everyone gets drunk at a wake."

"Maybe we can ask Fernando O'Brien's father," said Agnes. "Isn't that an Irish thing, wakes?"

Janie nodded, but didn't say anything on account of her mouth being stuffed full of cake.

The four women ate the cake for a few minutes.

"Eww, Janie," said Jenny through a mouth full of cake, "I know this cake is good, but making all those noises you sound like you need to go sit on the sex couch."

Janie finished chewing and swallowed her cake.

"At this point, I don't even care about the sex couch," Janie said, patting her belly. "I just want cake. And a margarita."

Agnes sat back from the cake.

"After all the Cocoa Puffs I ate last night, and the beignets and waffles this morning, and now this cake, I'm sweeted out, not to mention too full."

She wrapped her fork up in her paper towel and stuck it in the cup holder next to her seat.

"When you're done with your forks you can hand them to me," Agnes said, "And I'll stick them in this cup holder. Then I can wash them later."

"Here are the extras, Agnes," Janie said, handing Agnes the

handful of forks left on the front seat of the car. "They technically didn't touch my butt, so I don't know if you need to wash
them or not."

"I'll keep that in mind, honey," Agnes said, taking the forks
from Janie and sticking them in the cup holder.

Agnes turned and looked out the left-side window of the
car into the police station. Just behind the reception area was a
room with a large window, a window through which Agnes
could see Ida and Scott sitting across a table from Detective
Beauregard and Detective Drew. She wondered if they were
doing that good cop—bad cop thing with Ida. She hoped not. If
they were, she was pretty sure she knew which cop was the
good cop.

Oleen stopped eating the cake. She wrapped her fork in a
paper towel and handed it to Agnes, who stuck it in the cup
holder with all the others.

"I feel kind of ill," Oleen said, clutching her stomach.
"Instead of a muffin top I have a cake top. You know, I always
figured rooms for questioning suspects would be further inside
the building where no one could see. Let's check what's going
on, though."

Oleen pulled the binoculars up from where they rested on
her chest and put them up to her eyes.

"Why do they look so tiny?" Oleen asked.

"Turn them around, honey," said Agnes. "They're
backward."

"Been a while since I used binoculars," Oleen said, turning
the binoculars around.

"Old Beauregard is holding up a bag—like a clear baggie—
and it looks like it has Ida's atomizer in it."

"Now Ida's talking and pointing at the bag," Oleen said.
"She's gesturing a lot with her hands, so she's got to be telling a
story. She always talks with her hands when she tells a story. I
hope she stays on topic and doesn't start going on about her

ruined blouse she bought at Nordstrom Rack. I can't imagine how it could take so long just to have her identify her atomizer."

"Now Scott's whispering in her ear," said Oleen. "But we all know Scott can't whisper, so what's the point of that?"

"Hey, Jenny!" Oleen called, "The cute detective is standing up now and walking around the table. You could get a good look at him through these binoculars." Oleen held the binoculars out to Jenny, who waved them off.

"No men for me ever again, Mom," Jenny said. "Not even through binoculars."

"Well, I'll look at him," said Janie. "I may be married and pregnant, but I'm not dead." Janie took the binoculars and helped Oleen pull the strap up over her head. Janie held them up to her eyes.

"He's adorable, Jenny!" Janie said. "You're missing out."

"I'm good," said Jenny.

"I don't see why we had to wait so long. Scott," said Ida, touching Scott's arm as she sat down across the table from Detectives Drew and Beauregard. "I'm identifying an atomizer for goodness sake, not the stolen crown jewels."

"Shh," Scott said to Ida. Detective Drew tried to stifle a laugh by sneezing.

"So, do you know why we asked you here today, Mrs. McNair?" asked Detective Beauregard.

"Why, of course I do. Detective Drew told me. You have my atomizer, and it has my fingerprints on it."

"Detective Drew, huh?" said Beauregard, smirking at Detective Drew. "Sounds like you teach kindergarten or something."

"Can it, Beauregard," said Detective Drew. "Yes, that's why you're here. Take a look at the atomizer in the clear bag

Detective Beauregard has. We just need to make sure it's yours."

Ida pointed toward the bag.

"Can you turn the bag over so I can see the bottom?" she asked.

Detective Beauregard turned the bag upside down. There was a small chip on the bottom of the cylindrical, pink container. The ends were both rounded, and one end had a chip missing and was slightly dented.

"It's mine," Ida said, gesturing with her hands. "I got it out of my purse once in the parking lot of a church before we went in for a wedding. My wallet fell out of my purse, so I asked Delbert to hold the atomizer while I picked up my wallet. And, wouldn't you know, the man dropped it in the parking lot and it got chipped."

Ida shook her head.

"Now that we know it's yours, Mrs. McNair," said Detective Beauregard, "Can you tell us why it might have been stuck in the couch cushions backstage at the French—Canadian circus?"

"Just a minute, guys," Scott said. "I need to confer with my client."

Detective Beauregard rolled his eyes.

Scott cupped his hand around Ida's ear and whispered in an actual, quiet, whispering voice, "Tell them it's been missing from the bathroom since you looked for it there on Monday, but you have no idea who might have taken it or how it might have ended up in that couch. Then you're just omitting some facts, not lying. There were a lot of people at that baby shower, and they won't know when it disappeared, and they'll probably think someone who came to the baby shower took it."

Ida nodded. She was shocked that neither detective seemed to have heard what Scott whispered in her ear. Apparently, Scott's whispering skills only activated in police stations and courtrooms, kind of like how Superman couldn't fly until after he went into that phone booth and put on that tight little outfit.

"Well, I have no idea why it would have been back there. On Monday, before we left for the circus, I looked for it in the bathroom downstairs—that's where I keep it, but it wasn't there. I'd forgotten to put on perfume when I got ready in my bedroom, and I do that a lot, so I keep the atomizer downstairs. When I couldn't find it I figured I'd left it upstairs, but I haven't been home since, so I haven't checked."

"And when do you last remember seeing your atomizer," asked Detective Beauregard,

"Well," said Ida, "I'm not really sure, but I definitely haven't used it in a couple of weeks. At least not since Delbert and I went to that nice steak house in the middle of May. He broke two of my favorite mugs, so I guess that's how we ended up at a nice steakhouse." Ida shrugged.

"And has anyone you don't know been in your house recently? A repair person? Anyone who might have wanted to steal your atomizer?" asked Detective Beauregard.

"Frankly I don't understand why anyone would want to steal a dented pink atomizer," Ida said. "Particularly not some repairman. Also, you can buy an identical, brand-new, non-chipped atomizer at Target for $15, so why anyone would steal my chipped, dented one is beyond me."

"But has anyone out-of-the-ordinary been in your house recently?" Detective Beauregard repeated.

"We had a baby shower on Sunday for my daughter, Janie. There were mostly women there; family, family friends, and friends of Janie's. Oh, and Steve. But then everyone in my family was there on Sunday too, even all the rest of the men. It was like that *Intervention* show, but not cause I'm on crack. It's a long story, and I won't get into that now."

Detective Drew smiled. Then he walked around the table and stood next to the door, behind Scott and Ida.

"We'll need a list of everyone who was in your house on Sunday," said Detective Beauregard.

"Okay," Ida nodded. "Can I email it to you after I get home? My daughter Maureen has the baby shower guest list, and my brain is so addlepated at the moment it will be easier to just ask her. And I'll send a list of family members too. I don't understand how my atomizer has anything to do with that poor Sergei man falling from the sky, though," Ida said.

"We're following all possible leads," said Detective Beauregard.

58

TUESDAY

Detective Drew opened the door, allowing Ida and Scott to exit in front of him. After all three had left the room, Detective Drew let the door slam in Detective Beauregard's face.

"Thanks for coming," Detective Drew said.

"Detective," Ida said with a smile, touching Detective Drew's arm, "I'd like to apologize for our attire today. I'd never, ever wear this outfit out of my house, much less to be questioned at the police station," Ida said, gesturing down at her outfit. "I didn't want to sleep in my jeans, and Agnes only had long underwear pants—you know, all her other pants had buttons and zippers, and that's not comfortable for sleeping. I have no clue why she didn't have some yoga pants or sweatpants, or why she had long underwear pants in the first place. It's the South, it never gets that cold. And, frankly, these pants are causing me to sweat in a very unladylike way. Excuse me, I'm going to go get back in the car and sit in the air conditioning."

Ida walked through the front doors of the police station,

down the steps, and climbed into the front passenger seat of the car.

Scott and Detective Drew stood alone in the police station's waiting area.

"You know, your mom's hilarious," Detective Drew said.

"Oh, that's just Ida," said Scott. "Trust me, she's not trying to be. But one day I'll have to get her talking about movies in front of you. The way she messes up the names is truly spectacular. You might wet your pants and then have to borrow a pair of Agnes's long underwear."

Detective Drew laughed, then lowered his voice.

"I've been wanting to ask one of you something, I mean someone in your family because I like your mom and your aunt and I'd never want them to be hurt or embarrassed."

"Okaay," Scott said, drawing the word out until it was almost a question.

"Well, I figured you might be the best person to tell this to. I was at the Silver Kettle last week with my kids. On Wednesdays kids eat free and I have three; they all eat a lot. James, the oldest, he's six, just learned the word 'gay' from some kid at school, and he's been using it all the time. Not to stir anything up, but more just because he's proud he learned a new word. I was looking on Instagram on my phone on Tuesday and I follow Neil Patrick Harris because he's funny and always has pictures of his elaborate Halloween costumes, and there was a picture of him holding hands with his husband. James saw it and said, 'Look, Drew, those men are gay!' James was so proud of himself."

"Your son calls you Drew?" Scott asked.

"Long story. For another time," said Detective Drew, waving his hand in the air. "So, on Wednesday, we're at the Silver Kettle and across the aisle from us, I notice your dad and uncle are sitting in a booth. I didn't know they were your dad and your uncle until I met them at the hospital. Your uncle has a big mustache, which is hard to forget, so I knew it was him, and I knew it was your dad with him. They were holding hands. And James yells, 'Drew! Those men are gay just like the men on your phone!'"

Scott laughed.

"Gary and Delbert are very gay," he said. "Your son's got a good eye."

"I don't think they heard him. Gotta talk to James about yelling in public while pointing at people though. Wait, you know your dad and your uncle are gay?"

"Yeah," Scott said. "I've known since I was a kid. That was the topic of the intervention Ida mentioned. Ida and Oleen didn't know, and we kind of had a group reveal like people do when they tell the sex of their baby, only nobody clapped or said congratulations. Maureen caught Gary and Delbert together on Saturday afternoon. We decided we had to tell Mom and Oleen. It turns out most of the family already knew, but no one knew how to talk about it. I mean, what do you say? Hey, everybody! Did you know our dads are gay?"

"Ida and Oleen didn't know?" Detective Drew asked. "I wasn't sure, but I thought they might know, and your mom and dad and aunt and uncle might have some kind of arrangement."

Detective Drew held up his hands and made air quotes with his fingers when he said the word arrangement.

"No, there's no arrangement. And they really didn't know. I mean, maybe in the dark recesses of their minds. They know now, though. And let's just say things aren't too comfortable for them at home right now. Agnes and Ida won't let Oleen go home because they're afraid she'll kill Gary. But, now it's starting to seem like Oleen is dealing better and Ida is about to go nuts, even though at first it was the other way around. We'll see. Gary and Delbert have been having an on-and-off affair all during the forty-five or forty-six or whatever years they've been married to Ida and Oleen. It's a lot to take in."

Detective Drew whistled. "Now ain't that a kick in the head," he said.

"I love Dean Martin," sighed Scott.

"You know, I'm only telling you what I'm about to tell you because you're a lawyer, so I know you understand the importance of confidentiality, and you're not a suspect, and I guess I trust you. You know that Sergei guy was strangled, right?"

"Yeah," Scott said. "I kind of noticed all the red blood vessels in his eyes when I was stuck to his shirt button and couldn't get him out of my face."

"Well, he wasn't just strangled. He was bashed on the head first, or he hit his head on something, and that didn't kill him, and then someone strangled him, and that's how he died. I totally shouldn't tell you this, but I like your family, and I'm friends with Will and Leah. I just thought you might want to know. It was definitely murder, though we aren't sure how it happened or who did it. There are several people with motives."

"One thing I've been wondering," Scott said. "You know, when the corpse landed on us, Ida kind of got the guy's, uh, crotch in her face, and he was kind of, uh, you know- at the ready, if you get my drift. Is that normal? It doesn't seem normal."

"It's not," said Detective Drew. "But the initial tox screen—now, that's not the final, definitive one, but a quick one—showed he'd taken Viagra within an hour or so of his death. So if he were killed when he was still, uh, at the ready, that would explain why he was like that when he fell on Ida. When someone dies, blood flow stops, but especially if he was one of those guys who had one of those four-hour erections they warn you about on the commercials, then it's possible when rigor mortis set in that his, uh, groin, stayed that way."

Scott looked thoughtful.

"Since I've got you here, and you seem like you're in the mood to answer questions," he said, "Do you have any idea why Bill McGruder was traipsing around backstage at the circus like he owned the place? I mean, he's just the civic center event coordinator, so I don't get why the circus people would even let him back there or care much about him. Steve told me he heard that the French—Canadian Circus is considering setting up a permanent location here. Let's face it, not much goes on at the civic center anymore except lectures and different kinds of meetings, like crap with the Toastmasters' club, and weddings if you're a weirdo who wants to get married at the civic center, so that would make sense."

"Steve's right," said Detective Drew. "They are considering that. And if they do that, Bill McGruder will be out of a job unless the circus hires him as director of the facility. That would be a pretty important job—the circus is known world-wide, and he could get promoted eventually."

"Maybe he was back there trying to woo the director or performers or something," Scott said. "That sounds like something he'd do. Well, thanks, Detective," said Scott. "You seem like a cool guy, you should come grab a beer with Steve and me sometime, bring your son and we can test his gaydar."

"That sounds fun," said Detective Drew. "Maybe Will and Leah could join us. We could go to trivia or something."

"I'll be in touch," said Scott.

59

TUESDAY

"**O**h. My. God. You're not going to believe this," Scott said as he climbed into the driver's seat of Ida's Expedition.

"What? What is it?" asked Oleen.

"Detective Studmuffin. You won't believe what he told me! Also, he has three kids, and they call him Drew. Don't you think that's kind of weird?"

"You mean, kind of how you sometimes refer to your mom and dad as Ida and Delbert? Like that, you mean?" said Jenny.

"Who cares, Scott?" said Janie. "Just tell us what he said!"

"Detective Studmuffin said that the official cause of Sergei's death was strangulation, like we heard on the news, and like I knew it was because his weird eyes were all red and blood-vessely when I got stuck right in his face at the circus. But that isn't all that happened."

"Thanks for that image, Scott. You know how I throw up all the time. And I just ate a bunch of cake. When I throw up, it's going to be over the back of your seat and into your hair," said Janie. "I'll switch seats with Oleen just to make it happen."

"I look forward to it," said Scott. "I love red velvet cake, and that one looked so amazing I bet it would even be good the second time around."

Janie choked down a dry heave, and Agnes handed her a bottle of water.

"Detective Studmuffin told me that Sergei was bashed in the head first, or he hit his head on something, but he didn't die, and then whatever crazy loon killed him strangled him until he was dead."

"Oh my god!" said Oleen. "That is so gruesome. That's like something you would only see on *Law and Order Special Victims Unit*."

"Actually, Oleen," said Scott, "*Law and Order SVU* is only about sex crimes and crimes against kids, but you're right. It is gruesome."

"I can hardly imagine Mr. or Mrs. McGruder, or even one of those circus people, being that horrible," said Agnes.

"I know," said Jenny. "It's pretty disturbing to think we might know someone who would do something like that. Or even that you might have seen someone who would do something like that do a trapeze performance."

"And how about the fact that after Sergei was dead, someone dragged him up into the rafters?" said Oleen. "Wouldn't that be hard for a woman to do? It seems like it would be hard for a man to do, but how could a woman be that strong? Wait! There were some steep metal stairs in the front by the stage that led up to the rafters. Someone could have dragged the body up those. The stairs were really close to where we were sitting, and the body was stuck in the rafters right above us, so whoever did it wouldn't have had to drag poor Sergei that far across the rafters. Dragging him up the stairs would have been difficult, but not impossible. If you had just murdered someone, maybe that same adrenaline that helps people lift cars off other people in emergencies would allow you to drag a body up a steep set of stairs to the rafters, whether you were a man or a woman."

"Well, do you remember right after Julie Wellington got divorced?" asked Ida. "She started going to the personal trainer all the time, and he even had her do some bodybuilding. I bet back then she would've been strong enough to lug some man up to the rafters. Though I do have to say, I was so glad she got out of that because her arms looked way too pumped up. She kind of looked like the Terminator. I never was sure how she afforded all those personal training sessions. I looked into doing some myself, and those suckers are expensive! They can cost up to $100 an hour depending on the trainer. But I guess Julie did well in the divorce settlement. Thomas is a computer programmer, after all, and he used to work for Microsoft. And, apparently, he invented some sort of code that is now being developed so that Windows doesn't crash. Ever."

"Good luck with that!" Jenny said, laughing. "And Thomas Wellington is rich as hell. I read an article about him in *Forbes*."

Oleen looked impressed.

"My point is, the Wellingtons were very, very rich, which means now Julie is very, very rich, Ida said.

"Mom, first I am very proud of you for getting the name of a movie character right. And also, for discussing something involving technology in a coherent way." Scott said. "But, also, maybe it wasn't just one person. Maybe it was two. Or maybe it was even all four of them. But I haven't even told you the most scandalous part yet!"

"Cut the drama, Scott," said Janie. "What is it?"

"I asked Detective Studmuffin about why Sergei, uh, you know, would have been, uh, hard in the groinal region at the time of his death."

"The groinal region?" Jenny laughed. "I can't believe *you're* getting embarrassed, Scott."

"I'm not embarrassed," Scott said. "I did some reading, and

that would be weird because, at the moment of death, blood flow stops, and you know how that's, uh, caused by blood flow."

"Oh my god, Scott! I can't believe you asked him that. How did you even do that without dying of embarrassment?" asked Janie. "I saw how he looks, and I would have fainted if I had to say something like that to him. Plus, you barely know him."

"Well, we may know him better soon, because I asked if he wanted to get a beer with Steve and me, and then he said we should invite Leah and Will and go to trivia. So, Jenny, that means you're coming too. And, Janie, if you haven't had the baby, you can come. But I think Jason should stay home. Purely because I don't like him."

Janie rolled her eyes.

"Come on, Scott," she said. "You could be a little bit supportive and not say stuff like that all the time. I hate it when you do that."

"Even Mom, Oleen, and Agnes can come!" Scott said. "Detective Studmuffin likes them, and I told him that for his entertainment, one day I'd have Ida recite movie titles for him."

"Gee thanks, Scott," Ida said.

"You'll have to tell him the story of *The Fast and the Furious: Tokyo Drift*. That is the all-time most amazing tale, even going back as far as the time of the cavemen. It's the greatest story ever told." Scott sighed. "I love Charlton Heston."

"Well, I can't tell that story if your father's around," said Ida. "Or else I'm liable to bash him over the head and then strangle him if the blow to the head doesn't kill him. In fact, with what he's been up to lately I might do that anyway. I can get Julie Wellington to help me drag him up and stash him in a tree. Or that Rick guy from your gym. He looked pretty capable."

"Wow, Ida," Oleen said. "It would normally be me who you all would be afraid would commit murder. A few days ago I wanted to bludgeon Gary to death with a typewriter."

"A *typewriter*?" laughed Jenny. "Mom, do you even own a typewriter?"

"Maybe somewhere in the attic," said Oleen. "I think that happened on a TV show once. That's why I thought of it. But, now, I'm okay. I'm feeling calm, even. When I saw Gary staring at that cute detective's butt, I think I finally 'got' it. Up until then, I knew in my mind, but not in my heart. Gary's staring knocked something loose in my brain; hopefully not a blood clot or I might die soon, too, like that poor Sergei. But now I understand that, with me, Gary hasn't and can't ever live an authentic life. And I've decided I want him to be happy. Plus, let's face it. That detective does have a really cute butt. I think men and women alike can agree on that. Kind of how Steve's voice is something that people of all genders and sexual orientations can enjoy."

"Well, Oleen, I guess you and I have swapped bodies like in that *Freaky Friday* movie. That one with Jamie Lee Curtis and that Lindsey Linehan girl," Ida said.

Scott stifled a laugh.

"Because I'm ready to back over Delbert with my car about twenty-five times. Or maybe I should take him to a hockey game and stick ice screws through his clothes so he's stuck to the rink at halftime. Then the Zamboni can run him over. Since Zambonis are so slow he'll have about five minutes to see the end is nigh before it squashes him."

"You're brutal, Mom," said Scott. "Are you sure *you* didn't kill Sergei? Well, getting back to the actual murder and not your fantasy of how you're gonna kill Dad, Detective Studmuffin told me that from the quick tox screen there is evidence that Sergei had taken Viagra shortly before his death. Now, when someone is young and nimble enough to be swinging all over the place on a trapeze, it seems kind of odd to me that he'd need Viagra, but whatever. I heard some people use it kind of like a drug. The Viagra explains why Mom got it in the face."

"Eww, Scott!" said Ida. "I most certainly did not 'get it in the face!' In fact, I have never 'gotten it in the face,' in my life, thank you very much."

"Thanks for that image, Mom," said Scott. "I hope you know a good counselor, because soon I'm going to start having night terrors of that image, and I'll need someone to talk to. It can't be Steve because that image will give him night terrors too."

"Isn't Julie Wellington a therapist?"

"She used to be, but, after the divorce, she quit doing that and became a personal trainer," Ida said. "Just as soon as she stopped looking like the Terminator. In fact, I think she even became a certified Pilates trainer like that guy named Rick we saw at the hospital. The one who thanked Scott for the glutes."

"Let's get back on track, everyone," said Agnes. "So we have a dead man who was bashed in the head or hit his head and was then strangled til he died. We have someone or several someones carrying him up into the rafters where he stayed until he fell on you during the circus. And we have the fact that Sergei took a Viagra shortly before his death, so maybe there was some jealousy motivating that murder? Who knows. And then we have Matilda. Why was your atomizer in the couch, Ida? It had to be Matilda who took it back there. Who else could it have been?"

"I'm wondering if maybe she saw something," said Agnes. "I think we should call Piper and see if we can find something out."

"Well, Agnes, what are we going to say?" said Scott. "Hey, Piper, we were just wondering if your daughter saw Sergei get murdered and if your mom and dad did it. Tell us all about it!"

"I'm sure we can come up with something better than that, Scott," said Ida. "Maybe we can just ask Oleen. After all, she's the one who came up with that wonderful story about how Delbert cut off his finger. She does have a great imagination."

Oleen stuck her tongue out at Ida and then used her splinted wrists to make a rude gesture.

"I think we're just going to have to call Piper and inform her that Matilda stole the atomizer," said Scott. "I can't think of any other plausible reason we could give for calling her, since we aren't detectives, and I'm not involved in this case. We don't have any real reason to be questioning her. But, Mom, you could say you're upset about Matilda stealing from you and that you're concerned about her because you don't want her to 'go down the wrong path.' That sounds like something you'd say. You're going to have to be the one to make the call, Mom."

"But you're the lawyer, Scott!" said Ida. "I'm not even sure what I would say."

"Well, it would be bizarre if I called her," Scott said. "Besides, that's why we're going to tape the call for review later, using my special app for lawyers, and the rest of us are going to be in the room with the phone on speaker. I'll have a notepad nearby, and I'll write questions for you to ask if you can't come up with anything," said Scott

"Okay," said Ida. "I guess. But you better help me out, Scott, or I'm going to sound like a fool. And just don't make me talk about TV or movies."

"Mom, I doubt Piper is gonna want to discuss movies once you tell her her daughter stole from you," Janie said.

"Maybe you should mention that show, *Locked Up Abroad*, though," said Oleen. "You know, scare her a little."

"Okay, Oleen, but she's still in the country, so I don't see how that will help. Before we get home I have to call Delbert," Ida said as Scott backed the car out of the parking space. "I have to make sure he and Gary know to pretend he cut off his finger in case they somehow run into Piper."

~

Delbert was sitting on the front steps of his house when his cell phone rang. He'd been trying to prune Ida's rose bushes in such a way that she wouldn't even notice; that would mean he'd done an excellent job. But, after cutting off one small stem that happened to have a rose on top, he gave up, afraid he'd demolish the roses.

Delbert was tired of yard work. All he wanted to do was go back to the garage and continue working on that vintage Mustang, but he only did that with Gary, and Gary was never setting foot in Delbert's garage again. Delbert supposed that, eventually, the Mustang would gather dust, and once all the people on earth died off it would be overtaken by both kudzu and Ida's rose bushes, and it would be as though the car had never existed in the first place.

"Hello?" Delbert said, answering his phone without looking at the screen, sure there would be someone offering to sell him a timeshare on the other end of the line.

For someone who had put his name on the consumer do-not-call registry, Delbert sure did receive a lot of unwanted phone calls.

"Hello, Delbert? It's Ida."

"Hi, Ida," he said with a sigh. "You sound like you're in a car. I hope you're not texting and driving."

"Delbert, we're talking on the phone. How could I be texting? And, besides, Scott's driving."

"Yeah," said Delbert, knowing this wasn't a social call.

"This is going to sound weird."

Delbert laughed.

"And just why are you laughing?" asked Ida.

"After the past few days, I don't think anything anyone could do or say could sound weird to me. You could tell me you just went to Walmart to pick up Bigfoot and give him a ride home, and the weirdest part of that story would be you went to Walmart."

"That's true," Ida said. "I do hate Walmart."

From the front steps, Delbert watched Gary attempting to mow his own front yard. Gary had one of those non-powered push mowers that only old people and people from 1945 used. Delbert had no idea why Gary didn't buy a normal lawn mower. He could certainly afford to. Usually Gary asked to borrow Delbert's lawn mower, but today Gary was huffing and puffing across his yard, and after two hours he'd barely finished cutting half of it.

It was hot as Hades out, and surely those wind pants Gary had on couldn't be helping. Those kinds of pants made everything hot, and made you sweat in places you didn't even know you could sweat, plus Gary wasn't in the right physical shape to compete in an Olympic lawn-mowing event. Delbert shook his head.

"What's going on, Ida?" Delbert asked. "I know you didn't call just to chat."

"I don't have time to explain, so just listen and go with it, okay?"

"Okay."

"Well, Oleen sort of told Piper that you cut off your finger with a pair of hedge clippers and that Gary had to find the finger and put it in a cooler filled with ice and take you to the hospital so the doctors could reattach it."

"Uh, okay," said Delbert, staying calm. "That's a very interesting thing to tell Piper."

"We had to get rid of her, dear. I got called to the police station for questioning."

"You got what?"

"Anyway, tell Gary so he knows. You probably won't run into Piper, but in case you do just keep a washcloth or an ace bandage or something in your pocket so you can wrap your finger and pretend it's been fixed, okay?"

"Uh, okay."

"Bye Delbert."

"Bye," Delbert said, wondering why in the world the police would need to question his wife about a death she could not have been involved in.

Delbert stood up from the porch steps and walked over to his open garage. He pulled a couple of disposable shop towels from the box next to the bench and stuck them in his pocket. Then he went to the corner of the garage where his lawn mower sat. He wheeled the lawnmower out of the garage, across the yard, and onto Gary's driveway, where he left it, placing the two shop towels over the handle. Gary stopped pushing his manual mower, looked up, walked over to Delbert's lawn mower, grabbed one of the shop towels, and wiped his brow. Delbert watched Gary, then walked back across the yard and up the steps into his house, enjoying the cool breeze of the air conditioning on his face as he stepped through the front door. He'd tell Gary what Ida had said later. The chance of Piper McGruder stopping by was about as high as the chance of Delbert ever letting Gary into his garage again.

60

TUESDAY

I da and Scott sat down in the two chairs on opposite sides of Agnes's side table. Scott plugged in some sort of five-port USB charger, with five different cables coming out of it, and set it on the table. He handed Ida one of the cables, and she plugged it into her phone.

"We don't want your phone to die in the middle of the call," he explained.

Scott had already downloaded the call-taping app onto Ida's phone, and had logged in under the username "Scottald McDonald." It was a good thing Jenny hadn't seen that username, or the merciless teasing would go on until well after Janie's as-of-yet unborn child had graduated from college. Scott told Ida that the call to Piper had to come from her phone, not his because if it didn't, it would just be weird. That's why he had to put the app on her phone.

Ida looked down the list of file names in the app, of the calls Scott had already recorded. The one that stood out most to her was called "butt-touching notes."

"Scott?" Ida asked. "Why do you have a file on here called 'butt-touching notes?'"

"Oh, that," Scott said. "I like to give my call files names that immediately let me know what they are. That was a call with a client from a sexual-harassment case. Her boss kept grabbing her butt, which was apparently true because she got a lot of money in the settlement."

"Was Mr. McGruder her boss?" Oleen asked with a snicker.

Ida's phone lay face-up on the table with Piper's contact information pulled up on the screen. Oleen, Janie, and Agnes sat on the sofa facing the fireplace, and all three held yellow legal notepads and Sharpies. Jenny sat on the floor in front of Ida's chair, and also held a yellow legal pad and a Sharpie.

"Okay," Scott said. He held up his yellow legal pad and Sharpie. "I've got this notepad, and each of you has one too. We have Sharpies so the writing will be dark enough for Mom to see easily from a distance. If anyone thinks of anything for her to ask, write it down and hold the pad up for Mom to read. Got it?"

"This sounds like a game show," Ida said.

"Yeah," said Oleen. "*Jeopardy.*"

"Scott, why do you have so many brand-new legal pads and Sharpies?" asked Jenny.

"Kind of 'went shopping' at work last week. Shh!"

Ida breathed in deeply and made the sign of the cross over her chest.

"Mom, you're not Catholic and, also, you did that backward. I know because Steve's taken me to church a few times and he says I always do it backward."

Ida held her finger over Piper's phone number ready to touch it and make the dreaded call.

"Wait, Mom," said Scott. "First you have to hit the call button in the app. When that connects, you call Piper, and then you merge the two calls."

"You do it," Ida said, pushing her phone across the table

toward Scott. "That's so confusing I'll drop the phone and wet my pants."

"Don't wet your pants, Mom," said Scott. "Pants-wetting is Janie's exclusive domain."

"I'm sad to say it is," said Janie.

Scott hit the call button in the app and, once connected, called Piper, putting Ida's phone on speaker. After three rings, a voice that was not Piper's said, "Hello, Piper's phone."

Scott hit the merge call button, and a red light shone from the top-left corner of the screen of Ida's phone, indicating that the call was being recorded.

"Oh," said Ida. "Oh, hi, Matilda. This is Ida McNair. Remember me? You were at my house on Sunday?"

"Oh yeah. You wouldn't let me have any punch," Matilda said.

"Is your mom available, Matilda?" Ida asked.

"She's peeing right now, but I'll get her."

Oleen wrote "OMG" in large block letters on her notepad, then held it up for all to see. Jenny giggled, then covered her mouth to keep the noise in.

"Mom! Mom?" Piper yelled in a voice that was much louder than Scott's normal whispering voice. "Are you done using it yet? You've got a call from that Ida woman. The one who wouldn't let me have any punch at that dumb baby shower."

Ida heard the sound of a toilet flushing. Matilda must have either been standing right outside the bathroom door, or Piper didn't even bother to close the door when she used the bathroom, which Ida preferred not to think about.

"Hello?" Piper said, like a war-weary soldier returning from battle. "Hi, Ida, sorry about that. Matilda's kind of moody today."

"Today?" Oleen mouthed at Ida from the sofa. Ida waved Oleen off with her hand.

"How's Delbert doing?" Piper asked.

"Oh, uh, he's much better," said Ida. "They were able to reattach his finger. It looks pretty gross right now. He texted me a picture, but, uh, it should be just fine, and they expect he won't even have any nerve damage."

"That's good news!" Piper said.

"Yes," said Ida. "Listen, Piper, that's not why I called."

"Is everything okay, Ida? Is Janie okay? Did she go into early labor?"

"No, nothing like that," Ida said. "I'm calling because—"

Scott wrote furiously on his legal pad and held up the pad for Ida to see. Ida read the writing and continued.

"Because the police talked to me today and they had my perfume atomizer. The one I keep my Poison in."

"That's weird, Ida," Piper said. "Why would they have that?"

"Well, they said they found it backstage in the sex c— in the couch backstage at the French—Canadian Circus. Under some cushions."

Janie shook with laughter and whispered something into Agnes's ear, which set Agnes off giggling too. Janie stuck her face into a pillow to muffle her laughter.

"How did your atomizer get back there?" asked Piper. "Did you even go backstage? I don't see how you would have had a chance. I know Scott and Steve were back there after Scott beat those clowns up, but neither of them seems like they'd be too interested in smelling like women's perfume."

Scott scribbled on his notepad and held up the word "CLOWNS" with a circle around it and a line through it. He drew a frowny face next to it for emphasis.

"I didn't," said Ida. "That's what I wanted to talk to you about. I keep the atomizer in the downstairs bathroom, and at the baby shower Matilda spent a lot of time in there. After the baby shower I couldn't find the atomizer."

"Oh my god," Piper said. "Oh my god, now it makes sense. She stole it, didn't she?"

"I believe so, yes," said Ida.

"Oh my god. In a way, I'm relieved to hear that, because some things over the past couple of days haven't made any sense, and now I know I'm not crazy. But don't worry, I'm taking her phone away, and that girl will never get it back. At this rate, she's going to become a juvenile delinquent."

Jenny quickly wrote on her notepad, then held it up.

"Taking phone away = doubtful.

Juvenile delinquent = YES!"

Janie laughed and stuck her face further into the pillow.

"Well," said Piper, "As I mentioned earlier, we were supposed to leave for the beach early Monday morning. I mean really early, at like, 4 a.m. Andy is kind of fanatical about leaving early on car trips. It drives me nuts because I have no idea why it's necessary to leave so early when we can't check in to wherever we end up staying until around 3 or 4 p.m., but I sleep in the passenger seat so I guess I can't complain too much."

"That's so early!" said Ida. "I think Gary is like that too."

Oleen scribbled on the notepad, then held it up. It said:

"At 4 a.m., Gary drives in a nightshirt...and sweatpants."

Ida smiled and tried not to laugh.

"Andy didn't feel good on Sunday, so I really wasn't sure we'd even be able to go, but he felt better as the day wore on. On Sunday night, around ten," Piper continued, "Matilda couldn't find her phone, which made me quite happy because that phone is a pain in the ass. I wish Mom and Dad never gave it to her. Matilda whined, and Andy and I needed her to have her phone in the car on this trip because, otherwise, it would be hell on wheels."

Agnes widened her eyes and shook her head.

"Matilda looked everywhere, but she couldn't find the phone. I figured it was just somewhere on the floor of her closet under all those clothes, but then Andy asked her if she'd had it

when she went to the circus with my dad earlier in the evening
—Sunday evening, I mean."

At Agnes's house, everyone sat up straighter and listened
with rapt attention.

"See, Matilda had been begging Dad to let her go down
there and see backstage ever since he told her about the show.
She wanted to see the costumes. By the time we got back from
the beach trip, the one we'd planned to leave for the next day,
Matilda would be starting sleepaway summer camp and
wouldn't get a chance to go. So Dad agreed to take her on
Sunday night, right after we left Janie's baby shower. He said he
had to go get his laptop, though I think he said that to make it
seem like he wasn't making a special trip down there just for
Matilda. Not that Matilda would have felt bad if that had been
the case."

"That was nice of your dad," Ida said.

"Yeah, it was. Dad picked Matilda up around 6:30 and, at
that point, she still had her phone in her pocket. While Dad
went over to his office, he let Matilda go backstage in the circus
tent and look in the costume closet. When he came back, he
said she was lying on the couch playing on her phone."

Scott scribbled on his notepad.

"Don't lie on the sex couch."

Janie laughed into her pillow.

"Then Dad brought Matilda home. He took her to dinner
first and dropped her off back here around 8 p.m. He said he
somehow left his laptop backstage, even though that was what
he went there to get. I do that all the time, though—go to Target
to buy new sheets and then leave with everything but the
sheets—so I understood. Dad said he was going to go back
down and get it."

"I know all about Target!" Ida said. "I'm terrible about that,
too."

"Then Matilda realized a little while after Dad dropped her

off that her phone was missing," said Piper, "it was around 8:30 when she noticed, but lord only knows how it even took her that long, I had her search for it for a long time, but she couldn't find it. Finally, around ten, Andy said he'd take her back down to the circus to see if it was there. The tent might be locked up, in which case we'd just have to get it in the morning and leave later than Andy had planned. Andy was really good about it. He said if the tent was closed they could just go to Dairy Queen. There's one right next to the civic center, and he sure does love Blizzards. Personally, I think that was his true motivation for taking Matilda back down there, but I wouldn't say that to him."

"So, did they find the phone?" Ida asked.

"Actually, they did," said Piper. When they got back down to the civic center, the lights were on in the tent, but not in Dad's office, and his car was parked in front of the tent. Since Andy knew Dad was inside, he let Matilda run in to look for her phone by herself. While he was waiting, though, he saw something kind of weird."

Ida sat up straighter.

"What did he see?"

"Well," Piper said, "Andy parked a couple of spaces down from Dad's car. There aren't spaces, since it's not a parking lot, but he parked near Dad. Outside the lot, parked on the street, Andy saw a car that looked like my mom's car. You know she drives that bright green Kia Soul, so it's easy to spot. Andy peered at the car for a minute and decided it looked like Mom inside, so he got out and walked over. It was weird for her to be there so late, and he wanted to make sure she was okay. He said he startled her. She was staring at the tent, and she was eating French fries she was dipping into a milkshake. She's always done that when she's stressed. She jumped and then rolled down the window, and Andy asked if she was okay. She said she was—that she'd been visiting her friend Rose. Rose is the

Development Director for the civic center. After Rose's husband passed away a few years ago, she moved out of their house in the suburbs and bought a little condo down there by the civic Center. She can practically walk to work. Mom said she just wanted some Dairy Queen on the way home and decided to park near the tent because she liked 'the pretty colors.'"

"That sounds strange," said Ida.

"Yeah," Piper said. "Andy said he wondered if my mom and Rose had been smoking pot because that's kind of what mom smelled like, which would be really weird, but stranger things have happened. Andy left my mom with her fries and got back in his car. A couple of minutes later he saw some short, red-haired girl run out of the tent and toward the parking deck. I mean, *run*. And, a few minutes later, a blue Smart car pulled out of the deck and the same girl—the one with red hair—was driving it and appeared to be totally fine, so he chalked it up to it being a full moon."

"So, where was Matilda?" Ida asked.

"Andy started to wonder what was taking Matilda so long and was about to go look for her in the tent when Matilda came running out of the tent with her phone in her hand. She got in the car, and he said she reeked of perfume—perfume that smelled like mine. It was that Poison stuff you have too, Ida. When he asked her about it, she said she'd been in the costume closet and found it in there, but now I'm guessing it came from your atomizer."

"That sounds possible," Ida said.

"When they left, my dad's car was still there, but Dad's been so busy lately trying to schmooze his way into the directorship if the circus takes over the civic center, that it wouldn't be weird to me if he'd slept back there on that couch," Piper said.

"Dairy Queen was closed at that point, so Andy and Matilda got Frostys from Wendy's. Matilda loves Frostys, but she didn't eat any of hers so, when she got home, I ate it, which I shouldn't have done since I am about to be wearing a swimsuit and all. While they were gone I decided to make some red velvet cupcakes to take to the beach— we were going to stay with some friends there, and cupcakes travel so much more easily than a cake. I couldn't sleep, and that's the main reason I made them. I'd just finished using the stand mixer when Andy and Matilda walked in, and I offered Matilda the beater to lick. She loves to do that. This time though, she said, "No, Mom, eww, that looks like blood!" And then she ran upstairs to her room with her phone in her hand.

PART V

61

TUESDAY

"We're going to have to talk to Grace," said Oleen, after Ida had ended the call with Piper.

Ida noticed Scott labeling the call, "It's a Circus," before he signed out of the app on her phone. Though not a particularly clever or funny name, the way many of the names of his other files were, Ida did have to give Scott points for accuracy.

"We'll need to talk to Grace's friend, Rose, too," said Oleen, "Though it will be much easier to explain why we want to talk to Grace," Oleen said. "And we should talk to those circus people—Fernando and Katerina. And maybe even to Bill McGruder, but he's apparently so busy with his head up the butt of whoever is running the French—Canadian circus that I doubt he'd have had time to kill anyone. That, and with trying to lure twenty-two-year-old contortionists onto Scott's "sex couch."

"Ida," Oleen continued, "You and Agnes and I should talk to Grace. She must know, or at least suspect, that Bill has been making the beast with two backs with anything female that moves. Agnes, you can tell her that you once suspected

Herman of cheating. You know, find some common ground. Get her talking. Ida and I can't tell her that Gary and Delbert have been cheating on us for, like, six thousand years. She wouldn't consider that real cheating since they're gay."

Ida scowled.

"But I never suspected Herman of cheating!" Agnes said at the same time Jenny said, "The beast with two backs?" then shook her head and laughed until she cried.

"I mean, there was that one time I thought Herman was acting strange for a while," said Agnes, "But I never thought he was cheating. I doubt any woman would've put up with his antics long enough to get to the point of making the 'beast with two backs,' with him, as you say. It turned out he'd gotten into internet gambling. Thankfully, he didn't get too far into debt, but it was an addiction. He went to Gamblers' Anonymous for a while. Then he seemed to get over it, and he developed a peculiar interest in building ships inside bottles. You know those things? He must've made two hundred of them before he died. That's not attractive to femmes fatales who would've wanted to lure Herman onto the sex couch—making ships in bottles, that is."

Janie's cell phone rang, playing the music that accompanied Darth Vader's entrance into any scene in all the Star Wars movies.

Ida stared at Janie.

"He's on my list right now," Janie said, gesturing to her phone. "If he gets off my list his ringtone can be that song from *Dirty Dancing*—'Time of My Life,' or whatever it was called."

"Hi, Jason," Janie said. "No, I'm at Agnes's house. What's up?"

Janie listened for a moment, then her face turned red.

"Jason, I'm almost eight months' pregnant and you think going to Las Vegas with your friends TWO WEEKS before my due date is a good idea? You've gone insane!"

She held the phone up to her ear.

"No, that is most certainly not okay with me. No, Atlantic City is not okay with me either. Why do you need a 'last hurrah' with your friends before the baby's born? I can't have a 'last hurrah' with mine unless it involves drinking lemonade and barely being able to stand up from a chair. Lots of fun I am these days."

Janie took a sip of water from a bottle she'd stuck between the cushions next to her on the couch.

"You're an asshole, Jason. I know you're just going to do whatever you want to because you're just like that. Once you meet your daughter, maybe you'll realize the earth doesn't revolve around you. Oh, if you're not off gambling when she's born, that is. Fine. North Carolina. At least you could drive back fast. And three days only. One weekend and a Friday. Now I'm going. I'm hungry, and since I know you're going to go to dinner after work with the guys from the restaurant and drink beer until you die, I'm going to make other arrangements."

Janie hit the button on her phone's screen to end the call, and threw the phone across the room, where it became lodged between two throw pillows on Agnes's sofa.

"Now I'm gonna find him a ringtone that's just the word bastard repeated over and over. I can make one." Janie said.

"Well, that was pleasant," said Scott.

"If you say anything, Scott, I swear to god I'll have Mom help me kill you and she and Julie Wellington and I will hide your body up a tree next to Dad's."

Scott held both his hands up.

"Even I'm not that stupid," he said. "Well, Janie, how about you and Jenny and I head to my house? Steve will be home soon, and he'll cook us dinner. Then we can sit in the garden, and you can vent if you want. Or, if not, you can at least use my heated foot spa."

"I'm going with the foot spa," Janie said.

Scott's phone pinged with a text. He looked at his phone.

"It's Maureen," he said. "Allow me to quote from this message: 'Please help! No one's sick anymore, but Alex and I have to get out of here. Need real food. Is Steve cooking tonight? We will pay you cash money. Tomorrow morning we have to drive in the car for several hours. Help or we might die! Will leave kids with Alex's mom. If not, will kill kids in car tomorrow.'"

Scott tapped out a response, reciting as he typed.

"Where are you going?"

A second later, his phone pinged again.

"Gatlinburg?" he asked, reading the text. "Why the hell would anyone want to go there on purpose? It's super gay. And by super gay, I don't mean the amazing kind of gay like me. I mean lame, and stupid, and boring."

Scott responded, speaking as he typed.

"How long are you staying?"

When his phone pinged, Scott read the response with a laugh.

"A week? What can you do in Gatlinburg for a week? There are only so many airbrushed t-shirts you can buy and cable car rides you can take before you go insane."

The phone pinged again.

"We might go to Dollywood or Pigeon Forge," Scott read.

"Well, Dollywood might be hilarious, so that's much better," said Scott.

"Come on over," Scott said, as he typed the words. "We're having a party. Steve's cooking dinner and Janie and Jenny are coming too. Would ask Mike and Lauren, but I don't think engaged people leave their bedrooms for at least a month after they get engaged."

Scott's phone pinged again.

"Eww," he read. "I read Alex what you wrote about Mike, and he said he thinks the stomach virus is coming back."

"Come on, Janie, Jenny," Scott said. "I hope Maureen and Alex aren't gonna need to throw up in one of our bathrooms. Our maid service came today. The bathrooms won't look this good for a week!"

"You're so sensitive, Scott," said Janie.

"To the needs of his bathrooms," said Jenny.

After Scott had packed all his stuff back into his bookbag, and reattached Agnes's Apple TV and made sure it was working, he noticed Janie's phone still sticking out from between the two throw pillows. He grabbed it as he walked to the door. Jenny exited the house, and Janie followed her. Scott stopped Janie as she reached the front door and held her phone out to her.

"Here you go, Janie," he said.

"Keep it," Janie said. "I don't ever want to see it again."

"No, you take it, or I'll back over it with my car just because Jason's voice came out of it."

"Can't argue with that," Janie said with a shrug.

She took the phone from Scott and held it in her hand as she walked out the door.

62

TUESDAY

"Alright, Agnes," Oleen said as she stood up from the couch. "I know you never suspected Herman of cheating, and I'm sure he didn't, but we need you to take one for the team here."

"Okay," said Agnes. "You know, when I was in high school, I wanted to be an actress. I was always the lead in the school plays. I think I can still summon up my acting skills."

"So, Oleen, am I right that we're going to go visit Grace and then Rose?" Ida asked.

"I think that's the best plan, don't you?" Oleen said.

"We need to find out what made Grace go stare at the circus tent and eat French fries the other night," said Agnes. "Maybe Rose can tell us but, first, we have to see what Grace says, or Rose will think we're just odd since we don't know her at all. Also, I'd kind of just like to know if Grace and Rose were smoking reefer."

Oleen giggled at the word reefer. "We can't just show up at Rose's condo, and we don't even know where her condo is, except that it's near the civic center."

"Okay," said Ida, "To the car then, I guess. It's a good thing

Grace and Bill still live right around the corner. Oleen, how could we have gone several years without seeing Grace when she lives so close we could walk to her house?"

"I've run into her at the grocery store occasionally," Agnes said. "And I live at least ten minutes from all of you. Also, it's hard to want to be friends with someone who is homophobic when your son is gay and married to a man. I'd say that's why. It tends to make dinner parties awkward."

"We don't have dinner parties unless they involve a grill!" Ida laughed.

"Well, it makes cookouts awkward too," said Agnes. "Maybe even more awkward than dinner parties because everyone can just wander around in the backyard. At least at a dinner party you could seat Grace far away from Scott and his 'roommate.'"

All three women giggled.

"If we had it at your house, Ida," said Oleen, "We could cram her into the corner next to that big cabinet that holds your wedding china you never use. You know, where the corner edge can poke her in the butt all night."

Ida winced. "I did use that china once," Ida said. "The one time Delbert's parents visited. I never saw them again after that, and I never used that china again, either. It didn't go well."

"Good thing, if you ask me," said Agnes.

Ida turned off Agnes's street and navigated the familiar roads that led to her own neighborhood. She turned onto Magnolia Manor and stopped on the street in front of Grace's house, parking the car.

"Seriously," said Oleen. "How does a street name have Manor at the end? I thought it needed lane or road or boulevard or something at the end to be a legitimate street."

"The houses are a good deal larger here, dear. That's why," Ida said. "I mean, the McGruders have always had a large walk-in pantry, you know, with its own rolling ladder. You have to have a huge house to have one of those. And it's funny because I doubt either of them has ever cooked a thing!"

"Oh, the pantry," Oleen said. "The site of 'the incident.'"

"Huh?" said Ida. "What's 'the incident?'"

"You know!" Oleen laughed. "Scott's 'I love a pair of nice, shapely buttocks' incident."

"Oh, that. You know how Scott has always been so dramatic and made things up, dear," said Ida. "He just likes to tell that story and shake his rear end while he tells it, and then everyone laughs. It's like his party trick or something. Everyone knows he made that story up."

Ida, Oleen, and Agnes exited Ida's Expedition and walked up the stone walkway, then up the three steps to the McGruders' wraparound front porch.

Agnes had always admired wraparound porches, and this house had one on both the top and bottom levels. It was quite a beautiful house—light and bright with many windows. Agnes sighed. It also had a fantastic kitchen, and they'd probably updated it since Agnes had been here last.

Oleen knocked on Grace's front door and Grace opened it, not at all her usual put-together self. Instead of a brightly colored funeral dress she had on yoga pants and a long t-shirt. Seeing Grace's outfit made Ida look down at her own ridiculous clothing; she couldn't believe she hadn't thought to go home and change first. Maybe the fact Ida and Oleen both looked like they had just grabbed random items from the sale bin at Walmart and haphazardly put them on would make Grace feel more comfortable about being less coifed than usual. Ida was thankful Oleen looked just as hideous as she did.

Ida expected Grace to comment on hers and Oleen's clothing, but she didn't. She just motioned Ida, Oleen, and Agnes inside and invited them to sit on the couch. On Grace's coffee table sat a pitcher of what looked like sparkling grape juice, and an empty water glass.

"It's wine," Grace said, "But Matilda's here, and I don't want her to know that, so I poured it into a pitcher, and I'm drinking it out of a regular glass. She thinks it's sparkling grape juice, and she hates grape juice. Would you all like any?"

All three women nodded yes, and Grace took the pitcher into the kitchen and returned with three stacked glasses and the pitcher, which she had refilled with more wine. She poured three glasses of wine and passed them out, then refilled her own.

"I'm happy you showed up, actually," said Grace, taking a generous gulp of wine. "I'm so stressed out right now I hardly know what to do. Piper asked me to watch Matilda this afternoon because, since Andy had that virus and they didn't go on their trip this week, and since all that crap happened at the circus, she's been with Matilda nonstop and she just needed a break. She's out getting a massage. I completely understand. That girl can be a handful."

Agnes sighed.

"She's out on the back deck right now," said Grace. "She likes to go out there and take pictures on her phone. Probably spying on the neighbors and taking pictures like in that old Alfred Hitchcock movie."

"Back Window!" Ida said.

"I believe it's called *Rear Window*, honey," Agnes said. "But at least you got the window part right. And it was in the back." Agnes patted Ida's knee.

"I'm afraid she's hoping to see some murderer in the house behind us or something," said Grace. "She just keeps telling me dead people stink, and that's strange, even for Matilda. I think she acts out so much because her father's never home and, don't tell anyone I said this, but Piper's top priorities are the gym and Bloomingdale's. And so much has happened the past few days, I'm about to— I think my head may explode soon," said Grace. "I'm glad you're here because I can't talk to anyone about it. Not Piper, not Bill, not even Rose, and she's my best friend."

"What's going on, Grace?" Agnes asked, leaning toward Grace and patting her knee. "Are you okay?"

"Well, the other night I went to Rose's condo. Sunday night, yeah, it was Sunday. It's right by where Bill works, and Rose works there too, you know— she's the Director of Development and Annual Giving. Has been for years. When her husband, Fred, died a few years ago, she sold their house because it was enormous and she didn't need so much space. They only have one grandchild, and he and his parents live in Seattle. Their daughter is an only child, you see. So the condo is the perfect size for her, and it's cute too."

Oleen tapped her foot wishing Grace would get on with it.

"Anyway, you don't need to know all that. But on Sunday night I had dinner with Rose at her condo, and we went through more wine than I'd like to admit, way more than what I've had today. When we get all tipsy like that we tend to be more honest with each other than we usually are."

"I can certainly understand that," Ida said, gesturing to herself, Oleen, and Agnes. "We do that too."

"Well, I asked Rose how work was going, and she said she's planning to retire. I was shocked! I mean, Rose is older than I am. I'm sixty, and she's seventy-three, but she's in great shape and loves her job. And she's someone who I think would be really bored without a job to go to. You know, she loves being social and having something structured to do every day."

"That's interesting," Agnes said. "I wonder what would make her want to retire."

"Well, this is the part that bothers me so much," Grace said. "I asked her, and she was pretty drunk by then, but somehow Rose still manages to hold her tongue to a degree, even when she's drunk. I said. "Rose, why would you want to do that? You make great money, and you love your job!" And do you know what she told me?"

Agnes, Ida, and Oleen all stared at Grace.

"What?" Oleen managed to say.

"She told me that it has to do with Bill. With *my* Bill. She said he's been doing something unethical and she just can't stand it anymore. She said she's so tired of what he's doing that she just has to leave the place. She said maybe she'll take up a volunteer cause. She said she told Bill to stop and he didn't, and now she just wants out."

"What has Bill been doing?" asked Ida.

"Rose wouldn't tell me!" Grace said. "She said she didn't want to be in the middle of it and she also didn't want to somehow give me false information. She said if I want to know what's happening I need to go right to the source. She said that since she and I have been friends for so long, she went to Bill about whatever it is instead of reporting him, but since he refuses to stop she's just leaving since she isn't going to turn him in."

"Why wouldn't she tell you?" gasped Agnes. "That's got to be torture!"

"You may not know this," said Grace, "but Bill has had a couple of affairs over the years, and two were at work. Okay, more than a couple."

Oleen tried to camouflage her eye-roll by rubbing her eyes.

"I'm sorry, honey," said Agnes. "It's an awful feeling to think your husband is cheating on you. I once thought Herman was cheating on me, but it turned out he'd just gotten involved in internet gambling."

"Well, I know Bill has cheated. Several times. I won't go into it now, but I've wondered for a while if that's why the Wellingtons got divorced. Bill seemed way too close to Julie for a while. They started playing tennis together. I hate tennis, so Bill has always played with other people, but they've always been men.

Then he started playing with Julie, and she always wore that short little slutty skirt. Since then I haven't even been able to stand the sight of Julie Wellington! There's even some horrible picture on Bill's Facebook page where he's standing way too close to her, but there are lots of horrible pictures of him standing way too close to lots of women on his Facebook page. It's like he has no concept of personal space. I should confront him about it, but I've pretty much given up."

"I'm sorry, Grace," Ida said. "Do you think that's what he's doing now?"

"I think so," Grace said. There's some policy at work about not having romantic relationships, but now there are all those hot little circus numbers prancing around in their tiny leotards. And that show may permanently take over the civic center. It's almost a sure thing. Then who knows what Bill will be doing? That's why the other night I parked outside the civic center and tried to see what Bill was up to, but all I saw was that his office was dark and there were some circus performers leaving the tent. I bet he was out back having sex with some homeless woman in a dumpster!"

Grace began to sob.

"He'd rather be with a homeless woman than with me!"

"I'm sure that's not true, dear," Ida said, moving closer to Grace and touching her hand. "Homeless women aren't exactly known for their excellent personal hygiene, and Bill seems to go for women who take care of themselves. Like you. I mean, you always look fantastic."

Grace wiped her eyes.

"Thank you," she sniffled.

"I'm kind of mad Rose won't tell me, but I understand too," Grace said. "Who wants to be in the middle of someone else's marital problems?"

"That makes sense," Agnes said. "I certainly wouldn't."

"Everything's going to hell," Grace said. "With that and with the picture I found."

"Oh my god!" said Oleen. "Did you find a picture of Bill with another woman?"

"No," said Grace, "But I wish I had. That would be easier."

Grace reached into the pocket of her yoga pants. Oleen had no idea they made yoga pants with pockets, and she was about to ask Grace where she got them when Grace produced a folded-up piece of paper from the pocket of her pants.

"Here," Grace said, thrusting the folded-up paper at Ida.

Ida unfolded the paper as Agnes and Oleen looked over her shoulders. When the paper was unfolded completely, Ida smoothed it out on her lap, and all three women goggled at the image before them.

The picture was quite clear, even with the slight smudging that was probably the result of Grace's fingers touching the inkjet-printed image before it had dried. The photo appeared to have been taken from quite close up.

In the photo, crouched over Sergei's dead body, the trapeze artist Fernando was feeling Sergei's neck for a pulse and touching the back of Sergei's head. Fernando was staring off to the side as though looking to see if anyone might be coming, and his hands appeared to be covered with blood.

63

TUESDAY

"Oh. My. God," said Ida.

"You sound like Scott!" said Agnes.

"Grace!" Oleen said. "Where in the world did you get this? Did someone email it to you? I can tell you printed it because of the smudges. I print my knitting patterns out and always smudge them. Mike and Jenny make fun of me for even having a printer anymore."

"Why would someone email that to *you*?" asked Ida. "Is someone trying to blackmail you? Maybe over whatever Bill is doing?"

"Ida," Oleen said, "if someone wanted to blackmail Grace wouldn't they send her photos of something untoward either she or Bill was doing? That theory doesn't even make sense."

Ida shrugged. "I just saw an episode about blackmail on some show on Investigation Discovery. Also, in a murder, usually the husband or wife did it. Like, every time. That's what happens every time I watch a show on Investigation Discovery. And if it's not the spouse, it's the kids!"

"But Sergei didn't have a wife or kids, Ida!" Oleen said.

"That we know of!" Ida said. "And he's got a girlfriend,

doesn't he? Maybe Katerina did it, and she's framing Fernando!"

"You're nuts," Oleen said, looking at Ida and circling her finger around the side of her head in the international symbol for crazy.

"Ladies!" Agnes interrupted. "Let's stop and let Grace tell us what happened. "Where did this photo come from, Grace?"

"This is the part I don't want to say," Grace said, resting her head in her hands. She began crying softly again. "I wish someone had emailed it to me. But I found it on Matilda's phone."

"On Matilda's phone?" Oleen said in a voice eight octaves higher than usual. "Why would this picture be on Matilda's phone?"

"I'm not sure," Grace said. "And I certainly have no idea what to do about it."

Ida's eyes went wide.

"Piper told us Matilda went down to the circus with Bill on Sunday night because she'd been begging to go and wasn't going to have a chance to go later," said Ida. "That's the night the police say the murder was committed. Sunday night. Or maybe Monday morning, but they have to estimate the time someone died, and they don't always get it right. Scott told me that once. Piper said Andy took Matilda back down to the circus tent pretty late because Matilda left her phone down there when she'd gone with Bill earlier. She needed her phone for the beach trip the next day. Since Bill's car was there when Andy took Matilda back, Piper said Andy thought it was safe to let Matilda run into the tent alone. Bill's office was dark, and the tent was still open, and earlier Bill had taken his laptop to the tent so he could work there. So Andy figured that's where Bill was. Andy told Piper that after Matilda went into the tent it took her a long time to come back to the car, but he figured she'd just been poking around in the costume closet since she tends to get into things. He was about to go in and get her when she came running out with her phone. On the way home he got her a Frosty, and she wouldn't even eat it, and she usually loves those. And then, at home Piper was making red velvet cupcakes, and Matilda usually likes to lick the batter off the beaters, but Piper said when she offered one to Matilda, that Matilda said it looked like blood and ran upstairs."

"You don't think..." Grace said. "You don't think Matilda *saw* that man get murdered, do you? I mean, I know she acts weird sometimes, but I think that would be too much for even her to take. She *has* been subdued today, and she's only twelve, so I'm sure seeing that photo must have been awful for her. Or taking it."

"Oh god," said Agnes. "Are you saying Matilda gave you this picture? She showed it to you? Did she say what happened?"

"No," Grace said. "I found it on her phone. I have this older neighbor, Janice Zeblinsky. She lives next door, and she's always got fresh-baked chocolate chip cookies. She likes Matilda to come over and have cookies and talk with her. I never allow Matilda to take her phone there and be rude to Janice. She has to leave it here. Matilda does seem to enjoy the visits though."

"Maybe she told this Janice lady something?" said Oleen.

"I doubt it," Grace said. "I'll ask, but they just talk about art. Matilda loves art and Janice is quite a good painter. She even had an exhibit in New York once. I think Matilda wants to be an artist."

"So how did you get this picture from her phone?" Oleen asked, tapping her foot.

"Well, when Matilda left for Janice's, about an hour and a half ago, I noticed her phone sitting right there on the coffee table," Grace said, pointing to where the pitcher of wine now sat. "You know how Matilda doesn't always do what she's supposed to, so I figured it would be good to check her phone just to see what she's up to. I went on her phone to make sure she isn't talking to boys or sending them photos, or buying things she's not supposed to online or something. Her phone has a passcode, but Piper makes her keep it one that we all know, and Piper checks the phone. Matilda knows that if Piper ever tries to get into the phone and Matilda has changed the passcode that Piper will take the phone away. So I know the passcode and opened the phone."

"That was a good idea on Piper's part," Agnes nodded, surprised Piper had enacted such a rule.

"Well, I looked through Matilda's texts and emails, even the deleted ones, and through her browser history, and there wasn't much," said Grace.

"There were a lot of visits to art museum websites and a couple of apps where she makes drawings, but the drawings weren't weird or anything. In her photos there were a lot out the windows of her house, and some through neighbors' windows—spying and all—which Piper is going to have to talk to her about. The videos were mostly of Matilda lip-synching songs, ones with inappropriate lyrics so Piper will have to address that too. Then, I checked the deleted photos in case Matilda had been taking any inappropriate pictures of herself, which she hadn't been, and I found this picture. I don't want Matilda to know I've seen it until I have a chance to decide what to do, so I just emailed it to myself from Matilda's phone, and I printed it from my computer. Then I deleted the sent email off Matilda's phone and put the photo back into the deleted file. I saw on TV how to do all that. I think on some *NCIS* rerun. Then I printed the picture and made sure Matilda's phone was running the same apps it had been when she left, and I put it back on the coffee table. Matilda came home about ten minutes before you got here, and grabbed her phone, then went out on the porch. I saw her out there photographing some of my flowers, which is a relief because at least she's not trying to see into the neighbors' houses then."

"I guess she must have taken the picture," said Ida. "I can't see any other explanation. Thank god she didn't take a video!"

"I am thankful for that," said Grace.

All three women stopped talking as Matilda walked inside the house from the porch, clutching her phone. Then she went into the bathroom off the living room. Matilda closed the bathroom door behind her. No one spoke much while Matilda was inside, in case she could hear their conversation. Grace refilled everyone's glasses with wine.

"That phone is surgically attached to her hand, I swear," Grace said. "It was Bill's idea to give it to her for her twelfth birthday. I didn't think it was a good idea."

Grace shook her head.

The four women watched as Matilda emerged from the bathroom a few minutes later, picked up a bottle of bubble-blowing liquid off the side table, and went back outside onto the back porch. They could see her through the glass doors, blowing bubbles and popping them.

"Sometimes she acts so old and other times like such a little kid," Grace said, gesturing toward the porch.

"It's the age," Ida said. "That's quite normal."

"Excuse me," said Oleen. "I could do with a trip to the bathroom myself."

Oleen stood up, walked to the bathroom, and shut the door.

"Grace," said Ida, "I don't mean to overstep my bounds here, but do you think that red-headed trapeze girl, Katerina, might be the person Bill is having the affair with? Scott and Steve overheard a few things, and that's why I'm asking."

"Wait, what?" Grace said. "What did they overhear?"

"Well," said Ida, "Since we're all being honest here—and maybe we should have some more wine to help with that," she said, taking a sip from her glass, "After Scott attacked the clown last night, he and Steve went backstage. Remember, Scott was talking to you and they said Katerina acted very flirty with Bill, and then, well, they heard you getting kind of upset with him."

"Oh, that," said Grace, "I'd forgotten Scott and Steve were even there. I forgot anyone was there, I was so angry. Our whole marriage Bill has looked at other women, and I'm just fed up. I did think it was Katerina he was having an affair with, at least that night I did."

"Scott and Steve also heard you, well, yelling at her in the parking deck last night," Ida said.

"How did they hear that?" Grace asked.

"They got locked out of the building and it was raining so hard they had to creep along under the overhang to get back to their car in the deck. Before they walked out of the bushes, they heard yelling, and they didn't want to walk in on anything dangerous. They looked around the corner and saw you standing by Katerina's car and they heard you telling Katerina she'd better stop, and that you knew all about her. They said you said she'd be back in Russia soon, working for the state circus."

The toilet flushed and the three women heard the sound of running water. Oleen walked out of the bathroom and took a seat on the couch, taking a gulp from her glass of wine before setting the wine glass back on the coffee table. Ida looked at the glass sitting there on the wooden coffee table without a coaster and decided she didn't care about rings anymore.

"You know," said Oleen, "It's a good thing we quit talking when Matilda went into the bathroom because I could hear every word you said while I was in there. Also, just for your information, it's quite difficult to use the bathroom with two splinted wrists."

"Oh, I'll have to remember that!" Grace said. "That you can

hear everything in there. Not about using the bathroom with two splinted wrists. Once, right after the Wellingtons got divorced, Julie was here for some reason, and I was sitting on the couch with Rose talking about what a hussy she was. I hope Julie didn't hear me!"

"Well," said Oleen, "She might have, but that was a long time ago. Right now, though, I have something to add to your conversation. Grace, when I fell over on that tree up on the top floor of the civic center, it's because I was spying on Fernando and Katerina."

"I know that, Oleen," Grace said. "I didn't just fall off the turnip truck yesterday or anything."

"Well, they were talking about you," Oleen said.

"They were?" Grace asked, with genuine surprise in her voice.

"Yeah, Fernando was telling Katerina they better go to the police and tell them because you already knew, and you might have told someone or Bill might know now and tell someone because you might have said something to him. And Katerina said if anyone found out she'd lose her job. And then Fernando said she hadn't lost her job for dating Sergei, and Katerina said this was different. I think they must have some rule in the circus about romantic relationships too. They said something that sounded like "Bill's wife is the one." So I figured Bill and Katerina were having an affair, and that you knew and you were going to expose them."

"Oh," Grace said, putting her head back into her hands and beginning to cry again.

Being so used to handing Gary pillows to cry into, Oleen grabbed an orange throw pillow from the couch and gave it to Grace, who buried her face in it. Sobs shook her shoulders.

"I'm so embarrassed," she sputtered between sobs. "I hate that anyone saw me act that way. Yelling and being crazy."

Agnes patted Grace's knee, and Grace looked up at her, wiping tears from her eyes.

"It's okay, honey," Agnes said. "Thinking your husband is seeing someone else will make anyone crazy. When I thought Herman might be cheating, I purposely tripped the work colleague I thought he was having an affair with. This was at a company Christmas party, and her skirt even flew up, and everyone saw her underwear, but she didn't know it was me. And it turned out he wasn't even having an affair with anyone. I was mortified!"

Oleen eyed Agnes, mouth agape.

"If you've thought Bill has been having an affair with Katerina, your behavior makes sense," Agnes said.

"I did," Grace answered, "And that's why I confronted her, but now that I've spoken to Rose I think the woman he's sleeping with might be much higher up in the organization. Someone who, if anyone found out, he might even lose his job, and she might lose hers too. His last affair at work, at his old job, was with his boss, and she was ten years younger than he is! That's why he left to work at the civic center, and his boss was "relocated" to the Jacksonville office. If it gets out, it will be such a scandal!"

"Well, we know all about scandals, dear," Ida said, nodding at Grace.

"Huh?" Grace asked.

"But if you thought Bill and Katerina were just having an affair, Grace," said Oleen, "What was all that stuff about you knowing something about her, and telling her you'd looked her up and she'd have to go back to the Russian state circus?"

"Oh, that," Grace said, "I found out some things about her that I was trying to use as leverage to get her to admit to having an affair with Bill. But, like I said, after talking to Rose I don't think that's the case. I don't think she and Bill are having an affair. I still think she's a slut, though. I think she was seeing

Sergei and also having a thing with Fernando. Fernando must have caught them together and killed Sergei in a jealous rage."

"That would make sense," Oleen said. "I did see Fernando looking at Bill in a very angry way the night Sergei fell on us. Fernando must have thought Bill was having an affair with Katerina too. Three guys at one time? That's kind of gross."

"I'm not supposed to mention this," Ida said, "But one of the detectives told Scott that Sergei had taken a Viagra shortly before he died. So I bet Fernando walked in on Sergei and Katerina. I don't know why they picked the costume closet though. It doesn't seem like it would be very comfortable, and that's where your photo appears to have been taken."

"It does look like Fernando's in the costume closet in that photo," Oleen agreed. "And Fernando and Katerina did appear to have quite a close relationship, at least from what I saw the night Sergei died. Fernando was comforting her, and when I heard them arguing I could tell they had a secret."

"But what did you find out about Katerina, Grace? What was it that was so important you thought you could threaten her with it?" Agnes asked. "I'm dying to know, and maybe it's important!"

"Well, not threaten her, exactly..." Grace said. "But, aside from being a closet slut— no pun intended there—it seems that Little Miss Redhead has some secrets of her own."

64

TUESDAY

"Well, first," Ida said, "we're going to have to decide what to do with that photo. You're almost certainly going to have to take it to the police, but I can call Scott to help with that. It's evidence, and Fernando is clearly the killer, so if you don't turn it over to them it might be destruction of justice."

"Obstruction, honey," said Agnes.

"What?" said Ida.

"Obstruction of justice. It might be obstruction of justice."

"Either way, you'll have to give it to them," Ida said.

"They'll want Matilda's phone too," Oleen said. "At least on TV shows they always want phones and computers and stuff. They aren't going to take your word for it that it came from her phone."

"Well, we may have a time finding that phone," Grace said. "Maybe Matilda has it outside with her—probably—but she loses it constantly."

"Before we go to the police station or call Scott, though, what is this secret of Katerina's?" Agnes asked. "It's something you might need to tell the police too."

"Okay," Grace said. "Katerina is illegal. She's in the country illegally. And you know how things are now. If anyone finds out, she'll be sent back to Russia. My guess is Fernando either knows and thinks Katerina should tell the police, or maybe he meant they had to tell the police about their affair, though that doesn't make sense if Fernando killed Sergei, so I bet it's the illegal thing he thought she should tell the police about. Maybe he thought they'd go easier on her that way. I'm not proud of it, but I was going to threaten to report Katerina if she didn't admit to sleeping with Bill and promise to stop doing it. You know the circus was here for two months before the first show, for rehearsals and all. And it has something to do with the proposal to convert the civic center, I think, everyone arriving so early. I think it was for negotiating a price for buying the building or something like that. So Bill and Katerina had plenty of time to get to know each other."

"How did you even find out she's illegal?" Oleen asked. "I mean, I'm sure that's not something she tells people, and wouldn't that be hard to look up?"

"Okay, well, I'm not proud of this either. But I guess I'll tell you what I did."

"It's okay, Grace," Agnes said. "Desperate people do desperate things."

"Well, you know I don't work these days. I think I'm going to need to get a job because I'm bored. I try to volunteer, and that's satisfying, but it's not the same as having a workplace to go to every day. With staying home to raise so many kids I needed a break after the last one went to college, and I just never went back to work."

"Kids are hard work," Ida agreed.

Oleen tapped her foot wondering how a woman who arrived so early to every possible event could be so slow and meandering at telling a story.

Grace continued.

"The circus is interesting and, as Bill's wife, I've been allowed to wander around. I've gotten to know everyone, and everyone thinks of me as Bill's harmless little wife, I guess. But when I started to suspect Bill was having an affair with Katerina —that was a little over a month ago—I decided I wanted to find out everything I could about her. So one day, in the morning when the tent was open, and no one was in there, I went snooping around. I went to the director's office and rummaged through his desk and file cabinet, and I found personnel files. He had a copier in his office and I quickly copied Katerina's whole file, then put it back in the director's cabinet and shoved everything I'd copied into my purse."

"I'm impressed," Oleen said. "That's much better than hiding behind a potted tree."

"When I got home, I looked through the file and it had an employment contract Katerina had signed. So I scanned the contract, since my printer has a scanner built in, and I removed Katerina's signature from the contract using a program I have— it's like a simple version of Photoshop. You have to have a person's signature to get anything good from a background check. Then I filled out a background check form with a company that checks to see if workers are legal. I'm not entirely sure how on the up-and-up they are, but, oh well, they could get the information at least. I doubt they'd have cared if I forged the signature, but I thought I'd better be safe and at least use a copy of her signature. I think mostly people who are here illegally use the service to see if there are any records around that could jeopardize their being able to stay in the country, even though they're not supposed to be here anyway, but I don't care about that. Also, employers can use it to see if the people they hire are here illegally, I mean, if there are any records. But the company isn't there to turn anyone in.

"You do the entire process online, and I indicated I was thinking of hiring Katerina as a maid but wanted to be sure I was complying with labor laws. And since everything on their site is filled out online, I was able to transfer Katerina's signature from the old form to the new form using my Photoshop-like program. A few days later I got a report in my email with all her information. It said she came here to the US at the age of sixteen on a student visa. That expired when she was eighteen, but she never returned to Russia or applied to extend the visa like she was supposed to. Now she's twenty-four, and the United States is the country she lists as her legal country of residence, even though she's traveled all around the world with the show. So she's illegal here. But the company I used is very discreet and doesn't do any reporting, which has made me feel better now that I don't think she's having an affair with Bill. I'm glad I didn't ruin her life."

Ida stared, open-mouthed, at Grace.

"Did you see someone do that on TV too?" Ida asked.

"No," Grace said. "I just thought of it on my own. Desperate times call for desperate measures, as Agnes said." Grace shrugged, but there was a glow of pride in her eyes.

"You should be a private detective!" Oleen said. "But never hide behind a plant. I can vouch for that being a poor tactic."

"You've told that plant story a lot, dear," Ida said to Oleen. "As Scott said, maybe you need to find some fresh material."

"Ida, you know I've always had a tendency to repeat myself, so don't hassle me."

"You really do, honey," Agnes said. "But we still love you."

"Great, thanks," said Oleen, leaning back onto the sofa and crossing her arms.

"Grace," Agnes interrupted. "I think you're going to have to tell the police you know Katerina is illegal. You could say you overheard her talking to Fernando. I'm sure they'll believe you over them because you have that photo of Fernando and poor old dead Sergei. They won't believe anything Fernando says after they see that photo. In fact, they'll probably arrest him or, at the very least, question him thoroughly. No need to tell the police how you found out Katerina is here illegally. It's not a good idea, since it wasn't one hundred percent legal the way you used her signature. I am quite impressed you knew how to do that."

"Probably not," Grace agreed.

"Well, I can call Scott now if you like," Ida said.

Grace sighed.

"I suppose that would be best. Piper said not to expect her back for a very, very long time, so that shouldn't be an issue. I don't want to interrupt her spa visit to tell her that her daughter probably witnessed a murder. I don't think she'd find that very relaxing. I can't drive, though. I've been drinking for several hours, since Matilda got here a few hours ago. But, to be honest, I'm basically a functioning alcoholic so I can fake it at the police station."

Agnes, Ida, and Oleen all stared at Grace.

"Oh my god, I can't believe I said that out loud!" Grace said. "Forget you heard that."

"Heard what?" Oleen said.

Grace smiled.

"You're going to want to change clothes, though, Grace," Ida said. "Maybe touch up your hair and makeup, put on some real pants and stuff. Scott and I were there earlier, and I had on this outfit." Ida gestured down at her clothing. "And Scott had on shorts and a tank top. We don't want them to think we're all loony."

"Good idea," Grace said, turning to walk up the stairs. She got up three steps, then turned around.

"But what should I do with Matilda?" Grace asked. "I can't take her to the police station. I don't want her to know anything about this yet. Someone will need to watch her."

"Well," Ida said. "Agnes and I can take you to the station to meet Scott."

Ida turned and stared at her sister and, with a wicked glint in her eye, said, "I'm sure Oleen would love to look after Matilda. Oleen's got such a great imagination. Matilda will have a wonderful time."

65

TUESDAY

"Uh, of course, Ida," said Oleen, pasting on her maniacal grin and staring at her sister with shining, bemused eyes. "I'd love to look after Matilda while you all go to the police station. In fact, I think I'll take her over toward our houses, and see if Delbert and Gary want to go to that ice cream stand with the hot dog place attached. If Delbert is feeling up to it. You know, with his finger and all."

"Piper told me about Delbert's finger," Grace said. "That must have been so scary for both Delbert and Gary. I'm glad the doctors could reattach it, and there was no nerve damage." Grace continued up the stairs, and Ida heard the sound of a door closing.

"What the hell is wrong with you, Oleen?" Ida hissed through clenched teeth.

"The same thing that's wrong with you, I suspect," Oleen said back, smiling sweetly.

"Oh my god, now I've got to call Delbert. I'll be right back."

Ida stepped out onto the front porch and pulled up her favorites list on her phone. She hit Delbert's name, and the phone began to ring. She'd have to remember to remove him from her favorites list.

"Hello?"

"Delbert!" Ida whispered. "Delbert, what are you doing right now?"

"Watching the Braves' game. Why are you whispering?"

"Because I'm on Grace McGruder's front porch and Matilda is on Grace's back porch, and I don't want Matilda to hear me. I can't explain now. The point is, Oleen is about to bring Matilda over there so you, Gary, and Oleen can take Matilda to that hot dog and ice cream place. We needed a babysitter for her. We have to go back to the police station."

"There are lots of things you can't seem to explain lately, Ida," Delbert whispered back. "I don't even know why I'm whispering."

"You're one to talk about doing things you can't explain," Ida hissed back.

"Matilda?" Delbert said, pretending he hadn't heard Ida's comment, which rang a little too true for his tastes. "We have to help with Matilda? She's almost as much of a pain in the ass as Piper was when she was a kid."

"Well, you'll have to deal with it. Oleen can't do it alone. She might slap her, and with two wrist splints that could break Matilda's nose. The most important thing is you have to wrap your finger up like it almost got cut off with hedge clippers, and you went to the hospital and had it stitched and bandaged up and reattached. Use a lot of gauze and a lot of tape so none of it will fall off. Get Gary to do it for you. He's artistic. And put some ketchup on it or something because realistically some blood would have seeped through the bandage. And then act like it hurts and you can't use it. I never said which hand it was, or which finger, so do your left hand so you can still use your right."

"Ketchup doesn't look like blood, Ida," Delbert said, remembering Gary's accident with the flower delivery truck.

"Figure it out," Ida whispered back. "Use some of your car paint. "You can figure it out. You run your own business for god's sake."

"Fine," said Delbert. "How long do we have?"

"Maybe twenty minutes, max. But go for fifteen to be safe. I'll try to stall."

Delbert hung up the phone, stood up from the lounge chair in his garage, closed his laptop, sadly leaving the baseball game behind, and picked up his phone to call Gary.

I da hung up the call and stepped back inside just as Grace was walking down the stairs into the living room. Grace wore black Capri pants, a black and white horizontally striped sleeveless shirt, red low-heeled sandals with ankle straps, and a red scarf. Not a hair was out of place, and she'd touched up her makeup. Defined shoulders and arms shone out of her shirt. She didn't look a day older than forty-five.

"The straps of these sandals are too loose," Grace said. "It can be hard to keep them on, but they're my favorite sandals and I can't bring myself to retire them."

Ida looked down at her own outfit, which appeared to have come from the dumpster behind the Land's End store at the outlet mall. She smoothed her voluminous, fluorescent-pink t-shirt over her slightly protruding belly and sighed. She was changing clothes before she so much as left the neighborhood. She was tired of looking like a reject clown from a second-rate circus, while Grace and Agnes always looked perfect. Grace had on red lipstick. Maybe Ida should ask to borrow it and color the end of her nose red. Then the clown motif would be all set. Ida saw Oleen looking down at her clothes and knew Oleen was thinking the same thing.

"Okay well, Grace," Agnes said, "why don't you get Matilda and see if she can find her phone. I'll check the bathroom because I saw her take it in there. I didn't notice if she came out with it, though."

"I think I saw her take it back to the porch," said Oleen.

Grace sighed.

"What should I tell Matilda about why she needs to go with you, Oleen? This is a highly unusual situation. She only stays with Piper or me, or sometimes with one of my sons."

"Hmm," Oleen said. "Maybe you could tell her you have to do something boring she hates doing. And then offer her the chance to get out of it. I'll say I hate it too and I'll tell her she can go with me."

"Okay," Grace said, biting her lip. She walked to the door that led to the porch.

"Matilda!"

"Yeah?" answered a muffled voice.

"Would you come in here a minute? Bring your phone too."

There was much noise and rummaging around, and what sounded like the toppling of a chair. Matilda appeared in the doorway from the porch, closed the glass door, and locked it.

"I can't find it," Matilda said. "I bet it's in the bathroom." Matilda walked into the bathroom.

"It's not here," she said. "I always lose it."

"Matilda," Grace interrupted. "Listen, I have to go pick up a few things at Aldi, Agnes and Ida are going with me. There's this big sale on steaks and you know how men love steaks; including your granddad, Delbert, and Gary."

"Eww!" said Matilda. "I hate Aldi."

"I do too," Oleen said. "Your grandmother said you haven't had dinner, so I thought if you want, I could take you to that hot dog place next to the ice cream stand. We can get ice cream too."

Matilda looked at Grace questioningly.

"It's okay," Grace said. "We won't be too long."

"Delbert and Gary are going to come too," Oleen said.

"Ooh!" Matilda said, her eyes lighting up. "Delbert cut off his finger, didn't he? I'm going to ask to see it. This is awesome!"

Oleen smiled demonically, like she'd been sharing a cell with Charles Manson for twenty years.

"It sure is," she said.

"I can't go anywhere until I change clothes," Ida said.

"Neither can I," said Oleen. "I could do with a shower too, but it's so humid out it won't matter."

"Matilda," Grace said. "Did you leave your shoes on the front porch when you came back from Janice's house? Why don't you go get them?"

"But I can just put them on when we leave," Matilda said, staring at Grace with narrowed eyes.

"No, they're high-tops and you have to lace them up, and Ida and Oleen only live around the corner. You'll barely have time to get one on. Go outside and put them on and we'll be out in a minute."

Once Matilda had gone outside onto the front porch and shut the door behind her, Agnes said, "Let's all go back to Ida's and Oleen's, then. They can change, and while they do maybe Delbert can show Matilda around the shop. Ida can call Scott and tell him what's going on and then we can go meet Scott at the police station."

"You and Matilda can ride with us, Grace," Ida said.

"Okay," said Grace. "Piper and I are going to have to come up with a way for Matilda to keep better track of her phone, though. It was expensive! Andy and Bill won't be any help. They're never home anyway. I'm glad she can't find it now, though. That way she can't be rude when she eats with you, Gary, and Delbert, Oleen."

Oleen nodded.

"I bet she'll be sad she won't be able to take a picture of Delbert's injured finger," said Grace.

"I'm sure she'll live, dear," Ida said. It's pretty gross."

"That's what she'll be hoping," Grace said.

Agnes grimaced.

Ida, Oleen, Agnes, and Grace walked onto the porch where Matilda was bent over the railing and had her nose in one of the roses that grew on a bush next to the porch. Grace tapped Matilda on the back. Matilda jumped, then turned to follow the four women to Ida's car. Ida texted Delbert at a speed she had difficulty mustering in any other area of her life.

"ETA: 7 minutes."

66

TUESDAY

I da pulled her car onto Gardenia Lane. She'd driven as slowly as she could, and had been passed by a car full of teenage boys who had made a rude gesture at her. She could see the light on in the garage at her house, and saw Delbert and Gary silhouetted inside. She parked in Oleen's driveway instead of her own, to keep Grace and Matilda further away from where Delbert and Gary were preparing Delbert's finger. Ida looked at the clock on her phone. It was almost 7 p.m.

"Let's get Delbert and Gary and get cleaned up," Ida said, looking toward the garage. "When I called they were restoring the old Mustang."

"Wow," said Grace. "Delbert must have really wanted to work on that car if he's doing it with such an injured finger!"

"Uh, yes, he does love it," Ida said, smiling like an animatronic figure at Disney World.

"Grace, Matilda," said Oleen, "Why don't you come in with me for a few minutes while I change. You can hang out on the living room couch. I'll only be a minute. Agnes can go with Ida to get Gary and Delbert moving."

Grace and Matilda followed Oleen into her house, and Oleen got them settled on the couch with glasses of ice water. Then she went upstairs and searched through the piles of clothes on the floor of her closet for something appropriate to wear to babysit a minion of Satan. She chose a pair of red Capri pants, as she'd noticed that both Grace and Agnes had on Capri pants, so at least she knew she wouldn't be over or under-dressed. And, also, red was Satan's color. She chose a white button-down shirt and a pair of blue docksiders with red stripes. Oleen ran a brush through her hair, which, to her surprise, didn't look like that of a filthy mountain troll. Her makeup was toast, though, so she removed it with a wipe and quickly applied powder, mascara, and lipstick.

Ida led Agnes next door to hers and Delbert's house. As soon as they entered the house, and Agnes had closed the door, Ida said, "Will you go see if they're done yet? In the garage. They're making Delbert's finger look injured."

Agnes nodded, then went through the kitchen, out the door, and into the garage as Ida hurried up the stairs to her bedroom. Since Ida's clothes were all perfectly folded and in labeled drawers, it took her about two minutes to change into a new outfit. She went with black Capri pants, as Capri pants seemed to be the theme of the evening, and topped them with a three-quarter-length blue t-shirt that covered the tops of her arms, which she was afraid a small child would soon be able to swing upon for exercise. Ida sighed. Why couldn't she possess the fondness for the gym that seemed to run among the McGruder women, rather than the fondness for Snickers that seemed to run among, well, her?

Ida looked in the mirror, shocked that her makeup didn't look half bad after sleeping in it and wearing it in a hot car for part of the day. She touched up her concealer and eyeliner and pulled her shoulder-length frosted-blonde hair back into a low ponytail with a tortoiseshell clip. The makeup she could fix.

The hair she could not, as it looked like she'd just spent an hour under that bridge with Helen Hunt and Bill Paxton in that tornado movie; the one with the flying cows.

Ida rushed down the stairs from her room, through the kitchen, and into the garage, where she was surprised to see a very convincing, and bulky, bandage on Delbert's left index finger. Gary was spraying some dark maroon paint onto it in little spurts from an airbrush he used for touching up car paint.

"That looks great," Ida said, eyeing it from every possible angle.

"It does," Agnes agreed.

"Now, be careful, Delbert," said Ida. "Matilda has been talking nonstop about your finger and how she wants to see it. Who knows, maybe she'd even try to rip the bandage off, so, whatever you do, don't let her sit on your left side."

"Yeah, yeah," he said. "You all are nuts."

Ida noticed that Gary, though doing a good job with the airbrush, was sitting in a rolling chair about five feet away from Delbert's finger. Delbert eyed Gary like Gary were some scraggly hitchhiker he was trying to decide whether to let into his car; one who might have a small axe concealed in his pocket. Well, let them act crazy about the recent developments in their relationship. At least Ida was doing okay, though she supposed wanting to kill your husband and hoist his body into a tree, and also being glad you had a murder to distract you might not really constitute "doing okay."

"Okay, good enough," said Ida, as Gary put the airbrush away. "Let's go over to Oleen's."

"It's my house too," said Gary.

"Fine," Ida said, "Let's go over to Oleen and *Gary's*. You two and Agnes go on in and make small talk while I call Scott."

"And just what are we supposed to talk about?" Delbert asked.

"I'm sure Matilda will ask lots of gross questions about your finger and how it happened, so I suggest you two come up with something. Agnes can help. She supposedly tripped Herman's coworker at a Christmas party once, so she's good at making up stories."

"Mom!" Gary said, "I'm shocked!"

"She made it up," Ida said.

"I actually did do that, honey," said Agnes, "But it wasn't because I thought she was having an affair with Herman. It was because every time I saw her, she implied I was putting on weight, and I've never been able to put on weight. And also she was a bitch. I quite enjoyed it, to tell you the truth."

Gary stared at his mom, as she never used words like bitch, and he couldn't picture her purposely tripping anyone. But he guessed finding out your son was having an affair with your daughter-in-law's sister's husband could do that to a person.

Gary, Delbert, and Agnes left the garage to go to Oleen and Gary's house, while Ida stayed inside to call Scott. He answered on the second ring.

"Hello! Scott and Steve's House of Spaghetti and Foot Spas, may I help you?"

"Scott," Ida said, ignoring the greeting.

Scott worked retail all through college, and she supposed some habits never truly wore off.

"What's up, Mom?" he said. "You should come over. We're having fun over here."

Scott sounded a little like those young men who had filmed Sergei's dead body at the circus.

"Scott!" Ida said, "Are you drunk?"

"Just a little, Mom," Scott said. "I'm not drunk, though, I'm high. But don't worry, it's not Janie, Jenny or Alex. It's just Maureen and me. We couldn't take it anymore. I recently beat up a clown, and Maureen's been cleaning up vomit for forty-eight hours. I never do this, you know. Steve's cooking in, like, an industrial-sized pot. Spaghetti and meatballs. And Jenny's helping him make copious amounts of garlic bread. It smells excellent. You guys should come have some. But I'll tell you a little secret," he said. "Neither of them is too happy with me about the weed."

"Scott!" Ida said. "Where did you even get that?"

"Well, I haven't had any in maybe twelve years, but that guy at the gym, that IT guy who fixed my Apple TV, he does it all the time, and I asked him to bring me some. I told him he could use our house on Tybee Island next weekend at no charge if he brought it, pronto. So here we are. And it was gratis! You should come get some food, seriously! I'll even share my weed with you if you're nice."

"Scott, listen." said Ida, "We'll have to have a talk about this drug habit of yours later and, no, I don't want any. Pot *is* a gateway drug, you know. And I don't want you losing all your teeth to meth. But, right now, I need you to get out the Visine and put on some decent clothing. And, no, you don't have forty-five minutes to spend on your hair."

Scott was suddenly serious.

"What's wrong, Mom?" he asked.

"Grace McGruder found a very incriminating photo of Fernando on Matilda's phone. It shows Fernando all bloody and standing over Sergei's body."

"Oh my god!" Scott said.

Ida heard Scott cover the phone, and then his muffled voice yell, "Dude! Fernando did it."

He came back on the line.

"Sorry, Mom, I was holding my hand over the phone so you didn't have to hear me yell."

"Scott," Ida said. "I need you to meet us at the police station. Grace needs help turning this photo in. And you shouldn't be driving. If you got pulled over you'd be in big trouble. So we'll come get you. We'll be there in maybe twenty minutes. So figure out how to not look, act, or sound high."

"Okay, Mom. Got it." Scott giggled. "Don't act high. I won't bring my Snoop Dogg albums, but can I please sing 'Murder Was the Case That They Gave Me' for Detective Studmuffin? He'll really like it, and I promise it will only take four minutes and twenty seconds." Scott giggled again.

Having no idea what Scott was talking about, Ida said, "Put Steve on the line. And go get dressed."

"Aye-aye, Captain," giggled Scott. "Here's the Stevester."

Steve came on the line with an exasperated, "Hello, I can't believe him."

Ida explained the situation to Steve. Steve promised to fix Scott up as best he could in fewer than twenty minutes. She hung up the phone.

Ida had a cheating spouse who preferred Gary to her, a drug-addicted son, a pregnant daughter with a deadbeat husband, and another daughter whose idea of a good time was going to Gatlinburg. Walking out of the garage, she decided the day could only get better.

67

TUESDAY

Ida, Agnes, and Grace left Oleen and Gary's house, climbed into Ida's car and drove away. Oleen stood next to Gary and watched their departure through the front window of the house, considering bursting through the front door, jumping onto the back bumper of the car, and hanging onto the roof rack for dear life.

"They're going to Aldi," said Matilda. "To get steaks for all you men. I hate Aldi."

"No they're not," said Gary. "They're going to— OW!" Gary yelled as Oleen kicked him in the shin.

"I hate Aldi too, Matilda," Oleen said. "So let's go get some hot dogs and ice cream. Delbert, can you drive us? Matilda might enjoy riding so high up in your truck."

"Can I ride in the front?" Matilda asked.

"No, you have to ride in the backseat and wear a seatbelt," said Delbert, leading them to the garage and climbing into the driver's seat. "Kids aren't supposed to ride in the front."

Matilda scowled, but climbed into the backseat and fastened her seatbelt.

Gary climbed into the passenger seat, moving like he was

walking on pond ice that might soon crack. Oleen climbed into the seat behind Delbert, and next to Matilda. It was hard to climb into a high truck with two splinted wrists, and she couldn't pull the door closed at all, so Delbert got out and shut the door for her.

"Seatbelts, everyone!" Oleen called, as though putting on a seatbelt was a real treat. Oleen struggled with her seatbelt, since she could barely even find the thing you plugged the buckle into, much less use her fingers. Matilda reached over, took the seatbelt buckle from Oleen, and fastened it for her. Oleen stared at Matilda, wondering what had prompted such a civilized gesture.

Matilda frowned and said, "I wish I had my phone."

"I wish you did too," said Delbert. "OW!" Oleen kicked the back of his seat.

"We're going to that hot dog stand, Delbert, the one with the ice cream place attached. I bet it will be pretty busy. You have to go that way," Oleen said, pointing to the left.

"I know where it is, Oleen," Delbert said, sounding like the mountain troll Oleen had earlier feared she resembled.

"Can we turn on the radio?" asked Matilda.

"It's broken," said Delbert.

"Well, I heard something about you, Mr. McNair," Matilda said.

Oleen hoped to god Matilda wasn't about to bring up Delbert and Gary being gay. She was also shocked Matilda had called Delbert Mr. McNair. He was a pretty large man, and he'd sounded surly enough a minute ago. Maybe she was afraid of him.

"I heard you cut off your finger this morning with some hedge clippers, and that Gary had to find the finger and take it to the hospital in a cooler full of ice, and the doctors had to reattach it. I heard Oleen say so. But you didn't go to my dad's hospital," Matilda said, crossing her arms. "You should have.

He's a neurosurgeon. But I heard Ida say you don't have any nerve damage, so I guess that's okay."

"Yes, Matilda," Gary said, turning a little in his seat before realizing Matilda was sitting right behind him, and he couldn't see her. "It was horrifying. I was outside cutting my grass when I heard Delbert screaming. He was screaming so high and so loud that, at first, I thought he was a woman."

Delbert reached a stoplight, and Oleen noticed his hands gripping the steering wheel very tightly, his bandaged finger sticking up at an odd angle from the rest of his hand.

"I ran over and saw Delbert with a bloody towel around his finger, and he told me he'd cut his finger off. So I took off my t-shirt and made a tourniquet around his finger."

"Eww," said Matilda. "You took your shirt off?" Her face looked as though she had just smelled rotten eggs.

Delbert, who was still stopped at the light, and who had been watching Matilda in the rearview mirror, laughed.

"I had to!" Gary said, crossing his arms. "Otherwise Delbert might have died. I ran inside and found an old cooler I use for fishing, and I put a bunch of ice from the freezer in it. When I came back out, Delbert told me he could see the finger under the bushes, so I found it and put it in the cooler. It was still warm!"

The light turned green, and Delbert resumed driving.

"Did it hurt, Mr. McNair?" Matilda asked.

"Did what hurt?" asked Delbert, who was gazing out the window at a Jaguar dealership as they passed it. Oleen kicked the back of his seat again.

"OW! Yes, cutting it off hurt a little bit, uh, I think I was in shock, though, when I did it. I didn't feel much. It started to hurt on the way to the hospital. Gary drove me, but he got lost, so I was in a lot of pain for a long time."

Gary glared at Delbert, arms still crossed.

"Did getting it reattached hurt?" asked Matilda.

"Not too much," said Delbert. "I was awake, but my whole arm was numb from my elbow down to my hand. I couldn't feel anything, and they blocked my view with this little screen, I guess so I didn't freak out."

"It's okay, Delbert," said Gary, "It's okay to tell them you cried."

Oleen noticed Delbert grip the steering wheel even more tightly.

"I'm surprised they didn't put you to sleep," said Matilda. "My dad says neurosurgery is very complicated when you're trying to prevent nerve damage. He says they almost always have to use anesthesia and put the person to sleep. I asked him if I could come watch a surgery sometime, but he said no. I'll have to tell him how they did your surgery because Dad will be interested to know."

"Uh, no need to bother him with that, Matilda," said Oleen. "Look, we're here."

Delbert pulled into the parking lot of the hot dog and ice cream stand. It was very crowded, and they stood in line for a long time. Oleen could see Matilda trying to get a look at Delbert's bandaged finger, so she told Delbert what she wanted and had Matilda give Delbert her order, and she took Matilda to find a table.

They found a picnic table about twenty feet from the stand, and sat down on opposite sides.

"I like talking to you, Oleen," said Matilda. "My mom and my grandma never talk this much to me. I like talking to Delbert and Gary too. At my house, all I ever do is mess with my phone, and it gets boring. Dad's gone doing surgery and Mom is always at the gym. She makes me go with her and stay in this lame kids' club and when she's at home, she's on the phone with her friends."

Oleen felt a pang of sympathy for Matilda.

"That sounds lonely," Oleen said.

"Yeah, I guess," said Matilda, looking down into her lap. "It would be nice to have a sister, like you and Ida."

"It *is* nice to have a sister," said Oleen. "Most of the time. Don't tell Ida, but sometimes she's a little bit bossy."

Matilda giggled, and Gary and Delbert returned with a tray of food. Matilda began dipping French fries into her ice cream sundae.

"We just got everything at once," said Delbert. "Didn't want to stand in that line twice."

Delbert sat down next to Matilda, in the empty space on her left side, so his finger was as far away from her as possible.

"Mr. McNair?" Matilda asked.

"Yes?" Delbert said.

"Is Ida sometimes bossy?"

Oleen's sympathetic feelings toward Matilda wavered just a little. Delbert burst out laughing.

"Yes, Matilda," said Delbert, "Sometimes she is. She wants everything done in a very particular way. But I guess we can all be bossy sometimes. I'm bossy about how my car gets washed. I won't let anyone else do it except me."

"Yeah," said Matilda, "I hate when mom tries to organize my art supplies. She always does it wrong, and I can never find anything, so I guess I'm bossy too."

"Gary is bossy about anyone buying pajamas for him," said Delbert. "He always buys them himself because he only wears nightshirts."

Matilda made a face and giggled.

"Nightshirts? I thought only ladies wore nightshirts."

Gary threw a French fry at Delbert. It had ketchup on the end, and it hit Delbert in the bandaged finger. Ketchup dripped down Delbert's hand as the French fry dropped to the ground.

"At least no one will notice the ketchup with all the blood seeping through," Matilda said.

Oleen shook her head and laughed.

"Matilda," she said, "I'm bossy about Gary eating my snack cakes. I have to hide them from him."

"Oh, I found them in the back of the bathroom closet and ate them already," Gary said.

Oleen threw a French fry at Gary, but there was no ketchup on it, and it missed because, on account of the wrist splint, she threw it the way a T-Rex might throw a French fry at its spouse it had recently discovered had been living a lie for forty-five years.

"Ow!" said Oleen, waving her wrist in the air and wincing.

"Maybe you can bring me here again some-time," said Matilda, taking a bite of her hot dog.

"Maybe we can," Oleen said.

68

TUESDAY

"So, Grace," Ida said as she navigated her Expedition toward Scott and Steve's townhouse, "I want to warn you that if Scott seems a little, uh, unusual tonight, it's because he might be a little bit high right now. I feel like you should know, since you're still kind of drunk and all."

Ida gritted her teeth waiting for a response.

Grace sighed, "It's okay, Ida, we all have to get through the day. The other night, after Rose almost told me about Bill's big affair, I partook in some of the 420 myself, outside Rose's condo. It was just before I got my French fries and milkshake and drove to the civic center and watched the circus tent. I'd never tell Rose I do that stuff. She wouldn't approve."

"Scott mentioned 420 too," Ida said. "And also something about Snoop Dogg. I have no idea who these people are. Who names themselves a number?"

Grace giggled.

"Don't tell anyone, but I've started doing it regularly lately. The drinking just isn't cutting it anymore. I get it from some IT guy at Scott's gym, but *please* don't tell Scott. Once, I took a private Pilates lesson from some guy named Rick who teaches at Scott's gym. He came to my house for the lesson. I think he's an EMT or something, but he's an excellent Pilates instructor, too. I was a little drunk during my lesson and somehow let it slip that I wanted to buy some weed. Rick told me not to because it's terrible for my body and would negate the positive effects of the Pilates lessons, but he said he tries not to judge people, and he mentioned that this guy at the gym who's in IT could get me some. He gave me the guy's number, and I texted him."

"Yes, we've met Rick." Oleen sighed, resting her head in her hands.

"In exchange for the IT guy discreetly bringing it by every week or so, I pay for his weekly lawn and landscaping service," Grace said. "That way no money exchanges hands, and I tell myself that means I'm not doing anything illegal."

Ida was beginning to wonder if she should start a second career as a drug dealer. She'd have a beautiful lawn and access to vacation homes.

"Well, okay then," said Agnes. "So, you don't act drunk, and Scott won't act high. Or maybe if you both act that way you'll cancel each other out and you'll both seem normal."

Ida pulled her car into Scott's tiny driveway, and the back end of the car hung out onto the street. Ida didn't bother walking up to ring the doorbell. She just honked her horn twice.

The front door opened, and Scott stepped onto the porch wearing a blue seersucker suit, a pink bowtie, and blue and white Oxford shoes.

"Why is he wearing that?" Ida asked. "Does he have on spats?" she asked, squinting at the figure descending the front steps. "Oh my god, he does!"

Ida rested her head on the steering wheel. She considered banging it there, but she might cause herself a brain injury, and then she wouldn't be able to drive.

"Because it's summer, maybe?" said Agnes. "But you're right, I don't think it's the best wardrobe choice for this situation."

Steve led Scott down the steps and opened the first-row, right-side door of Ida's car to let Scott climb in behind Agnes and next to Grace.

"I'm so sorry," Steve said. "He insisted on wearing this and nothing anyone did or said could convince him not to. Believe me, we all tried. I even tried to spill spaghetti sauce on it, but he jumped out of the way, and I missed, and the sauce went all over the kitchen floor. He wore that outfit to some awful Kentucky Derby Party he dragged me to a few years ago. I will never go to one of those again. And I had the hardest time forcing him to leave the top hat and cane here. I'm not even sure why he has those. I don't know how you'll explain his suit, but it will be easier than explaining why he keeps singing 'Gin and Juice.'"

Scott giggled.

"You know why, Steve. Cause I got my money right here." Scott touched his finger to his temple and laughed.

Steve shook his head.

"It's okay if you don't bring him back," Steve said to Agnes, through the window.

Steve turned and walked up the steps to the porch, looked back at Ida's car, shook his head, then re-entered the townhouse.

"Seatbelt, Scott!" called Ida. Scott giggled and put on his seatbelt.

"So, Grace," he said. "Let me first apologize for being high."

Grace turned to the right and looked at Scott.

"It's okay, Scott," she said. "I'm drunk."

Scott made a move to fist bump her, which she awkwardly returned.

"Holla!" he yelled, as Agnes held her hands over her ears.

"Well, I'm going to be as serious as possible now," Scott said. "So let me see this picture, Grace."

Grace opened her purse and pulled out the folded piece of paper. She unfolded it and handed it to Scott. Scott took it and looked down at the image.

"Holy shit!" Scott said.

"Language, Scott!" Ida shouted from the driver's seat.

"Mom, you're taking a drunk person and a high person to talk to officers at the police station about a picture that shows what happened right after a murder we shouldn't know anything about, and you're worried about foul language?"

Scott and Grace giggled.

"Well," said Scott. "Fernando certainly looks guilty here. This is not good for him at all. You got this off Matilda's phone, Grace?" Scott asked.

"Yes," Grace answered. "But I have no idea where the phone is now. Matilda loses it constantly. I thought it was in the bathroom, but for all I know she knocked it off the side of the porch into the bushes. I just know she doesn't have it now."

"They're going to want that phone," Scott said, "But it can wait until they bring Fernando in for questioning, which they'll definitely do. They'll get him right before the performance, so he'll be at the station in his tight little trapeze pants, which will make my suit look positively pedestrian, chaps!" Scott said, affecting a British accent.

"Do not pretend you're British in the police station, Scott," Ida said. "No matter what happens."

"Fine," Scott said as Ida pulled into the police station parking lot and parked in the same spot Scott had parked in earlier that day.

"Now you all stay here," Scott said, somehow managing to put on his normal lawyer voice. "Only Grace and I should go in. Grace, don't act drunk."

"I won't," she said. "I have practice."

Scott and Grace walked into the police station and stopped at the front desk. Ida and Agnes watched through the front windows of the car and saw Scott and Grace sit in two chairs in the waiting area. After a couple of minutes, the doors behind the receptionist's desk opened, and Scott and Grace walked through the doors and down a hall. They were led by Detective Beauregard to the same room Scott and Ida had been in earlier in the day.

Ida watched as Scott and Grace took adjacent chairs on one side of the table, and Detectives Beauregard and Drew sat down opposite them. Detective Beauregard looked at Scott and said something. Scott gestured at his outfit and said something back. Detective Beauregard nodded.

Scott removed the folded-up piece of paper from his pocket, placed it on the table, and smoothed it out. The two detectives bent over the table and studied the picture. Detective Drew looked up and spoke to Grace. He appeared to be asking Grace a series of questions, which she seemed to be answering, punctuated by brief comments from Scott.

Way sooner than Ida had expected, Scott and Grace stood up from the table and walked back down the hall and out of the police station. They climbed into the car.

"Well?" Agnes asked.

"Well, the funniest thing ever is that Detective Beauregard complimented my suit and said he'd once worn a similar one to a Kentucky Derby party! Didn't even ask why I was wearing it!"

"And Scott didn't act high, and I didn't act drunk," Grace added.

Scott giggled.

"Scott!" Ida said, "Get to the point!"

"They were very interested in the photo. We told them it came from Matilda's phone and they wanted Matilda and her parents to come in immediately, and bring her phone. So I said Matilda and her mom are out of town, and they'd left soon after

Grace sent herself this photo. And I said Matilda took the phone, so they'll need to call Piper later to get them to come in with the phone."

"It is true," Grace added, "Because the hot dog stand and the spa aren't in the city proper, and the police station is, so both Matilda and Piper are technically out of town. And I know Piper always turns her phone off at the spa."

"They let us go, and Detective Beauregard told us not to leave town, at which point I had to sprint through the door and down the steps while covering my mouth to avoid laughing and wetting my pants at the same time," Scott said.

"Let's get out of here and go back to Grace's," said Scott. We shouldn't sit here for too long."

As Ida pulled her car out of the parking lot, Grace's phone pinged with a text. Grace looked at her phone.

"It's Piper," she said. "She's back at my house and wondering where Matilda and I are. Ida, text Oleen, please, and have her get Matilda back to my house. I'll have to come up with some reason why we all left."

Grace spoke as she typed.

"Went to dinner with Ida, Oleen, Agnes, Delbert, and Gary. Took Matilda. Also went to Aldi."

Grace's phone pinged again, and she read the text aloud.

"You hate Aldi."

"Delbert wanted steak," Grace said, giggling as she typed. "There was a sale, so we stopped there."

Grace's phone pinged and she read the response out loud.

"Eww, Aldi steak. Don't invite me to that barbecue. I'm going in your house now, Mom."

Grace typed, "Okay, but don't answer your phone. I've gotten five calls from the ballet asking for donations this afternoon. It's from this number." Grace looked at the number on the business card she'd taken from the front desk at the police station and typed it into her phone. "When they call, just hit decline."

Oleen studied Grace with growing admiration. She was way more clever than Oleen ever would have thought.

"Okay, I hate telemarketers," Grace read as her phone pinged.

"Agnes, will you text Oleen?" Ida asked. "I shouldn't text and drive, and I'd never do that with someone on drugs in my car, in case I crashed."

Scott laughed.

"It's not drugs, Mom! It's pot!" He giggled.

Agnes texted Oleen, "Come back to Grace's. Piper's there."

Then Agnes texted Oleen the information about dinner and Aldi.

Oleen sent back a thumbs-up.

"When you drop Matilda back off to Piper, Grace, come back to the car. We should all go talk to Rose and see if she'll give us the scoop on Bill and his affair. He might know something helpful about the murder that he doesn't even realize he knows."

"An affair? How lurid!" Scott said. "But Mr. McGruder has always enjoyed a nice pair of shapely buttocks."

Grace laughed out loud.

"Believe me," she said, "At this point, I'm not even sure he'd care if the buttocks were attached to a homeless woman in a dumpster."

Ida parked in Grace's driveway and, a second later, Delbert parked his truck on the street. "Stay here," Oleen said to Delbert and Gary, opening the door and motioning for Matilda to climb out of the truck behind her. Grace got out of Ida's car, and Oleen sent Matilda over to her. Then Grace and Matilda went into Grace's house, and Oleen climbed into Ida's Expedition.

"You can fill me in later," Oleen said, "But did it go okay?"

"Yes, but they're gonna want Matilda's phone, and no one knows where it is," Scott said. "She seems to have lost it again."

"No she didn't," said Oleen.

"Well, how do you know Sylvia Browne?" asked Scott. "Have you been channeling the dead again? And how's Montel Williams doing?"

"Sylvia Browne's not even alive anymore, Scott. And, no, Matilda didn't lose her phone," Oleen said, pulling an iPhone out of her bra, "I know, because I took it."

69

TUESDAY

"Oleen, first of all, I think that's called tampering with evidence or something," Ida said.

"Well, it wasn't evidence when I took it," said Oleen.

"That is true," Agnes said.

"And second," said Ida, "What is this with you hiding things in your bra? I mean, that's a big, rectangular phone, the biggest kind, that Plus thing. How did no one notice that thing in your bra this whole time? It's been a few hours."

"Like I told you before, Ida, when you're in your sixties no one cares about your boobs. If they see some weird shape under your shirt, they just assume it's part of a pacemaker or some oxygen apparatus; something that keeps you from dying. They're embarrassed or afraid it's dire, so they don't ask."

Scott guffawed.

"We aren't THAT damn old, Oleen," Ida said. "Even Agnes isn't that old."

"Uh, thanks?" Agnes said.

"And that's the second piece of evidence you've stolen in

your bra!" Ida said. "First that driver's license, and now that phone."

"Once again, Ida, I have no reason to think that license is evidence. Old red-headed hussy probably had it for sentimental reasons. If anyone asks me for either, I'll turn them over to the police."

"But no one will ask you because they'd never expect you to have them," Scott said, grinning and giggling at the same time. "You're an evil genius, Oleen! Who knew!"

"Listen, Scott, we don't have much time, so I need you to stay quiet and hear me, okay?" said Oleen.

"Grace is good with technology, better than I'd have suspected, but you're way above her in that regard. I'm *positive* there's got to be more on this phone, and Grace just didn't know how to access it. Even though I sort of like Matilda a little better after our dinner, she's still a grade-A snoop, and kids seem to exit the womb holding a smartphone these days, so she knows more about how to use it than you or I could ever dream of knowing. I bet there are more photos or videos on there and she knows how to hide them. Once, I saw a show on TV where some man had a pretend app that allowed him to store the sexual photos he was secretly sending to other men. And he had a wife!"

"Oh, sorry, Ida," Oleen said. "I don't think Delbert and Gary do that. At least I hope not. This app just looked like some boring weather app, so his wife never suspected a thing. If Matilda has one like that, then you have to find it, and we'll know what happened because my hunch is Katerina and Fernando were in this together. I think Matilda only caught part of what happened in that photo. It wouldn't surprise me if she has other photos too. Maybe she has no idea what to do, and that's why she hasn't said anything. She may be a pain sometimes, and a bit too precocious in some respects, but she's only a twelve-year-old kid. I'm way older than she is and, if I'd taken that picture, I'd be curled up in a corner somewhere."

"You wouldn't curl up in a corner, you evil genius, you."

"Just find something, Scott!" Oleen said. "I know you can do this!" She grabbed Scott's shoulders and shook him. "You can do it!"

Scott fidgeted and grinned.

"And I've got Alex and Jenny over there to help!"

"No more marijuana, Scott!" said Ida. "You need to be lucid."

"Okay, Mom," he said, rolling his eyes.

"Now go," said Oleen. "Go get in Delbert's truck. Have them take you home. Keep them there and feed them some spaghetti and meatballs, and they won't care about anything, even though it will be their second dinner. Take the phone."

Scott shoved the phone into the inside pocket of his seer-sucker suit jacket, exited the car, and hurried to the street to climb into the backseat of Delbert's truck.

Ida could see Scott and Delbert having what looked like a heated discussion as Delbert pulled away from the curb.

"Grace will be back soon," said Agnes, "But how did you get that phone, Oleen? You must have magical powers."

"Nah," Oleen said. "At Grace's this afternoon, when Matilda came inside from the porch to use the bathroom, I noticed she had her phone. I'd already decided we needed to get that phone. I watched the bathroom door, and she came out without it. Then she went on the porch to blow bubbles. So I developed a sudden need to use the little girls' room, and there it was, sitting on the edge of the sink. Since she loses it so much, I knew it wouldn't even enter anyone's mind that someone took her phone. Just don't tell Grace."

"Scott's right," Agnes said, "You are an evil genius."

Oleen sighed.

"Not genius enough to realize my husband of forty-five years has been gay the whole time and having an affair with my sister's husband, but a little evil, perhaps."

Ida scowled at Oleen from the driver's seat.

Grace left the house and climbed back into Ida's car, and Piper and Matilda stopped in front of Ida's car next to Piper's BMW. Matilda was fussing at her mom about something. They both climbed into Piper's car, and Ida swept out of the driveway so as not to block them in. Then Piper and Matilda pulled out of the driveway and disappeared down the street.

"She's upset about losing her phone, but it's her own fault," Grace said. "It will do her some good to spend a night away from it. But never mind that. There's something more important I should mention."

Ida turned the car slightly to the right and parked it on the street in front of Grace's house so she could give Grace her full attention.

"When I was out staring at the tent the other night, I didn't tell you this before, I saw Fernando come running out of a side exit and then go running back toward that hotel. You know, the one behind the civic center. The civic center owns it, or maybe it's just that the same company owns both. The hotel, I guess, is profitable because it's also a convention center, but the civic center has become a money pit. It used to be a big deal twenty years ago, but not anymore. I guess that's why they're thinking of making it a permanent home for the French—Canadian Circus. But the hotel is really profitable, with loads of conferences all the time, and all the attendees renting rooms there and eating in the restaurant, even though it's not that good. I think the performers are staying there right now, in the hotel, not the restaurant, but I guess if the show moves here permanently they'll have to find other places to live."

Oleen tapped her foot and looked at Grace, once again marveling at her ability to add so many unnecessary details.

"But getting back to my story," Grace said. "Fernando ran out a side door of the tent and back toward the hotel, and Katerina ran out the front of the tent and toward the parking deck, then got in her car and drove away. Something's been bothering me about her; maybe how she ran out or something, but I just can't figure out what it is, and I keep thinking about it. I wasn't completely focused at the time, you know, with the mind-alternating substances and all."

"Piper told us Andy saw Katerina run out out of the tent, but I don't think he saw Fernando leave," Agnes said. "Piper said Andy seemed to think it was a little unusual that Katerina was running, but he said it was probably because there was a full moon."

"Ha!" said Grace, "That's because that man's about as observant as a blind ostrich with its head in the sand. If it doesn't involve opening someone up and fixing them, he barely sees it. Trust me, anyone but him would have found it odd. I was high, and a little drunk, and even I noticed it was odd!"

Oleen wanted to add that maybe Grace had been seeing things, but she kept her mouth shut.

"I just can't figure out what bothered me so much about Katerina. It's driving me nuts. Maybe it will come to me if I quit thinking about it," Grace said.

"Let's go see Rose," Ida interrupted. "I know she didn't want to tell you who Bill's having the affair with, but maybe if we're all there and we explain she'll be more forthcoming. Who knows where Bill and this woman have been sneaking around? Maybe they were sneaking someplace near the tent the night the murder happened."

Grace winced.

"Sorry," said Ida. "That wasn't very sensitive of me, Grace. But I'm sure she wasn't a homeless woman in a dumpster, at least. What's Rose's address? I'll use my phone's navigation program."

Grace gave Ida the address, and Ida typed it into her phone and placed her phone into the holder that was affixed to her dashboard. Then she pulled her car away from Grace's house and headed toward Rose's condo.

70

TUESDAY

R ose lived in a second-level unit in a gated condo community that was only about a block from the civic center. Grace knew the gate code, as she visited Rose a lot. After passing the pool, fitness center, and enclosed dog park, observing the lush landscaping, and considering the prime location, Ida suspected Rose's now-dead husband must have had a whopper of a life-insurance policy.

They climbed the steps to Rose's unit. Oleen placed her right elbow on the right-hand railing, her splinted wrist sticking straight up. Ida took Oleen's left elbow and helped her up the steps because they didn't need any more dead bodies just now.

Grace knocked on Rose's front door, and the four women heard the sound of someone approaching the door from inside the condo, though the footsteps were muffled, either by carpet or by whatever footwear the person might have on. Rose opened the door.

Rose was a tall, thin woman, maybe five foot ten, with short steel-gray hair, and bright-blue, dancing eyes. She wore a pair of blue plaid pajama pants and a blue t-shirt. Blue Ugg slippers adorned her feet, making it difficult to hear her footsteps on the hardwood floors. The condo was much larger than it had looked from the outside, and was at least two stories, as indicated by the stairs Ida could see across the living room against the back wall. It looked like Rose could afford to retire if she wanted to.

"Hi, Grace," Rose said, "I got in my pajamas early tonight. I just had some takeout and was going to have a *House Hunters* marathon on-demand, but I can do that anytime. Those people are so ridiculous, refusing to buy a home because the hallway leading to the bathroom is the wrong color white." Rose shook her head.

"I once saw one where a woman said her biggest requirement was that the house not have a ghost in it," Oleen called from the back of the group. "No joke."

Rose chuckled.

"I see you've brought company, Grace," Rose said.

"I'm sorry I didn't call first," Grace said.

"Oh, fiddlesticks," Rose said, waving her hand in Grace's direction. "Do you ladies like wine?" she asked, gesturing to the group, and receiving three assenting nods in return.

"Then we're just fine," said Rose, walking through the doorway into the kitchen. "And I already know Grace likes wine!"

Grace cupped her hand against her mouth and loudly whispered, "It's true," before dissolving into a fit of giggles.

Agnes was pleased to see Rose's house did not have an open floor plan, and that her kitchen did not lead directly into her living room. Agnes peeked around the corner and was surprised to see that, just like at her house, Rose's condo had a galley kitchen. Agnes might need to get to know this woman better. She quickly moved away from the kitchen doorway so as not to be caught snooping, and sat down on the plush couches with the rest of the group.

Agnes heard Rose pop a cork in the kitchen, and then she returned with a tray on which sat an open bottle of wine, five wine glasses, and five coasters. Ida silently praised Rose for caring about coasters, even though she herself had decided they didn't matter anymore.

Rose poured each woman a cold glass of wine, and set each glass on a coaster atop the large, wooden coffee table. Each woman, in turn, picked up a glass. Agnes tasted the wine and noticed this wine was much better than whatever Grace had in that pitcher that afternoon. But who knew how old that stuff had been? Grace could have been drinking off that pitcher for a week, which wouldn't have done much for the flavor at all. For all Agnes knew, that stuff could have been some of the Everclear from Saturday afternoon at Jenny's house, mixed with some weak lemonade. Grace didn't seem to be very interested in flavor when it came to drinking, but rather in results.

Rose turned the TV to the Weather Channel, and muted it. The Weather Channel, Agnes thought, seemed to be everyone in the world's go-to channel for keeping a television on with the sound off. Remembering some of the awful elevator music they used to play in the 90s when displaying temperature forecasts, she understood why it needed to be muted.

"Do you all mind if I keep this on?" Rose asked, gesturing to the muted TV. "I'm interested to see if Jim Cantore blows away today. Those Midwest tornadoes are nasty, and he seems to think hiding behind dumpsters and under Dairy Queen awnings will keep him safe."

Oleen giggled as Jim Cantore appeared onscreen, leaning off the balcony of a hotel and gesturing toward a tornado in the distance.

"He's insane," said Ida. "You'd think as he's gotten older he'd want a desk job."

"Some people like excitement, I guess," shrugged Rose. "Though I'm not one of them."

After the women had watched Jim Cantore blow about on the balcony for a minute or two, and each woman had almost finished her first glass of wine, Rose set her glass on her coaster and broke the silence.

"I think I know why you're here, Grace, and why you've brought company. You know, I just now realized we never introduced ourselves. I guess that's a rude thing for me to do in the South. I think I may know who you all are, though. Are you Ida, Oleen, and Agnes?"

"Yes," Ida, Oleen, and Agnes said together.

"Grace has mentioned several times that she lives around the corner from identical twins, and also that she sometimes sees all three of you at the Silver Kettle on Saturday afternoons," Rose said, "Though she said she never says hello because she's usually a bit too impaired to walk to your table. She goes around noon, usually with Piper, because Piper doesn't really drink and can drive Grace home."

"Gee, thanks, Rose," Grace giggled, now even more drunk than she'd been in the car.

"We may all have to start making that a habit after the week we've had!" Oleen said.

"Ah, yes. I heard about that. You found out about your husbands," Rose said, nodding. "Grace and I discussed it on the phone this morning when she told me what happened last night."

Oleen, Ida, and Agnes exchanged open-mouthed, wide-eyed looks of horror.

"I go to the Silver Kettle myself," said Rose, "And I've seen Delbert and Gary there together acting a little too, well, I guess I'll say 'familiar.' I truly thought you two knew and you just had some kind of arrangement. But then, yesterday, I had this very gossipy waiter, Enrique, who I know quite well since I go every Monday afternoon, because there's Half-Price Happy Hour starting at 4 p.m. Enrique always works during Monday afternoon Happy Hour. He said he overheard you all at lunch talking to the waitress at your table. Was it Megan? I think that's who he said it was. He said you honestly didn't know. I'm so sorry, I think everyone assumed you did. Otherwise, someone would probably have told you. This has to be a terrible shock."

"Even I knew, and I know everyone thinks I'm homophobic and I don't even know Scott and Steve are married and I think they're just 'roommates,'" laughed Grace, making air quotes with her fingers when she said the word roommates. Then she giggled and gulped down her second glass of wine.

Ida, Oleen, and Agnes gaped at her.

Then Oleen laughed so hard she put her wine glass back on the coffee table, bent over, and slapped her knee.

"Oh my god! Grace, you know Scott and Steve are married? But I heard you refer to Steve as Scott's roommate when we were all at that garden club meeting a few months ago. And when Scott was young, you always acted like you didn't believe he was gay."

Oleen couldn't stop giggling, and soon Ida and Agnes were laughing too.

"Don't be dense, Oleen," Grace said. "As I've said more than once today, I didn't just fall off the turnip truck yesterday. That was all because of my mother. When Scott was little she was always coming by my house, and she really was homophobic and talked about Scott like something was wrong with him, so I just acted that way for her benefit because I didn't want to hear it. Hell, maybe that's why I have substance abuse issues now," Grace guffawed. "I guess, after a while, I stopped realizing I was doing it. And even now, when she's no longer with us, I guess I got so used to trying to mollify my mother that I suppose I did call Steve Scott's roommate that day, but out of habit. I think I was drunk that day. But what blind idiot wouldn't realize Scott is gay? Except maybe Andy, since, like I said before, he wouldn't notice anything unless it was inside someone's body and he was fixing it. Maybe next time Andy does a surgery we can stick a phone in whatever part of the body he's opened up, and it can have a video on it of Scott talking about how gay he is, and then we can ask Andy if he noticed Scott is gay, and Andy will still say no!"

At this point, all five women were laughing so hard that Ida blew wine out of her nose and Agnes stood up and sprinted to the bathroom yelling, "Depends don't help you get back into life. That commercial was a lie!"

"Just like those detergent commercials that say you can get ground-in grass and blood stains out of clothing," Ida said. "I wonder if I'll ever get my blouse back."

"No," said Oleen. "Give it up, Ida. You know, you keep going on about those detergent commercials being lies. Maybe it's time *you* get some new material to talk about."

Oleen smiled sweetly at her sister, and Ida scowled and took a long sip of wine.

Agnes returned, a look of relief on her face, and Rose brought out another bottle of wine. Agnes noticed Rose hadn't even finished half of her first glass. Maybe she'd been at Grace's earlier in the day before Ida, Oleen, and Agnes dropped by, and she'd had some of that awful pitcher wine, and that stuff had put her off wine for the remainder of her life. It wouldn't be a surprise.

Once each woman had a third glass of wine in her hand, and Rose had taken another small sip from her first glass, she said, "Well, I guess you came to find out what's going on with Bill. I know you all had that awful body fall on you, Ida and Oleen, and I'm sure you're concerned about who did that awful thing. I know Bill, well, to put it simply, can't keep it in his pants."

"I suppose he can't," Grace sighed. "We just thought maybe, well, if he's been sneaking around with some powerful female executive—he does seem to like that tent very much, you know

—that maybe he'd have taken her in there, to impress her or something. And maybe he's seen something he doesn't realize would even help with solving the crime. There is a pretty comfortable couch back there." Grace winced.

Agnes laughed. "Scott calls that couch the sex couch. He says it's 'where the magic happens.'"

"Eww," said Grace. "Remind me never to sit there again. But also, Rose, I just need to know who it is. I'm getting pretty sick of all this with Bill, and I'm thinking of getting out."

All four women stared at Grace.

"I think I've finally had it," she added.

"Good for you!" said Oleen, attempting to give Grace a thumbs-up with her right hand, then setting her hand on her knee as her wrist throbbed with pain.

"Well," said Rose, laughing, "I guess I have to tell you, seeing as we've all shared wine and watched Jim Cantore come within ten feet of a tornado together. Bill knows you're thinking of getting out, Grace," Rose said. "And, what's happened, it's not what you think."

71

TUESDAY

I da's phone pinged with a text. She looked down at it.

"It's from Scott," she said. "Since Scott has such a way with words, I'll just read it to you."

"Leah texted Jenny," Ida read. "They took Fernando in, and Will is observing through that two-way mirror thingy, even though he can't participate, and he shouldn't be texting Leah, so don't tell anyone. As soon as they got Fernando in the room —not the room we were in—this one is for hardened criminals and has that two-way mirror, apparently, so you know it's hardcore. Well, Fernando said, and this is priceless..."

"Get to the point, Scott," Ida said aloud. Ida spoke as she typed a message back to Scott.

"And?"

"Okay, Fernando said, and I quote—" Ida read. "You may think I look like some dumb Mexican, but I'm actually half Spanish and half Irish, and I have a theater degree from NYU. I spent five years training in Paris in acrobatics, and both my parents are in international law, so I suggest we all have some coffee while we sit down and wait for my lawyer to arrive."

"Damn," said Oleen. "He's crafty."

Ida sent Scott a smiley face back.

Scott replied with: "WTF, Mom, this is a murder we're talking about."

Ida sighed, put her phone on silent, and dropped it back into her purse. A couple of minutes later, she heard it vibrate with a text, but sometimes she found it was best to ignore Scott until he moved on to a new topic. He tended to talk, or text, in circles if you didn't.

"Alright," Rose said, "Well, I'm not positive Bill is even having an affair, Grace. I mean, it's completely possible because, let's face it, it's Bill. He once accidentally hit on Agnes's husband many years ago when he was drunk because for some reason he mistook Herman for a woman."

"Herman never told me that!" Agnes said. "It must have been at one of those barbecues you all always have, Grace," said Agnes. "I bet Herman had on an apron."

"It was at that Memorial Day barbecue, long after you three and most of the other women had quit coming," said Rose. "I kept going to give Grace moral support.

"The issue that's making me want to quit my job is a financial matter. Financial and legal, and I'm sorry I let you think it was that Bill's having another affair—it's the other stuff that's making me not want to work with him."

"Huh?" Grace replied. "Oh my god! Is he using business funds to hire prostitutes? I saw something on *Inside Edition* once about a man who did that."

"No, no," Rose said. "It has nothing at all to do with sex. It's worse? Maybe better? Compared to using business funds to hire prostitutes, I'm not sure.

"Well, what happened," Rose said, "is, you see, my office is just down the hall from Bill's, which is only relevant because we've developed quite a good working relationship in the couple of months he's worked there, because we've known each other a while and feel comfortable with each other. Sometimes we just stick our heads into each other's offices if one of us needs to ask the other a question."

"As the Director of Development and Annual Giving, I have access to all the donor logs, and also to the accounting software we use—I input all the donations, and I have an administrator login to the software because I'm the only one at the civic center who even uses the accounting software. The rest of the accounting is handled by the hotel and convention center, and they have an entire accounting department. Well, to be more accurate about the software, I import transactions from the bank account the civic center uses to handle donations into the accounting software and then it also shows up in the hotel's accounting logs, though I must say there aren't nearly as many donations as there used to be."

"Yeah, I can imagine," said Grace. "I know it's not for-profit and more a showcase for cultural affairs, but mostly now it seems like they hold meetings there for various organizations, which isn't a compelling reason to donate money: so some group from that Meetup website can use the meeting rooms for free."

"When we got the software, everyone was given an individual login. As I said, I have an administrator login, too, but only because I'm the only person at the civic center who uses the software. That's in case there's some problem I can't fix from my individual login, and then I can log in as an administrator and see what's going on and try to fix it. Only an administrator can make any big changes, like deleting information or changing how things are set up. We all have individual logins because then we can't cause some huge problem by accidentally deleting or changing important stuff.

"I hadn't had to use my administrator login in about a year, because that was the last time I had an issue with the software, but, about a week ago, the software started acting funny, and I had to log in as an administrator to see what was wrong with it. While I was trying to figure out the problem I noticed something peculiar. The numbers looked a little weird when I compared the donation logs to the imported information from the bank account. I have to do that anyway, and I was waiting for tech support to call me back, so I did it then, when I was logged in as an administrator. It was odd. Each donation amount on the log was exactly three cents more per dollar than the amount that showed up for that donation in the accounting software. I had no idea why."

"That's really weird," said Oleen. "I wouldn't know what that meant either, and I used to be a CPA."

"Well, if someone donated, say, ten dollars, then there would be an extra three cents added for each dollar. That would make the ten-dollar donation into a donation of ten dollars and thirty cents."

Oleen nodded to show she understood.

"I started going back and comparing the donation logs to the entries in the accounting software and discovered that these discrepancies began about two months ago. As I said, they showed up just around the date Bill started working at the civic center, but when I first saw it had been going on for two months it didn't mean anything to me. I didn't connect it to Bill at all. I did the math, and the missing three cents from every dollar of each donation totaled $150. That doesn't seem like a lot of money, but the civic center doesn't get a lot of donations and, really, there shouldn't be any money missing, period. The added three cents for each dollar came out of the money that was already in the bank account."

"That sounds like stealing!" said Oleen.

"Oh, it was stealing, and wait until you find out how much money was stolen in all. I thought maybe there was some kind of bad glitch in the software, or with the bank or something, because that day was the first time it had ever shown up in the software even though the discrepancies started a couple of months ago."

Grace's eyes were wide.

"I figured the issue wasn't visible from the individual accounts, but only from administrator accounts. So I called this guy I know, Terrence, he's the head of the accounting department at the hotel and convention center. You know they're owned by the same people, but I think I said that already. I might be going senile. Anyway, I asked him to look at the software from his individual and administrator logins, since our systems are connected. I thought maybe the problem could just be with my computer or my accounts. He said he hadn't logged in as an administrator in about three months. I know you'd think he'd need to more often than that, but the software usually runs smoothly, and unless there's an issue there's really no need."

"This sounds like a movie," Ida said.

"Well, Terrence called me back a couple of hours later and said it wasn't a glitch in the system. He found the same three-cent discrepancy in the accounting software there, and it appeared in every transaction at the hotel and convention center. When he looked at the information in the software from his individual login, it appeared normal, but when he logged in as an administrator, he could see the three-cent difference added to *every dollar of every transaction*. And when I say every transaction, I mean conference payments, restaurant food sales, even buying a water bottle from the in-room refrigerator in one of the hotel rooms."

"Are you— Are you saying Bill had something to do with this, this discrepancy?" Grace asked.

"I'll get to that," said Rose.

"First, Terrence told me that since the hotel and convention center does such huge amounts of sales every day, the missing money there, just in two months, totaled about $10 million!"

Agnes whistled. "That's a lot of three cents," she said.

"Especially in only two months!" said Oleen. "I'm assuming the $10 million was taken from the money already in the hotel's bank accounts, so why didn't anyone notice sooner?"

"Good question," Rose said. "Because, well, Terrence isn't proud of this, as he's very meticulous. He usually stays on top of both the online bank accounts and the accounting software numbers, making sure everything matches. But Terrence's wife died six months ago, and he says he hasn't been very "with it" since then. He's let some things fall by the wayside. I do understand, though. When Fred died I didn't function normally for a long time."

"I understand, too, honey," said Agnes, "I was the same way when Herman died."

"Well," Rose said, "Terrence and I agreed it wasn't a mistake. Someone had done it on purpose and must have hacked into the administrator accounts and made it so the discrepancy wasn't visible from any of the individual logins. And on top of that, they also had to have hacked into the server for the hotel and convention center, which the civic center shares. The person who did it, we discovered, wrote a program, like a virus, that upped the cost of everything sold by three cents without it being visible to anyone. Not to cashiers, not to front-desk attendants, not to anyone. And the difference didn't even show up on receipts. Instead of charging customers the extra three cents, the program pulled the three cents from the bank accounts, but it pulled the money in large amounts, because constant three-cent changes in the account balances probably would have raised a red flag with the bank. Instead, the collective gobs of three cents appeared as transfers which went to some bank account not associated with the civic center or the hotel, and transfers like that wouldn't look suspicious to the bank, since the accounts had been added as authorized to receive transfers, also courtesy of the same person who hacked everything.

"Now, that was still really dumb, because you'd think whoever did it would have considered that, at some point, we'd have to use the administrator login, or we would look at the bank account information and notice the missing money, but I suppose most criminals aren't known for their forethought."

"I wonder why they didn't just charge the extra three cents per dollar to the customers, if it wasn't showing up on the receipts," said Ida. "People aren't going to remember an extra fifteen cents added to the cost of something they got out of the hotel refrigerator when they look at their bank statements."

"Ida," Oleen said, "Think about it. What if some huge organization booked a conference there, and spent ten or twenty thousand dollars, or even more? That would be an extra three hundred or six hundred dollars or more they were charged, and most places would notice that."

"Oh, I guess you're right, dear," said Ida.

"You are correct, Oleen," Rose said, "Either way is stupid, but not involving customers would at least keep the problem in-house. Fortunately, Terrence and I go way back. We were in college together and have managed to somehow remain friends all these years, which seems a miracle in and of itself. So, since we have such a history, I explained to him that I suspected Bill. Terrence knows you're my best friend, Grace, and that Bill is your husband, so Terrence and I agreed not to tell anyone and to try to figure this out before taking any further steps, to disrupt your life as little as possible."

Grace began to cry into her hands again, and Oleen handed her a throw pillow.

"He's going to go to jail!" Grace howled.

"At least he can't have affairs in there," Oleen said, as Agnes and Ida glared in her direction.

"Well, I guess he *could*," Oleen continued, "But not the kind that are to his liking."

Ida reached across the coffee table and hit Oleen over the head with a pillow.

"Shut up!" she said, not even trying to whisper.

Grace sobbed harder.

"It's okay, Ida, she's right. I've seen *Midnight Express*. I know."

Then Grace sat up and wiped her eyes, realization replacing the despair on her face.

"Wait a minute, Rose," she said, "That money thing—it had to be done with some kind of hacking into the accounting system and messing with it, right? So why would you suspect Bill? He's clueless about that stuff."

"Ah, yes," said Rose, "And the answer is two words: Thomas Wellington."

"Thomas Wellington?" Ida shouted. "Of Thomas and Julie Wellington? Julie's ex-husband?"

"The very same," Rose said.

"I don't understand," Grace said. "Thomas Wellington is mega-loaded. What would he care about getting $10 million from the civic center? That's, like, change to him."

"It wasn't Thomas who wanted it, Grace," Rose said. "It was Bill."

"But why?" asked Grace. "We have enough money. We aren't super-rich, but he doesn't need more money. We've got loads in our retirement accounts. He especially doesn't need money if he got it illegally. And he and Thomas are friends, but not close friends. I don't understand."

"I talked to Bill about it, Grace," Rose said. "I had the same questions. I went into his office one day last week, sat down in the chair across from him, presented him with the documents from both my donation logs and the transaction logs from the hotel and convention center, and said, 'What's going on, Bill?

This has to involve you. Terrence and I have been through it a hundred times. What are you doing?"

"Oh my god!" Grace said.

"He didn't even try to deny it, Grace," said Rose. "Just put his head in his hands and sat there for a minute. Then he explained, even confirming the whole scheme was his idea."

"Was he trying to get enough money to run off to some island nation with a twenty-two year old?" Grace asked, nose scrunching as though smelling the dumpster in which she suspected Bill of cavorting with a homeless woman.

"No," Rose said. "Are you really thinking of divorcing him, Grace?" Rose asked.

Grace blushed.

"I'm seriously considering it," Grace said. "I'm so done with all these affairs, but I haven't said it out loud to anyone until today. How would he know that? Rose, you said earlier he knows."

"It seems Bill found a card for a divorce attorney in the top drawer of your desk," Rose said.

"Why was he even in my desk?" Grace huffed.

"Well, whatever the reason, he found the card and decided you'd probably go through with it, as his behavior of late has been quite poor, and he didn't want to split half the assets with you. So he decided he needed to make some money he could hide— money he could keep offshore, and then after a year or two he could start slowly moving it back into the country and use it to keep up his current lifestyle. He thought that, because of how many times over the years he's behaved poorly with other women, you could have some concrete evidence of his affairs. I was surprised he told me that. He said that, since you had stayed home all those years and raised five kids while he worked, you might get a lot more than half of everything. So, he was preparing himself. I mean, $10 million wouldn't last forever with Bill's love of luxury, but I think he was planning for this scheme to go on much longer than it has."

"Well, he's sealed his fate now! I don't want to be married to a convicted felon! And I'm not going to blame it on myself like some weak woman saying if I hadn't decided to divorce him this wouldn't have happened. This happened because Bill's a huge ass." Grace said. "The doubt I've been feeling about getting out seems to be slowly oozing away."

"You go, girl!" Oleen said.

This time Ida didn't tell her to shut up.

"But, more importantly, how does Thomas Wellington figure in?" asked Ida.

"Grace," Rose said, "Julie didn't have an affair with Bill. That's not why the Wellingtons got divorced. I know you've never believed that, but it's the truth. Julie told me all about it one night, and I swore to keep it to myself. She did play tennis with Bill a few times and thought he was creepy and way too 'familiar' with her, so she told him to find a new doubles partner. She preferred one who didn't like to slap her on the butt every time she scored a point. That's not at all why they got divorced. They got divorced because of something Thomas did at his last job, and Julie made me promise not to mention it because, when they got divorced, she had to sign a non-disclosure agreement."

72

TUESDAY

When Delbert pulled his truck up to Scott and Steve's townhouse, Scott instructed Delbert to park on the street. Even in a state of impairment, Scott couldn't stand the thought of the back of a gigantic truck hanging off the end of his driveway, but he didn't bother to say anything about it.

Scott led Delbert and Gary up the steep steps to the front door of the townhouse and into the living room.

"It smells like reefer in here, Son," said Delbert, waving his hand in front of his nose.

Scott, Jenny, and Maureen all giggled.

"Reefer?" Jenny asked. "Have you been smoking some, Uncle Delbert?"

"I can't believe you're doing this around Janie and the baby!" Gary said.

Scott waved his hand.

"Oh, we're not. Janie was out in the garden earlier using my amazing heated foot spa."

"It *is* pretty amazing," Janie said.

"But now she came inside to hang out on the couch with

Jenny and Maureen, so I'm just doing it out on the deck, with the door closed, I might add. Even I know babies shouldn't be around smoke, Gary."

"It only smells in here," Scott continued, "Because I smell like it. The smell wasn't so bad before I went to the police station, but now it's not so good." Scott looked glumly at the floor. "Maureen attempted it once, but she didn't inhale. I'm waiting for her to get invited on *The Arsenio Hall Show* to play the saxophone. She is looking quite presidential at the moment."

"Arsenio Hall! Wow, Scott, that's a blast from the past," Janie said.

"I'll have you know, Janie, that being high vastly increases my pop culture knowledge. Now, I haven't been high since I was in college, but one night back then, some guys and I were discussing 1980s sitcoms, and I was able to deduce that *Family Matters* was a spin-off of that show *Perfect Strangers*. Where those two dudes lived in the high-rise and one was, like, from another country. Harriet from *Family Matters* was their elevator operator."

"Wow, that is so enriching to my life," Janie said.

"You love it," Scott said, picking up his cane and top hat from the corner, where Steve had tried to hide them from him earlier.

Then, holding the cane with two hands, and placing the hat atop his head, he began a vaudeville-style performance of the song "Putting on the Ritz", singing loudly and shuffling his feet back and forth.

"Can we tranquilize him?" asked Delbert. "Jenny, do you take Xanax?"

"Nope," said Jenny. "Klonopin. And he's not getting any. I might need it when his singing causes me PTSD."

"Delbert, Gary, would you guys like some spaghetti and meatballs?" Steve asked. "I still have a lot left."

"Yeah, that would be great. I don't care if it's second dinner. Just don't tell Oleen," Gary said.

Steve set Delbert and Gary up at the dining room table with plates of spaghetti, utensils, paper towels, and a bottle of Heineken each. Then he walked back into the living room and sat down on the couch next to Alex. Scott approached the table and pulled out the chair next to Delbert's.

"You smell like a dirty old skunk, Son," said Delbert. "Can you go sit in the living room?"

"I'd rather be a dirty old skunk than a lying weasel," Scott said, grabbing his hat from his head and holding it to his heart, then sweeping away into the living room.

Delbert thought the move would have been better if Scott had been wearing a cape.

Delbert scooted his chair to the left so he was no longer sitting directly across the table from Gary. Gary glared at Delbert, but didn't say anything.

"You guys making any progress?" Steve asked Jenny and Alex. "I know he was supposed to help," Steve said, gesturing at Scott, "but I'm assuming that's out."

"He's helping the way a cat helps you read the newspaper," said Jenny, who was sitting on Alex's other side. "Best to just keep him over there. Otherwise, every five minutes his face pops up between us from behind the couch, and he says, 'Whatcha doing, guys?'"

"I thought marijuana was supposed to make you mellow," said Alex.

"Have you ever seen Scott act mellow?" Jenny asked.

"That is a fair point," Alex said.

"Who knows," said Jenny. "It's Scott. He could be mellow but just needed an excuse to perform that song."

Alex stared down at Matilda's phone.

"We found a fake app," he said. "It looks like Spotify, see?"

Jenny pointed the app icon out to Steve.

"But if you look very closely," Jenny said. "That little O is really an A, only the little tail is so tiny you can't tell."

"Spatify?" Steve laughed.

"I guess they had to change it in some way to get it into the App Store," Alex said. "The icon looks identical, otherwise. But Jenny and I looked up the description of this app, and it's for concealing photos and videos, I guess of stuff you don't want other people to see. Matilda's real Spotify app is in her music folder."

"We have the app open, and there's not a passcode since that would be a tip-off to anyone messing with it that it's not Spotify," said Alex.

"That and the fact that it's called Spatify." Steve laughed. "But I didn't notice that until you pointed it out to me, so I guess most other people wouldn't notice either."

"Yeah, and you're pretty observant," said Jenny.

"There are so many songs and stuff in here that it's taking forever," said Alex. "You can search almost all the same songs, artists, and albums you can on the real Spotify, and there are tons, only none of the songs actually plays any music when you click it. When you touch the names, they either bring up a blank screen or a photo or video. So far, when we *have* found photos and videos hidden behind some of the songs, they've mostly been of Matilda lip-synching songs with lots of curse words in them. And then there was one video where her mom was on the phone, and Matilda must have been recording from around the corner, but the conversation was boring. It was about how bad some guy in her mom's hot yoga class smelled. Don't know what she was planning to do with that."

"Extortion!" Jenny said, with wide eyes. "We have to try to think of what song she might have chosen to use as a cover for murderous photos and videos. How does one choose such a song?"

"The one good thing is we can view her search history, and

so we've been checking the songs in that, but there are quite a few. It's taking a lot of time," Alex said.

"Well, keep looking, Steve said. "I'll try to control Fred Astaire over there," he said, waving toward Scott, who had returned to the table and was now dancing behind Delbert. As Scott sang the Judy Garland classic, "Get Happy," Delbert swatted at Scott with his left hand and continued to eat his spaghetti and meatballs with his right hand.

"I can't believe even whiffing that stuff made me feel so sick," said Maureen from the other couch. "And I only took one puff and barely inhaled. How could Scott have smoked so much? I don't feel high, I just feel nauseated. I cannot take anyone in our house having any more stomach issues or I'll die."

"If he ever does this again, I'm going to kill him," Steve said. "And you can take a video of the murder and hide it on Matilda's phone."

"Wait, what?" Grace said, thinking she hadn't heard Rose right. "Why did Julie have to sign a non-disclosure agreement when she got divorced?"

"Well," said Rose, "Remember just before Thomas retired when he ran that huge microchip manufacturing business? He founded the business, but you know how those things work."

Ida had no idea how those things worked, but she kept listening and didn't ask any questions.

"He was the CEO, but the board decided he wasn't performing well enough, so they replaced him. That can happen when a company becomes publicly traded; it can even happen to the founder. He can be forced out as CEO because the real people the company has to please are the shareholders."

"Shareholders?" asked Ida.

"The people who own stock in the company. When you own stock, you own a tiny little piece of the company, and if the company does well, your stock makes you money. So I guess Thomas wasn't making the company enough money. So, they replaced him and moved him to another position. He was some real high-up executive there. I think they demoted him to Vice President of Finance or something, right under the CFO, but he wasn't allowed to make any important decisions, and his income plummeted."

"Okay," said Grace. "He obviously did something. What did he do?"

"Ahh," said Rose. "It seems our friend Thomas was embezzling money from the company. He was angry about being displaced as CEO and, according to Julie, he said it was 'his money anyway.' I have no idea how much money he took. But that company is well known, and it would have been a huge scandal if the public found out that the founder and former CEO was stealing money from the company. And I think the company's main worry was it would tank the stock prices."

"You sure do know a lot about business, Rose," said Ida.

"Thanks, Ida," Rose said, smiling. "That's how I know Terrence. We went through our MBA program together, many moons ago."

"So why did Julie have to sign that agreement?" Grace asked.

"Thomas got caught, and Julie found out," Rose said. "Julie thought something weird was going on and had some good sources. She knew the wife of one of the company executives. She and Thomas used to have dinner with the woman and her husband, and the woman told Julie things her husband had said about Thomas being unethical. Then Julie didn't want to be with Thomas anymore, since he was a crook. To avoid embarrassment for the company, and also to avoid their stock prices dropping, the company demoted him, but he quit right after that. I guess because he started the company and then he had to work for other people there, so I kind of understand why he quit. That would be really infuriating if you started the company.

"They took his pension and severance package to cover some of the money he stole, and allowed him to pay the rest back in a lump sum. He could more than afford it. Julie was smart and had a good lawyer. Her lawyer got her way more money than she would have gotten in a typical divorce settlement—way more than half. They held it over Thomas's head that Julie could leak the story to the press. So, in exchange for obscene amounts of money, including setting up massive trusts for each of their adult children, which stupid Thomas apparently never did when the kids were little, Julie signed an agreement that she would never talk about it. Grace, don't you dare mention it to Bill, even if you're mad!" Rose said. "Don't any of you tell *anyone*, either," Rose said, looking at Ida, Oleen, and Agnes. "It could get Julie into loads of trouble."

"I won't," said Grace.

"We won't," Ida, Oleen, and Agnes said together.

"If he has so much money, why would he bother helping Bill steal money from the civic center?" Agnes asked. "I figured he might be getting a cut in exchange for doing the technical work but, really, why bother at all? As Grace said, it sounds like $10 million wouldn't be worth it to him."

"I think Thomas does these things for sport," Rose said. "To see if he can get away with them. But, Grace, just so you know, I did see Bill take one of those little Asian girls from the show into his office—twice. One of the girls who stands on the balls and rolls them around. He should be more discreet."

Grace stood up.

"Well then, having someone stand on his balls shouldn't be

a foreign concept to him," said Grace. "I want to call him right now and tell him to go to hell."

"Don't you think you should calm down a little first, dear?" Ida asked. "At least sober up a bit? You can come stay at one of our houses for a while. We can let Rose get back to *House Hunters.*"

Grace hung her head and began to cry again.

"Okay." She sniffled.

As they herded Grace out the door, Agnes said, "Thanks for the wine, Rose. And the company. That was fun. We should do it again."

"Yes, let's," Rose answered. "Grace can set it up. Seems like she'll need it once she talks to Bill. Here, let me walk you out."

Rose stood up from the couch and followed the other women down the steps, still wearing her pajamas and Ugg slippers. The group reached Ida's car, and Ida climbed into the driver's seat, with Grace in the passenger seat, and Oleen and Agnes in the second row. Rose stood at Grace's open window, patting her arm. Grace had her arms on the dashboard and her head down between them.

Ida heard her phone vibrating in her purse for what had to be the fifth time now.

"I'm so sorry, Grace," Rose said.

Without warning, Grace's head shot up, and her eyes got wide, causing Rose to jump back from the window.

"I remember!" Grace said. "I remember!"

"Huh?" asked Ida.

"Katerina, I remember what was bothering me about Katerina!"

"Well, what is it?" Agnes asked.

"Her hands!" Grace said. "Her hands! They were covered in blood!"

"So they did it together!" Oleen said. "Katerina and

Fernando did it together! We should go confront her before the show, so she can't get away!"

"We have to, or she'll run off back to Russia!" Grace said.

"I can't drive," Ida said. "I'm too drunk. "Can anyone else drive? I actually don't even know why I got in the driver's seat."

Everyone shook their heads.

"I think we all drank too much," said Oleen, "But I don't think Rose did. Rose, you didn't even finish one glass of wine, did you?"

"You're observant," said Rose. "After Grace and I had so much the other night I didn't feel so much like drinking today. I'm not drunk at all."

"Then you'll have to drive us to the circus tent," said Oleen. "Get out, Ida."

Ida climbed out of the driver's seat, stumbling a little, then climbed through the door of the third row of seats.

"Come on, Rose," Grace said, motioning to the driver's seat, "Get in."

"I've got to get my driver's license, Grace," Rose said.

"You don't need it," Grace said. "It's just over a block away."

"I know, but the only time a policeman ever stopped me was because I had a broken tail light. This was before I moved here to the condo. I was just driving to a neighbor's house down the street, and I didn't have my license, and it was a big rigmarole. I actually got a ticket! For the broken tail light and for not having my license!"

"Come *on*, Rose!" Grace said. "She'll get away!"

"I'm getting my license!" Rose said, firmly, hurrying away from the car and back up the steps to her condo.

Once Rose had gone, Ida pulled her phone from her purse to see what wisdom Scott had to impart. She noticed a number of texts with just emojis, many featuring a rude gesture. Then one from just a couple of minutes earlier that said, "Alex and Jenny found a video! It was hidden behind Pharrell William's song 'Happy.' A red herring if I've ever seen one. That Matilda is an evil genius like Oleen, and when she's in her sixties she'll hide things in her bra."

Ida shook her head and looked up at the door to Rose's condo, which was still closed, then down at the clock on her phone, which read 8 p.m.

~

Once Alex and Jenny had found the video, which had a still frame of the circus costume closet visible, Scott turned on the Apple TV in the living room and fiddled with it until the TV mirrored the screen of Matilda's phone. Then Alex pressed play on the phone's screen.

A video of the costume closet started to play. The perspective of the closet made it look like it had been filmed through an opening in the side.

"How come you can see in through the side of the closet?" Delbert asked. "What kind of closet has an opening in its side?"

Alex paused the video.

"It's not a closet, really," said Steve. "It's an area set in the back left corner backstage with two screens next to each other on the right side and on the front. The back and left walls form the other two sides of the closet. On the very left side of the front, the left-hand screen has a flimsy door. You can push it inward or outward to enter and exit the closet. I noticed all this when I was backstage with Scott, because that Katerina woman came out of the closet, and then went back in."

"Kind of like Dad!" Scott cackled. "Enjoying being back in the closet, Delbert?"

"Delbert will always deny our love," Gary sighed. "But he can do whatever he pleases and stay in that closet his whole life." Gary crossed his arms and glared at Delbert.

"Son," Delbert said, "Unless you want to get killed inside a closet I suggest you shut the hell up."

"Guys, guys," said Alex, holding up his hands "Can we please table all this for a while? Let Steve finish."

Scott laughed. "Sure thing, Sheriff," he said to Alex.

Neither Delbert nor Gary looked happy, but neither said anything more.

"Go ahead, Steve," said Alex.

"Matilda must have been the one to film this, and she has to have been standing on the right side of the closet, at the place where the two screens meet. If she filmed through the crack where the screens meet, this is the view you'd get. The entrance was all the way around the corner from where Matilda has to have been, and, if she was standing around the side while filming between the screens, no one would have seen her."

"Let's watch, Alex," said Gary.

Alex pressed play again.

Sergei and Katerina appeared on screen, in the back of the closet, shoved in amongst some clothes, doing something they shouldn't be doing in a costume closet.

"So much for the sex couch," Scott said. "Apparently the sex couch is very last year. Now it's the sex closet. Or the steam room!"

"Shut up, Scott!" said Gary, who was craning his neck to watch the screen from the dining room table.

After a couple of minutes of shenanigans in the back of the closet, a male voice sounded from offscreen.

"Hey! Hey! What are you doing in there? Get out of there!"

"Oh shut up," said Sergei with a Russian accent, turning his head to the left so his blond hair covered one of his deep-blue eyes. "Go away. She doesn't like you. She isn't interested."

Katerina didn't turn around, though her bare back was visible amongst the clothes.

"I said get out!" the voice boomed.

"And I said screw you!" Sergei responded.

"You're not even good at your job!" shouted the voice. "Don't think I haven't seen you missing cues!"

"That voice sounds kind of familiar," said Scott. "Maybe it's Fernando?"

"I can't tell," said Steve. "It's a little muffled."

"Well, don't think I don't know all about you and the money either, old man!" Sergei yelled. "I was outside your office the day that old lady talked to you about it. At first, I thought you just had no age preference since you bang everything that moves, but then I realized it was a lot more interesting, so I stayed to hear the whole story. I put my ear up real close to the door after that lady closed it. You two talk so loudly you were easy to hear. I'd just gone up there to ask that old lady if she could bank draft my check so I could make a donation. My mom said I should."

"The money?" Jenny said, looking around the room to see if anyone understood, which apparently no one did.

Then a man's back vaulted into view of the camera, launching itself at Sergei, knocking him against the back wall with a sickening thud as the back of his head was jolted and slammed into the edge of a small set of shelves that was attached to the wall. Sergei slid down the wall to the floor. Katerina, who had jumped back when the man attacked, bent over Sergei, touching his face and the back of his head and feeling his wrist for a pulse. The man just stood there, staring down at an unmoving Sergei. Then Katerina stood upright, blood covering her hands. She looked at the figure who had attacked Sergei, then grabbed a tank top off a nearby rack and pulled it on over her half-removed bra and her jeans. Shaking, she ran out of the costume closet, clearly terrified.

"Wow!" said Janie. "That guy was as fast as Dad was when he dove onto Jenny's couch the other day. I think we had a side view for a minute, but that guy was so fast he was just a blur."

"Shhh!" said Delbert.

The attacker stood, his back still to the camera, panting and looking down at Sergei, who was still lying on the floor, his head propped against the wall. The attacker turned around and, for a second, the camera caught his face. The man did not have olive skin and dark hair. He was not stocky and muscular. The man was thin, with fair skin and salt and pepper hair.

"Holy Shit!" said Scott. "It's Bill McGruder."

73

TUESDAY

In the video, Sergei lay on the floor, and Bill bent down to check his pulse. Bill's facial expression was a mixture of surprise and horror. Bill moved like a robot, then disappeared off the left side of the screen. A moment or two later, Fernando walked into the frame from the left.

"Katerina?" he said. "Sergei?"

Fernando walked further into the closet and saw Sergei lying on the floor.

"Oh my god! Sergei!" he said.

He bent down and felt Sergei's neck for a pulse and Sergei made a small noise. A muffled noise came from the left side of the screen. Fernando felt the back of Sergei's head, and when he pulled his hands away they were dark red.Fernando felt the back of Sergei's head, and when he pulled his hands away, they were dark red.

A muffled sound came from the left side of the screen.

"I'll be back, man," Fernando said to Sergei. "Hang in there. I'll get help."

Fernando stood and looked around, blood covering his hands.

"Matilda must have taken a screenshot of this part of the video, for some reason," said Scott. "This part of the video looks like the photo Grace had."

"I accidentally take screenshots a lot. I can understand," said Jenny.

"Shh!" Gary hissed.

Fernando stood, frozen, looking down at Sergei. Then he ran out of the frame, off the left side of the screen.

About twenty seconds after Fernando's exit, Bill McGruder appeared from the left. He was holding a long blue scarf and he knelt down next to Sergei, wrapping the scarf around Sergei's neck.

The sound of heavy breathing could be heard as the view of the camera flipped around and showed the inside of the tent and then the landscape outside. Whoever was holding the phone was running away. The screen showed a quick progression toward a Range Rover, still accompanied by the sound of heavy breathing.

"I was about to come look for you, Matilda," they heard Andy say, as his face appeared on the screen.

Then the video ended.

"I can't believe Matilda saw all that," said Janie. "I feel sick myself, and I wasn't even there."

"Well holy hell," Scott whistled. "Old Bill McGruder likes to corner men in both pantries and closets! I'm calling Detective Studmuffin."

Scott grabbed his phone and made the call, speaking quickly and explaining what they had just seen. He had just hung up the call when his phone pinged with a text.

"It's Mom," he said. Scott read the text out loud. "We know who did it. Rose got her driver's license, and we're headed there before she gets away and escapes the country."

"Who's Rose?" asked Alex.

"She works with Bill," said Steve.

"What is Mom talking about?" Scott asked. "Isn't Rose Grace's friend? Why does Rose want to escape the country?"

Scott texted back, reading as he typed.

"Don't confront anyone. And don't leave the country with Rose. He could be dangerous. Wait for us. We're coming, and we're bringing the police. Detective Studmuffin is on his way. We saw it all. Matilda caught it on video."

~

Rose drove the car out of the condo complex, her driver's license tucked into the pocket of her pajama pants.

"It's deceptively hard to drive in slippers," she said.

As Rose inched the car forward, Ida read Scott's text out loud, but no one seemed to be listening.

"Hurry, Rose!" yelled Grace, as they stopped in front of the exit gate and waited for it to open.

"I'm going as fast as I can," Rose said. "I'm not a magician. And don't even suggest I break through this gate. It's made of metal, and I don't think this car could stand up to it, even though it's very big." Rose patted the steering wheel of Ida's Expedition.

The gate opened at the speed of a baby crawling across the road. When it was just wide enough for Rose to squeeze the car through, she moved through it slowly, and drove out of the complex through the gate.

"Gun it, Rose!" shouted Oleen, as Rose drove the block-and-a-half to the civic center, keeping well under the speed limit.

"This isn't the *Dukes of Hazzard!*" Rose said.

"If you get pulled over, you *do* have your driver's license," Grace said.

"Why did Scott say he?" Ida asked, shaking her head, "Fernando is in custody."

No one paid attention to her.

Rose reached the front of the civic center parking lot. The tent was visible, as was the front of the building itself, but the lot's parking arm was down to keep patrons of the show confined to parking in the deck.

"Drive through the arm!" Ida said. "It's only wood. It won't even hurt the car."

Rose stopped the car about a foot from the arm and looked thoughtful for a moment, then hit the accelerator, ramming Ida's car into the parking arm. The arm only splintered and didn't break off.

"Back up and do it again!" Agnes shouted.

Rose backed the car up about five feet, then gunned the accelerator and drove straight into the parking arm, which broke off with a loud "thwack," and flew off to the right, landing in a cluster of bushes.

"Park in front of the tent!" said Oleen. "The show hasn't started yet. We'll get her while she's backstage. This is way better than *House Hunters*, Rose! This is Hussy Hunters."

Rose stopped the car and put it in park just as a gigantic red minivan came careening into the lot behind them.

The minivan swerved in to the spot to the right of Ida's Expedition, and skidded to a stop with the front right tire balanced halfway on and halfway off the curb.

"It's them!" Ida shouted. "Maybe we can find out what Scott was talking about."

The five women exited the car, only Rose doing so without a considerable amount of swaying and giggling. They walked around to the right side of the minivan and stood on the sidewalk next to it. As they watched, the side door of the minivan slowly and mechanically opened, and, after what seemed like two hours, a gaggle of people burst out with extreme effort, as each one had to bend down to avoid knocking his or her head on the van's doorframe.

First to exit was Maureen, who looked pale and disoriented. Then Steve, in his jeans, t-shirt, and Teva sandals. Jenny climbed out, shaking her knees as though they pained her. Gary stepped out of the van wearing a pink polo shirt, tan shorts with little cars embroidered on them, and brown sandals with black knee-high socks. Delbert came next, wearing his grease-stained blue denim overalls and black tennis shoes. Last to exit the car was Scott. He was dressed in the same blue seersucker suit and pink bowtie he'd had on earlier at the police station, along with the blue and white saddle shoes with spats. But now he sported a top hat, and he was carrying a cane. He did a little dance on the sidewalk holding the cane horizontally in front of him and shuffling back and forth with the energy of a large puppy. He held out his hat as the finale. Steve closed his eyes and shook his head, wincing.

Janie hoisted herself out of the passenger seat, assisted by Steve, and Alex jumped from the driver's seat, ready to chase someone. The side door of the minivan slowly and mechanically closed.

"I'm sorry you had to crouch, Jenny," said Maureen. "Jack's car seat and Devin's booster seat take up a lot of room. I didn't really fit in the booster, but I think if I'd had to crouch I would've thrown up."

"No problem," said Jenny. "If I exercised more, my knees wouldn't hurt so much."

The passengers from the minivan stood in the parking lot and looked at the line of women on the sidewalk. Ida, Oleen, Agnes, Grace, and Rose stared back at them. Rose was still wearing her blue plaid pajama pants, blue t-shirt, and blue Ugg bedroom slippers.

Rose waved at the crowd on the pavement.

"Hi, I'm Rose," she said.

"Hi, Rose," everyone responded, as though welcoming her to a twelve-step meeting.

Scott watched Ida, Oleen, Agnes, and Grace wobbling and poking each other.

"You're drunk!" he shouted and pointed.

"And you're high!" Ida lobbed back.

"Whoa, boy, is he high!" Alex said. "We had a tough time getting him to climb down off the back bumper of the van. He had interlocked his cane under the roof rack and was going to ride here on the back bumper of the van. Janie convinced him to get in the car by telling him he'd lose his top hat that way. He wasn't going to until Jenny pointed out that it would be like that scene in *Bridget Jones's Diary* when Renee Zellweger loses her scarf in the convertible with Hugh Grant. Apparently, it's a known fact Scott despises Hugh Grant, though I never knew. Then Scott sneered, climbed down, and got into the back of the van with his top hat and cane."

"Doesn't pot make you mellow?" called Rose.

"I see you've never met Scott," said Steve.

"I suppose I haven't," said Rose.

"What are we doing standing around? We have to get her before the show!" Oleen shouted.

"Get who?" asked Scott.

"Katerina!" said Agnes, Ida, Oleen, and Grace.

"She and Fernando did it together!" Grace said. "And she's illegal. They've got him, but if we don't catch her, she'll run back to Russia."

"Katerina and Fernando didn't do it!" said Scott. "It was Mr. McGruder! We saw it on video!"

"Mr. McGruder?" said Grace. "Bill?" Bill McGruder? *My* Bill?"

"Yes!" shouted everyone who had climbed out of the van.

"It was about money. Not about an affair. I don't understand at all," said Jenny.

"I do!" said Grace.

A police car careened into the parking lot with its siren

blaring and lights flashing. It shot up to the curb to the left of Ida's car.

Detectives Beauregard and Drew jumped out of the car and ran to the gaggle that had converged next to the minivan.

"Get back in your cars!" Beauregard shouted. "This is a matter for the police."

"The police who dragged Fernando in?" Scott asked.

"Ignore him," Steve said to Detective Beauregard.

"Bill's probably in the tent," said Grace. "Feeling up all the performers, or out back in the dumpster with some homeless woman."

"Huh?" said Beauregard.

"He's not in the tent!" shouted Detective Drew. "There he is, coming out of the civic center. I've called for backup."

All thirteen people, and Detective Beauregard, looked to where Detective Drew was pointing.

Bill McGruder stood outside as one of the doors of the civic center closed behind him. He stared at the group in front of him.

Then Grace shot out of the crowd and launched herself at Bill, running toward the civic center with shocking speed and agility. Bill stood there, unable to move. Just as Grace was about to reach the doors, he seemed to understand what was happening, and he turned, opened the door, and ran back inside.

"You!" Grace shouted, pulling open one of the doors, "I'm gonna kill you, Bill!"

And with that, Grace barreled through the door of the civic center and up the stairs after him. She was followed inside by a motley crew of fourteen people who bolted after her, trailing behind her as she flew up the first set of steps, Bill McGruder leading the way like a pacesetter in a marathon training group.

74

TUESDAY

Bill clambered up the stairs and rounded the corner from the first flight to the second. Grace could hear the pounding of many footsteps behind her as she tailed him.

"You rotten piece of shit!" she screamed at him. "We won't be splitting anything in the divorce since you'll be in jail! I hope you get a REAL NICE cellmate! One who goes for older men!"

Grace kicked off her low-heeled sandals, one of them flying back and hitting Gary in the face, but the buckle got stuck in his mustache, and the shoe dropped to the floor.

"This thing is always handy," said Gary, to no one in particular, as he rubbed his mustache.

At the second-floor landing, Janie stepped out of line and bent over, panting.

Jenny led her to a bench at the edge of the hall as the herd thundered by.

"I can't run," Janie said. "I'll have this baby right now, and having my baby at the civic center while chasing after a murder suspect isn't exactly what I've been dreaming of."

"I'll stay with you," said Maureen, who looked green. "I feel like I'm gonna throw up."

Jenny grabbed a trash can that was sitting outside a closed office door waiting to be dumped by a custodian, and set it down in front of the bench.

"You should be fine here," Jenny said. There's no way he could get down here with everyone tailing him."

Alex walked back down the steps.

"I'll stay with them," he said, sitting down on the bench next to Maureen.

"Thanks," said Jenny, continuing her sprint up the steps and disappearing up the second flight of stairs and onto the next landing.

Bill, followed closely by Grace and Detective Drew, had skirted past the fifth set of stairs when Scott, still on the fourth set, tripped over his own shoelaces and fell into Detective Beauregard's back, both of them clearing the top step and sprawling in a heap on the fifth-floor landing. Steve stopped to see if Scott was okay, but Delbert, Gary, Ida, Oleen, Agnes, and Rose sprinted past them. The women were a bit unsteady on their feet, but still ran uncommonly quickly.

"You okay?" Steve asked Scott.

Scott rubbed his head.

"Yeah," Scott said. "I think it's wearing off, though. This is not good. I had no idea Mom could run so fast."

Detective Beauregard jumped to his feet. Then he held his hand out and helped Scott up.

"You're high!" Beauregard said. "I thought you were high at the police station. Don't think I didn't do enough of that stuff in my younger days that I don't recognize the smell. But you're way too old for that. Haven't you ever seen *Reefer Madness*?"

"Oh shut up!" Scott said, conking the detective over the head with his cane.

Beauregard slipped backward, mouth forming an o, and fell

onto a cushioned bench which sat against the wall. His head hit the bench cushions, which protected him when he slammed into the bench beneath. Beauregard slid to the floor and rolled on to his left side, his gun sticking noticeably out of the holster on the right side of his body.

Steve leaned over and checked Detective Beauregard's pulse, his breathing, and the back of his head for any signs of bleeding.

Scott retied his shoes.

"He's fine," Steve said. "And, boy, are you lucky he is. You and I are going to have to have a serious talk about your recent behavior, Scott. I think this whole thing with your dad has sent you off your rocker."

"Well, can't help it now," Scott said, darting up the next set of stairs, followed closely by Steve.

Up ahead, Bill had reached the sixth floor. He used his keycard to enter the reinforced door. Grace slammed into the door just as it automatically closed and locked behind him. Detective Drew caught up to Grace, bending over and resting his hands on his knees.

"How are you not winded?" he asked Grace.

"Adrenaline," Grace answered. "And I run a lot. For exercise. This door is super-thick," she said. "Like a bank vault. They store overflow art from the museum up here. You won't even be able to shoot the handle off the door or anything."

"I was not going to try that," said Detective Drew. "But okay."

Ida, Oleen, Agnes, Scott, and Steve came careening around the corner and skidded to a stop behind Grace and Detective Drew on the stairs. Then Delbert and Gary arrived, Gary slamming into Oleen's back.

"Dammit, Gary!" Oleen said. "I know that was you. I felt your giant mustache!" More feet skidded to a stop at the very back of the crowd, from which came a woman's voice.

"Let me through," Rose said. "I have a keycard. I grabbed it when I went back in to get my driver's license, just in case," she said, pulling out a lanyard with a white keycard attached. "See, it pays to be a law-abiding citizen."

Rose handed the keycard to Detective Drew, who moved it over the reader. The light on the reader flashed green, and the door clicked. He turned the handle and opened it, then handed the keycard back to Rose, which she returned to her pocket.

Detective Drew didn't bother telling them to stay back. He made a motion for them to be quiet and follow him.

Behind the detective, Grace, Delbert, Gary, Scott, Steve, Ida, Oleen, Agnes, and Rose followed. The lanyard of Rose's keycard became stuck on the door handle as she vaulted through the door. It was pulled violently out of her pocket and clattered down the stairs behind her.

"Screw it," Rose said, and followed Agnes into the hallway, holding the door handle and letting the door close quietly behind her.

The hallway was dark, except for the small spotlights that illuminated the area inside the glass windows, showcasing the artwork in an eerie, yet beautiful way. Everyone except Grace, Rose, and Oleen stood staring through the window, mesmerized by the sheer breadth and scope of the pieces.

Then Gary pointed through the window and shouted, "There he is! Behind that painting of the water nymphs."

"There's a door that way!" Rose shouted, pointing to the left. "And a door in the same place on the other side. The hallway goes all the way around. The artwork is in the middle. There's a freight elevator that way," she said, pointing to the left again. "It's right by the door on the other side. Bill knows it's there, so that's where he'll go."

"I'll sneak up on him from the back," Detective Drew said. "I'll approach the elevator from the left side, since he'll be slightly to its right."

Detective Drew headed down the hallway to the left, and around the front side of the enclosed space in which the artwork was housed. Everyone else burst through the door a few feet down the hall to the left, and into the vast storage area, thundering like a running heard of brontosauruses. Once inside the room of artwork, Agnes, Oleen, Ida, and Grace turned right, creeping around paintings and statues to see where Bill might be hiding, since their galloping feet had probably drawn him out from behind the painting of water nymphs. It was highly unlikely he had a weapon on him, because he didn't own a gun, and Grace figured she could easily kill him with her bare hands.

Gary, Delbert, Scott, and Steve ran to the left, the plain tiled floor magnifying the high-pitched, skidding sounds their shoes made. They turned down a row of paintings, all of which featured ominous-looking clowns, some with blood dripping down their faces. Rose stood in the hallway and guarded the door to the stairs in case Bill came back.

Scott grabbed Steve's hand.

"I'm closing my eyes," he said. "Get me off this row, now."

Scott leaned onto the cane he held in his left hand, and breathed in a fast and shallow manner like he was about to deliver a baby.

"It's okay," said Steve, taking Scott's right hand. "Keep your eyes closed and I'll get you away from the paintings."

The men continued down the row, which ended in a large cluster of statues.

"You can open your eyes, Scott," Steve said. "They're gone."

Scott opened his eyes, his breathing slowing as Delbert shouted,

"I see him! In the middle of that cluster of statues. Behind the one of the Gryphon!"

In an uncharacteristic fit of bravery, Gary rushed forward toward the place Bill was hiding and knocked hard into an enormous statue of a standing naked man. The statue fell face-first into the ground, breaking at the waist. A small curved, yet still sharp piece of the statue broke off, and skittered across the floor, landing just next to the statue behind which Bill was hiding. Bill jumped from behind the statue of the Gryphon and grabbed the sharp, curved piece which had broken off the statue of the naked man.

Gary, who was now only two feet away from Bill, stood stock-still, unable to move. Bill threw his arm around Gary's neck, holding the sharp, curved piece just below Gary's Adam's apple, looking ready to draw blood.

"Get away!" Bill shouted. "Get away, or I'll hurt him!"

"Oh my god!" Scott said, pointing to the thing Bill was holding against Gary's neck. "You're holding him up with a penis!"

Scott bent over laughing with his hands on his knees and then managed to stand up.

"You're right, Son," Delbert said. "That's what broke off the statue."

"Gary does like a nice penis," Scott guffawed.

"Shut up, Son!" said Delbert. "This isn't the time!"

"Let him go, Bill!" Scott shouted. "You'll just be in more trouble if you hurt him!"

Bill glared at Scott with hatred in his eyes. "You think," Bill spat at Scott, "that just because you have a nice pair of shapely buttocks I'll let him go? Well, I won't!"

Delbert, Steve, Scott, and even Gary, who was being held at penis point, exchanged wide-eyed looks.

Scott smiled. "I told you so," he said.

Delbert could see Detective Drew sneaking toward the doors on the other side of the glass behind where Bill stood, still holding his arm around Gary's neck, the sharp end of the broken-off genitalia scraping against it. Gary wept softly.

"Please don't, Bill," Gary sniffled, but he didn't have a pillow to cry into this time. "Bill," Gary whispered through his tears, "we've known each other for years."

"I don't care!" Bill shouted, as he moved his hand and pushed the broken penis more tightly to Gary's neck, prepared to slice the sharp end across it if anyone tried to capture him. "You all stay away or Gary here gets it. I'm not going to jail!"

A sudden, deafening boom sounded. A barely audible shattering sound, followed by a release of pressure from his neck caused Gary to let out a high-pitched scream and jump away from Bill and onto Delbert's shoulder. Gary sobbed as tears and nose drippings oozed down Delbert's shirt and onto his overalls. Delbert awkwardly patted Gary on the back.

Scott and Steve yelled in surprise, ducking back onto the row of clown paintings. Scott shut his eyes and leaned onto his cane with his left hand again, grabbing Steve's hand with his right. Steve pulled Scott into a protective hug and Scott dropped the cane.

"I hate clowns, Steve," Scott said, almost hyperventilating.

Detective Drew flattened himself against the back wall of the art storage area, having snuck in as the thunderous boom and Gary's escape distracted everyone. In the spot where he had been standing just a moment before, Bill McGruder lay on the ground where he had fallen, clutching his right foot and screaming in agony.

And there, in front of them all, feet wide apart, hands clasping a still-smoking gun, stood Jenny.

75

SATURDAY, ABOUT TWO WEEKS LATER

T he Silver Kettle was crowded at 2 p.m. on a Saturday afternoon. This time was later than when Ida, Oleen, and Agnes usually came to the restaurant, but it was okay because they had company, and it was a special occasion. Well, if you could call dissecting the details of a murder and of how someone you knew shot the perpetrator a special occasion.

The large group sat at an enormous table on the patio, something Ida, Oleen, and Agnes had never done before. Whenever they drank a lot, they liked to be at the table right next to the bathroom, but there were no tables inside the restaurant large enough to accommodate a party of sixteen.

"So, Steve," Ida said from Steve's right, "did you and Scott enjoy your anniversary trip?"

"It was great, Ida. Thanks for asking," said Steve. "It's so nice to have that house down on the island. Scott did have to wrangle a bit with the IT guy from his gym. You know, the one he got the marijuana from. He had to move that guy's weekend out a little, but Scott promised to leave a lot of top-shelf alcohol in the house for him, so he relented. It was great to get away from all the craziness."

"It sure was!" Scott interrupted, from Steve's left. "Just four days at the beach, nice dinners, sunsets, and no drugs ever again!"

"I will say, though," said Steve, "That there was far too much gloating about the fact that the 'shapely buttocks' incident did, indeed, occur, and that Scott never lied about it or made it up. I think the gloating may have lasted the entire drive down there."

Scott laughed.

"I told all of you," he said, affecting the dramatic face Meredith Baxter had employed in the horrible movie Steve and Jenny had watched the night Sergei died; the face Meredith had used when she told the police her granddaughter had been kidnapped and wasn't just lost in the Catskills. Parroting Meredith, Scott announced in a dramatic, slightly hysterical voice, "I told you! I told you all! But you wouldn't listen!"

Then Scott laughed so hard he snorted.

"I can't believe that it was true!" Oleen said. "It's so bizarre. Maybe Bill didn't hit on Herman by accident. I suppose we should apologize to you, Scott, for not believing you, but that will only encourage you."

"Don't tell him that, Oleen! It really will encourage him," said Ida.

Across the table from Ida, Steve, and Scott, Jason dipped a tortilla chip into some cheese dip, put the chip in his mouth, and closed his eyes.

When he had finished chewing, he said, "This cheese dip is *amazing*."

"Wow, Jason," Scott said, "I thought the Ancient Egyptians constructing pyramids without the use of modern machinery and equipment was amazing, but I suppose that cheese dip is on par."

From Jason's right, Janie flung her left hand out in a stop gesture. "Not today, Satan!" she said in such a venomous voice that both Scott and Jason silently continued eating their food.

Scott turned to the dark-skinned man on his left.

"So, Fernando, what was it like being in the slammer?"

"Frustrating," said Fernando. "Once my lawyer arrived, that Beauregard guy kept saying I killed Sergei in a fit of rage because even though he was dating Katerina, I was having a secret affair with her. I kept saying, 'Dude, I'm gay.' Sergei was the only trapeze guy who wasn't gay. I told Beauregard I've been dating someone for two months, ever since I arrived in the city. I explained to him I've been seeing this great guy from my gym, my Pilates instructor, who's also an EMT, but he wouldn't believe me until Rick came down and verified what I said."

Rick squeezed Fernando's left hand under the table.

"Are we just dating?" Rick asked, rubbing his head with his left hand. "I've been telling people you're my *boyfriend*," he said in a whisper.

Rick blushed all the way to the top of his bald head.

Fernando looked embarrassed. "Okay, I've been telling people that about you, too. Boy, what a relief!" he said, leaning his head against Rick's shoulder.

"I'm glad you're staying here, long term," Rick said.

"So am I," said Fernando. "I'm glad the circus is staying here permanently. I like it here."

"I'm glad, too," said Scott. "The civic center sucks. So, what happened to Katerina, lover boys?"

"She went back to Russia to live with her family for a while," said Fernando. "She was deported, but she may have to come back and testify about Sergei's murder. I'll probably have to testify too, now that I think about it. There's a special visa for people who aren't citizens but are witnesses to or victims of serious crimes. After they testify it's even possible for them to apply for extended visas and green cards, so Katerina could do that, but I'm not sure she'd want to live here again after what happened. We've messaged each other some. She's traumatized."

"I can imagine," Scott said. "I guess a whole lot of us may have to testify. Ugh."

"She's also grateful to your aunt for giving her Sergei's driver's license. She asked me to thank Oleen for her."

"I'll tell Oleen she said so," said Scott.

"Hey, Scott!" Rick called across Fernando. "Thanks again for those tips on my glute workout. It's improved my ability to hold Pilates poses."

"Sure thing!" Scott said, saluting Rick. "By the way, Fernando, Oleen saw you and Katerina talking in the turret on the top floor of the civic center. How did you get up there without a key card?"

Fernando looked down at his plate.

"I sort of stole one," he whispered.

"You stole one?" Scott said. "But you seem so, so...nice!"

"I actually was trying to be nice. The first day I arrived here, I settled my stuff into my hotel room, and then went to Gray's Gym. The same one you and Rick go to. It's not far from the hotel, and I read good reviews of it online. Well, that day, I was on the Stairmaster when I noticed Rick. He was walking into one of the exercise studios, and I knew right away I wanted to talk to him. I did about five more minutes on the Stairmaster, so I wouldn't seem obvious, then got off the Stairmaster and snuck over to the door Rick had gone through. I could see through the glass in the door that he was the class instructor. A sign outside the door listed Rick's name and showed the time and that it was a beginner's Pilates class. I saw his next class was two days later, and I decided to go."

Both Fernando and Rick turned pink.

"I noticed Fernando right away when he came to class," said Rick. "I wanted to talk to him, but I was so nervous that after class, I turned away from the group and picked up a clipboard and pretended to be looking at the papers on it, hoping everyone, including Fernando, would leave. I felt so embarrassed I figured he'd be able to tell. But when I looked up, everyone was gone from the room except him. Fernando said he was a trapeze artist at the French—Canadian Circus, and he wanted to ask me some questions about how he could use Pilates to improve his performance on the trapeze. He asked me to go for coffee, so after we had each gone and cleaned up some, we went to the Starbucks around the corner from the gym."

"Slick one, Fernando," Scott said, holding up his fist for a bump, which Fernando didn't return.

"After we went for coffee, I felt let down because the whole thing seemed so professional I thought Rick wasn't interested in me," Fernando said.

"I was! So much!" said Rick. "I felt so flustered I didn't know what to do but act professionally."

Rick's cheeks turned a deep crimson.

"I know I said we should get coffee so I could ask professional questions," said Fernando, "but I figured it would turn into a social visit because it seemed like such a flimsy excuse that Rick would know I really asked because I liked him, but we were both so awkward it didn't."

"I thought maybe you liked me," Rick said, ruffling Fernando's hair," But I didn't want to get my hopes up because I never meet anyone I really like, and it seemed too good to be true."

Fernando smiled and continued.

"About the keycard. The day after Rick and I met for coffee, I was sitting on a bench near Rose's office, and I guess I looked sad because Rose asked if I was okay and, for some reason, I said no. I always say yes when someone asks me that. Rose invited me into her office to talk about it, so I told her how I felt, and she was helpful and said I should ask Rick to do something he wouldn't see as a professional meeting. Someone knocked on the door, then, and called Rose out of her office, and a thought popped into my head. I'd heard about the artwork on the top floor of the civic center, and I was interested in seeing it but didn't know how I'd ever get the chance. Then I thought asking Rick to go look at it would be a great idea; you know, cool and unusual, but I knew it would be locked up tight. As I heard Rose talking in the hall, I saw a file cabinet drawer labeled "keys." I stood up and looked through it, on the off chance she had a key to the top floor, which I doubted.

But somehow, at the bottom of the drawer, I found a keycard with "art" written on it in faded permanent marker. I figured because it looked so old, it wouldn't even work anymore. Maybe they'd changed the keycards or something. I stuck the keycard in my pocket and shut the file-cabinet drawer. Rose came back, and I thanked her for the advice and left.

"The key card did work!" said Rick, "because after the next Pilates class Fernando invited me to see the artwork. We went that night, and the artwork and the view from the turrets was so beautiful we started picking up dinner after Fernando's practices and sneaking up there and eating every night I wasn't working, at my EMT job, I mean. That's how we discovered how much we like each other. All those dinners."

"I tried the keycard on the top-floor door in the evening the day after I took it," Fernando said. "I was shocked it actually worked. And I discovered it also opened all the other doors in the civic center, which didn't seem like the best security idea, but whatever."

Rick smiled at Fernando.

"Get a room, you two!" Scott said.

"Well, to be fair, the top floor was kind of like getting a room. Eventually," Rick said.

"Yuck. Don't tell me that story. So, you used the keycard to go to the top floor when you and Katerina needed a private place to talk, Fernando?"

"Yes," said Fernando. "The night Sergei fell from the rafters. I guess Grace told Rose that Katerina and I had been up there. Rose called me into her office a couple of days ago, and told me she knew I'd been up there, and it was okay. She knew I had taken the keycard the day we had our chat, because I hadn't shut the file cabinet drawer all the way, and Rose is very observant. She looked through the drawer and saw the keycard was missing, but she figured I'd taken it, probably to impress Rick, since the drawer was shut before I came in. She said she decided to let it go, even though she shouldn't have, because she likes to see love. Rose said she was glad Rick and I had gotten together, but that they would be changing all the door locks soon because of the murder, and then my keycard wouldn't work anymore, and she couldn't let me have another one. I like Rose. She's kind."

Further down the table, Ida turned to her right and poked Oleen, gesturing toward Delbert, and then toward Gary, who were sitting at exact opposite ends of the gigantic table. Gary was to their right, and Delbert on the other end, right between Rick and Janie. Ida had noticed Delbert staring at Rick and Fernando, who were being appropriately affectionate with one another while in public, unlike how Delbert and Gary had reportedly acted every time they had gone to the Silver Kettle together, and held hands and made goo-goo eyes at each other.

"Do you think this feud, or whatever you call it, is ever going to stop?" Ida asked Oleen.

"I don't know," Oleen said. "What will we do? Where will we all live? You and I don't think about it by drinking. Maybe they don't think about it by staring silently and hatefully at one another."

Gary and Delbert glared at each other, neither moving nor speaking, shooting invisible beams of hatred at one another from their eyes. You could feel it.

Gary sat with his arms crossed, observing everyone at the

table, remembering in flashes how Bill McGruder had held the cracked penis to his neck. Gary thought he might need to see a therapist like he did back when the flower delivery truck hit him, the only other time in his life he'd thought he was going to die. The thought of crying on Delbert's shoulder, and of Delbert patting him on the back did cheer Gary up a little, though.

Next to Jason, and across from Fernando and Scott, Agnes turned to her left and said, "I'm so glad you came today, Rose. You're a lot of fun. And your busting through that parking arm was nothing short of magnificent!"

"It's a good thing the arm was blue like Ida's car. They never did figure out who did it," Rose said. "I've had more fun in the past two weeks than I've had in the past two years. That sleuthing thing was a blast, even though I did run up six flights of stairs with no bra. But, when you're my age, no one cares about your boobs anymore.

"You should talk to Oleen about that," Agnes laughed. "The idea seems to be an obsession of hers."

"Well, the *House Hunters* marathons you, Grace, Ida, Oleen, and I have been having have been great too, Agnes. And Grace even suggested we invite Julie Wellington sometime, if you can believe that!"

"Really?" asked Agnes. "I thought Grace hated her."

"Well, she did when she thought Julie had an affair with Bill, but she and Julie used to be friends, and Grace said she's tired of drama and conflict. She wants to smooth things over with Julie. It's fun to have more female friends. And I'm also very happy for Jim Cantore's family that those tornadoes in the Midwest seem to be over. I'm sure all they do is worry."

To Rose's left, Grace sat answering questions about Bill and Matilda.

"So, Bill's in jail then?" Maureen asked.

"Yes, and because of that video, there's not much he can do.

I've heard he won't talk. I haven't been to see him. I've had my attorney visit with divorce papers. Bill hasn't signed yet, and I don't know exactly how that works when your soon-to-be-ex-spouse is in jail for killing someone in a costume closet at the time you're trying to divorce him, but I guess we'll see."

"Did he say why he bothered dragging Sergei's body all the way up to the rafters?" Maureen asked. "That seems like a weird thing to do when you could drag the body outside and hide it where it would be less likely to be found, and much easier to do."

"I asked him that when he was clutching his foot in agony after Jenny shot him," Grace said, raising her margarita glass toward Jenny, "And he just mumbled something about it being all he could think of. Who knows? Seems like a lot more work than many other things he could have done. No wonder he was saying his back hurt for the next couple of days. Maybe one day I'll want to see him. Maybe. But right now, he makes me feel gross and dirty."

"I can understand that," said Alex. "How's Matilda? And how are Piper and Andy and your other kids?"

"Well, Matilda is seeing a child psychiatrist, and a psychologist, and she and her parents are all going to family therapy together. Matilda finally talked about what happened the day after we caught Bill, and she is, understandably, scared, anxious, and depressed. She's taking medication to help her with these feelings; medication the doctor said she wouldn't always need to take. But, as soon as Matilda talked about it, I guess the shock wore off, and then she refused to get out of bed. Matilda lost interest in art, in summer camp, and even in her phone! Not caring about her phone was a red flag something was very wrong, and after two days of her not getting out of bed, Piper and Andy realized they had to do something.

"Andy has taken a leave of absence from work, and I think Piper has finally woken up from her happy housewife thing, though she never has seemed happy to me. They're all spending time together, for once. And Piper and Andy are discussing how Andy can change his job role so he can be home more. In a way, I think Bill's being a murderous idiot is going to save Matilda's childhood, and Piper and Andy's marriage. Don't tell anyone I said this, but Piper and Andy have kind of sucked in the parenting department for a couple of years, ever since Andy became Chief of Neurosurgery and started being gone all the time. I really think Piper has been depressed too, but she hasn't talked about it with me. My guess is Piper was only a year or two away from having an affair, with how little Andy was home. And you all know Matilda wasn't on a good path."

Maureen nodded.

"What about your sons?" asked Alex.

"Well, they wouldn't like me telling you this, but every day at least one or two of them calls me, and we spend an hour or two on the phone with one of them crying. I've cried enough I don't have any tears left. Except for sometimes, like when I hear a song Bill and I both loved or something like that. I've been talking to the boys a lot more, and it seems we may actually start spending time together!"

"That's great, Grace," said Maureen, "though I'm sorry about the circumstances."

"How was Gatlinburg?" Grace asked. "You went just for the weekend, right?"

Alex and Maureen looked at each other.

"It was airbrushy," said Maureen.

"And funnel cakey," added Alex. "And also full of cable-car rides. Meh."

Delbert sat quietly at the end of the table, munching on chips and guacamole. He stared down the table at Gary. He was both glad Gary wasn't dead, and also never letting Gary into his garage again.

Next to Delbert, Jenny asked Detective Drew, "So, you have kids? Scott was going on about how your kids call you Drew, but keep in mind Scott is rude," she said.

"I do have kids," Drew said. "I have three, and they do call me Drew."

"But you're not married?" Jenny asked.

"No, and I never have been," he said.

"Me neither," said Jenny. "Once I thought I might, but I'm glad I didn't. It wouldn't have been right."

"You know, you're a good shot," Drew said. "Will has told me so before. Were you actually aiming for his foot?"

"Somewhere in the vicinity," Jenny said. "I thought it would have been fitting to shoot him in the groin, but I couldn't figure out how to do that without hurting Gary, so the foot it was. I didn't want to kill him, just make him let Gary go. There were so many people around I knew I wasn't in any danger. I was just lucky Beauregard had his gun on him when I ran by, and that Rose dropped her key card down the stairs. Otherwise, I wouldn't even have gotten up there, much less been able to shoot Mr. McGruder in the foot."

Drew laughed.

"Would you like one?" he asked, holding the margarita pitcher out to Jenny.

"No, I'll stick with water," Jenny said. "To tell you the truth, I don't drink."

"Neither do I," Drew said, holding his water glass out and clinking it against Jenny's.

"Cheers."

CPSIA information can be obtained
at www.ICGtesting.com
Printed in the USA
LVHW021043150820
663273LV00029B/2431

9 780578 694467